The
Reversion

The Reversion

Book I

Of

The Stonemont Series

Steven C. Smith

To my wife, Kelly, and our children, Aedan, Brody and Morgan, who have become almost as interested as I in developing and living a preparedness lifestyle. You are the loves of my life and the reasons for my efforts.

A Word of Recommendation

Steven "Craig" Smith is a masterful and eloquent story-teller. I was honored to read a "proof" copy of *The Reversion: Book I of the Stonemont Series* - a series which I am anxious to continue - and rarely have I so enjoyed a book.

"Craig" has an exciting and accurate knowledge of survival skills, combat skills and mind-set, weapons, military and police tactics, and of "the good, the bad and the ugly" of when things get "down and dirty". He knows and writes about the real stuff – not the "bull-stuff".

Only one problem – it kept me awake reading it, and I didn't get much sleep until I finished it! When is number two coming out?

Jim "Ronin" Harrison
Montana, 2017

Called "one of the most dangerous men alive" by Bruce Lee, Jim Harrison is one of the true legends of martial arts, combatives and survivalism. Known for his notorious battles during the "Blood-n-Guts" era of American karate. he has been called the closest thing to a modern samurai the 20th century can produce.

He was 3-time U.S. Karate Champion, 3-time All-American Grand Champion, undefeated U.S. light heavyweight Kickboxing Champion, and coach to the undefeated U.S. Professional Team.

He has trained U.S. Army Special Forces, Rangers, SEALs, Marine Scout-Sniper/Recon and members of First Special Forces Operational Detachment-Delta (Delta Force).

He has provided personal security for Chuck Norris, Linda (Mrs. Bruce) Lee and Prince Mikhail Matijasevic.

He was awarded a Ph.D. (Research, Analysis and Instruction) by Yudanshakai University, and was inducted into the International Karate Hall of Fame with Chuck Norris and Bruce Lee.

He is the founder of Bushidokan, Ronin Jutsu and Sakura Warrior Arts.

Forward

Among the many novels in the SHTF/TEOTWAWKI genre, *The Reversion* stands apart – and, perhaps, alone. This is not just because it is well written, not just because it tells a great story, and not just because its character development is exceptional - although those would be enough. *The Reversion*'s singularity lies in the lessons it teaches and the preparedness path it suggests.

One of the copy editors with whom I am acquainted said that *The Reversion* makes you laugh, cry, realize what is truly important, laugh and cry some more, and, finally, realize how thankful you should be for what you have (and that does not, necessarily, mean the creature comforts of today's world). Another, an experienced prepper and disaster preparedness instructor, said he learned something new on almost every page, and a third said it had drastically changed how he thought about preparedness. Those are all true and important, but what truly sets it apart is something more – or, actually, several "somethings more".

The Reversion does not follow the survival learning curve of the unprepared or minimally-prepared, as so many excellent books have already done so well. Rather, it is the story of a man who was prepared, and of how his preparation and foresight provided not only a safe haven for him and his family, but a re-start point for those who come together to survive the collapse of the world around them. As such, it is an unbelievably positive book about an unbelievably negative circumstance, and carries within it the lessons of preparedness and survival that every person should strive to learn.

Tightly woven into the story are threads of history, morality, politics, economics, philosophy and comparative justice – the kind America was founded on, the kind they had devolved to under the weight of an increasingly liberal and socialist society, and the kind that might re-establish a society reflective of America's original ideals. As these threads are woven into the fabric of the larger story of survival, the realization emerges that a great catastrophe enabled the return of what makes us, as human beings, truly happy and fulfilled, and that, perhaps, only a great catastrophe could.

The Reversion, written by an expert in survival and preparedness with an interesting government and non-government background, is destined to be an instant classic in the preparedness/survival genre. More than a good story, it is a manual and a resource for all who are interested in these fields, and deserves to be kept on your desk or chair-side table where it can be read, re-read and referred to often. That's where mine is, and I'm about to start reading it for the fourth time. And I can't wait.

John Middleton
Somewhere in America
2017

"A prudent person foresees the danger ahead and takes precautions. The simpleton goes blindly on and suffers the consequences."

Proverbs 27:12

1

Jim Wyatt stood in line reading the menu on the wall and enjoying the smell of barbecue. An iconic barbecue restaurant in a city known for barbecue, Joe's Kansas City sat on the border between the affluent Johnson County, Kansas to the south and the working-class Kansas City, Kansas to the north. A few blocks east, the "big" Kansas City began at the Missouri state line, where the large medical centers and transitional neighborhoods quickly gave way to the sprawling parks and glass skyscrapers of downtown, then spread out to decaying residential and industrial areas to the east. Thus situated, Joe's drew an eclectic crowd of barbecue zealots. Doctors, lawyers, mechanics, sheet metal workers, secretaries, cops and pretty much anyone who liked great barbecue flooded the place every lunchtime, filling the tables and forming a line that stretched out the door for the better part of two hours each day.

Wyatt rarely ate here, not because he didn't like barbecue – he was a barbecue lover just like any other born-and-raised Kansas Citian - but because he didn't like to stand in the line. Today, however, he had come past before the rush started and took a chance. Finding himself only about a dozen people back from the order counter, he waited patiently, enjoying the aroma and watching the people around him. There was a certain energy about the place, and he realized that people always seemed happy when they came here, as if they were all part of a private club about to enjoy something special together. He didn't feel like part of the club, but he enjoyed the feeling around him anyway.

He was still studying the menu, trying to decide between a large beef sandwich and a rib platter, when the lights went out. He heard someone behind him make the obligatory "forgot to pay the light bill" comment, to which several people chuckled, but he kept looking at the menu, hoping it wouldn't be long before the interruption was fixed.

The restaurant had been a gas station before its transformation, and the large windows gave plenty of light for both patrons and those preparing the food to continue what they were doing, so it was a minute before he noticed the beginning of a murmur. Looking around, he saw a number of people looking at their phones and wondered if they were all reading some news alert.

"Damn thing won't even turn on," said a voice behind.

"Neither will mine," said another.

Wyatt turned around and saw the man behind him punching buttons on his cell phone. Others in the restaurant were doing the same.

He pulled his own phone out of his pocket and found it blank and unresponsive. Looking out the plate glass windows, he saw no cars pulling into or out of the parking lot, which was odd, though an old pick-up truck drove by, its passing announced by its faulty muffler.

The murmur grew louder as people kept trying to bring their phones to life, and the line stopped as the cash registers and drink machines sat dark.

"What the hell is going on?" asked the man who had first noticed his phone had quit, to no one in particular.

Opinions came quickly.

"Transformer probably blew," said one.

"Cell tower probably went out," offered another.

"Aliens."

"Just my luck."

Wyatt stood there watching and listening, thinking to himself, when the manager came out and banged on the counter.

"Sorry folks. We're not sure what the deal is, but hopefully it'll get fixed pretty quick. Until then, our registers, drink machines and anything else electrical are out. That means we can't take credit or debit cards till the power comes back on. Sorry." He looked over the crowd. "For those paying with cash, we can still serve orders with what's already made up."

Several people in front of him and a large number behind him started to dwindle away, grumbling, which put Wyatt closer to ordering. He watched the growing irritation around him as he waited his turn, then, getting to the counter, adjusted his order in light of what he thought might be happening. "You have plenty of ribs?" he asked the manager.

The man nodded. "Yeah, we're good on meat through lunch. Fryer stuff will run out soon, though."

"Okay, give me six slabs, four large beef sandwiches, a quart of beans and a quart of coleslaw."

The man squinted at him. "You got cash, right?"

"Yep."

Wyatt looked around the restaurant while he waited for his order. The people were getting more anxious as they talked to each other and several came in complaining that their cars wouldn't start. Time to get

8

out of here, he thought.

"Here you go, buddy," said the manager, handing him two bags, "Let's call it a hundred even."

Wyatt nodded, counted out some bills and picked up the sacks. "Good luck," he said, looking at the manager.

"Uh huh," said the manager. "Next!"

Wyatt carried the bags out to his car and tried to start it, with no success. He had figured as much, but thought he ought to try anyway. He got out and opened the trunk.

The additional food was going to add quite a bit of weight, but he felt it would be worth it. He needed something to eat on his way home anyway, and the ribs would be a treat to his family tonight - if he made it home tonight.

Opening a small trunk locker, he pulled out an empty tactical pack into which he transferred the food and two water bottles from the case he always carried in the trunk. Another two bottles went into the side pockets of his cargo pants and two more into the side mesh pockets of his JIC, or "just-in-case" bag. He'd always been a big believer in having plenty of pockets.

Unzipping a side pouch of the pack, he withdrew a Smith & Wesson SD40 which he fastened butt-forward onto the left side of his belt in a nylon holster with an extra magazine pouch. The weight evened out the weight of the 1911 Government Model which he was already carrying on his right side, making him feel more balanced than usual. With one in each pipe and an extra magazine for each, that put forty-eight rounds ready to go.

His years in law enforcement and other things had taught him that it was better to carry several guns and need none than to carry one and need more. Today, two would have to do. Driving his Acura instead of his Excursion, he had not brought a rifle, which he now regretted. He looked around as he pulled his shirt over the guns, but saw that no one was paying any attention to him.

Leaving the bags in the opened trunk, he unlocked the passenger door and removed the registration and insurance cards from the glove box. It probably wasn't necessary, but trade craft died hard. He left the license plate on. If the power came back on, he'd come back and get the car. If it stayed off, it wouldn't matter. A couple of ball point pens and a Snickers bar went into his shirt pocket but he left the change in the ashtray. Locking the door, he returned to the trunk, pulled a boonie hat out of the pack and stuck it on his head. No reason to add sunburn to other problems.

He stood there for a minute, thinking and watching the crowd around the restaurant which was growing in both size and unease, then slung the pack onto his back, settled it on his shoulders, cinched the waist belt inside the butts of the pistols and fastened the chest strap. Next, he slipped his arms through the shoulder straps of the tactical pack, wearing it in front, and secured it with carabiners to the main pack. Rolling his shoulders back, he felt pretty well-balanced.

There was a school of thought that you should be able to run with your bag, but Wyatt figured that if you had to run very fast or very far you were counting on luck and hope that you were faster than anyone trying to catch you, and he'd rather have a few extra pounds that might keep him from having to rely on luck and hope. Slow and sure was how the tortoise had beat the hare, and it had always served him well.

Wyatt looked around the parking lot as more people began coming out of Joe's and milling around, being joined by others whose cars had stalled nearby and were walking toward the restaurant. Some were just irritated and confused, but he could tell that others were getting agitated and angry. Time to get going.

He closed the trunk and thought about his wife and kids. Kelly was smart and tough. He knew that she was either home or not far from it, since she hadn't told him she was going anywhere. Communication was an important part of their family life. If she was home, she'd wait for him to get there. If she was at the grocery store or Costco, she'd get herself and the kids home and wait for him. She had carried a Springfield XD .40 since he had taught her to shoot several years earlier, and she wasn't easily intimidated, so he wasn't worried. His immediate problem was just getting home.

He looked at his watch to find it had stopped at 11:08.

"What do you figure happened?"

Wyatt turned toward the voice and saw an older man in an old Ford pickup looking at him. The truck was running.

Wyatt thought he knew what may have happened, but didn't think it would be wise to start talking about it where others could hear. He shrugged. "I don't know. What do you think?"

The man looked at him slyly. "Well, seeing the way you're all geared up, I think I'm thinking the same as you. EMP."

Wyatt turned to look at the crowd around the restaurant parking lot, relieved to see that no one was paying attention to them. "Yeah," he nodded, turning back to the man, "that's what I'm thinking."

The man squinted at the crowd. "How far do you have to go?"

Wyatt shrugged. "Not far. Twenty, twenty-five miles."

The man nodded. "That's good." He sat for a minute, looking at the growing crowd. "Well, I don't want to seem unfriendly, but since you look like you're set up all right, I've got a family about an hour north of here and I'd better get to them." He looked over at the crowd again. "I figure it will be a while before all those fancied-up people realize their cell phones and auto clubs can't help them."

Wyatt looked at the crowd, then back at the man. "Yeah, you'd better get out of here before they see your truck is running. And you'd better be careful. You've got some bad areas to get through. You have some protection?"

The man chuckled and held a shotgun up just high enough for Wyatt to see. "Yep, this and a bad attitude. Got me through a lot in life. Probably get me home."

Wyatt stepped to the door of the truck and offered his hand to the man, who took it. "Thanks for stopping. You take care, and take care of the family. I have a feeling things are going to change in a big way, and not for the better."

"Yep, I think so too." The man looked out into the distance, then back at Wyatt. "You know, my family always thought I was crazy talking about this stuff. Wish I had been."

Wyatt nodded. "Me too."

"Well, good luck."

"You too." Wyatt slapped the roof of the pickup and stepped back to watch the man drive off.

He turned back toward the crowd and figured the time. It was late April and would start getting dusk around seven thirty and dark by eight. He wondered if he could get home before then. Then a thought occurred to him that there might be an easier way.

Walking two blocks east, he came to a thrift store he occasionally shopped at for old books. People were milling around the small strip mall in which it was located, especially around the liquor store and the Chinese restaurant. The restaurant seemed peaceful, but the liquor store was starting to have some problems with the day-drinkers showing up for their noon fix and getting slow, cash-only service. He walked over to a row of bicycles for sale, inspecting each one, and found a beat-up

11

mountain bike with air in both tires. After a bit of haggling, the thrift shop manager accepted forty dollars cash and five minutes later he was pedaling south.

As he rode, Wyatt thought about the situation. From what he had read, the pattern of disruption would indicate an EMP, as opposed to a simple electrical disruption. Whether the cause was a nuclear strike or a coronal mass ejection didn't really matter at this point, though the differences had been debated in the preparedness circles for years, but this seemed to have the earmarks of a HEMP – a high altitude nuclear detonation causing an electromagnetic pulse. What mattered was that many of the things people relied on in their daily lives, in some cases for life itself, were simply not going to work for a while, perhaps a long while.

He knew he had been lucky so far. It had happened in the morning, giving him a start to get home to his family. It had happened at a good location. Just a few blocks to the west, north or east would have been in areas where street robberies and drive-bys were common, and a guy like him on a bike would be a prime target. Joe's was right on the edge where going to the south put him on a route through some of the most affluent and peaceful suburbs in the city. Plus, he'd found a rideable bicycle, even if the seat was torn and already uncomfortable. All-in-all, things were going fairly well in a bad situation.

As Wyatt followed the tree covered Mission Road through the bedroom communities of Fairway, Mission Hills and Prairie Village, he saw people out in their front yards talking to their neighbors, all of whom stared and some of whom waved at him as he rode by. He knew he must look a bit strange to them.

Vehicles were stalled along the road, with their drivers and occupants either waiting in them or walking along the sides of the road, and it took him a while before he realized he was able to hear much of their conversations because the air was devoid of mechanical sounds. No cars. No air conditioners. Nothing. Occasionally, kids on bikes would ride by in small groups, their yells and laughter testifying to the fact that they thought this was all great fun, an interesting break in an otherwise boring day. Seeing a Prairie Village police car at the side of the road gave him an idea and he headed toward the police station.

Several minutes of uphill pedaling, heavy breathing and disgust at himself for getting out of shape brought him to the combination police station and city hall. He rode into the parking lot and took the bike up the steps and into the building with him. He wasn't about to risk losing it with another twenty or more miles to go.

Inside, groups of people stood around in the dark hallways, some talking in hushed tones, others talking louder and obviously anxious. Wyatt walked over to a calm group, which included a police captain, an older sergeant, a young patrolman and what appeared to be several public works employees.

"Howdy," Wyatt said as he approached the group, pushing the bicycle. "Any idea what's going on?"

The men quit talking, looked at him and then at each other. Finally, the captain answered. "Who are you?"

"I was just riding home after my car died and figured you all might know more than most of the people wandering around."

The captain looked at him, trying to decide how to answer. 'We're not sure yet. Obviously, we have a power outage, though we don't yet know how wide spread it is."

"Are your radios working?" Wyatt asked.

The captain looked at the officers and back at Wyatt. "No."

"Emergency radios? HAM?"

The captain looked hard at Wyatt, obviously irritated at being questioned by a civilian. "That's classified information."

Wyatt nodded. "That means no, right?"

"That means it's classified information is what it means," snapped the captain. "And like I said, who are you?"

Wyatt looked back at the captain. He'd had his run-ins with officious ranking officers while he was on the job, and this one had all the markings. Shorter than average with an immaculate uniform that had probably never been dirty. Lots of patches and shiny badges and bars. He had never liked these guys, though he had sometimes found them humorous, and he liked them even less since he had left law enforcement and seen them through civilian eyes. Most of them were little martinets with limited field experience and large egos resulting from years of bureaucratic and clerical power. "I'm a citizen, captain," he answered evenly. "A citizen asking a question."

The captain took a step closer to Wyatt and pointed his finger at Wyatt's chest. "Like you said, you're a civilian and you don't need to be here or to be questioning me." He looked at the bulges under Wyatt's shirt. "Are you carrying a gun?"

Wyatt thought for a moment about saying no, he was carrying two,

13

but he just met the captain's glare and said "Yep."

"I'm going to need you to surrender it. Now."

Wyatt smiled and shook his head, glancing at the other officers, who looked like they would rather be somewhere else. He looked back at the captain. "It's fine where it is, captain."

He looked at the man who appeared to be the senior public works employee. "What do you figure?"

The captain angrily cut off the man's answer. "You're under arrest." Then, to the sergeant and patrolman, "Disarm him and put him in a holding cell."

Wyatt looked at the two officers, who made no move toward him, then looked back at the captain. "Kansas is a constitutional carry state, captain. Unless the Constitution has been revoked, I'll keep my gun."

"This is an emergency!" snapped the captain, his face beginning to flush. "I have the authority to disarm any citizen I feel is a threat to the safety of this community. You will surrender your weapon or these officers will disarm you and put you in a cell!"

Wyatt controlled the irritation he felt building within him at the thought of this sawed-off office boy trying to lock him up and keep him from getting home to his family. He slowed his breathing, noted the positions of the others, and squared on the captain. "I was on the job back in the days when even captains were cops. I figure you for one of those who made their rank writing tickets and kissing ass. You've got an attitude that's about to get you into trouble, and if you try to push this, you're not going to like what happens."

He watched the captain turn red and the sergeant try to suppress a smile, then waited to see if anyone was going to make a move. No one did. Turning back to the public works man, he asked "So, what do you think?"

The man pushed back his ball cap and scratched the top of his head before replacing it. "Well, like you said, we've got no power, no communication. Most of the vehicles won't start, though we have a tractor and a couple of four wheelers that will run." He paused, looking at the others, not wanting to go on, but knowing he should. "Guess I'd figure an EMP, though I know that sounds crazy"

Wyatt nodded slowly. "That's what I figured. Do you have an emergency plan for this?"

Both the public works guy and the sergeant shook their heads. "We had a conference coming up next month with DHS about it, but we're pretty much in the dark right now," said the sergeant. Then, realizing what he had said, "Yeah, really in the dark, but it's not so funny I guess."

Wyatt looked around, thinking about how much to say. Deciding, he looked back at the sergeant and public works supervisor. "You've got no power, no communications, no outside help coming, an inner city of almost half a million people who are going to start spreading out in a couple of days when they run out of food, and a small department that's about to get smaller when your people either don't show up for their shifts or head home to take care of their own families. What are you planning to do?"

The sergeant and the public works supervisor looked at each other. "Well, that's what we were talking about," said the sergeant. "What we were trying to figure out." He shook his head. "I just don't know. You seem to know a bit about this. You got any ideas?"

Wyatt looked at the captain, who continued to glower at him, then back at the others. "If this really is an EMP, this city is going to start to explode within a couple of days, maybe sooner. You all won't be able to stop it or even help much."

He saw their disappointment but acceptance of that truth and continued. "Your first responsibility is to your families if you can get to them. Then to your neighbors and communities, in that order. Don't sacrifice yourselves and the help you can give your family by trying to be a hero here. It won't help and it will only hurt your family's chance of survival."

He paused and saw that they were all listening to him, even the captain. "There are a couple of grocery stores nearby," he continued, "and a number of smaller convenience stores and restaurants. These are going to be swamped and then overrun in a day or two if order hasn't been maintained. I would suggest that if you can get to them you do so, and organize some kind of security and distribution system for those who come. That way, as many as possible can be helped without the strongest taking advantage of the weakest. Then, take what food you can carry and get home to your families. What you do from there on depends on how prepared you are and what options you think you have. That's up to you. Also, I'd take whatever weapons, ammo, medical supplies and anything else you think you could use from here. If things get back to normal, you can bring it back. If it turns out to be a long-term situation, you're going to need everything you can get."

All the men were silent. Then the sergeant spoke. "You really think it's going to be that bad?"

Wyatt looked at him and nodded. "Yeah."

The sergeant seemed to slump in resignation. "Yeah, me too. What are you going to do?"

"I'm headed home."

The men looked at each other for a moment, then the sergeant spoke to the young patrolman. "Jacob, the rest of us live fairly close, but you're quite a ways from your family. I don't think anybody would object if you took one of the ATVs and headed home." He looked around and saw everyone agreed.

Wyatt looked at the patrolman. "Where do you have to go?"

The patrolman was shaken, but answered, "Garden City, on the Missouri side. It takes me about an hour. But my family's going to be okay till I get home. I think I ought to stay here and help for a while."

Wyatt shook his head. "The longer you wait to head home the worse it's going to get. Gangs could start spreading out in a day or two, as soon as they see there's no organized police presence, and even good people stuck on the highways will start to turn ugly soon. Riding or driving any working vehicle after a day or so will make you a target, and there will be a lot of them out there ready to take a shot at you."

The patrolman looked from Wyatt to the sergeant and nodded. "Yeah, I guess so. Just seems like I ought to try to help a bit while I'm here, before I go running off."

The sergeant shook his head. "You're not running off, Jacob, you're going to help your family. To protect and provide for them like you should. You're not going to make much difference here, but you can make all the difference in the world there. It's the right choice. They need you." He turned to the captain. "You have any problem with Jacob taking one of the four wheelers with a couple of weapons and some ammo?"

Wyatt noticed the sergeant had not prefaced the question by calling the captain by his rank.

The captain looked as if he had lost his place in things, but finally stammered, "No, no ... no problem."

Wyatt spoke to the patrolman. "If you leave now, you might make it with no trouble. If you stick around for a while, you're asking for trouble on your way home. I'd get going, if I were you."

The patrolman nodded slowly. "Okay, thanks."

Wyatt turned the bike around and nodded to the men. "I'm headed home. Good luck to you. I think we're all going to need it."

16

The sergeant nodded. "Yep."

As Wyatt exited the building he noticed a small crowd forming, apparently from stranded motorists and neighbors who lived nearby. Swinging a leg back over the bike, he dug a barbecue sandwich out of the front pack and pushed off.

The next leg on Mission Road was mostly downhill, making up for the mostly uphill grind of the previous hour. It had been thirty years since he had been on a bicycle, and his legs were feeling it, not to mention every other muscle in his body.

As he coasted past neighborhoods and small shopping centers, he slowly ate the sandwich and watched the people he passed, seeing pretty much the same thing he had seen since leaving Joe's. This was an affluent area, and people tended to think themselves through problems rather than reacting emotionally to them. He knew that most of them would be slow to accept the possibility that help would not come soon, and would, as a result, become victims of the thousands that would undoubtedly pour out of the city in the next week or two. He wished he could stop and explain it to them, but he knew that most of them would not believe him and it would just slow him down. The knowledge that he was looking at people who would most likely be dead within several months saddened him, but he pushed the thought from his mind and kept riding.

As he followed the descending Mission Road to his turn onto Indian Creek Parkway, he thought about what he would need to do when he got home. Kelly would probably be there with the kids, waiting for him. The kids wouldn't be worried yet, but Kelly would know something was wrong and would be preparing for a night without electricity. She would undoubtedly be tightening up security at the house, preparing some food for the night and having the kids get out lanterns and flashlights. The dogs provided good outside security, and they had built the house with security in mind. He would just build on the preparations they had already made and fill in the cracks as he found them.

Turning south for a mile and then west, he looked with pleasure as the homes became larger and the landscaping more expensive. He and Kelly had worked hard and been smart with their money. As a result, they had been able to first buy a house in this area, then finally move out of the suburbs to sixty acres of beautifully rolling hills outside the exurban ring. A mixture of pasture and tillable land with a fringe of forest, their

17

property sat atop a hill that overlooked the surrounding area, with two stocked ponds and a natural spring that fed into a year-round rock bottom creek on the west side.

They had built their dream house of natural stone and timber, much of it with their own hands, on top of the hill to enjoy the views it gave them on every side, but also with an eye on defensibility. They hadn't mentioned that part except to a few trusted friends with whom they shared the same social concerns, but he knew that the coming weeks and months would show the wisdom of that decision.

Turning south again, Wyatt was glad to have another long downhill stretch as the road reached miles into the outer suburbs, through the exurbs, and finally to a mixture of acreages and farmland. Here, the peddling got harder because the wide street had turned into a two-lane blacktop, but he was energized by the knowledge that he was close to home and he doubled his effort as he rode the miles, trying to take his mind off the burning in his legs and lungs by thinking about Kelly, the kids and the barbecue in his pack.

The residential lots had given way to larger acreages, and he watched the cows, horses and other animals go about their business in the surrounding fields, blissfully ignorant of the concerns of mankind.

After what seemed like an eternity, he finally found himself pedaling up the long hill to the gate of the place they had named "Stonemont" from the many stones that dominated the dome of the hill and from which the first floor of the house had been built. At first, the name had been kind of a joke, a small jab at pretentious estate names, but it had caught on and soon became the name by which their place was locally known. Eventually, Wyatt had even placed plaques bearing the name in the stone gate pillars.

He stopped at the iron gate and opened it, pushed the bike through, then closed the gate behind him. Pushing the bike up the long driveway, he felt himself start to relax, even though his legs felt like putty that might not get him to the house. The place had always felt like a haven to him, a place where the outside world could not intrude, and now it felt even more so. As he reached the side veranda and propped the bike against the wall, Kelly came out of the side kitchen door with their three kids spilling out around her.

"Daddy, the TV doesn't work!" exclaimed their six-year-old, Brody.

Their four-year-old daughter Morgan smiled shyly from behind Kelly's leg and nine-year-old Aedan ran up with an excited smile. "Hi daddy! We've got a bunch of solar lights and the LED lanterns ready in case the lights don't come on before dark."

Wyatt tousled Aedan's hair. "Good thinking, buddy. We sure might need them."

"Hi Babe," he said to Kelly, grabbing her around the waist. "Glad to see you're home."

Kelly returned the hug and laughed at the squeeze he gave her on the side the kids couldn't see. "I'm glad you're home too. I was getting a little worried." She looked toward the bicycle. "Nice bike."

Wyatt started shrugging off the packs as he entered the house, with Kelly and the kids trailing along behind. "Yeah, I was clear up at Joe's Kansas City when everything went off. Got it at the thrift shop up there. Good thing, too. I'd still be a long ways away without it."

He set his main pack by the door and carried the tactical pack to the large kitchen table. "How's everything around here?"

"Fine. I was in the middle of giving Morgie a bath when everything went off. I was going to run to the store, but the car won't start. And none of the phones are working. How widespread do you think it is?"

Wyatt looked at his wife and liked what he saw. He'd first noticed her because of her looks, but had soon come to appreciate her many other virtues. "Hard to know. Did you try to start the truck?"

She shook her head. "No. When nothing would work, I thought I'd wait till you got home." She looked at him closely. "What do you think? EMP?"

He nodded his head and smiled. "I knew I married you for your smarts." He grabbed her, kissing her and squeezing her again. "That's what it looks like to me. I'm going to go try the truck."

Letting her go, Wyatt went into the garage and got into his Ford Excursion. Saying a silent prayer, he put the key in the ignition and turned it. The engine roared to life.

He let it run for a minute then turned it off. There had been an ongoing discussion in the preparedness circles as to which vehicles would run after an EMP and which would not. Some felt that garaged vehicles might have a chance, but he had gone the extra mile and lined his four-car garage with steel mesh, grounding it with steel rods driven twelve feet into the earth, creating a large Faraday cage.

At the time, he had questioned the expense and the amount of work involved. Unlike most of his other preps, this was not something they would really have a use for except in case of an EMP. Now, he was glad he had done it. Several motorcycles, two ATVs and an older F-150 crew cab also started, as did his beloved compact John Deere tractor.

He stepped out of the truck and saw Kelly standing in the doorway. "Looks like we're in good shape," he said, following her back into the kitchen.

He opened the tactical pack and started pulling out the ribs, beans, slaw and remaining sandwiches, placing them on the counter. "Here, I brought dinner." He stopped and leaned back against the counter, looking at Kelly and putting out his arms. "Come here."

Kelly walked into his arms and rested her hands on his arms as he rested his on her hips. "You think we have time for that?" she smiled.

Jim chuckled. "I wish." Then he looked at her seriously. "There's no way to know how serious this is yet. We'll be fine, but we need to make a few changes starting right now."

Kelly looked up at Jim's face. Ever since they had started dating he had made her feel safe. He knew things that most people didn't, at least in her circle, and he always seemed to be in control of his world. At first, a lot of it had seemed weird to her, even paranoid, and she had teased him about it, even argued a bit. But little by little she had learned more about him and the life he had led, though she knew he hadn't told her everything. She had never known anyone like him, and others had said the same thing about him to her. If there was a problem, Jim knew what to do. "Okay. What do you want me to do?"

"First, get your gun and keep it on you. Always. I don't think it will get bad quite yet, but no use taking chances. We'll keep the driveway gate locked and the kids close to the house where we can always see them. I'm going to add some lights and additional alarms around the place. The dogs will let us know if anyone comes around, but we'll bring Max inside at night." He paused, looking at her with a smile. "But the main thing I want you to do is to meet me upstairs after we tuck the kids in tonight."

She giggled and stretched up to kiss him. "Mmmm, I think I might like this emergency."

2

Christian Bell lay motionless under the low hanging branches of a large pine tree, watching the road below him. The day before yesterday had been a hell of a day and this one was shaping up to be just as interesting.

He had been watching his coffee cup filling from the machine in the ER galley when the lights and everything else went off. The emergency room had been slow, and most of the doctors and nurses had been chatting or browsing the internet, so the sudden blackout was greeted with laughter and jokes, an almost welcome break in an otherwise boring day.

It hadn't taken him long to have a pretty good idea about what had happened. His radio and pager had both blacked out, as had both his personal and security cell phones, and, from what he had heard around him, so had everything else. The standby generators had not kicked on, and, checking the Jeep, he found it to be dead too. He had walked through the hospital, followed by people attracted to his flashlight, until he found the other officer. Together, they had checked the elevators, extracted several visitors who had been trapped, and returned to the security office where they found the safety manager waiting for them and pacing nervously inside the ambulance bay.

"Where have you two been?" the manager had demanded. "All the electrical systems are down and the emergency generators didn't come on."

Christian walked past the manager into the security office and started unbuttoning his shirt. "Getting people out of elevators and yes, we know."

"We need you posted at the entrances."

Christian looked at him. "Why?"

The manager started getting flustered, not liking having his authority questioned. "We're not sure what's going on. We can't raise anybody outside the hospital. We need to secure the facility."

Christian checked the shirt pockets for anything he wanted to take with him and hung it on a hook. Then he turned to the manager. "Jeff, look outside." He put his hand on the manager's shoulder and turned him toward the windows. "Do you see any cars moving?"

Jeff looked out at the normally busy street below them. "No. So what?"

"Did they ever talk about EMP at any of those seminars and conferences you were always going to?"

Jeff started to look less confused and more concerned. "Yeah."

"Well, I think that's what we've got."

"Then we need to secure the hospital!"

"Why?"

"In case people try to get in here!"

"Well, Jeff, if people are hurt or sick I hope they do get in here. Maybe they can get some help, at least for a while. And if a big bunch of bad guys try to get in here, what would you like us to keep them out with, our personalities and these cute little Tasers you let us carry?"

"You're an ex-cop. Don't you have a gun in your car?"

Christian scoffed. "You mean the gun you would have fired me for having if I'd brought it in an hour ago?"

Jeff chewed on his lip, not knowing what to say. Then, "This is different. This is an emergency!"

Christian shook his head. He had tried to get the hospital to allow the security officers to carry firearms for several years, with no success. The answer was always cost and liability, the last refuge of the corporate administrator. "And, of course, it wouldn't have been an emergency if someone had walked in yesterday and pointed a gun at us, right?"

He turned away. "You better get your head around this, Jeff. Anyone who was on life support upstairs is either already dead or soon will be. You have no lights, no air conditioning, no refrigeration for food or meds and a whole bunch of people in the building whose cars won't get them away from here. You're the big emergency management guy, so I hope you can find something in one of your manuals to tell you what to do. I can't do anything here, so I'm going somewhere I can. Good luck."

With that, he had turned around and walked out to his truck.

It had only taken him a few minutes to change out of his duty boots and into some hikers, throw a lightweight field jacket over his t-shirt and put his gun belt on. He had taken to wearing a separate gun belt several years before because it allowed him more versatility than hanging holsters, mag pouches and other things directly onto his regular belt. Plus, it was more comfortable. His uncle Jim had introduced the concept to him and he thought about Jim now.

Pulling his AR out from behind the seat, he laid it in the bed, then hauled his rucksack out of the truck box. He was strapping it on when he saw a paramedic walking toward him, also wearing a backpack and carrying a rifle. The man looked to be in his mid-twenties, several years younger than Christian's thirty-two.

Christian nodded at the paramedic and chuckled. "I feel like I'm looking in a mirror."

The paramedic smiled as he walked up and stuck out his hand. "I'm Mike. I thought I was the only one like me around here."

Christian shook his hand and nodded. "Secret's out, I guess. Where you headed?"

Mike looked around slowly. "Not really sure yet. How about you?"

Christian tightened the waist belt and chest straps of his pack. "My uncle lives down in Miami County. We always said that if anything like this happened I'd go there." He looked at Mike. "You have family around here?"

Mike shook his head. "Nope. My folks are in South Carolina. My sister's at school in Georgia. An ex-girlfriend is all I have here." He laughed. "Or had."

"What do you have there?" Christian looked at the rifle Mike carried in his right hand. It was a bolt action with a camo stock and a serious scope.

".308".

"You a hunter?"

"Sort of. Sniper."

"Army?"

"Marines."

Christian nodded, locking his door and picking up his rifle "Well, you're welcome to come along with me if you want."

Mike nodded and smiled, slinging his rifle over his shoulder. "May as well."

They had walked until dusk, making good time and taking only normal precautions when meeting others along the way. The situation was still new and most people were shocked and confused, not yet understanding the full scope or ramifications of what had happened.

The walk had given them a chance to get to know each other a bit.

Mike had left college out of boredom after his sophomore year and joined the Marines. His natural athletic ability and attraction to challenge had taken him into Recon, but he had soon become disillusioned with how the military was being used and didn't re-up when the time came. He had followed a nurse from California to Leavenworth, Kansas and become a paramedic, which appealed to his desire to help people. The girl didn't last, but the job did, and he found himself in the Midwest just marking time until he decided what he wanted to do next.

Christian shared a brief synopsis of his history, saying little more than he had been a cop and wasn't anymore.

At dusk, they had found a stand of pine trees overlooking an interchange of secondary highways and slid in under the lower branches, making themselves comfortable and taking turns on watch through the night.

The following day was a repeat of the first, with bright Kansas sunshine and miles of highways littered with increasingly confused and worried people. By sundown, they had reached the intersection of highways 7 and 10, which Christian explained was getting close to the outskirts of Olathe and still a couple of days walk to his uncle's.

There was a collection of people at the intersection who had come together out of their mutual fear, so they pushed on a couple more miles to find a more easily concealed and defensible position. Having made do with protein and candy bars from their go bags the night before and through the day, they built a small fire and cooked up several packets of instant oatmeal from Christian's bag and an Asian noodle Knorr's side packet from Mike's. After eating, they cleaned their stainless steel bowls, drank their evening ration of water, put out the fire, then, after it got dark, moved several hundred yards farther on in order to throw off anyone who might have been watching them. Again, they rotated watches throughout the night.

Christian was on watch at daybreak. Within a few minutes, the rear door of an SUV on the highway below him opened and a man got out. The man walked a short distance behind the vehicle and into the ditch, then stood there for a couple of minutes, obviously answering nature's morning call. The man then returned to the vehicle and several minutes later two women got out of the SUV and walked across the ditch and into a stand of trees. After a few minutes, they emerged and returned to the vehicle where the man was now removing things from the rear cargo area and an attached rental trailer.

Christian lay motionless under the pine tree with just his eyes above the crest of the small hill, watching the road. The man and two women were removing boxes and plastic tubs from the vehicle, going through some and setting others aside on the shoulder of the highway.

The sound of breaking glass drew his attention to the east, where he saw several men milling around a car about a quarter of a mile away on the opposite side of the divided highway, leaning into the car and throwing things out onto the ground. He watched as the men finished with the car and started walking in the direction of the SUV, whose occupants were still going through various boxes.

Without turning, he spoke quietly to Mike. "You awake?"

"Am now."

"We have some activity on the road."

Mike rolled smoothly from his back to his stomach, bringing his rifle up as he looked through the scope. "Looks like mom and dad and daughter. Daughter's cute."

"Look down the road to the right."

Mike swept the road with his scope until he acquired the three men walking toward them. "Uh huh. Three fine citizens."

He studied them for a minute. "The big guy in the white t-shirt looks like a prison tat map. The one in the red shirt is drinking from a bottle and has a pistol stuck in his belt, Mexican style. The third guy's wearing a camo t-shirt and looks fairly clean. I make tats as the leader."

Christian watched the family as they continued going through their boxes, pulling out things and setting them aside. "They'll get here in a few minutes. Let's wait and see how this plays out. Are you ready to go?"

"When you are."

It took about five minutes for the looters to realize there were people at the SUV and another ten for them to begin approaching them from across the median. The family was oblivious to the trio's approach, since they were on the ditch side of their vehicle and intent on sorting out their things. Tats and camo came around the front of the SUV and red shirt came around the back. By the time the family realized they were in the pincers of the three, it was too late.

Christian and Mike watched as the three looters approached the family. The father placed himself between his family and tats and camo, who he obviously felt were the greater threat. Tats was talking while red shirt moved up closer to the women. Christian had seen this cat and mouse act a hundred times. The bullies always liked to make their victims squirm before they struck, the only variable being how serious the attack would be.

The situation was obviously escalating between tats and the father when tats kicked the father in the groin and followed up with a hard punch to the side of the head. As the father collapsed, tats mounted him, holding him down.

The mother and daughter rushed to defend the father but were grabbed by the others, red shirt grabbing the mother by her hair and pulling her into a choke hold and camo throwing the daughter to the ground, straddling her and pinning her wrists to the ground above her head with one hand as he put the other on her throat.

The girl was screaming, trying to squirm loose and kneeing camo in the back, while the mother was kicking in the air and trying to scratch at the face of the man holding her.

Christian got to his feet. "Let's go."

The screams and crying of the women combined with the muffled struggles of the father covered the noise of Christian and Mike's footsteps, and the attackers were unaware of their approach until they heard Christian say, "Good morning."

The thugs jerked away from their victims, the two on the ground standing up, and each starting to reach for a weapon until they saw the rifles pointed at them.

The women took the opportunity to break free of their attackers, the daughter delivering a kick to camo's leg as she got up.

"Sorry we're late," said Christian. "Is this the before-breakfast dance?

He looked at the group. "You idiots - that would be you, you and you," Christian indicated each thug with the muzzle of his rifle, "real slowly, lace your fingers behind your heads and get away from these nice people."

As the thugs slowly complied, the women quickly rushed over to the father, helping him up.

Christian glanced at the family, confident that Mike was watching the thugs. "Are you folks okay, I mean considering you've just been knocked around by these ass-hats?"

The women nodded, though each was trembling. The father managed a feeble "Yeah."

Christian returned his attention to the thugs, who were now standing with their hands behind their heads. He stepped closer. "Let's see if you assholes can follow a few simple instructions. Get on your knees."

Camo glared at him. "Who the he'll are you? You ain't no cops!"

The muzzle of Christian's rifle struck camo in the solar plexus before camo could react. The stock of the AR didn't lend itself to a butt stroke, but Christian's brutal kick to the groin collapsed camo to the ground gagging.

"I'm the guy helping you get on your knees," said Christian. Then he looked at the other two. "Anyone else need help?"

Tats and red shirt got on their knees, watching Christian closely.

"Very good," said Christian. "You two must be the smart ones." He motioned with the muzzle of his rifle, "Now, everyone on their stomachs, hands behind your heads, eating dirt and ankles crossed." He jabbed camo with his rifle. "You too, tough guy."

All three lowered themselves to the position Christian had told them to, camo with some difficulty.

"Very good. I think you guys have done this before. Now, I think you were all reaching to give my friend and me something when we interrupted you. I think I'll just see what it was while you boys lay real still, just like you were dead, if you get my meaning."

Mike moved around to cover the three prone thugs while Christian let his AR hang, drew his pistol with his right hand and approached camo. "You first, princess. Lay there just like sleeping beauty."

Christian searched camo, coming up with a Glock 9mm, then searched the other two, finding a .38 revolver and a large hunting knife. Putting these in his waistband and pockets, he took three cable ties from his pack and secured the thugs' wrists behind their backs. He then took a length of paracord and, cutting it into three sections, tied the crossed ankles of each. Tats tried to kick, which earned him an extra length of cord tying his ankles to his wrists.

Christian straightened up. "Okay, boys, you just lay there for a while and think about what you've done wrong, and what might happen next."

With that, he turned back to the family, who were beginning to calm down. A large lump was forming on the left side of the father's face, and the daughter was attempting to hold the front of her blouse closed where it had been torn open. The mother seemed okay, though disheveled. He extended his hand to the father. "I'm Christian Bell. This is Mike ..." He turned toward Mike and paused, realizing he didn't know his last named,

"Mike Carpenter," Mike said, nodding to the family and smiling.

The father accepted Christian's hand. "Bill Garner. This is my wife, Ann, and our daughter, Tracy. Thank you," he paused, taking a deep breath, "for what you did."

Christian and Mike both nodded to the women, who nodded back.

"Believe me, it was our pleasure. You all get stuck out here while traveling?"

Bill nodded. "We came out to pick Tracy up from school. She just graduated from law school and we were headed back to Ohio when our vehicle went dead."

"So, you've been sitting here since the day before yesterday?"

Bill nodded again. "Yeah. There were other people around here who stalled out too, but they all started walking after the first night. I guess they lived closer around here, or at least had an idea where to go." He looked down the highway. "We're a long way from anywhere we know, so we decided to wait and see if help came along. This morning we decided we'd better get some things together and start walking." He looked at the three men on the ground. "Then they showed up."

Christian nodded at Mike. "Mike is a paramedic. Let him take a look at your face and any other injuries you all have, then we need to talk."

Mike slung his rifle and did a quick examination of Bill's face and Ann's neck. Neither required any treatment, though both had some swelling and the start of some bruises. Tracy had disappeared inside the Suburban and re-emerged wearing a blue University of Kansas sweatshirt, replacing her torn blouse. She had some scratches on her back and throat, which Mike cleaned and put antibiotic cream on.

After being satisfied that none of the family was seriously injured, Christian looked at each of them, then spoke to Bill. "We have to decide what we're going to do with them."

Ann spoke up. "Shouldn't we just hand them over to the police?"

"I wish we could," said Christian. "The problem is that we don't know where the police are, or even if there are any police anymore."

"What do you mean?" asked Bill.

"Since Mike and I started walking the day before yesterday, we've passed several abandoned police cars. No sign of anyone. The shotguns were taken out, but otherwise they were just locked up sitting there."

"Surely there's a police station we can take them to."

Christian shook his head. "You were on the highway when your car shut down, so other than yourself and the few cars around you, you don't know the extent of it. We came from a hospital in Leavenworth. That's about thirty miles from here. Everything shut down, and I mean everything. Even the police substation across the street. No electricity anywhere. No radio communication. All vehicles stopped. And come to think of it, I haven't noticed any planes flying." He wondered how to express what he thought had happened.

"EMP", said Ann, as if reading his mind.

Christian looked at her. "You know about that?"

"Mom's an electrical engineer," said Tracy. "She's been warning us about this for years." She looked her mom apologetically. "I'm afraid we didn't pay much attention."

"A coronal mass ejection, a CME, was a virtual certainty," said Ann. "But from what we're seeing, cars not running, radio communications still off, I'd say we have a nuclear induced EMP."

Christian looked at her with new respect. Ann looked like she would be most comfortable baking cookies or organizing a charity event, but there was obviously a lot more to her than that. He nodded. "That's what I've been thinking. We can assume that it's wide spread, but we don't know how wide spread or whether we are in the middle of it or on the edge of it - or which edge. Would you agree with that?"

"One hundred percent," replied Ann. "There's no way to know at this point, at least until we make contact with an unaffected area."

Christian nodded again. "That's what I mean. What happens to these three depends entirely on what we do with them."

He looked at each member of the family individually, then continued. "We can't take them with us. They would slow us down and we don't have the resources to properly guard, feed and otherwise care for them. And they would remain a constant danger to us. We can't just let them go, because we know they would be a danger to anyone else who came into contact with them. Essentially, we would be responsible for any harm that came to those people, and from what we've seen from them that harm could be great."

"Couldn't we just leave them here tied up?" asked Tracy.

Christian shook his head. He saw that Bill was about to say something, but he wanted to make their choices clear before opening it up for discussion. "No. If we did that someone might come along and untie them, not realizing who or what they are, and that person might get hurt or worse. It would be like leaving a booby trap behind. And if no one found them they would die of dehydration in a few days. We would essentially have tortured them to death. And finally, I don't feel we can morally kill them, since they didn't kill anyone here. That's what we have to discuss. You were the victims here, so you need to be involved in making the decision."

Everyone was silent for a few moments. Ann and Tracy were both looking at Bill, who was looking at the three on the ground. After another moment, Bill looked at Christian. "You've described the quandary very well, young man. I'm a lawyer. In fact, I've been a judge for the past fifteen years. The question of just punishment for criminal actions is one that has been asked for thousands of years. The answers to that question have been many and varied."

He looked back at the three thugs. "If what we suspect is true, we find ourselves in a time like those before functional central, or even tribal government. At that time, and even during the first evolutions of authority, retribution for wrongs was largely felt to be a personal matter. Punishment was decided and administered by the victims or their representatives."

Bill looked around at the others, then continued. "Christian has listed the unacceptable choices. Unacceptable, at least, to us at our current understanding of civilized and humane behavior. But he has not, and I expect purposefully, suggested the solution which best satisfies the demands of justice while also serving to warn others of criminal threat." He looked at Christian. "That solution is to mark and disable them."

Christian nodded.

"Have you given thought to what should be done, specifically?"

Christian nodded again. "They need to be marked in a way that brings attention to them and can't be hidden easily. And they need to be physically disabled in a way that reduces their threat to others in the future."

He paused, looking at each of the family members in turn. He was fairly sure that Mike would understand the necessity of what he was about to propose, but questioned whether the family would. He was about to go on when Bill spoke again.

"Historically, marking has included the removal of various body parts, including the ears and nose, as well as permanent marking of the skin such as tattooing or branding, usually on the face where it cannot be easily hidden, except by the wearing of a mask, which alerts others in itself. Disabling has included cutting the tendons of the hamstrings, castration, the breaking of bones and joints, and, more recently, limb punishment shootings, which includes kneecapping but also the shooting of elbows, wrists and ankles depending on the severity of the violation." He looked around at the group. "In answer to your unasked question, yes, I believe this is appropriate in this situation."

"I agree," said Christian. "But I think each person should have the opportunity to either include or exclude themselves from this decision."

Christian looked at Mike, who just nodded. Bill nodded. When he turned to Ann and Tracy, he was surprised but glad to see both of them nod yes.

Christian looked at Bill. "Judge, in the absence of any sentencing guidelines, I'd be interested to know what your suggestion would be for punishment. "

Bill remained quiet for several minutes while looking at the three thugs laying on the ground. Then he turned back to the others. "I've spent a few minutes thinking about what they did, and what I believe in my heart they would have done if they hadn't been stopped. I have also thought about what they may well do to others if the punishment we administer is not sufficient. But there is one more aspect I would like to consider before coming to a conclusion, and that is intent."

He looked at his wife and daughter, his eyes welling with tears. "We know what they said before the physical assault began, but after that all I could hear was him telling me they were going to make me watch before they killed me. And I heard your screams." His voice choked. "Did they say anything to you?"

Ann and Tracy looked at each other, their eyes also brimming with tears, but mouths set in anger. Ann spoke. "The one who was holding me said I was next, after they were done with Tracy."

Tracy was unable to keep her tears from spilling over any longer, but as they trailed down her cheeks her eyes showed plainly that they were tears of rage, not fear. "The one who was on me said I was a fighter, but he was going to take the fight out of me and the others could have me when he was done."

The group looked at each other closely, then at the three on the ground. The family's initial shock was dissipating and giving way to a deep rage. Christian was the first to speak.

"Judge, I think we all knew what their intentions were, but, in my opinion, this new information, the fact that they plainly told their victims what they intended to do, removes any reasonable doubt and should be taken into consideration for appropriate punishment. I withdraw my objection to execution."

Everyone looked at Christian, no one speaking for a full minute as each internalized the full meaning of what he had said, and came to their own acceptance of it.

Finally, Bill said quietly, "We'll carry out the sentence as soon as we're ready to go."

It took the better part of an hour for them to go through both the Suburban and the trailer, deciding which things were the most important to take with them.

Tracy had a backpack from school, into which she placed all her socks and underwear, some t-shirts, her toiletries, a pair of leather sandals, two sweatshirts and an extra pair of jeans. She stuffed her personal papers and a few thumb drives with pictures on them in a side pocket, along with her jewelry and a few small mementos from school. She put on a pair of low hikers, a KU ball cap and a lightweight jacket.

With Christian and Mike's help, Bill and Ann fashioned two packs out of a couple of Tracy's heavier jackets, which they filled with their own clothes and personal items they had brought on the trip, along with the small amount of snack food they had with them and some bottled water.

With preparations completed, Christian and Mike walked over to the three prisoners. Christian cut the line between tat's wrists and ankles and they turned all three onto their backs. A mixture of rage and fear showed in each pair of eyes as the thugs glared at their captors.

Christian stood over them, looking each one in the eyes. "You probably heard us talking earlier. That was your trial."

He turned back to the Garners. "If anyone wants to remove themselves from this, say so now."

No one said anything. They just kept looking at the three on the ground. Christian drew his pistol and walked to stand over tats.

"Wait."

Christian turned toward the voice. It was Bill who had spoken. Christian had half expected someone to have second thoughts, but had expected it to be one of the women.

Bill walked over to Christian and held out his hand, palm up. "It was my family they intended to rape and kill. It's my job to do this."

Christian started to hand him his pistol but Bill shook his head. "No, the one they were going to use on us."

Christian nodded, re-holstering his own weapon and removing the Glock he had taken from camo from his waistband. He racked the slide, ensuring there was a round in the chamber, picked up the one that had ejected off the ground and reloaded it into the magazine, then handed the gun to Bill butt first. "You know how to use this?"

All eyes were on Bill as he accepted the pistol from Christian. "It's been a long time, but yes."

Bill looked at the three attackers on the ground, then walked slowly over to tats and looked down at him. "You were going to rape my wife and daughter and make me watch. Now, you watch, so you can anticipate your own punishment."

Walking to camo, Bill pointed the pistol at camo's groin. "You were going to rape my wife and my daughter. I find you guilty." The sound of the pistol was startling in the surrounding silence, but was drowned out by the screams of the would-be rapist. Blood leaked out of the holes the bullet put in his jeans, splashes being sent over the ground as he thrashed and tore against his bonds. Tats and red shirt also started bucking, trying to get away from the fate they now realized was theirs.

Bill stepped over to red shirt, who had turned back over onto his stomach and was trying to inchworm himself away, grunting and wheezing with the effort. Bill walked slowly around him, as if studying him, then delivered a crushing kick to his ribs. As red shirt contracted into a fetal position on his side from the blow, Bill placed his foot on his shoulder, rolling him back over onto his back, then slid his foot to red shirt's throat and leaned down to look into his eyes.

"You were going to rape my wife and my daughter. I find you guilty."

The blast was as loud as the first one, but red shirt had trouble screaming with Bill's weight pressing onto his throat. As Bill lifted his foot, red shirt's strangled gurgling turned to a combination of a wail and a howl as he curled into a trembling ball of pain. The muzzle had been so close to red shirt's groin the flash had burned his trousers, emitting a thin whiff of smoke from the singed fabric.

Tats had been watching the punishment of his fellow gang members, and was having difficulty maintaining a defiant facade. He had always thought himself tough, but he had always been the predator, never the prey. Since he was a teenager, he had reveled in his ability to frighten and intimidate others. He had enjoyed watching their discomfort and fear, then their panic and emotional collapse as he had released his full sadistic personality on them. Now things were reversed, and his mounting terror came wrapped in confusion over his new reality. When Bill came to stand over him, tats' feeble attempt at a kick came more from fear than defiance, a sign of the mental reversal he was now experiencing.

Instead of standing over him, Bill sat on tats' stomach, straddling him and pinning his head to the ground with a fist full of hair and the pistol barrel pressed hard into his throat. Though tats tried to buck Bill off and bring his legs up to either knee Bill in the back or wrap his legs around Bill's head, his bound wrists and ankles didn't allow him the leverage.

Bill leaned forward to lock eyes with his prisoner. "I want you to think back a few hours. Think back to the time when you came into our lives intending to destroy us. You saw us as victims, just as I'm sure you've viewed many others over the years. You felt you could take whatever you wanted from us, our property, our dignity, even our lives, simply because you wanted to and you brought force. The lives of others meant nothing to you, because you think with the primitive, destructive mind of a sub-human brute. Well, today, force has been brought against you, and will be applied with the same mercy I'm sure you've shown others."

The others watched solemnly as Bill handed down the sentence to the man beneath him, Christian and Mike with approval, Ann and Tracy as if they were seeing a part of their husband and father they had never seen before, but also with approval.

Bill continued. "In a moment, I'm going to geld you with a bullet. I have no doubt the pain will be horrendous. But I imagine that the horror of what has happened to you will surpass even the greatest physical pain. You will realize that one of your intended victims, one you so enjoyed exerting power over, has destroyed you as a man, and there is nothing you can do about it."

Bill paused, watching the fear build in the criminal's eyes, then continued. "After I shoot you, I'm going to allow you to live for a while. Not long, but long enough for you to experience the feeling of helplessness and hopelessness you intended for us." Bill moved the gun from tats' throat to his groin. "Now, is there anything you would like to say?"

Tats was trembling, finally understanding the reality of the situation. He was no longer thinking, his mind fracturing into broken pieces he wasn't able to put back together. "Please... please..."

"Okay," replied Bill, "since you asked nicely."

The sound of the shot only slightly preceded tats' screams. He bucked in agonized frenzy, almost throwing Bill off, but Bill remained on his chest until the thrashing subsided as shock set in. Bill then got up, never taking his eyes off of tat's face until he turned back to the others.

Everyone was silent as Bill walked over to his wife and daughter, extending a hand to each. "I'm sorry."

Both women moved past his extended hands, folding themselves into his arms. As the family embraced, Bill kept repeating "I'm sorry, I'm sorry, I'm sorry..."

Ann was the first to pull away, and she looked Bill sternly in the eye. "You have nothing to be sorry for."

"Yes, I do." He looked closely at each of them. "I've allowed myself to hide behind the law and the thin veneer of what I believed was a civilized society, a veneer I saw torn away every day in my courtroom. By doing so, I abdicated my primary responsibility to provide for the safety and security of my family. I placed your welfare in the hands of a society I saw fail on a daily basis." He nodded at Christian and Mike. "If they hadn't come along, I would probably be dead now and I can't bear to think what would be happening to you. I can only ask that you forgive me."

Tracy just hugged her dad tighter, but Ann knew that she needed to address her husband's feelings now, not later. She drew away and looked him in the eye.

"Listen to me. You are the strongest and the bravest man I have ever known. You have stood by your principles, provided for us, protected us and lead us as a family in the world we knew. Don't you ever think you haven't. And don't you ever apologize for being the best man I have ever known." She took a deep breath before continuing. "What happened today came out of a new world we are apparently living in, and, now that we know it, there is no one I would trust more than you to keep us safe."

Bill looked at his wife for a moment and slowly nodded. "There's one more thing I have to do."

He extracted himself from Tracy's arms and walked toward the three criminals on the ground. His first shot took red shirt in the forehead. Moving to camo, who was still writhing on the ground, he lifted the pistol and put one round into his chest. Camo shuddered and stopped moving.

As he moved over to tats, Ann walked over to him and put a hand on his arm. He turned to see her standing beside him with her hand out.

"I've been your partner for thirty years," she said. "I'm your partner now. He hurt you. He's mine."

After a moment's hesitation, Bill handed the gun to her. "Are you sure?"

Ann nodded. "It's mine to do."

Taking the gun from her husband's hand, she walked slowly toward tats. Standing at his feet, she watched as his eyes locked on hers. He seemed to sneer until she raised the gun to point at his face. She pulled the trigger, surprised by the recoil and realized that she had missed his head. Holding the pistol in only her right hand, she had flinched, missing her intended target and hitting him in the left shoulder, making him writhe and scream in pain.

Walking around to his head, she held the pistol in a two-handed grip as she had seen her husband do. Leaning down until the muzzle of the gun was only a few inches from tats' face, she waited until he stopped flopping around and his fluttering eyes once again met hers, then pulled the trigger.

The blast sounded more muffled to her than the others had, and she didn't notice the blood spray and bits of tissue that blew back onto her. Holding the pistol in place for another moment, she saw the locked-back slide and the head wound beneath it. Then she straightened up and turned to face Christian, Mike and her family. "Let's go."

3

Jim Wyatt shut off the tractor and looked back at the area he had just tilled. About four acres, it quadrupled the space of his existing garden, which was now beginning to sprout its many rows of tomatoes, cucumbers, zucchini, corn, beets, beans, potatoes, carrots and melons. Until three days ago, it had been more than enough to satisfy the needs of his family, supplemented with meat and dairy products from the grocery store and their freezers. Now, without a commercial supply chain to rely on, he knew they would have to grow a lot more, not only for their immediate needs, but to can for later and to use for trade.

It was still early enough to get in a second crop, which meant they would have fresh vegetables from June through the first frost in October, and more to set up as stores. Plus, the apple, peach, plum and cherry trees he had planted several years ago were starting to show good fruit. He hoped that would be enough, as he didn't want to deplete the food bunker's stock if he could help it. Looking around the property, he figured he could add another twenty acres of food production in the future, but this patch was about all he'd be able to get in right away.

He was taking off his hat to wipe his forehead when he saw Aedan charging across the yard, followed closely by Brody and not so closely by a slower but determined Morgan.

"Daddy, daddy! There's some people coming down the road!"

Jim smiled. "Do they look like friends or enemies?"

Aedan stopped, excitement beaming from his sweaty face. "I don't know. Mommy said to come tell you!"

"Mommy said to come tell you!" echoed Brody.

Jim chuckled, put his hat back on and shut off the tractor. "Well, let's go see what they look like."

He pulled his AR out of the scabbard on the tractor and started walking toward the driveway that ran by the side of the house. As he approached the house, he shooed the kids inside and heard Kelly tell him to be careful, to which he gave a wave while slinging the rifle around his neck and unconsciously touching the butt of the pistol on his belt.

He kept an eye on the road as he walked down the long drive, hearing the dogs come up behind him. As he neared the iron gate, he saw the people approaching, three men and two women. One had a familiar walk. He opened the gate and stepped through, then waited for them to get within talking distance.

"About time you got here, boy!" he yelled with a smile.

A grin broke out on Christian's face. "Been trying to get here, but got held up a bit."

The two men walked to within handshake distance, but threw their arms around each other instead, Wyatt slapping Christian's back. "Damn good to see you." He let him go and looked at the others. "Who'd you bring along?"

Christian gestured toward Mike. "Mike came with me from the hospital. These other three are a package we picked up along the way - Bill, Ann and Tracy. Folks, this is my uncle Jim."

Wyatt nodded with a smile. "Well, if you're with Christian and he's not holding a gun on you, you must be alright. Let's get up to the house and get you all something to eat and let you sit down."

Christian nodded toward the dogs, who were sitting attentively on either side of Jim. "Is it safe? What the heck do you feed those things?"

Wyatt laughed. "Unfriendly strangers. But they just had a couple, so you should be okay for a while."

Jim came back onto the deck with two more beers, gave one to Christian and sat back down. "I didn't think it would start so soon."

After Christian had arrived with the others, Jim and Kelly had arranged for all of them to get showers and be provided with new clothes, then have time to relax and decompress before dinner. Some of Jim's clothes had fit Mike, who settled into a spare bedroom with its own bathroom while Kelly took the Garners down to the finished basement which had more room and a full bathroom of its own.

Christian had stayed with Jim while Kelly started preparing dinner, and had been telling him about his trip for the past hour. He had covered the incident with the family and the thugs in detail, including his opinion of their guests.

Jim took a long pull of his beer. "So, you think they're good folks?"

Christian nodded. "From what I can tell. It hit them hard, but they came through tough. Every one of them. I was surprised."

"How about Mike?"

Christian shrugged. "I don't know him well. He was a paramedic who came into the ER a lot. Always seemed like a good guy. Says he was a sniper in the marines. Doesn't talk much, but he was ready to go when things got real and has acted right all along. So far, I'd say he's solid."

"Good." He looked over at Christian. "You staying?

"Hell yeah, I'm staying. Somebody's got to watch your back. Besides, where else am I going to find good cooking like Kelly's?" He was quiet for a moment. "And you always said family is what's important when things get bad. Well, you're my family, and like the guy in that movie said, if this ain't bad, it'll do till bad gets here."

Jim laughed. "Glad you remembered that. About family, I mean. Good. Tonight, we'll just relax and make our guests comfortable. I have a feeling Bill will want to talk a bit, and I'd like to talk to him too. Tomorrow, I want to go over some things with you. How we're set up and what our plans are."

"What about Mike?" asked Christian.

Jim thought for a moment. "I'll leave that to you. If we're going to do what I think is going to be necessary, we're going to need more people, as long as they are good people and have skills to contribute or the willingness to learn them. I imagine Mike has skills that we could use here. If you keep thinking he's a good guy, let him know we'd be happy to have him stay."

Dinner had been hamburger steaks cooked on the grill, smothered with mushrooms, grilled onions and melted Swiss cheese, green beans, carrots and grilled corn on the cob with iced tea and lemonade, eaten at the long table for twelve Jim had built on the expansive stone veranda he had also built along the side and back of the house. A pergola covered with wisteria and honeysuckle shaded the entire deck and a stone outdoor fireplace, today unused, dominated the far end. It was the family's favorite place to sit during nice weather.

Table talk had been relaxed, if a bit subdued, everyone thinking about the Garner's ordeal and what it indicated about the new reality they faced. Jim and Kelly had inquired about the Garners' previous work, to which the Garners answered politely, and the Garners complimented the house and grounds, to which Jim and Kelly responded in great detail in order to relieve the Garners from having to make too much conversation. Mike mainly ate, smiled and looked at Tracy while the kids ran around, chasing, and sometimes being chased by the dogs.

When the meal ended, Ann and Tracy helped Kelly clear the table and do the dishes while the men remained, enjoying the relaxation. Finally,

Christian and Mike got up to straighten out their gear, leaving only Jim and Bill at the table.

Jim could tell that Bill wanted to talk, but also knew he might feel a bit hesitant, so he broke the silence. "Did Kelly get you all settled in okay?"

Bill nodded. "Yes, very well." He paused for a moment, looking down at the table then back up. "Jim, I want to thank you for taking us in like this. We all want to thank you. I know it must be a great imposition."

Jim waved it off. "No imposition at all. We like having company and the kids always love it when other folks come by. It gives them new people to show off for." He chuckled, then became more serious. "I'm just glad you all hooked up with Christian. He told me everything that happened."

Bill watched the kids playing for a few moments. "Did he tell you I killed three men?"

Jim noticed that Bill had not mentioned his wife's part in the killings. "He told me you blew the nuts off of and then executed three dirt bags who were going to gang rape your wife and daughter and probably kill all of you. Is that about right?"

Bill nodded. "Yes."

"Christian said it was justice. Sounds like justice to me."

Bill nodded again, though more in thought than agreement. "I was a judge for almost fifteen years. I dealt with these people all the time. Sometimes, I was able to sentence them according to what I felt was justice. Sometimes I was constrained by sentencing guidelines or deals the prosecutors felt were necessary." He took a deep breath. "And sometimes their crimes were so heinous, so inhuman, no sentence would have been justice."

Jim said nothing, giving Bill time to talk it through.

It took a minute before Bill continued. "What I did yesterday, I would have to go back several hundred years to find precedent for. Yet it felt just. Still, I wonder whether it really was just or simply felt like it because it was personal."

Jim was quiet for a minute in case Bill had more to say, then leaned forward, forearms on the table. "Christian used to be a cop. So was I. We both did it because we wanted to help people, to stand between the good folks and the bad guys and hold the bad guys to account. We both left in disgust because we discovered it was all a big game that had little to do with justice and a lot to do with who knew who, what political point was in play and how much money you had. We got tired of taking out the garbage for a dysfunctional society that seemed intent on creating an endless supply of new garbage."

He leaned back again and continued. "The majority of people you sentenced during those fifteen years went on to hurt more people - many more people. The three you took care of yesterday will never hurt another person. The rest of good society owes you a debt of gratitude."

Bill shook his head slowly. "Is that what we've returned to, then?" he asked. "A society in which individuals take retaliatory action on their own? Where a gun at the side of the road takes the place of a court of law?"

Jim nodded. "That was more justice than I saw coming out of a lot a court rooms in my time, and you just said the same thing yourself a minute ago. Let me ask you something, Bill. Who were the victims out there yesterday?"

Bill looked at him, giving a small shrug. "My family and I."

"Exactly. You know what used to get me? When something horrendous would happen to someone, and when it got to court, if it got to court, it was 'the state of such-and-such versus so-and-so'. The state, which had not protected the victim in the first place was now taking the victim's place in seeking justice. In the end, the lawyers got paid, the judge got paid, the court reporter got paid, everybody who shuffled some papers got paid, the crook either went to prison or didn't, and the victim went home with nothing but the state's pompous assurance that justice had been done. No offense, Bill, but I think that system would have made our founders want to puke, and was part of what was bringing this country down even before this happened."

Both men were silent for a few minutes. Jim got up and came back with a bottle and two glasses. He poured two fingers into each glass and set one in front of Bill before sitting down to his own. "I drink Wild Turkey. One-o-one to celebrate and eighty-six on more serious occasions. This seems like an eighty-six night."

Bill smiled and picked up the glass. "I'll drink to that." He took a sip of the bourbon and gestured at the property with a sweep of his hand. "You have a beautiful set up here. Christian said you saw all this coming."

Jim shrugged. "Well, I was afraid something was going to happen. I didn't know what it would be, but with the economy, the corruption in the government, international problems and our own societal troubles here at home, I wanted to separate and protect my family from whatever came down the road. I wanted to be self-sufficient and not have to rely on outside providers, especially the government. I decided to prepare for an EMP because I figured if we were prepared for that we'd be prepared for anything. And look what we got. How about you?"

Bill took another sip of the bourbon and looked down at his hands. He shook his head. "Ann told me something like this could happen. She was starting to get interested in all that preparedness stuff and even had me watch a couple of National Geographic shows about it. I'm afraid I didn't take it very seriously. It seemed like a lot of tinfoil hat stuff to me. So essentially, I was prepared for everything just going along the way it had been. I had insurance, savings and a retirement plan. Something like this just seemed impossible, like science fiction."

Jim nodded. "I think most people felt that way. Christian told me you all are from Ohio. What are you going to do?"

Bill was quiet for a moment and shook his head. "I don't know. Ann tells me this could last for years. That seems unbelievable, but I know it's true. I don't know how we can get back home, but I'm not sure what else to do."

Jim took a sip from his own glass. "Bill, trying to get back to Ohio would be suicide, at least right now. Those who made projections about something like this estimated a die-off of fifty percent of the population within six months and up to ninety percent within a year from dehydration, starvation, disease and all the violence that will come with societal collapse. We're back in the frontier days, but with three hundred million more people, few who can provide for themselves, many of whom have psychological problems, and millions who are just mean and waiting to prey on the vulnerable. You don't want to be out traveling in that, especially with two women."

Bill nodded his head. "I know you're right. But I don't know what else I can do."

Jim drained his glass and set it on the table. "Well, you all are welcome here until you decide. We can talk some more tomorrow. I have an idea."

4

Jim awakened earlier than usual. Everyone had turned in soon after dinner and the last thing he remembered was talking with Kelly in bed. The next thing he knew he was waking up to the faint light of dawn.

Kelly was still asleep, as was his left arm that had been under her head all night. Gently, and as quietly as he could, he pulled his dead arm out from under her and got dressed in the dark using his right hand. His arm started the electric buzz in time for him to put on his boots and gun belt, and he went downstairs to the large kitchen and hearth room. Making a cup of instant coffee, he put a large percolating coffee pot on the gas stove for when the others got up and went out to drink his first cup on the deck.

It looked like it was going to be a beautiful day. The sky was showing the pink and purple tones that resulted from clouds in the east, and the west was starting to change from dark to brilliant blue. He knew it would be warm later, but it was still cool and the slight breeze made the hot coffee taste just right. He thought about how drastically things had changed over the past few days, yet the world continued on in all its beauty as if nothing had happened. And he thought that put things into an important perspective.

He watched the sun creep a bit higher, then finished his coffee and walked out to the attached garage addition he had added a year ago coming off the back of the house. The garage had four bays with a large open apartment above it that would accommodate six with its own kitchen and bathroom. What no one but Kelly and the contractors who poured the foundation knew was that it also had a full basement. The addition had interior steel doors to each level of the house, basement, ground and second floor, but he didn't want to bother anyone who was still asleep and wasn't yet ready to let anyone else know about the bunker.

Entering the garage through the pedestrian door, he walked over to a large wooden work table in the far corner. Moving several items off it, he lifted one end and tilted the table so that it rested on its top and rear legs. Rolling back a large black mat that had been positioned under the table, he lifted a sheet of heavy plywood by a hinge at its midpoint, revealing a closed, inward swinging steel door beneath it. Unlatching and lowering the door, he flipped on a light switch and descended into the bunker on the metal ladder set into the concrete shaft.

In the past, he had always had mixed feelings when entering the bunker. On one hand, he felt good that his family was well provided for in case of any emergency. On the other hand, he had occasionally wondered if he'd been a bit nuts to spend this much money on a "what if?". Now, all doubt was gone and he was glad he had followed his instincts.

The bunker was large, measuring the full twenty-four by forty-eight-foot footprint of the garage above it. Indirect low voltage lighting gave the space a pleasant glow, unlike the harsh lighting of many such shelters, and the soft whir of fans could be heard as they circulated air in and out of the bunker. Walking to a desk on the near wall, Jim turned on a laptop.

The day after the event, Jim had opened the large Faraday room he had constructed at the far end of the bunker. In theory, the entire bunker was a Faraday room, as was the garage above it, but he believed in redundancy whenever possible. You just never knew.

Inside were numerous shelves of electronic equipment, including laptops, televisions, radios, walkie-talkies, wireless alarms, surveillance systems, inverters and controllers for the wind and solar power systems and more. He had been relieved when he powered up the laptop and found it functional. Theoretically, he knew the specially designed room should protect his equipment, but seeing was believing.

Bringing up the surveillance program, he found that all four of the cameras he had installed were working. Today, he would install more, and he would keep doing so until he had the entire property covered.

Walking through the bunker, he made a quick mental assessment of what they had on hand. Most of the bunker was taken up by shelved food storage. Six bunks built against the far wall served as shelving for tents, tarps, sleeping bags and other outdoor equipment. A separate area held a row of metal gun lockers.

It took him about forty-five minutes to remind himself of what they had and make mental notes of what they should try to pick up wherever they could. Glancing back at the laptop, he noticed that Christian and Mike had come out onto the veranda. None of the other cameras showed any activity so he picked up the laptop and climbed out of the bunker, securing it behind him.

Max and Pink joined him as he exited the garage and walked up to the veranda. "I figured you boys had decided to sleep all day."

Mike smiled from behind his coffee cup as Christian made an exaggerated show of looking at the sky. "Well, uncle, if sun-up is all day I must have missed lunch and supper so I guess I'd better finish breakfast and get back to bed."

Kelly came out of the kitchen door and put a large platter of biscuits on the table. "Is he giving you guys a hard time?"

Christian laughed. "He's trying to, but I think he just needs a good morning hug."

"Oh yeah? From me or you?"

Jim came up behind her and put her in a bear hug. "I'll take it from you. He's too ugly."

Kelly spun around in his arms and kissed him quickly, then ducked under his arm and headed back to the kitchen. "We've got work to do," she said with a smile over her shoulder.

Jim grabbed a biscuit and sat down at the end of the table. "You guys get some sleep?"

Both nodded. "Like a log," said Christian.

"Yes, sir," said Mike.

"Good, 'cause we have a lot to do and go over today. Christian, have you made a decision on what we talked about?"

Christian nodded. "I've told Mike we'd be happy to have him stay with us if he'd like to."

Jim looked at Mike.

"Yes, sir. I appreciate the invitation. From what Christian has told me, you've really thought this through. I'd like to stay for a while and will be happy to help any way I can."

"Good, then we're happy to have you. I just have one question and one request."

"Yes, sir?"

"First off, family is the most important thing. What about yours?"

Mike stopped smiling and looked out across the field as if trying to see a great distance. "My family is in South Carolina. My two older brothers are there with my parents and they're both tougher than me. They've been fine while I've been sent all over the world, so I imagine they'll be okay now. And they'll get my sister back one way or the other" He looked back at Jim. "We've got some land, and we're pretty well set

45

up. I want to try to get home eventually, but I don't think now is the time. Maybe in a year or so when everything settles out."

Jim nodded. "In a year, the major die-off should be over. But organized groups will be better established and some may not take well to an outsider coming through their area. You're kind of trading one problem for another."

"Yes sir, I've thought about that, but it just seems better to me."

Jim nodded again. "Well, it looks like you've thought this through. We're glad to have you. Now the request." He smiled. "I wasn't in the military, so I won't give you that 'Don't call me sir, I work for a living' jazz. But I also come from a southern family. Our ancestors first came into the country in Virginia and the Carolinas and had plantations in South Carolina until after the war, when they moved to Tennessee and then on to Missouri. Anyway, I grew up in a family where 'sir', 'ma'am' and 'miss' we're a central part of our dialogue. But I never took to a grown man calling another man 'sir', because it implies inferiority and superiority, and in my world men are judged by their character and actions, not their job or position. So, what I'm saying is that if you're bound and determined by upbringing and training to call me sir I won't be offended, but if you find you can break loose of that, then 'Jim' will be fine."

Mike gave a big grin and laughed. "My dad always said pretty much the same thing, and it always irked me to have to say it to some two-legged horse's ass in the military." He nodded. "Thanks, Jim."

Jim nodded back. "Good deal. Have a biscuit."

After breakfast, the morning was spent touring the property, showing Mike and the Garners the different areas of Stonemont.

A short distance from the main house was a stone and log guest house, built in the same manner as the main house, in which, it was decided, the Garners would stay. It would afford them privacy as a family, and provide a tactical outpost to the main house.

Beyond the guest house, a pasture sloped gradually to the lower field which included the acres Jim had just finished tilling and a large pond they had stocked with bluegill several years before.

Eventually coming to the tree line that marked the property's southern boundary, they followed it west to a creek that followed the low area between their own hill and the one to the west. Following the creek a quarter of a mile, they came to a series of ascending natural terraces that climbed to the western field which included fenced areas for several cows and the family's three horses.

As they walked back toward the house and neared the large barn, a structure that had been on the property when the Wyatts bought it, they saw several empty corrals and a chicken yard and coop with several dozen chickens clucking and pecking around.

Returning to the main house, Jim explained that they had designed the house themselves after years of talking about what they wanted. The first floor had two-foot-thick walls, constructed of natural stone on both interior and exterior sandwiching reinforced concrete in between. The second floor was constructed of filled concrete blocks faced with nine-inch logs on the outside and reinforced wallboard on the inside. The thickness of the walls provided insulation in addition to security, keeping the house cool in summer and warm in winter. Functional steel shutters were fitted into each window and door, secured with large bolts set into the concrete sections of the walls.

The central part of the first floor was a large, two story main hall dominated by a huge fireplace. Off the hall was an office, a dining room, a front room, a library, a mud/utility room and the kitchen/hearth room. The upstairs consisted of five bedrooms and a walkway which overlooked the central hall. The deep veranda on which they had eaten supper and breakfast ran across the rear of the house and around the east side.

During a quick lunch of sandwiches and sweet tea, Jim laid out the plans for the afternoon. Kelly, Ann and Tracy would get the guest house opened up and cleaned in preparation for the Garners to move in. Christian would go with Jim to check on a couple of neighbors, and Mike and Bill would stay at Stonemont for security

When lunch was over, the women headed for the guest house and the men headed for the garage. "The dogs will give you plenty of warning if anyone is coming," Jim told Mike and Bill. "I don't really expect any trouble yet, but better stay alert. Kelly is carrying her pistol and has an AR with her."

He handed Mike a MURS radio turned to the same channel as the one he was carrying. "These are pretty good, but we're going to be right at the edge of their range, so we may or may not be able to hear you if you call."

He turned to watch the women and kids as they arrived at the guest house. "This is too big a place for one man to cover adequately. From now on, we always need at least two men on the compound and will establish a twenty-four-hour watch." He handed Bill an AR he had brought from the house. "Are you familiar with these?"

Bill took the rifle and shook his head. "No, I've only seen other people use them. I've never touched one before."

"Well, this afternoon will be a great time for Mike to start training you on it." He looked at Mike, who nodded. "I can't think of a better teacher than a recon marine. We should be back before dark, but until then, you're in charge of security, Mike."

"Yes, sir." Then, at Jim's grimace, he smiled. "Okay, Jim."

5

As he turned the Excursion west out of Stonemont, Jim explained to Christian what they were doing.

"I want to check on a couple of neighbors. We're going to the Samuels' first. You might remember them from when you spent summers here." He glanced at Christian with a smile. "At least I'm sure you remember their granddaughter. They were okay when I checked on them the day after the event, but I want to check on them every few days. Then we'll go over to the Eddington's a couple of miles back the other way. They weren't home when I checked before, so I'm hoping they've made it back."

Christian looked at his uncle. "How bad do you think it's going to get?"

Jim thought for a moment, bringing the picture together in his mind. "It's going to get bad. Real bad. It's been what, four days? I imagine the city is starting to come apart. Most people are out of food and haven't had clean water for a couple of days. People are already starting to die of dehydration but don't know it. Some may be heading to the creeks and rivers, but most won't know how to process it to drink. They'll start dying of intestinal problems and starvation. Some who don't already kill for fun or profit will be killing for food and water. Kids and old people will be among the most vulnerable. Some will be abandoned and some will be the cause of death for those trying to take care of them. There's no police, no fire protection, no ambulance service, no light at night and no government help coming. It's already bad, and it's going to get worse."

Christian was quiet for a moment. "You've really thought about this."

Jim nodded slowly. "I have."

"What about the suburbs?"

Jim gave a small shrug. "Things will be a bit better there, I think, at least for a while. Most people in the suburbs tend to be more prepared than those in the city. They don't live so much day-to-day. They are better educated, possess better social and coping skills, and are generally in better health. Plus, they have a much higher percentage of intact families with fathers present, and more integrated support groups like churches, school organizations and the like. They're not so dependent on government and social services. But they'll run out of food and water pretty soon too, except for the preppers, who will soon stick out like a sore thumb because they're not suffering like the rest. Then, their friends and neighbors will start coming to them for help, and they'll have to decide whether to help or not. If they try to help, they'll soon be starving with the rest unless they have enough stockpiled to feed everyone they know, everyone who knows everyone they know, and everyone who just happens to come by. If they decide against helping, they're going to have to defend themselves against everyone who comes for their stuff. That means probably having to kill some people, maybe a lot of people. All while other people are trying to kill them for their food. Of course, they can try to leave, but if they don't have a place to go or a way to carry enough supplies they're in the same boat as the rest of the refugees." He turned into the Samuels' long drive. "Yeah, it's going to be bad."

Ralph Samuels was walking back from the barn when Jim pulled the Excursion up to the side of the house under the shade of a massive oak tree. Coming to the Samuels' had always reminded him of going to visit his grandparents on their farm. The barn was red and the house was white, with a screened side porch that served as the main entry and exit of the house, and that, of course, through the kitchen. Only strangers came to the front door, and the slamming of the screen porch door let everyone know when someone was coming or going.

Ralph gave them a wave. "Howdy, Jim. You're just in time for lunch."

Jim smiled as he and Christian got out of the truck. "Thanks Ralph, but we just ate. We came by to say hi and see how you were doing." He nodded toward Christian. "You remember my nephew, Christian?"

Ralph looked at Christian with a sly smile. "I remember a wild young whipper-snapper who broke his arm falling out of my barn loft when we found him up there with my granddaughter, but this monster can't be him."

Christian smiled big and held out his hand. "Afraid so, Mr. Samuels. Good to see you. And I'm sorry about breaking that chair I fell on."

Samuels chuckled. "Oh, that's alright son. At least you didn't break the anvil." He looked Christian up and down. "And I think you're big enough now to call me Ralph. Come on. Even if you just ate, you ought to have room for pie."

The slamming screen door announced their entry and Mary Samuels met them as they stepped into the kitchen. "Thank goodness it's you, Jim. I heard voices and thought Ralph was talking to himself again."

Ralph chuckled. "She still thinks the voices she hears are coming from outside her head." He kissed her on the forehead and winked at Christian.

Mary swatted him with a dish towel. "And if you'd stop talking to yourself, the voices in my head would go away."

She smiled at Jim, then looked at Christian. "And it looks like you brought an eating machine with you, Jim, and just in time for lunch."

Ralph nodded at Christian. "This is Jim's nephew, Christian. The one Becky mooned over every summer for so many years. Remember?"

Mary took a step back and looked Christian up and down. "Oh, do I remember. Every summer, we'd spend the first month hearing her talk about you, the second month not seeing her at all because the two of you were out gallivanting around, and the third month watching her mope around like a sick calf because she missed you." She chuckled. "How's your head?"

Christian made a show of gingerly touching the back of his head. "I think it's about healed, ma'am."

She laughed and patted him on the arm. "Ralph always said he could see a head-shaped dent in his anvil. Said a broken arm served you right for denting his anvil and leading Becky astray. Well, sit down. You both look like you're starving."

After convincing Mary that they had just eaten, Jim and Christian each had a large piece of apple pie and coffee while the Samuels ate lunch.

Ralph dug into a large slab of ham, then looked at Jim. "It looks like this EMT thing of yours is still going on."

"EMP," said Mary.

Ralph looked at her. "What?"

"EMP. EMTs are those fellas that ride on the ambulance. What Jim was telling us about is called an EMP."

"Oh. Well, whatever it's called, it doesn't seem to be over." He looked back at Jim. "You really think it's going to last as long as you said?"

Jim shrugged. "I don't know. But I think we'd better plan on it lasting quite a while. How are you all doing?"

Ralph took a drink of milk. "We're fine. Kind of reminds me of when we first moved here. Candlelight baths and all that. I think Mary likes it. Every time I fall asleep she tries to fiddle with me."

The dish towel made immediate contact with a resounding slap on Ralph's arm. "If I touch you, it's only because I'm trying to find the switch to turn off the sawmill I'm sleeping with. Besides, these gentlemen don't want to hear that nonsense, and Christian is too young anyway."

Ralph gave a sly smile. "Not from what I remember. Or from what I overheard Becky tell you."

A second strike from the dish towel was caught in one of Ralph's large hands and used to pull Mary to him as he held her and kissed her on the cheek. "Don't be ashamed honey. It's not your fault I'm irresistible."

Jim and Christian laughed, watching the antics of the older couple.

Mary finally pulled away and made a show of smoothing her hair and dress. "Irresistible, my eye. I can resist you just fine, thank you." She turned around and started clearing the table.

"We're worried about Rebecca and Becky, though," said Ralph. "It's just the two of them and Bobby up in Topeka. We think they're pretty well set up, but we don't know if they're going to stay there or try to get here."

"Who's Bobby?" asked Christian.

Ralph and Mary looked at each other, then Ralph answered. "Bobby is Becky's boy." He hesitated, then went on. "Becky had a boyfriend in college, up at Washburn. She got pregnant, and when she told him she was going to keep the baby he decided that didn't fit into his plans. She moved back in with her folks and finished college. Then when Robert was killed by that drunk driver, it left just the two of them and Bobby."

"When was the last time you saw them?" Jim asked.

"A couple of weeks ago. They would come down every month or so and we'd go up there every now and then. They have a nice house in south Topeka."

"Ralph says he's going up there tomorrow to try to get them," Mary said, her voice and the look on her face showing the worry she felt. "He won't let me come with him."

Jim and Christian looked at each other. Neither was very familiar with Topeka, but both knew it was large enough to have serious problems. Jim thought for a moment, then looked at Ralph. "How about if we go up with you? There could be trouble up there, and more guns is better."

Ralph looked at Jim as if he wasn't sure. "It's not your problem, Jim. They're my family, and I don't want you all putting yourself at risk for us."

Jim set his coffee cup down on the table and looked Ralph hard in the eye. "You're kidding, right? And you wouldn't want to help me if the tables were turned?"

"That's what I told him," said Mary.

Ralph stared at the empty milk glass in his hands. It had never been his way to ask for help with personal problems. Cutting hay, sure. Or fixing the roof on the barn. That was just what neighbors did. But he felt that this was a family matter and he didn't want to put friends in jeopardy, even if he thought their help might make the difference.

He looked up at Jim. "And what if we don't make it and you get killed, too? What will Kelly and the kids do?"

Jim pushed that thought aside. "We'll try not to let that happen. Now, things are probably already getting bad, and they're just going to get worse the longer we wait. We'll pick you up tomorrow morning around sunrise."

He turned to Mary. "You ought to be ready too, Mary. We'll take you over to our place to stay while we're gone."

"Oh, Jim, I'll be okay here. I'm here by myself all the time when he runs into town or to the sale barn."

Jim shook his head. "It's a different world, Mary. We'll pick you up in the morning."

The rest of the afternoon was spent checking the Eddington's place, where they still found no one, and installing more surveillance cameras at Stonemont.

Kelly had the Garners moved into the guest house, where they had given the place a quick cleaning and put on new bed linens. Mike had spent his time identifying potential shooting positions around the compound and scouting the property for likely attack channels, making mental notes on how to fortify the former and tactically manage the latter.

When they gathered that evening for dinner, Jim explained their trip to Topeka the next day. Though Kelly was worried, she understood the need, and knew she would want someone to try to get her kids out if things were reversed. She gave him one piece of advice: "Don't get killed."

Mike and Bill would remain at Stonemont and continue weapons training while Kelly, Ann and Tracy would start an inventory of food and supplies in the bunker. The reality of the new world was setting in.

6

At first light, Mike, who had taken third watch, awakened Jim and Christian. Within a half hour they were headed to the Samuels' and a half hour after that had dropped Mary off at Stonemont and were headed west.

The rising sun threw long shadows ahead of them as they kept their speed around sixty. The blacktop back roads were in good shape and the lack of other traffic made it easy to keep their speed up, as generations of Kansas kids with pickups had long known.

They passed through Baldwin City without incident and continued west on 56 Highway. Everything seemed normal except for the lack of even the minimal normal traffic and the absence of the glow of mercury vapor lights that usually illuminated the farm and ranch buildings a short distance off the roads. Cattle and horses grazed the tall green grass, corn and wheat fields were beginning to show their colors, and an occasional farmer or rancher could be seen walking to or from a house or barn. As the shadows in front of them started to shorten, they came to Highway 75 where they turned north toward Topeka.

Driving north, they began to see traces of smoke coming from chimneys. Almost all farmhouses, old and new, had fireplaces, and the older ones had fireplaces and wood stoves still in the kitchens. More people could be seen walking around, and at one point an old GMC pickup pulled out of a side road and passed them going south with a wave.

As they approached the town of Lyndon, Jim slowed to forty miles an hour. The houses were closer together here, with many properties running from a couple of acres to ten or twenty rather than the hundreds of acres of the rural farms and ranches.

As they passed through Lyndon, they drove slower still. Everything seemed normal, if you forgot that all the cars had been parked in their current positions since the event. Jim was sure that many had stalled out while driving, but small-town people were the kind that pushed them out of the way and into a parking spot. He knew the cities would not look like this.

They saw a number of older vehicles driving around, as well as a couple of tractors and one riding lawnmower, and the looks they got were only those given to obvious strangers on any normal day.

They picked up speed as they left Lyndon and within twenty minutes were entering Carbondale, another small town, though bigger than Lyndon. Carbondale was much like Lyndon, with a bit more pedestrian traffic and a few more running vehicles. They drove slowly through the town, drawing the normal stranger stares, when Jim slowed down even more. "Look up ahead."

Christian and Ralph switched their attention from watching out the side windows to looking forward. A large Caterpillar back hoe was parked across the road just on the other side of the city limit sign. Several vehicles bracketed the Cat, and several men stepped out into the road. Two were wearing uniforms and were carrying rifles in addition to their side arms. The largest man was wearing a white Stetson and gave a wave that seemed friendly but obviously meant stop.

Jim stopped about twenty feet from the men, but kept the Excursion in gear with his foot on the brake. "Stay cool but be ready," he told the others.

The man in the Stetson walked slowly toward the Excursion as the other two men separated to cover each side. They held their rifle muzzles down, but were obviously ready.

Jim figured the man coming toward them to be about six foot four and two hundred and sixty pounds. He'd obviously eaten well the last few years, but still had the light step of forty pounds ago and the muscle to move it. Genetics and hard work grew them big in Kansas. As the man approached the driver's window, Jim could see the Sheriff Department patches on his shoulders and a gold star above the left breast pocket.

The man smiled and nodded as he stopped at Jim's window. "Morning, gentlemen. I'm Sheriff Freelove." He looked inside the Excursion and saw the rifles. "I wanted to make sure you really wanted to go into Topeka before we moved our Cat out of your way. but it looks like you're ready for what you might run into."

Jim nodded back. "Morning, Sheriff. I'm Jim Wyatt from Miami County, this is my nephew, Christian, and back there", he gestured to the back seat, "is Ralph Samuels." He motioned to the sheriff's badge on Freelove's shirt. "Christian and I both did the job in Jackson County, Missouri. We're headed into Topeka to bring Ralph's daughter, granddaughter and great-grandson out and back to their farm."

56

Sheriff Freelove nodded. "No offense. We just don't know you and we're being careful."

Ralph's voice came from the back seat. "No offense taken, Sheriff. We're just getting to know you, too."

Jim, Christian and the Sheriff all looked back at Ralph and saw he was holding his shotgun, not exactly at Sheriff Freelove, but definitely in his general direction.

Jim and Christian raised their eyebrows at each other and Freelove chuckled. "What part of town do they live in?"

"Southwest," Ralph replied. "Have you heard if there's any trouble around there?"

The Sheriff looked up the road as if he was trying to visualize Topeka from where he stood. He shook his head. "I haven't been up there myself, but the word I'm getting from some coming south is that the south side isn't too bad yet. Topeka PD and the Highway Patrol sealed the bridges, only allowing people to travel from where they don't live to where they do live. Of course, that was a couple of days ago and those guys may have gone home to their families, so things might have changed. Plus, the county jail is south of the river and they let the inmates out when they couldn't feed them anymore, so they're roaming around, and a lot of them aren't local so they have nowhere to go."

"You think there's any law enforcement at all?" asked Jim.

The Sheriff shrugged. "Hard to say. A lot of TPD officers live outside the city. We have several who live here and they all stayed home after the second day. I'd guess if there are any guys left up there it's not many."

Jim thought for a moment. "What's the roadblock for?"

"We want to be able to manage any refugees coming out of Topeka. This is the first step of what you might call our filter, to let decent folks through and keep the dregs out."

"Will there be any problem with us getting back through?"

The Sheriff straightened up and shook his head. "Nope. I'm your filter and you're good to go. Give me a minute and we'll get our Cat out of your way."

He turned away and walked over to the other man in uniform, talked for a minute, then returned. "Would there be any problem with my chief deputy going with you? We'd like to see for ourselves what's going on up there, and it wouldn't hurt for you to have a local uniform with you in case you run into any of the local boys, not to mention having another gun."

Jim shook his head. "No problem at all. We'll be happy to have him. He can take the seat behind me so we'll have a non-driving AR on both sides." Jim nodded up the road. "Anything special between here and Topeka?"

The Sheriff motioned for his chief deputy to join them. "Not really. You'll see the exit for Forbes Field up a ways on the right. I'm sure the airport's closed, but there's an Air National Guard unit stationed there. From what I hear, they've secured the base and don't come out. I'd say if you don't mess with them, they probably won't mess with you. Just stay on seventy-five into Topeka."

As the chief deputy came up, Sheriff Freelove made the introductions. "Glen, this is Jim and Christian in front. They're both former deputies from Missouri. Back there is shotgun Ralph." He laughed. "His muzzle kind of wanders around, so I'd be careful." He nodded his head at the deputy. "Gentlemen, this is Glen Davis, my chief deputy. He knows Topeka pretty well, so he ought to be a help."

The deputy returned nods, climbed into the back seat and got settled as they waited for Freelove to get the Cat moved. When the way was clear, they returned Freelove's wave and continued north on highway seventy-five, following the western jag until they entered the suburbs of Topeka.

Things were starting to look different, with more people visible. Small groups walked the streets and larger groups milled around in the parking lots of strip malls, many of which had obviously been looted. No vehicles were moving, and the looks they received were different than what they had seen in the small towns. They could see the smoke from a number of fires to the north, and the sound of breaking glass drew their attention to a group of men entering a hardware store.

"Inmates from county," said Glen, recognizing the apparel from the Shawnee County Jail.

Jim pulled the Excursion into the parking lot, but stopped well back from the groups of people by the stores. Most of the businesses had already been sacked, and the remaining probably would be soon. He looked in the rearview mirror at the deputy. "You're the law here, Glen. It's your call."

Glen thought for a moment and shook his head. "This is probably going on all over. I don't think we're at the point of shooting looters, and we don't have any place to put them. Plus, dealing with this stuff will hold us up from getting to Shotgun's family. Let's go."

Jim nodded and pulled back onto the road, following Ralph's directions toward southwest Topeka. The scene remained pretty much the same as they passed more strip malls and businesses. As they turned a corner, Christian pointed up a hill ahead of them. "Black and white," he said, indicating a Topeka PD patrol car angled in the roadway at the top of the hill

Jim drove up the hill, slowing down as they got closer and stopped about twenty feet away from the squad car. The car was angled away from the curb, putting its driver's side toward them, and the trunk was open.

"Christian, Ralph, you're security while Glen and I check this out."

They got out and Christian and Ralph took positions to each side of the Excursion while Jim and Glen slowly approached the police vehicle. They soon caught the smell of decomposition that both of them recognized.

As Glen walked around the front of the car, he stopped. "Here he is."

Jim walked around the rear of the car until he saw the body. The officer lay curled up, clad only in boxer shorts and socks. Several days of heat and wild animals had left few identifying features, except for the assumption that it had been a male due to size, boxers and hair length. A pool of dark, congealed blood had collected in a low spot in the pavement about a foot from his body, the blood run beginning under his torso. Most of it had seeped through the blacktop or been lapped up by animals, but the stain and a small amount of sludge remained.

Jim nodded, looking around. "So somehow, they got the jump on him, gut shot him, took his uniform and left him here to bleed out. Which means there's a cop killer around here somewhere, maybe wearing a police uniform."

Glen nodded. "Looks that way." He went back to the car and got in, looking around. "Ignition's on. Light bar is activated." He thought for a moment and looked ahead. About ten yards up was a battered blue pickup sitting on the shoulder.

Exiting the patrol car, he walked to the pickup. An expired Nebraska license plate was hung on the bumper by some wire. In the bed were an assortment of rusted tools, tow chains, empty beer cans and a bald spare tire. A bumper sticker on the back window said "OUTLAW". Inside the cab was the usual trash he'd seen in hundreds of dirt bag car stops. Something whispered to him inside his head and he walked back to the patrol car.

He stood at the open driver's door for a minute, looking in and trying to hear what the whisper was telling him. Suddenly, it clicked. This was a two-man car. The way the computer was positioned told him that.

Walking around to the passenger side, he opened the door and looked inside. Laying on the floor was a small spiral notebook, the kind many cops carried for personal notes instead of the larger pads they kept for official notes and court reference.

Glen opened the notebook to find neat, obviously female handwriting. He looked inside the front and back covers for a name but found none. Leafing through the pages he found it to be a collection of lists, appointments and personal thoughts like "Capt. is an idiot." He flipped to the last entry. "Matt asked me out again. Maybe. Pulling over blue PU. shit everything off". The last words were scribbled uncharacteristically and was the last entry. He looked up. "Jim."

Jim walked over to Glen, who handed him the notebook. "It looks like there was a second officer. A female."

Jim looked through the notebook, also reading the final entry. He handed it back to Glen. "If they took her, I don't know how we could find her." He looked around, thinking and noticing that several acres of woods lay at the bottom of the slope down from the road. "But if this happened right at the time of the event ... if it was me, I'd want to get off the road as quick as I could, especially with a prisoner." He nodded his head at the trees. "Let's go take a look."

They made their way down the embankment, looking carefully at the ground for any sign while watching the tree line. As they reached the trees, they saw what appeared to be a natural separation of vegetation leading into the woods and stepped into the relative cool of the shade, stopping to listen and let their eyes adjust to the dimmer light after removing their sunglasses.

They made their way slowly through the woods and found her in a small clearing about fifty yards in, hanging by her handcuffed wrists from a tree branch.

Her uniform was gone and her legs were dark with the post mortem pooling of blood. The unnatural paleness of her torso showed evidence of a savage beating and dried rivulets of blood ran down her legs to her feet, where droplets had fallen to the ground.

Both men stood there, enveloped in a crushing sadness tinged with anger.

Finally, Jim spoke. "I had hoped to never see anything like this again."

Glen nodded slowly. "Yeah."

Jim lifted the body, taking the weight off the cuffs while Glen unlocked them, then lowered the dead woman to the ground. He looked at her hands and wrists closely and tested the movement in her arms and legs, assessing the status of rigor. "She lasted a long time. I'd say she hung there alive for a couple of days. Probably died yesterday."

He had become inured to violence and human suffering as a young police officer, but had been able to regain most of his humanity years later. Sometimes he thought that when his hard shell had cracked it had exposed an inner empathy that was even greater than when it had first been lost.

He knelt by the dead officer, looking at her face and imagining the suffering she had endured; the fear, hopelessness, despair and loneliness she must have felt. Without thinking, he placed his hand on her head, stroking her hair back from her face. "God was with you in your suffering, little one. Now you are with him in his eternal love and peace." He looked at her for another moment, patted her head softly, then rose to his feet.

Glen was silent for a moment, then spoke. "You believe that? What you just said?"

Jim looked at him, then back at the woman and nodded slowly. "Yeah. I didn't always, but I do now."

Glen shook his head. "I've never seen anything like this. I've been a cop for over twenty years, and I've never seen anything like this." He looked at Jim, his eyes showing his rage. "How can people ... anyone. ..." He stopped, not able to find the right words, unable to continue.

Jim knew how seeing something like this for the first time could affect a man. He had seen it change many men, destroying some. "There's no answer for that, Glen, except that there's evil in the world. We can't ignore it and we can't turn away from it. We have to face it, recognize it for what it is and fight it like we always have, because there's also good in the world, and the good is worth fighting for." He looked back at the body. "Come on, let's get her back to her partner."

They carried her back up to the road and told Christian and Ralph how they had found her. They had no way of burying the dead officers and nowhere to take them, so they put the female in the patrol car and covered the male with a blanket. Siphoning gasoline from the patrol car, they dowsed both it and the blanket and lit them.

They stood there for several minutes, watching the funeral pyres, quiet in their own thoughts, then turned away and returned to the Excursion.

They rode in silence, the only sounds being the tires on the road and Ralph's occasional direction to Jim. Beneath the silence lay a deep and growing anger at what they had seen and an increasing realization that this was now a world without law or even the civilized facade the law had tried to enforce. As they made the last turn, Ralph said "It's about half way up the block on the right side."

Jim pulled over and looked at the neighborhood. It was a new development of mostly two-story houses. Small trees were planted close to the curb in front of each house, and only a few cars were parked in driveways. He watched for a few minutes, looking for movement or anything that seemed out of place. Other than one man coming out of a house to smoke a cigarette and a border collie chasing something across a yard, everything was quiet.

Jim turned to the other men. "We'll drive up and back into the driveway like everything is normal. That will put the tailgate toward the garage for loading. Ralph, you go on up to the door and see if they're there. Christian, Glen and I will stay in the truck and watch the neighborhood. We don't want some good Samaritan with a rifle to think we're home invaders and take a shot at us. When you get in, open the garage door and we'll come in that way."

They drove up the street slowly, watching the windows of the houses for any movement. Driving a bit past the house, Jim stopped, put the Excursion in reverse and backed into the driveway, stopping a few feet from the garage door. He looked in the rearview mirror at Ralph. "You're up."

"Okay." Ralph got out of the Excursion and walked up the front walk calling Rebecca's name as he approached the door. He kept calling as he knocked on the door and soon heard the noise of bumping and dragging from behind the door, along with Bobby yelling "Papa! Papa!" In a moment, the door opened and all three rushed out to hug him.

Rebecca wrapped her arms around his neck, almost choking him in her attempt to hug him tightly enough. Becky held onto his side while Bobby took turns hugging him around the waist and jumping up and down yelling, "We thought you were robbers!"

Ralph hugged them all tightly, closing his eyes in a silent prayer of thanks and waited until he could speak without choking up. Then he peeled Rebecca and Becky off and looked them up and down. "So, you're all okay?"

Rebecca nodded. "It's been a tough few days and I was starting to worry. We were down to drinking the packing water in the canned vegetables." Then she looked around him. "Whose truck is that? Is mom with you?"

"Nope. It's Jim Wyatt, his nephew Christian and an Osage County deputy named Glen. We came to take you back to the farm. Come on, let's go open the garage and get you loaded up."

As they walked through the house, Ralph saw the exterior doors all had furniture stacked against them. "Have you had trouble? " he asked, nodding at the doors.

Rebecca shrugged, "Not really, but we wanted to be ready. Dad, what's happening?"

"I can't really explain it, but Jim says it's something called an EMP. Short answer is all power is out, maybe for years."

She looked at him, stunned, unable to make such an unthinkable scenario real in her mind. "Years?"

"That's what they say. Come on, let's get started."

They went through the garage and rolled up the double door, only then seeing the men getting out of the Excursion. Ralph made the introductions and the men entered the garage." Rebecca hugged her dad again. "I can't believe you're here." Then she turned to the others. "Thank you so much. I don't know what to say except thank you."

Jim nodded and smiled. "It's our pleasure, Rebecca. There's no way we'd leave some of our own out here." He looked at the two women and young boy. "Now, we're going to have to hurry so we can make it back before dark. We don't have a lot of space, so I'd suggest you pack up as much as you can of the most durable clothes you have, especially winter clothes. Also, any medications you have and all your important papers like birth certificates, licenses of any kind and property deeds or mortgage papers." He thought for a moment. "And all pictures and any small things with sentimental value. Weapons, ammo, gold, silver and any gemstones, too, and may as well bring any cash you have, though I don't know what good that will be."

Becky spoke up. "We have some food stocked up. Should we bring that too?"

"We'll see what kind of room we have left after everything else is packed, but you're going to be okay for food when we get back. Maybe you can bring some favorites."

"And bring some of Bobby's favorite toys." said Christian. Everyone turned to see him smiling at the boy.

"Thank you, Christian." said Becky quietly.

"Is there anyone in the neighborhood you want to leave your extra food with?" asked Ralph.

Rebecca scoffed. "Not a single one has come over to check on us or see if they could help, except for the jerk across the street who was always trying to put the moves on Becky and I whenever he thought his wife wasn't looking. And he made it real clear what payment he expected."

"Okay," said Jim. "Then let's see how fast you can get ready to go."

It took a little over an hour for the women to collect what they would take and load it into the Excursion. In the meantime, the men kept watch and loaded the family's bicycles onto the roof and tied them down.

The hour had been an emotional roller coaster, especially for Rebecca. The excitement of escaping from a disaster she did not fully understand to returning to the safety of her parents and the family farm, coupled with the sadness of leaving the home she and Robert had built, caused such a mixture of emotions that she had a hard time concentrating. She had decided, at Jim's suggestion, to leave her extra food on the front step. Jim had said that it might keep people from breaking in, but in any case, to keep food she wasn't going to need from people who would soon be starving wasn't the right thing to do. She agreed.

As they got into the Excursion, Rebecca stopped and turned for one last look at the house that had been her home through so much happiness and so much sadness. Maybe it was time for a new start, she thought, as she climbed into the middle of the second-row seat between Glen and her dad.

As they pulled out of the driveway, Becky, who was sitting on top of the cargo in back with Bobby, saw the jerk across the street come out of his house to watch them. Distracting Bobby to something else, she flipped the guy off with a smile.

7

The trip back had been quicker than the trip to Topeka. Dropping Glen off at the Caterpillar roadblock and taking a rain check on Sheriff Freelove's invitation to supper, they had arrived at the Samuels' place at dusk and were able to unload and get to Stonemont just before dark. Everyone had been waiting up for them, but they had been tired from a long day and Jim had told them to hit the sack and they would talk in the morning at breakfast.

Now, Jim stood on the stone veranda looking out over the field at the rising sun and drinking his first cup of coffee of the day. Max and Pink came running up for their morning pats on the head, then ran off again to continue their playful patrol.

He enjoyed these morning minutes alone, and this morning it was even more important to him than usual. What he had seen yesterday had surprised him. He had not expected the brutality of the police officers' murders so soon. And he had expected neighborhoods like Rebecca's to be more united and mutually supportive. Instead, it seemed as if families were holing up as individual units when they should be working together, building mutual support groups and developing sustainability plans.

Yet, in his heart, he knew he shouldn't be surprised. Society, particularly urban and suburban society, had long been moving in the direction of personal isolation. The more densely you packed people, the more distant they grew from each other psychologically and emotionally, and the more superficial their relationships became. Even the children had become more isolated from their parents as a result of public school curriculums, an increasing importance placed on sports and other non-family activities, and laws infringing on parental rights. Too many parents had turned into chauffeurs instead of guiding and nurturing moms and dads. Moms had been replaced by pre-school and school teachers, dads by soccer coaches and taekwondo instructors. In the cities it was worse, where jobs had been replaced by government checks and fathers replaced by nothing.

Under the veneer of neighborhood groups and friendships, competition and jealousy lurked and drove much of the consumerism that had supported the economy while driving individuals into debt. Now, with a real disaster to deal with, this was going to cause these people to turn on each other soon, and then become easy victims for stronger and more organized groups which would surely find them. He thought about the horror he knew was coming, and when he thought about the children, a crushing sadness came over him. He had to force himself to stop thinking about it.

The sound of the kitchen door made him turn to see Kelly coming out. He always liked the way she looked in the morning, wearing one of his t-shirts and barefoot, her blue eyes still sleepy and blonde hair a semi-mess.

"Hey sexy," he said. "I see you're wearing one of my favorite outfits."

He held his free arm out for her to step into. He had met her when she was twenty-six, twenty years his junior, started dating her after she had joined his martial arts class at twenty-eight, and married her when she was twenty nine. That had been fifteen years ago, and she looked better than ever. "What are you doing up so early?"

She snuggled into him. "Max woke me up barking at something. Is everything okay?"

"Yeah, he probably just saw a coyote or something. I'm afraid he dug up one of your hydrangeas."

She snuggled deeper into his side. "That's okay. Why are you up so early?"

Jim shrugged. "Getting to be a habit, I guess. Just thinking about yesterday."

"Was it bad?"

He nodded. "Worse than I had expected this soon. But we went through a couple of small towns that had it together. I hope most are like that."

They saw Mike step out of the woods to the east and watched him walk toward them, his AR slung across his chest.

"Morning Jim, Kelly." he called out when he got within talking distance.

"Hey, buddy." Jim responded. "How's everything?"

Mike unslung his rifle as he stepped up onto the patio. "Max and Pink had something over in the east woods. I'm not sure what it was, but I'm going to go back in a bit when there's better light and look at the tracks."

Jim nodded. "The Eddington place is on the other side of our fence. I'm going back over there today to see if they're back."

Kelly stretched up to give Jim a kiss. "I'm going to go get dressed and

66

get breakfast started."

Jim poured another cup of coffee and sat down at the table. "So, how did everything go around here yesterday?"

Mike cleared his rifle and placed it in a rack on the wall, then sat down with a cup of coffee he had poured himself. "Pretty well. Bill is a quick learner on the weapons. I only had him fire a few rounds because I didn't want to call too much attention to us, but his weapons handling is good and he's already pretty good on the target."

He took a sip of coffee and looked out over the fields. "I can see why you picked this place. It's the highest ground in the area, with natural defensive features everywhere except on the east. And I went down into your bunker for a minute while they were doing inventory. It's amazing. You really planned for this."

He paused for a minute, then continued. "There's something I'd like to say while it's just you and me here."

Jim looked at him over his coffee cup. "Go ahead."

Mike looked into his coffee cup, then back up at Jim. "I want to thank you for taking me in. I've been thinking about what things might have been like if I hadn't hooked up with Christian, and I'm afraid I might have reverted back to what I became in Iraq."

His eyes became distant for a moment, then he focused back on Jim. "Uncle Sam taught me some good skills for a situation like this, but the price was a big slice of my humanity, if you know what I mean. I just wanted to tell you that I think that being here with you and your family saved me from backsliding to something I never want to be again, and to thank you for that. And I want to tell you that I'm here to do whatever I can, whatever you need me to do."

Jim looked at him for a minute, then nodded. He could well understand the younger man's feelings, as his own years in law enforcement had carried much the same cost. He reached his hand out and placed it on top of Mike's two hands holding the coffee cup. "Until the day comes when you want to try to make it back to your own family, we're your family, and you're ours."

Mike nodded, his eyes serious. "Thanks."

The kitchen door opened and Christian came out. "If you two are done holding hands, I'm going to get a cup of coffee."

Breakfast became a meeting. After the platters of eggs, bacon, biscuits and pancakes had been devoured, Jim asked Kelly about the supplies inventory, to which Kelly answered they had a little over two years of food for the current group, following a normal diet.

"The problem," she said, "is that we're going to be doing more physical work than usual, which means we're going to need more than the normal daily calories."

Jim nodded. "That means more protein and fat, which means animals, which means hunting for the short term and breeding for the long term."

He turned to Mike. "Mike, are you a hunter?"

Mike nodded. "I used to do some before I went in the military."

"Good. You're in charge of hunting, and teaching hunting and weapons to everybody. The kids can be trained on pellet rifles when you get the time.

"The deer population has exploded around here over the past few years due to a decrease in hunting, so there are plenty around. Start taking a few, but not close by. Go out a ways so they don't learn that this is a danger area, because we might need them closer in later on. In addition, we'll plant some corn along the tree lines so they'll get used to coming here to eat. I want everyone to get familiar with the process of hunting, shooting, dressing, cooking and eating game."

He looked around the table to see if anyone looked squeamish, but no one did. Good. "Also, train everyone to take some smaller stuff like rabbits and squirrels. Again, not close by."

Mike nodded. "Will do."

"For fruits and vegetables, we planted peach, apple, plum, pear and cherry trees a few years ago and they're starting to produce pretty well. The extra acres I tilled a few days ago will let us plant a lot more vegetables, and hopefully we'll be able to get a good crop to put up at harvest."

Jim turned to Christian. "Christian, you're in charge of security. All the lighting at Stonemont is low voltage LED, so the solar panels and wind turbines can run them all and still have reserve. We have more lights in the bunker and plenty of wire. Plus, we have solar powered lights, trail cameras and battery operated wireless surveillance cameras and alarms. I'd like you to do a complete security survey of the place and add what's needed to get us sewn up tight. Let me know if we need anything else."

Christian nodded. "You got it."

Jim addressed the group as a whole. "The women will be responsible for supplies, inventory control, meal preparation and physical maintenance of the property. That means keeping everything running. I would like all of you to be armed whenever you are outside your home. And from now on, we will consider the main open area around the main house, the guest house and the barns as the security zone. No women or children outside the zone without an armed man." He started to continue, but Tracy raised her hand.

"No offense, Mr. Wyatt, I mean Jim, but you seem to have the women doing all the cooking and cleaning like in the old days. As much as I appreciate what you've done for us, if this is going to be a throwback to 'Little House on the Prairie', where the women do all the work while the men go running around, then I'm afraid I'm not interested."

"Tracy!" a shocked Ann exclaimed as the table fell silent and Bill put his face in his hands.

"Well it's true, mom. Women can do anything a man can do, and I'm not going to throw away all my hard work to revert to a second-class citizen."

The table remained silent as everyone stared at Tracy, then looked at Jim.

He thought about going through all the reasons for such a separation of labor, but knew that words never changed anyone's personal perspective like experience and reality did. He leaned back in his chair and smiled. "Well, Tracy, if you think that so-called woman's work is less important and more tedious than the running around we men do, I assure you it's not. Actually, the traditional roles reflect the high esteem and value a culture places on women who themselves value those roles for the sake of their families. However, if you would prefer to join us men in our jobs, and can do everything we do, we welcome you to join us. Can you tell us what your particular strengths or specialties are?"

If the table had seemed silent before, it seemed even more silent now. Everyone turned to Tracy, who seemed both surprised and confused. "Well, I uh ..."

Jim let the silence last for a moment, then waved his hand and smiled. "That's okay. We'll find out as we go along."

8

The next week was busy, and spent solidifying the things Jim had laid out at the breakfast meeting.

In the compound, Kelly and Ann had developed a regimen that brought daily life to a level as close to pre-event as they could. Meals were planned out a week in advance, with attention paid to variety and proper nutrition.

Kelly had started a medicinal and culinary herb garden in some raised beds Jim had built next to the patio, and made daily work schedules for Aedan and Brody, which included emptying trash cans, collecting eggs from the chicken house, feeding the dogs, and setting the table for each meal. Morgan stuck to the boys like glue, trying to do everything they did and learning in the process.

Jim and Mike had gone to the Eddington's again, only to find that they had still not returned. Concerned about the animals and potential looters, they broke open a large bag of food for the family's dogs and entered the house to secure the guns, which they took with them. They saddled the Eddington's three horses and two ponies and Mike rode one and led the others back to Stonemont where they were turned in with the Wyatts' horses. Jim left a note on the kitchen table, letting the Eddington's know what they had done.

Christian completed his security survey, and had added lights and cameras to several areas, including the barn. For fire suppression, and Kelly's request for more household water, he had installed a second two hundred seventy-five-gallon caged water tank on the roof of the main house, bringing the total amount of gravity fed water to five hundred and fifty gallons. He also added a second fifty-five-gallon barrel to the guest house.

Mike had made a wide-ranging tactical assessment of the surrounding area out to a mile from the compound and had prepared a plan to maximize their defensive capabilities and develop approach channels.

Jim, Bill and Tracy helped as each job required, with Jim constantly making mental notes to himself about things that needed to be done and possible improvements to be made. Together, they all planted the acres Jim had recently plowed in corn, beans, peas, beets, potatoes, onions, tomatoes, squash, zucchini and wheat.

In the evenings, they all gathered for supper on the veranda with the happy, satisfied weariness that came from hard, productive work. They would cover what they had done that day, tell stories, and watch the kids run around with the dogs, expending even more of their seemingly endless energy. After supper, some stayed at the table to talk or just relax, while others went off to other things.

Jim had declared Sunday to be a day of rest. It had always been a day for church, Sunday dinner with family and relaxation when he was growing up, and he knew that it served a valuable purpose for recharging physically and mentally. As he had gotten older, he began to see a greater purpose.

As a Christian, he had read the Old Testament extensively and realized that, while he was not bound by the laws given to the Hebrews, many of them had a purpose, indeed a blessing, attached to them that transcended denominational religion. A day of rest was one of those. God had demanded that the Hebrews work only six days and rest on the seventh as an act of faith that God would provide for their needs. Having seen God provide for him many times throughout his life, often in miraculous ways, he felt that observing a day of rest, a Sabbath, was appropriate. He had established such a day on Sunday at Stonemont, letting everyone know that they could observe it however they wished, but were welcome to join his family after breakfast for Bible reading and discussion.

.

Jim still rose early on Sunday and was having his first cup of coffee on the veranda when the kitchen door opened. He turned with a smile, expecting to see Kelly, but was surprised to see it was Tracy.

Tracy smiled. "Hi. I hope I'm not bothering you."

Jim shook his head. "Not a bit. Want some coffee?"

Tracy nodded, poured herself a cup from the percolator and sat down. She looked out over the compound for a minute, then at Jim. "I wanted to thank you, and to apologize."

Jim looked at her. "For what?"

"Well, first I want to apologize for being such a snark last week with that 'women are as good as men' stuff."

Jim smiled at her but said nothing.

She looked down at her coffee cup, then back up. "And I want to thank you for letting me try. I had expected you to argue, or to knuckle under like so many men do. Instead, you gave me a chance to prove what

I claimed, and to learn something about myself, and about others."

Jim remained silent, sipping his coffee and watching her.

Tracy took a drink of her coffee and continued. "I enjoyed working with you guys, but I know I didn't keep up and you all had to slow down to let me stay with you." She hesitated for a moment. "Can I ask you how old you are?"

Jim smiled. "Sixty-two."

Tracy shook her head. "You're almost forty years older than I am and you still worked rings around me."

She looked out at the field again, then back. "This week made me realize that I've lived a life that didn't really call for a difference of the sexes. Most of my life has been about the mental, not the physical, at least not about anything really physically hard. In sports, we accepted, even demanded, lower standards, just like in the military, without admitting to ourselves or anyone else that it was because we couldn't keep up with men physically. Even when I'd ask a guy to do something for me I told myself it was just for convenience and not because I couldn't do it myself."

She took another sip of her coffee and continued. "I've learned a lot this week. I learned that men can do things women can't. I've learned that men should be appreciated for what they can do. And I've learned I don't make a very good man."

Jim started to say something, but Tracy held up her hand. "Please, I'm almost done."

She looked down at her coffee, then back at Jim. "I also learned that I missed being around the other women, talking about the things we talk about and doing the things we do. And I think the biggest thing I learned, something that surprised me and for which I will always be grateful to you for letting me learn, is how much you men really respect and appreciate the women for who they are and what they do. I never knew that."

Jim smiled and nodded. "Yes, we do."

Tracy nodded back and smiled. "I see that now." She took a deep breath. "Well, if you think you can do without me, I think I'd rather go back to where I'm appreciated for what I am rather than tolerated for what I'm not."

Smiling, Jim leaned forward and took her hand in his. "Tracy, there are male lions and female lions. Neither is better than the other. Each is unique and perfect for what it is. And no matter how hard they might try, they can never be the other. You're a good woman. Your husband and children are going to be very lucky, just like we're lucky to have you with us now."

Tracy's eyes welled up with tears and she was about to say something when they heard the kitchen door open and Christian's voice.

"Jim, every time I come out here you're holding hands with somebody else. I'm telling Kelly."

The day was beautiful. Breakfast was about an hour later than usual because it was Sunday, but was as good as ever, and Aedan, Brody and Morgan were excited that the eggs were ones they had gathered themselves. After the table was cleared and the dishes done, Jim sat down at the table and opened up the family bible, surprised that everyone else joined him.

He started with a prayer, thanking God for his protection and providence, then asking for guidance and continued blessings in the days ahead. The chorus of "Amen"s also surprised him.

"This last couple of weeks has brought a few particular biblical principles to my mind," he began. "Among those are, of course, the Ten Commandments, which give us the basics of God's laws for a righteous life. In addition to those are his rules for preparedness as exhibited by Joseph in Egypt and, of course, the entire wisdom of the book of Proverbs. Next is Jesus' parable of the good Samaritan, in which we are told to care for our neighbor."

He shuffled through the bible to a page he had marked. "And finally, this verse from James 1:27, 'Religion that God our Father accepts as pure and faultless is this: to look after orphans and widows in their distress and to keep oneself from being polluted by the world.'"

He closed the Bible and looked around the table. "I won't bore you with my personal story, except to say that God brought me out of a destructive life many years ago, and, as a result of my listening and trusting in him instead of trying to fight for everything myself, he has given me a life which I can only describe as unbelievably happy and fulfilling."

He looked around the table. "I also believe that he brings certain people into our lives for his own purpose, and I believe he has brought you all into our lives, and perhaps us into yours, for a purpose he will reveal and assist us in."

He paused again, letting the right words come to him. "Our

73

forefathers came to this country in order to escape religious persecution and to establish a new community in which people could worship as they chose, was founded on God's principles, and would spread the Gospel of Jesus Christ. It doesn't matter how many people have tried to deny that over the past fifty years, that's the way it was. Those who decided it was necessary to create a new nation put their faith in God and petitioned him for his guidance and blessings in their endeavors.

"Based upon the principles and worship of God, our nation and its people prospered and became greater than any other in history. Then we, as a nation, lost our way. Our society turned away from God, even making mention of him in our schools illegal. Society celebrated consumption over production, celebrity over ability and the government collective over the family."

He looked at each of his children, then out across the compound and surrounding fields, then back at those at the table. "The Bible tells us that God promised not to send another flood, but I don't remember it saying anything about something like this. I'm not necessarily saying that this is from God, but what I am saying is that this is a reset point from which a renewal of proper values and principles may be able to be established."

He hesitated for a moment, then rose to his feet, looking at Kelly before continuing. "I've said before that we have been blessed, and that's certainly true. But with blessing comes responsibility, which is a blessing in itself, to pass on that blessing to others."

He walked to the edge of the terrace, looking toward the city he couldn't see.

"Every morning I come out here and think about the children in the cities and suburbs who, even now, are starting to suffer unbelievably. I think about their hunger and their fear. I think about their mothers and fathers, who I hope are doing their best to keep them safe, and who are undoubtedly experiencing fear and despair themselves."

He turned back to the group. "I know we can't save, or even help, everyone. But that doesn't mean we can't help some, and that's what we're going to do. Stonemont is going to help everyone we possibly can, starting this week, because some people can't wait any longer."

He looked at Mike and the Garners. "I know this isn't what you all necessarily expected when you came here, so if you feel this isn't for you, I fully understand. We will enjoy having you with us for as long as you want to stay, and when you feel it's time for you to leave Stonemont we will equip you to the very best of our ability. We will consider you extended family wherever you go."

He paused for a moment to let that sink in. "If, on the other hand, you feel that the mission of Stonemont as I've described it is something you also believe in and would like to be a part of, we welcome you to join us in it. I can't promise what will happen, but I promise that we will do our best in the endeavor."

He stopped, sitting back down at the head of the table and looking at those around him.

Kelly smiled and nodded her head.

Christian was the first to speak. "I'm with you all the way, Jim."

Mike nodded his head slowly. "Me too."

No one spoke for a moment, then Bill leaned forward, looking at Ann, Tracy and then at Jim. "For years, I've made my living talking. First, as a lawyer trying to convince people my client was right, and then as a judge trying to explain the law and the justice of my decisions. But I don't think I could have said it any better than you just did, Jim."

He looked at his wife and daughter again, who both nodded, then turned back to Jim. "Ann, Tracy and I have been talking about this very thing for the last few days. In fact, what you said so closely approximates what we have said ourselves, it was amazing to hear you say it. So, without making a big speech, I'll just say that we are with you, and are proud to be with you."

Jim smiled and looked around the table. "We'll start tomorrow. Let's enjoy the day, and then I want to talk more after dinner."

The rest of the day was spent relaxing and playing with the kids. For supper, Jim built a fire in the patio fire pit and everyone roasted their own hotdogs and brats. Bowls of corn, baked beans and coleslaw were placed on the self-service table along with iced pitchers of tea and lemonade. It was the most relaxed and happy Jim had seen the group since it had all started, and he knew it was because they now felt like a group and had a purpose ahead of them.

Kelly came up beside him and put her arm around his waist. "We're going to need everything."

He draped his arm over her shoulders and nodded. "I know."

After supper, everyone returned to the table after the dishes had been cleared. Jim could feel a new energy in the group, one of belonging and purpose. He remembered that energy from the units he had served in years ago, and knew the importance of it in unit cohesion and mission success.

"I want to lay out the general parameters of what we will be trying to accomplish and how we will try to accomplish it," he began. "We will have several tasks tomorrow, all of equal importance because they are intertwined.

"First, we want to recon the suburban area and make contact with groups or individuals there. If they are self-sufficient, we want to establish relationships with them. If they are having a hard time or unable to take care of themselves, we want to give them the help they need, if we are able to, up to and including bringing them back to Stonemont. We will take some supplies with us, including food, water and some basic medical supplies."

He looked around the group. Seeing that they all seemed receptive, he continued. "Our top priority will be children without parents, whether orphaned, abandoned or lost. Next will be families with children. After that, adults without children. This final group we can offer some limited immediate assistance to, but we don't want to use up resources that will be needed by the groups with children. We will offer adults assistance only if they want to come and contribute at Stonemont. Reliance on government or someone else is what put many of these people in their current situation, and we're not going to just start that all over again. Any adult who won't work for their own food isn't worth helping. Even the Bible tells us that those who don't work shall not eat, unless they're sick."

"Jamestown came to the same conclusion after their experiment with collectivism failed and a lot of them starved," said Bill.

Jim nodded. "Exactly. In order to do this, we are going to need some supplies. Here's what we need most - everything. I can't imagine anything we won't need. However, let's first concentrate on food, medicine, cleaning supplies, tents, blankets and sleeping bags, soap, toothpaste, shampoo, vitamins, well, anything that can keep a person warm, clean and healthy."

Christian put a hand up. "Are we going to break into businesses?"

Jim nodded. "If we have to, but I doubt we'll have to break into any. I imagine most will have been broken into already if they weren't guarded. We won't go into any independently owned businesses yet, though, since some may have local owners who just haven't gone back to them yet. We'll focus on the large chain stores."

Bill raised a hand. "What if they've already been cleared out?"

Jim shrugged. "I doubt if they will be, except maybe for the food. And if people have taken things to help them survive, good. That means they're taking care of themselves. But I don't think most people will be looking for the things we are, at least not yet. And we won't empty any place of anything. We need to leave things for individual scavengers. Taking everything could amount to killing them."

He paused for a moment. "There is one exception. Firearms and ammunition. We will take all we find. Those who know how to use guns probably already have them. Those who don't won't be looking for them. And we can't take the chance of them getting into the wrong hands."

A murmur of agreement went around the table.

"Now vehicles. Although all the TEOTWAWKI books had cars going kaput after an EMP, most of the scientific literature maintained that vehicles would be generally unaffected. Of course, this is the same scientific community that warned us of a coming ice age until they changed their mind to global warming until it was discovered that all their data was faked. So here we are with a big 'Who knows?'. Our experience, however, has been that newer vehicles aren't running."

"What's teotwawki? " asked Bill.

"It's an acronym for 'the end of the world as we know it'," replied Jim. "There are a lot of people who have thought about, written about and prepared for something like this for years. Some thought the economy was going to collapse, some thought a civil or third world war was coming, and some expected an EMP. Collectively, they were called 'preppers'. Some were kind of nutty, but most were just regular people who realized that if something bad happened they had better be able to take care of themselves, and they prepared to be able to do so."

"Like you," said Bill.

Jim nodded. "Yep."

"And the rest were like us. I mean me."

Jim shrugged. "Well, to be honest, most people who did well in the system tended to trust the system. After all, it had always worked pretty well, and most people were too busy doing other things to really pay attention to what was going on in the world. For some, it was job or family responsibilities, for others, bread and circuses."

Ann nodded. "Panel et circenses."

"What's that?" asked Tracy.

Ann turned to her daughter. "When Rome was in decline, it kept its citizens, particularly its newer citizens, distracted with games and satisfied with food it provided to them. It kept them from paying attention to the growing corruption that lead to Rome's fall. Today we do it, or did it, with sports, entertainment and reality shows."

Kelly nodded. "Three weeks ago, most men could tell you all about other grown men they had never met playing a game with a ball, and most women could tell you all about who was dancing with a star, getting a rose from some momma's boy or the latest diet craze."

Jim nodded. "Those who were really paying attention to what was happening here and around the world knew it couldn't keep going the way it was. Anyway, we need to find more vehicles that will run. That probably means older cars and trucks, but the most useful to us will be diesel trucks. Gas engines will be okay for a year or so, but then the stored gasoline will be so bad the engines won't run well, if at all. Diesel has a much longer shelf life.

"That brings us to people. While we will help everyone we can, according to the categories and parameters I laid out, there are certain skills we should look for to add to our community, or at least to our mutual assistance contacts. The ones that immediately come to mind are doctors, nurses, dentists, engineers, builders, carpenters and, referring back to our previous subject, mechanics – especially diesel mechanics. This isn't meant to be a comprehensive list, and we'll all have plenty of ideas and questions, so we'll have to make decisions as we go. Are there any questions or suggestions now?"

"Where are we going to put the people we bring back?" asked Tracy.

"Tents, for now." answered Jim. "So, just like before all this started, our first stop is Wal-Mart."

9

They left right after breakfast. Jim had explained that their first task would be to scout area stores, particularly the large box stores, to see whether they had been looted and what supplies remained.

Jim had selected Mike, Bill and Ann to go with him. Mike would be the main gun, though all were armed with an AR and a pistol. Ann would deal with any women that needed special contact and Bill would help as needed.

Driving north, they passed farm houses that were beginning to show signs of daily activity. Jim waved to those outside as he passed and told the others to do so as well, explaining that they would be contacting these people in the next day or so. It took them about fifteen minutes to reach the first housing developments, large million dollar homes on acre lots, and another five to make it into the more closely grouped neighborhoods and the Wal-Mart in far south Overland Park.

Pulling into the expansive parking lot, Jim thought at first that the store remained secure. Except for the lack of people walking around, it seemed like a normal day. Jim pulled into a parking spot so the Excursion wouldn't draw attention and they all got out, locking the vehicle behind them.

"We'll go in a diamond formation," Jim explained to Bill and Ann. "I'll lead, Mike will follow about fifty feet behind me, and each of you position yourselves about half way between us, but out to the right and left. Focus on your own direction point, but stay aware of everyone else's positions. Allow your rifles to hang by their slings, but keep your hand on the grip and finger off the trigger."

Everyone nodded, and he continued.

"When we turn them on, hold your flashlights in your off hand, higher than your head and away from your body. And be careful not to light each other up. We'll go down the aisle leading from the door, clear everything back to the electronics department, across the back and back to the front through the grocery department, across the front and then come back to this door. If everything is clear, we'll each get some baskets and get started."

Everyone nodded again.

"Okay, let's go."

They walked through the parking lot in formation, slowly enough to watch their direction points but quickly enough to avoid making themselves easy targets. As they approached the doors, Jim saw that they were standing open. He stopped and went to one knee, motioning for the others to come to him.

"The doors are open, and I'd say there's a good chance that somebody or a number of somebody's are in there. This store is set up with the groceries to the far right, clothing in the middle, and sporting goods, pharmacy and such to the left of where we'll be going in. After we get our baskets, Mike and I will head to sporting goods for guns, ammo, tents and camping equipment. Bill and Ann, you head left for vitamins, painkillers, allergy medicines, body wash, toothpaste and brushes, shampoo and anything else that makes sense to you."

Everybody nodded that they understood.

"Now, when we enter, we're going to be backlit by the sunlight and we'll make excellent targets if anyone is in there waiting, though if anyone is they're probably down at the grocery end. Mike and I will go in first." He looked at Mike. "I'll go in right and you follow to the left."

Mike nodded.

"We'll wait for a bit and listen. When we feel it's clear for you to come in, one of us will clap twice. When you come in, get away from the door and come to us as quickly as you can."

Bill and Ann nodded.

"It's going to be dark in there compared to out here," Jim continued, "so as soon as you get inside take your sunglasses off. Everybody ready?"

They all nodded.

"Okay, here we go."

Jim ducked in the door, quickly moved about twenty feet into the store and knelt down behind an ice freezer against the wall to his right. Mike went in behind him, advancing twenty feet further to the left. Both remained silent and listened.

After a minute, Jim advanced about twenty feet beyond Mike and took a knee between a barbecue display and a rack of swim accessories. Again, they waited silently, listening. Finally, hearing no unidentified noise, Jim nodded to Mike, who clapped his hands twice.

Bill and Ann came in, making more noise than Jim would have liked, and ran to Mike, who then had them take their positions on the wings of the diamond.

After another minute of listening, Jim signaled everyone to get to their feet and they started moving slowly toward the back of the store.

As their flashlights illuminated the areas around them, Jim was amazed at what he saw. Other than a few clothes scattered on the floor, the store looked as if it were simply closed. When they arrived at the electronics section, he saw the rows of black televisions hanging untouched on the wall. Merchandise still sat on shelves or hung on hooks untouched. There had been no looting or vandalism. He led them over to the grocery section, where they found aisles and aisles of empty shelves. The people had taken what they needed to survive and left the rest untouched. He knew it would be a much different story farther into the city.

He led them back to the front and past the long line of dark and silent cash registers to complete a circuit of the store, arriving back at their entry door.

"Okay," he said, keeping his voice low. "We may be alone, but still be careful. Bill, I want to change plans a bit and have you stay posted at this door to let us know if anyone is coming in. I don't want to be surprised. Ann, that means you'll have to make double trips." Both nodded. Jim could see they were both hyped up a bit from the unusual situation.

Jim then turned to the empty store and spoke in a loud voice. "If there's anyone here, we're not here to hurt you or take anything from you. We're going to be picking up some things we need and then leaving. If you need help, we'll do everything we can for you. Just holler out and we'll wait for you."

A minute went by with no response, and Jim turned to the group. "Okay, let's go."

Bill posted on the door and Jim, Mike and Ann got their carts and headed to their areas.

Arriving at the sporting goods department, they found shelves of tents and sleeping bags, and an untouched glass case of ammunition. The people in this area had houses to live in, and if they were campers they already had equipment. Many didn't own guns at all, and if they did, most weren't the type to think of ammo at this point. Jim nodded to Mike. "Take it all. Even the calibers we don't use may be good for trade later."

Mike broke the glass case and loaded the ammo into two carts. "Don't worry," he called to Bill and Ann, "it's just us."

They went through the aisles, loading their carts with tents, sleeping bags, camouflage clothing, rain gear and assorted camping supplies. Some freeze-dried food had been left on the shelves, which they threw in.

Leaving sporting goods, they took their carts to the front door, picked up two new carts each, and went to hardware, where they loaded rope, twine, duck tape, bungee cords, tie downs and a variety of hand tools, then headed to electronics where they loaded up all the batteries. An idea occurred to Jim, and they returned to the front door to find Ann bringing her third and fourth cart up.

"How much more is there?" Jim asked Ann.

"I can fill up as many more carts as we have time for," she answered.

Jim turned to Bill. "Everything good?"

Bill nodded. "Yep."

"Okay. Ann, go ahead and fill up some more." He turned to Mike. "Jeans, underwear, socks, work shirts, t-shirts and anything else that makes sense. Let's go."

It took them another hour to gather everything they thought they could take. When Ann had finished with soaps and pharmaceuticals, Jim had sent her to collect underwear and socks for the women and girls. Another hour was spent loading the back of the Excursion and strapping large plastic totes filled with the overflow onto the roof. When they were done, there were three levels of twelve totes on the roof, held down by a spider web of bungee cords. Mike looked at it and shook his head. "I saw things like this in Afghanistan, but I've never seen it here before."

From Walmart, they headed west, their target destinations two churches that were in close proximity to the road Jim had ridden through the suburbs on the day of the event.

Within ten minutes they were pulling into the almost empty parking lot of the first church, a large modern structure with a small metal cross on the roof. The sign by the street had indicated it was Family Church with a Dr. Harold Hanson as its senior pastor. A few cars were scattered around the parking lot, and three gleaming black vehicles, a Suburban and two Tahoes, we're parked in a line close to the door.

Jim pulled up in front of the main door, but stopped about twenty feet short of the sidewalk. He waited a few minutes, then got out and tapped the horn a couple of times. He left his AR in the truck and covered his pistols with his shirt.

Another minute passed before the door opened and a large man emerged, surrounded by four others. The man had a deep tan and was wearing a black silk shirt, khaki shorts and leather sandals. He wore a gold chain around his neck, another on his right wrist and an expensive gold watch on his left. The four men with him wore black BDUs and boots, with pistols holstered on their web belts.

"Greetings, brother!" exclaimed the man, with a big smile. "We're happy to see you." He nodded toward the totes on the Excursion's roof. "Have you brought offerings?"

"We came by to see how you are," replied Jim. He nodded his head toward the black SUVs. "Has the government shown up?"

The man looked at the vehicles then back at Jim. "No, no. Those are mine and my family's - the senior pastoral staff."

Jim looked at the vehicles and again at the man's expensive jewelry. "Pastoring must pay pretty well."

Irritation flashed quickly across the man's face before he recovered his smile. "We simply strive to do God's work, brother. I'm Pastor Harold, senior pastor here at Family Church." He nodded again at the totes. "What have you brought for God's people?"

Jim saw some people opening the front door and looking out. One of the men in black immediately walked to the door and tried to usher them back in, but several pushed past him.

Hearing the commotion behind him, Hanson turned toward the people and raised his spread hands. "Men and women, God is faithful and our prayers have been answered. These good people have been sent by the Lord to help us in our time of need."

"Do you have any food?" called out a woman.

"How many people do you have?" Jim asked.

Hanson turned back toward him. "We have forty faithful souls, Plus eleven pastoral staff and six on my security team."

Jim looked at the four black clad men surrounding the pastor, and wondered where the other two were. "Why do you need a security team?"

Hanson looked as if the question were naïve. "Brother, in this age of evil, the shepherd must be protected even as he protects the flock." He half-turned and indicated the security team with an outstretched hand. "These good men serve the lord by serving me in that capacity." He smiled. "Their reward shall surely be great in heaven."

Jim nodded slowly. "Interesting. How much food do you have?"

Hanson made a face that looked pious, resigned and hopeful all at once. "We are even now coming to the end of our food stocks." Then his

83

smile returned. "But we are grateful that God in his mercy has chosen to send you to our aid."

Jim nodded absently and spoke above the pastor to the people behind him. "Folks, we were just heading back to our place with a load of clothes and stopped to see if you were okay. I'm afraid we don't have any food with us, but we can bring you some in the morning if you can hang on."

A murmuring came from the crowd and irritation once again flashed across Hanson's face.

"Our food's been out for two days," yelled one man. "Our children are starving!"

Jim raised his hands to the crowd. "Folks, we'll be back in the morning. Hang on till then."

"Is there nothing you can give us now?" asked Hanson. "God will reward you many times over for every mercy you offer."

Jim looked at him and smiled. "Tomorrow morning, pastor. Be ready for a memorable day."

Jim turned and walked back to the truck. Getting in, he spoke to Mike. "Watch those jokers. If any of them pull a gun, take 'em out."

Mike nodded. "Okey dokey."

It took them less than five minutes to get to the next church, a beautifully traditional building of brick and stone with tall stain glass windows and a white steeple. A one-story school building sat separate.

As they pulled into the parking lot, they saw children playing on a playground, watched over by a number of adults, and more adults and teens working in a field next to the church. Some were turning the dirt with a shovel, followed by others breaking up clumps with hoes, and still others smoothing it with rakes to prepare it for planting.

"This looks a lot different than the last one," said Jim, parking the truck and shutting it off. "Let's all get out. Leave your rifles in the truck and keep your pistols under your shirts."

As they got out, they saw a man walking toward them. The man was stocky, broad in the shoulders and wearing a blue work shirt, jeans and work boots. As he approached them, a wide smile broke out on his sun darkened face and he held out a callused hand.

"Hello!" he said. "Welcome to Redemption!"

Jim shook the man's hand and introduced the group.

The man shook each hand with an earnest smile. "I'm Pasquale Paoli, the caretaker. Do you all need help? We don't have much, but you're welcome to share what we have."

Jim thought what a difference this was from the last place. "Thanks, but actually we came by to see how you all were doing and if you needed any help."

Paoli shook his head. "Thank you, but so far we're doing okay. We have always kept a food pantry for those in need, and some of our local families have come together to stay at the church, bringing food in with them." He turned toward the people working in the field. "And as you can see, we are trying to start a garden, though we can't claim to be very good farmers yet."

Jim looked over the area. The people were working hard, and were as dirty and sweat stained as Paoli, yet they were obviously in good spirits as evidenced by an occasional laugh or good-natured ribbing. "How are you for seed? What are you planting?"

Paoli shrugged. "Some of the members brought in seeds they had at home. It's kind of a hodge-podge, really. Some tomatoes, cucumbers, zucchini and the like. We'll plant what we have and pray for success. The Lord fed thousands with a few loaves and fishes, so we'll see what he does with some Burpee seeds."

A bell rang from the church.

"That's the lunch bell," said Paoli. "Would you like to join us?"

Everyone said thank you and followed Paoli to a large water barrel where they washed their hands, then through a side door into a fellowship hall beneath the sanctuary. Long tables ran the length of the hall, where those who had already gone through the food line were taking seats. They stood in line with Paoli, who seemed to have a smile, a word of encouragement and a pat on the arm or back for everyone. Finally getting their paper plates with baked beans, corn, a small piece of meat and two crackers, they followed Paoli to a back table where he sat them down and promised to return in a minute.

Paoli walked to the food line and held up his hands, gradually quieting the chatter of the crowd. "Friends, we have guests with us today," indicating those from Stonemont. "They came to see if we needed help. What a blessing that God has shown us there are others out there offering help."

He bowed his head and gave the blessing for the meal, which was followed by a chorus from all in the hall, "In Jesus' name, Amen."

Paoli returned to the table and sat down.

"I thought you said you were the caretaker, " said Jim.

Paoli smiled. "Indeed, I am. It is my responsibility to care for the church, which is the body of believers, and of the building we use. Some call me pastor, but it is the same thing."

"You're named for the Corsican patriot?" asked Bill.

Paoli looked up in surprise. "You are the first to catch that. Are you a political historian?"

Bill shook his head. "Just an amateur. Pasquale Paoli was a fascinating man, a man of his own star and the author of the Corsican constitution."

"Yes. I can't claim to be the man he was, but it was for him my parents named me."

"Have you been here since it happened? " asked Ann.

Paoli nodded and swallowed a spoonful of beans. "Yes. I was in my office when everything went out. One of our maintenance men was here and we tried to get things going, but no luck. Bible school was going on, so a number of parents and kids were here, and as the days went on others gravitated here as a kind of headquarters or sanctuary, like the old days when everyone gathered at the church during emergencies. After a week of no improvement and no help coming, we realized we were on our own and had better start planning how to take care of ourselves. You saw our efforts when you pulled in."

"What's this meat?" asked Bill.

Paoli paused before answering. "Venison. The woods around here are thick with deer, and I have a bow."

Bill smiled. "It's good. I'm glad we stopped by."

"Have you been joined by many non-members or started any outreach?" asked Jim.

Paoli nodded. "We have had a few come from the surrounding neighborhoods looking for help. Some left after seeing how little we had to offer and some stayed, becoming part of us." He hesitated, then continued. "I did walk over to another church to make contact with them and try to establish a relationship, but their pastor didn't seem to be interested. "

"Family Church?" asked Jim.

Paoli nodded. "You know them? "

Jim shook his head. "Nope, but we just met them. I didn't take to the pastor much.

Paoli didn't say anything for a minute, then "Are they okay over there?"

Jim shrugged. "Hanson and his security detail seem to be doing fine, but from what we could see, his flock isn't doing so we'll. We're going back tomorrow."

"To take them food?"

"No. To bring them out. We'll give some basics to anyone who wants to stay, but the ones I could see looked like they wanted a better alternative than just holding up in there. We came to see if we could help anyone by bringing them back to our place, so any who want to come under our conditions certainly may."

Paoli looked thoughtful. "What are your conditions?"

"As far as a legal code, we figure the Ten Commandments are fine. As to how to relate to others, the Golden Rule covers it. And finally, we will care for those who can't take care of themselves, but those who are able to work must work."

Paoli nodded slowly. "A biblical model."

"If any wanted out of that other church but didn't want to come with us, would you be willing to take them in?" Jim asked.

Paoli thought for a moment. Although the guests seemed like good people, he didn't know them and couldn't judge their real intentions yet. Now, Jim had asked him a question that seemed to clarify the visitors' position while calling on him to declare his own. Again, he nodded. "We would not turn anyone away who came to us for help," he answered carefully, "but our resources are already thin, and more people would stretch those resources even more."

"How much more of that field are you going to turn and plant?" Jim asked.

"As much as we can, but it's going more slowly than I thought it would. And I'm not sure how far our seeds will go."

Jim looked at Paoli closely. "I don't mean to pry, but how long do you think your food will last?"

Paoli didn't answer immediately, remaining quiet and staring at his beans. Finally, he spoke without looking up. "I'm not sure, but I think a couple of months."

Jim thought for a minute. Stonemont didn't have the resources to feed this number of people for more than six months, and that put them in the middle of winter. Then, they would all starve. They couldn't let that happen.

"Pasquale," he said, "we'll be back in the morning. I have an idea."

10

Pasquale Paoli was praying at the sanctuary rail when he first heard the engine. At first, he couldn't identify it, so he rose from his knees and went outside.

As he exited the church, he saw a tractor turning off of the main road, pulling a large contraption behind it. Preceding it was the red Excursion the people from Stonemont had arrived in the day before. He watched as the tractor and SUV came up the hill and pulled into the church parking lot. Both vehicles shut down, and Jim Wyatt and some others got out.

"Morning Pasquale!" called Jim, as he and the others approached. "We thought we'd stop by and lend a hand with your garden."

Paoli stood transfixed. He had just been praying for God's guidance and assistance, but God had rarely answered his prayers so quickly in the past.

Jim stuck out his hand, which the still stunned Paoli shook, and made the introductions. "You remember Ann from yesterday. This is Christian, my wife Kelly, and the guy walking over from the tractor is Ralph. Folks, this is Pastor Pasquale Paoli."

Everyone shook hands, some again and some for the first time.

Paoli looked at the group. Clearly moved, he shook his head slowly. "I don't know what to say, except thank you, and thanks be to God." He glanced back at the church. "We're just starting to get up. Can I offer you some breakfast?"

"No thanks, Pasquale. We had something on the way. Also, on the way, we made another stop at Wal-Mart and pretty much emptied their seed inventory and gardening tools. There are both hybrid and heirloom seeds, so you'll want to keep those separate for seed harvesting, but they'll all be good to grow for this season. Ralph will till a few acres and help you with all that."

Paoli was trying to keep his composure but was starting to visibly shake with emotion. He had known in his heart that they didn't have enough to make it through the winter, even if their garden produced as they hoped. The people from Stonemont had very possibly saved the lives of everyone at Redemption.

Jim stepped up to Paoli, placing a hand on each massive shoulder and looking into his eyes.

"Pasquale, remember what I said yesterday about our guide for dealing with others?"

Paoli nodded. "The Golden Rule. 'Do unto others as you would have others do unto you.'"

Jim nodded. "That's the one." He slapped Paoli on the shoulder. "Well, here we are."

An hour later they were once again pulling into the parking lot of Family Church. They had unloaded the seeds and hand tools from the Excursion and left Ralph behind to till the field and give advice on preparation for planting. Pasquale had agreed it might cause a problem if he went with them, but a Redemption member who was in the Kansas National Guard had asked to come along. Jim looked in the rear-view mirror at him. "I'm sorry, buddy, what was your name?"

"Josh, sir."

Jim chuckled. "No 'sirs' around here, son. Jim will do and we're happy to have you. You're checked out on that AR, right?"

Josh patted the AR they had loaned him. "Yes, sir. Jim"

Jim pulled the Excursion up in front of the church again, heading in so the doors could provide some cover when they got out, and turned off the engine. "Everybody stay in the truck. If his little storm troopers come out with him, wait for my sign, then Christian and Josh come up on my wings. Kelly and Ann, you stay put until we secure things. We need you for the women and kids."

The front doors of the church opened as Jim was getting out of the truck, and Hanson walked out flanked by the same four of his security detail they had seen yesterday. Today, he was dressed in a black golf shirt, black slacks and black loafers without socks. The same gold jewelry sparkled on his neck and wrists.

"Hello brother!" Hanson called with a big smile, striding purposefully up the front walk. "This is the day the Lord hath made, and we welcome you in it!"

Jim nodded. "Uh huh. We've brought some food for your people. How are they today?"

"We're fine," answered Hanson, smiling even bigger, "and under the Lord's protective care. I always tell my people that faith will see us

89

through, no matter how dark the evil one's attacks may make it appear, and our sacrificial giving will be returned to us a hundred-fold." He raised his hands, as if giving a benediction. "We praise God that he has sent you to us in our time of need, and I can assure you that your generosity will be returned to you many times over."

Jim nodded slowly. "Yeah, well, we have some food for your people. If you want to have them come out, we'll issue some meals to each of them."

Hanson lowered his arms and shook his head. "That won't be necessary. My men can take it in to them."

The bodyguards started to move forward, but Jim stopped them. "No, that's alright. It'll be easier to have them come past the truck in a line. Besides, we'd like to meet them."

Hanson's face flashed the mixture of anger and confusion he had displayed the day before, and he seemed unsure of what to do or say. The security detail seemed edgy and looked back and forth between their pastor and the outsider who was daring to challenge him.

Jim looked at each of them, gauging their mindsets. The two to his left appeared unsure of what to do and showed signs of wanting to back away. The two on his right, however, were staring at him hard, obviously offended that anyone would question their boss. Both looked as if they wanted to crush the outsider, and one was moving his hand closer to the gun at his waist.

"Pastor," said Jim. "do your men believe in Jesus?"

Hanson lifted his chin as if offended. "Of course they do. I would not have a non-believer on my staff."

"That's good," Jim said, nodding to his right, "because that one on the end is about to meet him."

The guard on the end froze as Jim pulled his shirt back from his pistol. Jim raised his hand and Christian and Josh got out of the Excursion, taking their positions.

Hanson turned pale under his tan. "What is the meaning of this? How dare you bring weapons to the house of God!"

"Well, we just wanted to fit in, pastor, so we thought we'd dress like your men. Now, if you would be good enough to have them remove their weapons, very slowly, and lay them on the ground in front of them."

Hanson looked back and forth between the man in front of him and his own men. Beads of sweat had started to form on his forehead and his breathing had suddenly become fast and shallow. He was beginning to feel faint, confused and frightened by the sudden turn of events and the loss of the control he had become so used to. Minutes before, he had been secure in the belief that he could convince and manipulate people as he pleased, as he always had. Even in these dire circumstances he had had no doubt he could get his way with these outsiders and maintain control over the members who remained inside. Now, he felt everything suddenly spiraling out of control and, for the first time in his life, he felt personally threatened.

The fear almost paralyzed him, but he raised his hands. "Please, there's no need for this. I have money. I have other things you might want." His mind searched frantically for the thing that would buy him out of this. "I have...I have women inside. You can have your pick."

Jim's stomach turned with disgust and anger rose within him. He had felt something was wrong when they were here yesterday, but he couldn't put a finger on it. Now, it was clear. He drew his pistol and let it hang in his hand at his side. "Your men have ten seconds to lay their guns down, or we will disarm them."

Hanson looked frantically around. He could not understand what was happening. The situation made no sense to him. He could not think. Slowly, he brought up his clasped hands as if in prayer. "Please ... please... I beseech you ..."

The sharp cracks of two rifle shots interrupted Hanson, and Jim looked over to see the guard on the far right crumple to his knees, his hands clutched to his chest and his pistol laying on the ground beside him. Christian was holding his rifle on him in case more shots were necessary, and Josh had his weapon shouldered covering the others.

Jim looked down at the now kneeling Hanson, who was starting to cry, then at the remaining security guards. "I figure you're down to about two seconds."

The three standing security men slowly removed their pistols and laid them on the ground.

Jim nodded. "You guys aren't as stupid as you look. Now take off your duty belts, drop them on the ground, take two steps forward and lay face down on the ground with your wrists crossed behind your backs.

The guards looked at each other, hesitating.

Jim raised his pistol. "I'm not going to say it again."

Slowly, the guards got down on the ground and crossed their wrists behind their backs.

Jim took several steps toward them. "Now listen closely. If you do what we tell you, you might live through this. If you don't, you won't. Lay still while we cuff you. Try to resist and we'll shoot you."

Christian went behind the three and flex cuffed them.

"Him too," said Jim, indicating Hanson.

Christian flex cuffed Hanson and pulled him to his feet.

Hanson tried to pull away from Christian, turning to Jim. "Please, I'll take you inside. I'll take you to them. I'll tell the guards to cooperate."

Jim scoffed. "Yes, you will take us to them. As far as getting the guards to cooperate, don't worry, we'll handle that." He grabbed Hanson by the back of his shirt and shoved him toward the church door. "Let's go."

They entered the building. "Which way?" asked Jim.

Hanson turned toward him. "It's not what you think. I swear. We had to keep them separate to keep them safe."

"Keep who separate?"

"The men. The women. The children. We had to separate them in order to keep them safe, to minister to their needs." Hanson had started to regain some of his composure, obviously convincing himself of the rightness of his actions by repeating a claim he had invented to excuse them.

Jim stopped and put his face within inches of Hanson's. "You separated the men, women and children?" he whispered, his eyes boring into Hanson's. "You separated families?"

Hanson recoiled from the fury of Jim's question, and his composure started to crack once again. "We had to! Don't you see? We couldn't save them, couldn't provide for their needs while they were together working against us!"

Jim stayed within inches of Hanson's face, anger continuing to build within him. Sensing the evil in the man, he wanted to overcome that evil and fill the man with his rage. Holding the man's eyes in the grip of his own, he spoke very quietly. "Men first. Take us to the men."

They walked through the cavernous entry hall, then down a side hallway and up some stairs to another hallway, their steps on the tile floors echoing off the block walls. At the end of the second hallway, a guard stood in front of a double steel door.

The guard seemed confused as the group approached him. The pastor was walking strangely, and he didn't know any of the people with him. "Pastor? Is everything alright?"

"Everything's fine," Jim said as he walked to within ten feet of the guard and pointed his gun at the guard's face. "Take your gun belt off slowly and put it on the floor."

The guard hesitated at first, but complied and was quickly flex cuffed.

Opening the doors, the group was hit with the stench of unwashed bodies and human waste. Hollow-eyed men stared at them from around the room, some sitting on the floor, some laying down and some staring out the non-opening windows. The room was bare, except for the men themselves and five-gallon buckets that served as toilets.

Jim looked at Hanson. "Where do they sleep?"

"Here," replied Hanson, slowly. "They sleep here."

"I don't see any beds."

"We didn't have any beds," Hanson stammered. "We were working on it. I mean, we were trying to make it as nice as we could for them. For all of our people."

"Where do they eat?"

Hanson started to shrink within himself, beginning to understand the extent of his captor's anger. "Here," he said, lowering his head. "They eat here."

Jim looked at him for a long minute, then turned to the men in the room. "Can you men walk?"

A general murmur of affirmation came from the group, and those who were sitting or lying down got to their feet.

"Good. Let's go get your families."

Similar scenes awaited them at the women's room, where they secured the sixth guard, and the children's room, in which two of the mothers were currently caring for them. After allowing a few minutes for an emotional reunion of the families, Jim spoke to the group.

"Folks, we're from a place called Stonemont, a bit south of here. From now on, you're free to do what you want, but we have some food for you and will arrange for everyone to get cleaned up and get some fresh clothes. After that, you can all decide whether you'd like to come with us or take off on your own. We'll get you to the food in a minute, but first there's something I want to see and think you might too."

He turned to Hanson. "Take us to your family quarters, and the guards' too."

Hanson looked dazed, unable to process the sudden change in his position or imagine what his future might now be. With a lethargic nod, he led off slowly.

After several turns, they came to a hallway carpeted in red and adorned with rich brocade wallpaper. A velvet rope spanned the entrance, a small gold placard hanging from it indicating "Private".

Jim unhooked the rope from one wall and let it fall on the floor, kicking it to the side. As they walked toward the large double wooden doors at the end of the hallway, they looked at dozens of professionally taken photographs of Hanson, some by himself, some with his family and some with famous religious and political leaders, but always smiling. Hanson had taken the classic "Me wall" and extended it to a "Me hall", obviously meant to impress those he welcomed into his private domain, and probably to feed his ego as he left and returned to it each day.

Jim stopped the group, seeing that many of the former members were following them. Looking around at the pictures, he spotted one of Hanson alone, his smile even bigger than normal. The plaque on the base of the frame indicated that the church had just reached five thousand members and Hanson had been declared pastor of the year by some national group. A pair of doors in a recessed alcove appeared to their left.

"What's in here?" Jim asked Hanson.

"Our, I mean the dining room. It's where the guards stay."

"Stayed," Jim corrected. "You have a key?"

Hanson bowed his head. "In my pocket."

Christian reached into Hanson's pants pocket and came out with a small ring of keys. "Which one?"

"The one with a zero on it."

"Appropriate," said Christian, finding the key and unlocking the door.

They entered a large room dominated by a massive dining table surrounded by eighteen richly upholstered chairs. Covering the table were boxes and cans of food stacked several feet high. Along the walls were cots on which the guards had slept, separated by more stacks of food and cases of water.

Jim turned to Hanson. "Well, pastor, you certainly were prepared."

"That came from us," said a voice from the back. A man came pushing through the crowd angrily. "We brought that."

A general grumble through the crowd agreed with the man and he continued. "When we came to the church after the power went out, pastor said we should bring all our food in to the church. Something about bringing everything into the storehouse and claiming God's promise to provide for us in return."

"Has he been rationing this out?" asked Jim.

The man gave a scornful laugh. "If you call it that. We got peanut

94

butter on crackers and a cup of water in the morning and the same at night. If we worked during the day, we got a granola bar for lunch. I don't know about the women and kids."

"We got the same," said a woman. "The kids got dry cereal for breakfast and peanut butter on crackers for dinner."

Jim looked at the food and at the crowd, then raised his hands to quiet the chatter. "Folks, we're going to take a little break. We'll divvy up this food later, but for now come on in and get a bottle of water and something to eat. And make sure the kids get a candy bar or something. They deserve something special."

He turned to Christian. "Go out and help Josh bring the live ones in here."

Christian nodded and left.

11

The rain had started before dawn and showed no sign of letting up. He had hated rain when he was younger, as it always seemed to get in the way of life. Now, he liked it. He had come to recognize and appreciate it for what it was, a life sustaining process that not only provided the water necessary for the growth of the food they ate, but an enforced break in the otherwise constant activity of life. He had learned from the animals who stayed in their shelters when it rained, and now when it rained he retreated to his office, to think about things that had happened and plan for things that might, and sometimes just relax.

When they had built Stonemont, he had designed his office, his lair, as Kelly jokingly called it, to span the west side, with windows on both the front and back of the house, and more windows on the west end bracketing a large stone fireplace in the middle. This way, he could keep an eye on the property in three directions by simply walking across the room. Floor to ceiling shelves on each side of the doorway on the east wall held the books he had accumulated over the years, spanning a wide variety of subjects with a major focus on history and politics, and pairs of wing back chairs with occasional tables sat in front of both the north and south windows. Due to his dislike for desks, three deep leather couches formed a horseshoe facing the fireplace.

It had been a month since they had gone to the churches and a lot had been accomplished in that time. In a few minutes, the others would arrive for a situational meeting, each bringing the others up to date on their areas of responsibility. They worked closely together on most days anyway, but he knew that things could slip through the cracks and people could be left out of important loops if they didn't sit down regularly to share their progress, needs and concerns with each other.

As he waited, he thought he could almost imagine that the recent past hadn't happened, that things were as they always had been. They had planned and prepared Stonemont to accomplish just that and, for the most part, they had succeeded. Now, the challenge would be to see what they could build from here on.

The door opened and Kelly came in carrying a spiral notebook. "Hi honey. Whatcha doin'?"

He smiled, patting the spot on the couch next to him. "Waiting for a good-looking blonde to come along so I can corrupt her."

She laughed, sitting down where he had patted. "I think you took care of that years ago, but I could always use a refresher."

He chuckled back at her. "How did I get so lucky?"

She leaned over and gave him a kiss. "It wasn't luck. It was a devious plan on my part."

The door opened as they were about to kiss again. "Finally, I walk in and catch you playing handsies with your own wife."

"Great timing, Christian. Is this why you're an only child?"

Christian laughed. "My parents always told me it was because I was so perfect they knew they couldn't be satisfied with any others, but now that I think about it you might have a point." He sat down on the sofa to the right of theirs and stretched. "But I know you love me anyway." He winked at Kelly.

Jim was about to reply when the others arrived. Mike took a seat with Christian, and Bill and Ann took the remaining sofa.

"Pardon the stocking feet," said Bill. "We left our boots and ponchos in the mud room. It's a good day if you're a duck."

"Or a bean," added Ann.

Jim chuckled. "You're making me hungry. There's coffee here if anybody wants some. Except for Christian. None for him. He's been getting smart with his uncle."

The small talk continued until everyone got situated and Jim started the meeting.

"It's been a busy month and I think, all and all, we're doing pretty well. I'm sure there are some things we can improve on, so let's get started. Kelly, as head of operations, let's have you start."

Kelly opened her notebook. "The two main areas are people and supplies. On the people side, we now have twenty-two families living in tents in the compound, three from Family Church and the remainder are those our scout parties came into contact with on their probes." She nodded at Mike, who ran the scout teams. "In addition, we have four single men and two single women. So far, everything seems to be working out fairly smoothly. Most are pitching in and working, and getting along well with each other."

"Most?" asked Jim.

Kelly nodded. "There are two families who seem to be having some problems understanding the expectations here." She looked at a page in

97

her notebook. "The first are Michael and Linda Kant. They have two teenage boys."

"What's their problem?"

"General attitude, basically. The adults both seem to be very opinionated, argumentative types. They rub people the wrong way, and apparently argue with each other pretty loudly late at night. When people are living close together in tents, this becomes a problem. Michael works okay, but Linda seems to do more sitting and talking than working."

Jim nodded. "How about their kids?"

"Someone suspects the older one of stealing. No apparent problems with the younger one except for kind of an attitude."

Jim looked at Christian. "We'll have a talk with them." Christian nodded. "What about the other one?"

Kelly again looked at her notebook. "Tom and Patty Cramer. Two daughters about ten and twelve."

"And their problem?"

"Tom works hard sometimes and sometimes doesn't. Patty thinks she and her girls are special. She doesn't like to get dirty, but talks a lot and seems to be trying to form a social circle around her."

Jim looked at Christian. "Them too."

"You seem to have pretty good information," said Bill, his eyebrows raised in a question.

Jim thought for a minute, deciding how much information to reveal. "One of the families who came in are friends of ours. We offered to put them up in the house, but when we discussed the difficulties of filtering newcomers they volunteered to stay in the tents and keep us informed about what was going on there, at least until the fall." He smiled at Bill. "You must have been a pretty good judge, the way you saw that."

"And you must have been a pretty good whatever you were," Bill replied, his statement implying a question he'd been wondering about.

Jim shrugged. "Maybe. Anyway, back to you Kelly."

"Our scouts continue to make contact with outsiders, who are becoming more marginal, by which I mean in worse shape and needing more care. One of the women is a nurse practitioner, and we're setting up a clinic, but we are going to need more medical help. Also, some recent arrivals have indicated that they had heard about us, so the word may be out and we might be dealing with a greater influx soon."

She looked at her notebook again. "On the supplies side, our fields seem to be coming along nicely. We don't know what the yield will be yet, but I think we should till all available acres for winter wheat and future plantings.

"Finding that Wal-Mart truck, and Christian's idea to look for trucks and bring them in has been a godsend. So far, we have nine trailers in the compound. Two from Wal-Mart, one Home Depot, one Del Monte foods, one Hy-Vee grocery, three from national haulers with mixed or unknown loads, and one tanker of diesel fuel that Ralph says is about three quarters full. We haven't been able to go through them all yet, but just figure department, hardware and grocery stores on wheels. When we find a truck, Ralph goes out with his old Peterbuilt, jacks up the trailer, pulls the tractor out with his, hooks his up and brings it in. He gets a ten percent interest in every load he brings in."

"Ten percent doesn't sound like much," said Ann.

"We offered him twenty-five, but he said he was just driving a truck so ten would be plenty," replied Kelly. "He's a good man and does business like in the old days. Also, he found and fixed up another old truck and gave it to us, for which we will give him ten percent of whatever we bring in with it."

"On the diesel, how many gallons is that and what's it's storage capability?" Jim asked.

"Ralph says the average tanker will hold about eight thousand gallons, so say six thousand. Stability, he says, could be anywhere from one to five years, depending on if we can find certain additives."

Jim nodded. "Very good. Ann, how about energy and engineering?"

Ann opened her folder, but spoke from memory. "We have almost all of the solar panels operational, and they are more than adequate to power the existing lighting and security systems. The current battery banks are also adequate, and we have some spares, but I would suggest that deep cycle batteries be high on the acquisitions list in order to be ready for expansion.

"The existing wind turbines aren't really needed right now, but will come into play when the days get shorter and the wind picks up during the colder months. We have three more in storage, but no reason not to pick up more if we run across them. Same goes for solar panels, charge controllers and inverters. Some will be fried, but hopefully some won't be. It depends on where and how they were stored. Plus, we should also pick up all the low voltage lights and wire we can.

She looked down at her notes. "On water, I've completed the ram pumps which bring water up from the creek to the tanks on the hill. This gives us gravity fed running water to the main house, the guest house, the compound camp and the fields for irrigation. Pipes to the houses and the camp are filtered, but I'd still suggest that all water for drinking, cooking or washing dishes be run through the Berkeys and Sawyers."

Jim nodded. "Sounds good, Ann. Any specific ideas on where to look for these things?"

"For the low voltage wire and consumer quality lights and fixtures, the big box stores are a start. Also, the hardware and lawn care stores. We're not going to find professional quality stuff there, but it's a start. Some of the inverters and charge controllers will be shot, but some may not be. For batteries, big box and automotive stores. They can be either six-volt or twelve-volt, but they have to be deep cycle, made to charge and discharge repeatedly. Regular car batteries won't do."

"Okay." Jim said, turning to Christian. "What's our security situation?"

"We're well covered as far as lights and alarms go. I agree with Ann about getting as many more lights as possible, but for now we're in good shape. The thing that most concerns me now is our perimeter and manpower. The dogs, wireless alarms and trip-wired lights will give us warning if intruders get within a couple hundred yards of the compound, the dogs sometimes farther out, but that's just warning, not perimeter protection. I think we need to consider building fortifications around the compound and channeling obstructions farther out."

"What's that?" asked Bill. "Channeling obstructions?"

"It's impossible to build a defensible wall around the entire property," explained Christian. "Instead, by using the natural terrain and constructing strategically placed barriers, we can direct any approach or attack along certain channels which we can more easily defend. It won't fool or deter experienced fighters, but it simplifies things in most cases and allows a small force to defend a larger area."

Bill nodded in understanding and Christian continued. "As Kelly said, we can probably expect more people to head our way as they hear about us. Some will be good folks and some won't. Most will probably be coming up the road, and I don't like the fact that they can get right up to our front gate before we make contact with them.

"Our place is about midpoint of the top of a "T", with the Samuels' place at the west end and the Eddington's at the east. I think we should put a reception point, maybe just an empty trailer for now, about a half mile down the approach road, where we can stop and filter any newcomers before they get to our main gate. Longer term, the main gate needs to be fortified along with the rest of the compound. Also, since the Eddingtons haven't come back, I think we should consider their place as possibly abandoned and put a caretaker in there for security."

He checked his notes. "Finally, manpower. Currently, we're able to keep a one person watch from dusk till dawn, but we really need at least two and ideally more. Mike and I are working with some guys we think may be suited for the security and scout teams, and we're cross training them for both. We're going to start folding them into the watch rotation as seconds, which will allow us to see how they do and let everyone get to know them and get a feel for them. Now, Jim, this is up to you, but I would like every able adult from eighteen on up to be scheduled into the rotation."

Jim nodded. "I think that's a good idea. I don't want to require anyone to serve in security or scouts because some people just aren't cut out for it, but taking turns at watch makes sense. You and Mike put together a quick training class for it and start getting everyone in the rotation right away. It will give us a better look at them too. Anything else?"

Christian shook his head. "That's it for now."

"Okay, start implementing everything you've mentioned. I'll think about who to put in the Eddington's place, and I have one thing to add for you. Dogs."

"Dogs?"

"Uh huh. You can't beat dogs for making noise and going after what they don't know. Max and Pink do a great job, but we need more. There are a lot of loose dogs around now and they'll be going wild pretty soon. Let's get as many German Shepherds and Rottweilers as we can and start a breeding and training program."

"Just those two breeds?" asked Christian.

"Yeah, and I want them mixed. That gives a dog with the best traits of both, but heavier than a purebred shepherd. That's what Max and Pink are. We could fold in Belgian Tervaruns and Malinois if we come across any, but I doubt we will. I want the natural traits and instincts of the Shepherds and Rotts, and the Belgians are close."

Bill spoke up. "Aren't Rottweilers dangerous?" he asked.

Jim shook his head. "No. They got a bad rap from a movie years ago and some morons who raised them to be mean because they wanted a tough dog, but they're very family and kid friendly. They were originally bred as butcher's dogs in Germany, to herd livestock and pull the butcher's heavy carts, and their loyalty, intelligence and natural protective instincts are second only to Shepherds. Breeding them with Shepherds gives you a great dog with great instincts."

He turned to Mike. "How are we doing with weapons and the scouts?"

Mike leaned forward, resting his forearms on his thighs. "I'll start with weapons. We hit a jackpot with Bass Pro a couple weeks ago. It had already been entered, probably numerous times, but obviously not by groups who came prepared to stock for the long haul. All the survival food was gone, of course, and they had made a bit of a mess. All the handguns in the glass cases were gone, but most of the long guns were still there. Somebody had run a chain through them in addition to the normal locks, and I guess the previous visitors weren't as prepared as we were with bolt cutters. Plus, we were able to open the gun room in back.

He checked a pad in front of him. "Total count was forty-three AR platform rifles, twenty-nine in 5.56, eight in .223 and six in .308. It's good to have them all, especially the .308s, but we'll need to be careful to keep the 5.56 and .223 separate."

"Why is that?" asked Bill.

"They're the same caliber," replied Mike, "but different chambering characteristics. You can run .223 through a 5.56 chambered weapon but you don't want to do it the other way around too much."

Bill nodded as if he understood and Mike continued.

"We also got sixty-two shotguns, mostly in twelve gauge but some in twenty and .410, fifty-six bolt action and semi-autos in .308, 30.06, 30-30, .243, .270, .22 and a few others, eighty-six pellet rifles, and more ammo than we've been able to categorize and count so far. Oh, and we also got a bunch of compound bows and arrows. I don't know much about bows, but I picked up a couple of books about it."

Jim smiled. "That's alright. We know a bow hunter. Remember Pastor Pasquale? I'm sure he'll teach us."

Mike nodded. "That's right. Good deal. We also took all the camo - loads and loads of it. We have enough to outfit hundreds, and some of it is cold weather stuff. Boots and socks too."

"Very good." said Jim. "Are there many clothes left? Or anything else we can use?"

Mike nodded. "There are a lot of clothes left. Also, some camping equipment and a lot of assorted stuff we might want if we have the room."

"Okay. We'll see if we can get one of the trailers emptied into the barn and schedule a trip back there in a few days. In case you don't fill it up, you might be thinking about other stops you'd like to make as long as you've got the trailer out. How about scouts?"

"Like Christian said, we're cross training some guys as scouts and security, since many of the skills are shared and the better each one is at the other the better they'll be able to deal with those of any adversaries. I think we need as many more as we can find and train, as long as they are quality people, and to that end I have a suggestion. I think we should open it up to women."

Jim cocked his head at him. "Tell me your reasons."

"Security is not going to be like law enforcement, and the scout teams are not going to be like military special ops. Brawn is not going to be nearly as important as teamwork, smarts and attitude. To be honest, I can see where women could be value enhancements in domestic situations here and with surveillance and contact activities with the scouts."

Jim thought for a minute and looked at Christian. "What do you think?"

Christian nodded slowly. "It makes sense," he said, looking around at the others, then at Jim. "There were a lot of problems when women came into law enforcement due to affirmative action, because a lot of them simply couldn't do the job physically and they were taking the slots of male applicants who could have. Here, it's different. They wouldn't be taking anybody's place, they'd simply be adding their abilities to others on the team. They won't be able to do everything we can, but that doesn't mean they can't do a lot. And like Mike said, there may be situations a woman is actually better suited for. I'm for giving it a try."

Jim sat thinking while the others watched him. Finally, he looked up. "Okay, we'll give it a try. A couple of parameters, though. Only women between eighteen and forty, and none with children."

Both Mike and Christian nodded and agreed.

Jim looked around the group. "Okay, anything else?"

"Actually, Aedan has something he'd like to show you," said Christian.

Jim's eyebrows raised. "Yeah?"

Christian smiled. "Yep. He's chomping at the bit. We'll need to go outside."

They left the house and walked across the compound as a group. It had stopped raining, but their steps made small sprays in the wet grass and splashes in the occasional puddles. Aedan walked importantly between Christian and Mike, smiling up at each of them and back at Jim and Kelly. In his hands, he carried a long bundle wrapped in burlap.

"I think this should do," said Christian, stopping the group about fifty yards from the apple trees.

As the group waited there, he continued walking toward the trees. Reaching them, he removed an empty pop can from a bag he was carrying and stuck it on a branch about head high. After setting five more at different heights, he walked back to the group and nodded at Aedan. "All right, buddy, show them what you can do."

Aedan untied the bundle, revealing a high-powered pellet rifle with a scope.

Kelly looked over at Jim, who looked back and shrugged.

Aedan handed the rifle to Christian, who broke open the barrel, loaded a pellet, closed it and handed it back. Laying the burlap on the ground, Aedan sat on it and brought the heavy air rifle to his shoulder.

"He knows that a good sniper never gets any wetter than necessary," Mike said to the group with a chuckle.

Aedan held the rifle steady with his elbows pressed against his thighs, looking through the scope. He took a deep breath, let half of it out, waited two seconds and squeezed the trigger. The rifle made a quiet noise and a can jumped off its limb. His face broke into a huge smile and he handed the rifle to Christian, who reloaded it and handed it back.

Taking aim a second time, Aedan squeezed the trigger again and another can flew off its branch. Four more shots took down the four remaining cans and Aedan turned around to the applause and shouts of approval from the group. "Christian and Mike have been teaching me," he said with a grin.

Christian tousled Aedan's hair and Mike patted him on the shoulder. Aedan looked up at each of them, his smile getting even bigger.

"Aedan has something to ask you," said Christian.

Aedan looked at his parents, becoming serious. "Rabbits and squirrels and raccoons and other things get into our crops and eat them. I can shoot them and keep them from eating our stuff and we can eat them instead." He paused, as if unsure whether he should say what he wanted to say next. "Mike says I could shoot even better and farther with a .22."

Jim smiled, looking at Aedan, who stood expectantly fidgeting, then at Mike and Christian. Finally, he nodded. "Mike, I have an additional assignment for you. I would like you to form a junior scout program, age seven and up, boys and girls. Use the air rifles we got from Bass Pro and teach them some sniping, tracking and woodcraft skills."

He looked back at Aedan. "And get Aedan the best .22 rifle you can find. He's our first junior scout and our new field warden."

The sun started to break through the clouds as they walked to the collection of tents in which recent arrivals were staying. Children were running around playing and women were setting out lunches on three long tables. Each adult would get a canned meat sandwich, pork and beans and a serving of canned fruit. Each child would get as many peanut butter and jelly crackers as they wanted, canned spaghetti rings and some fruit. The women set the food out on the table on plastic plates so that each person could come past and get theirs. Drinking water was dispensed at the end from a large tank fitted with a Sawyer filter.

Tracy was at the table, having brought the food down from the main house with the help of a couple of the other women, and was organizing the preparation and setting out of the plates. She smiled as she saw them approaching. "Hey you all! Are you coming to join us for lunch?"

"That depends," said Mike. "What's on the menu?"

"The best cuts of Spam you'll find this side of a Kansas City steakhouse. Plus, you get to eat with me!"

Mike laughed. "How could I resist that?"

They all lined up and got their plates and cups of water, then sat at a picnic table under one of the sun shades that had been erected around the common area. They watched as the kids were called in when fathers arrived from their work unloading one of the trailers into the barn, and families got their food and found places to sit at the tables to eat.

Jim watched as the families got situated. He enjoyed seeing the family unity that was obvious as fathers joined their wives and kids for lunch, and he reflected on how it resembled a simpler time when families focused more on each other than on their activities. He was glad to see that some families said grace before eating, and that everyone seemed to get along.

"You look happy," said Kelly.

Jim turned to look at her and smiled. "I am. You look happy too."

"I am." She looked around at the people eating, then back at him. "It's hard to put into words, but I feel good about all this. It seems like we should be scared, or at least worried, but it just feels good."

"Great purpose focuses the mind," said Bill. "It reduces one's attention to the most basic elements of life, and joy is found in the simplicity of satisfying one's central physical and spiritual needs without worrying about the superfluous."

The table turned silent, everyone staring at Bill. "Who said that?" Christian finally asked.

"I did," Bill replied with a smile. "Just now."

Everyone laughed.

"Well, I think that pretty much sums it up," said Ann. "I'm not thinking about the latest project deadline, shopping for a new outfit for a charity banquet or trying to figure out when I can pick up the dry cleaning. I'm enjoying being with my family and friends. It feels strange that I'm actually relaxing."

"Me too," said Tracy. "I'm not dreading spending the next year as a go-fer in a Cincinnati law firm. I can't believe I'm saying this, but this is nice."

They ate as they watched the people around them. Families talked among themselves and with others as they ate. Most were smiling, and kids ran around away from the tables after they had finished eating. At one point, they heard a man and a woman arguing from several tents over, and Tracy identified them as Michael and Linda Kant. Others turned toward the argument for a moment, then turned away, ignoring them.

Jim watched as the families finished eating and the women collected the plates and cups, taking them to a large plastic tub full of sudsy water where two women were washing them, one was shaking them then rinsing them in another tub and two others were drying and restocking them. "It looks like everyone is working well together," he said, "except for her." He pointed at a dark haired, overweight woman in a low-cut black sparkly blouse sitting on a blanket on the ground. She was looking up and talking to the people walking around her and stroking the hair of a little blonde girl whose head was in her lap. "Let me guess. Patty Cramer?"

Kelly looked where he was pointing. "Yep. You're good."

He chuckled. "So you keep telling me." He pointed to a man clearing the dishes off the Cramers' table. "And that would be Tom."

Kelly nodded. "Two for two. Would you like to guess my weight now?"

Jim made a show of slowly looking her up and down, then cocked his head. "Perfect."

"Unbelievable!" she laughed. "Three for three!"

Ann jabbed Bill in the side. "Listen and learn, your honor."

"I already came up with one brilliant saying today, dear. As Dirty Harry said, a man must know his limitations."

Jim laughed as Tracy and Mike asked "Who?" in unison, and, seeing that the lunch break was coming to a close, he got up and walked to the main serving table.

Holding up his hands, he called out, "Folks ... folks…" and waited for everyone to stop talking and turn toward him.

"For any of you who arrived in the last couple of days and don't know me, I'm Jim Wyatt. This is my family's place. We're glad to have you here, and happy to see that everyone seems to be getting on fairly well. It's been a rough couple of months and we're still getting things organized, so if there's anything you need just come see me or any of the people under that shade over there and we'll see if we can get you fixed up."

Greeted with affirmative murmuring, he went on. "For those who don't know, our rules are fairly simple. The Golden Rule pretty much covers it - just be nice and help each other out. That, and every able adult has to work and do their share. I'm not big on shirkers. We offer charity to children and those who aren't able to take care of themselves, but able adults need to pitch in and do what's right."

He paused for a moment to let that sink in, then continued. "Mike shot a pretty good-sized buck and we've got him prepared, so I want to invite everyone up to the house tonight for a barbecue. Just come about supper time. Have a good day and we'll see you then."

The afternoon was spent unloading a second trailer into the barn and inventorying the contents. They took out several cases of canned corn, green beans and baked beans for the barbecue, plus a case of KC Masterpiece barbecue sauce. Jim, Christian, Mike and Bill butchered the buck and started a fire in the patio pit, over which a large grill would be placed when a thick bed of coals had been established. Several of the women from the camp had come up to the house to help, and their kids played with Aedan, Brody and Morgan while they helped Kelly, Ann and Tracy get everything ready. Christian and Mike drove the Excursion over to the Samuels' and brought Ralph, Mary, Rebecca, Becky and Bobby back for the get together. When they arrived, Mary, Rebecca and Becky pitched in to help while Bobby played with other kids and Ralph joined the men on the patio.

"How's everything over at your place?" Jim asked Ralph as he handed him a glass of lemonade.

"Everything's fine," replied Ralph. "It's good to have the girls back and Bobby follows me around like a shadow."

"It's good for him to be around a man, finally."

Ralph nodded. "Good for me, too. It's nice to have someone who wants to learn about everything. He makes me think about things I haven't thought of in years. Good little worker too. Helps me out a lot."

"You ought to bring him over sometimes and let him play with the kids."

"I will. He's always asking to come with me when I go out salvaging, but I tell him it's too dangerous. Mind if I bring Mary and the girls over too? I worry about them when I'm gone."

"You bet. We need to keep in better contact. Which brings me to a couple of things I want to talk to you about. Let's sit down."

The men sat in a couple of large Adirondack chairs, setting their glasses on the wide wooden arms and looking out on the compound.

"I always liked these chairs," said Ralph. "Been meaning to make me a couple for about thirty years now."

Jim laughed. "Well, when you get around to it, make me a couple more too."

"Okay. Hope you're not in a hurry." He took a drink and let out a loud breath of satisfaction. "I'd forgotten how good iced lemonade was."

"We've got several cases of it. I'll send some home with you." Then a thought occurred to him and he felt ashamed he hadn't thought of it before. "Do you have ice?"

Ralph laughed. "I don't know what I'd make it with since the electricity's out."

"Don't you have a generator?"

"Sure. But it runs on gas and we ran out about a month ago."

"What do you do for lights?"

"What we did when I was a kid. Lanterns, candles and we go to bed when it gets dark."

Jim thought for a minute and then called Christian over.

"I was planning on running up to see Pasquale tomorrow,' he said, looking up at his nephew, "but something more important has come up. I'd like you to take some of those Harbor Freight solar kits we have stashed in the bunker and install them over at Ralph's place. Take enough batteries to run his refrigerator, fans and some low voltage lights around his place. Take as long as you need to set him up right."

Christian nodded and smiled. "Sure thing. We'll get them set up real good."

"Now, Jim, there's no need for that," said Ralph. "We're doing fine."

"How the hell can you be doing fine without iced lemonade, Ralph?"

"We didn't have ice when I was a kid."

"Well by all means let's do everything like when you were a kid. Are the ladies looking forward to that long snowy walk to the outhouse every night this winter?"

"We have indoor plumbing and you know it. And it's good exercise hand pumping the water from the well."

Jim nodded thoughtfully. "So, indoor plumbing is okay, but electricity isn't. Makes perfect sense."

Christian tried to suppress a smile and Ralph looked exasperated. "Oh, alright. And thanks. Then you keep my cut of the next two trucks."

Jim waved it away. "I don't want anything. I don't need them and it's the neighborly thing to do."

"Well I can't take them and all of Christian's work for nothing."

"Then how about helping me when my mare foals?"

Ralph thought for a moment and shrugged. "Okay. It doesn't seem like much, but okay."

Jim smiled and leaned back in his chair. "Good. Remember when you helped me with her when she foaled a couple years ago? Looks like I'm all paid up now."

Christian laughed and walked off.

Ralph sat there realizing he had been set up and shook his head. "You know, for having such a nice wife, you sure are sneaky."

Jim laughed and took a drink. "Now, what I wanted to talk to you about. Our scouts have been seeing an increasing number of people coming out of the city, and as time goes on they're becoming less savory. We're starting to get some at our gate. How about you?"

Ralph shook his head. "Not yet. You must be taking them all in."

"Yeah, so far. But I'm worried about having them get right up to us before we can talk to them and get them sorted out. It was suggested at one of our meetings that we put a checkpoint up the road about half a mile so we can make initial contact farther away from the property, but I wanted to talk to you first since it's your road too."

Ralph nodded. "That makes sense to me. Do you need my help?"

"I thought we'd put a trailer on each side of the road and fill them with dirt. Could you do a little grading with your dozer and fill the trailers?"

"Sure, no problem. You said there were a couple of things."

"The Eddingtons aren't back. It's been almost two months and I imagine it means they're not coming back anytime soon, if at all. I don't like having an empty house or unattended land next to me, so I was thinking about putting someone in there, maybe a family. I wanted to see what you thought about it and if you had any suggestions."

Ralph sat for a minute and took a sip of his lemonade, then nodded. "I agree. And I think I might have a suggestion if you would want to wait a little while."

"Who?"

Ralph lifted his chin to indicate something out in the common area. "You see who Christian's walking with?"

Jim looked out and saw Christian walking toward the house with a young boy. "Bobby? You mean Christian and Becky?"

"Yep."

"I knew they saw each other a little when they were younger, but now?"

"Yep. He swings by quite a bit when he's doing his perimeter checks." He smiled. "I feel real safe. I think Becky does to."

Jim shook his head. "I'll be darned. I had no idea."

Ralph chuckled, "And I'm sure you told your family all about your love life, right? I bet by the time Christian finishes the real thorough job I know he's going to do at my place you might have your family for the Eddington place."

They relaxed through the rest of the afternoon, putting more wood on the fire as each load of logs turned into coals and the sun started to dip below the tips of the western trees, throwing welcome cooling shadows over the patio. When the coals were thick enough they lifted the heavy eight-foot grill and placed it over the fire pit to heat.

The camp tenants started to arrive, the women shepherding their kids and some of the men carrying the long serving tables up from the commons to place near the pit. Kelly led the women in setting out the containers of lemonade and the huge platters of venison the men had cut earlier. Soon, everyone was milling around with red plastic cups of lemonade, laughing and talking, the recent hardships seemingly forgotten as an aura of celebration surrounded them all.

Once everyone was there, Jim held up his hands to quiet the group. "Folks, one of the best things about a barbecue is watching and smelling the meat cook, and we'll get that started in just a few minutes. But I want to say a few things first."

He looked out over the crowd, and at the individual faces of those to whom Stonemont had become a refuge. "It's been tough lately, and we can thank God and our hard work that we've survived so far and are doing as well as we are."

A soft murmur of agreement ran through the crowd and he continued.

"You've been working in exchange for food and a safe place to live, and there's nothing wrong with that. That's essentially what we all do when you get right down to it. However, the way we've been doing it is collectivist in nature, where people do what they can and get what they need. But that's not what built America in the first place and it won't be what rebuilds it the way it ought to be rebuilt.

"If you know your history, you know that the inhabitants of Jamestown starved because of their communal economy, and it was only by changing to a capitalistic model that their fortunes were reversed and became the seed of the America we knew.

"Our country prospered like no other until capitalism and self-sufficiency gave way to a growing desire for security, entitlements and governmental inclusion in every aspect of life. The loss of personal liberty and responsibility came about slowly, over a period of many years, and the result was a nation of people who had lost the understanding that protecting and providing for their own security and the security of their families was their own responsibility."

The crowd was quiet.

Jim went on. "We cannot continue that mentality. The catastrophe we have experienced has thrown us back to the reality that providing for ourselves and our families is our own responsibility. In order to do that, we don't have to invent something new. We just need to return to the original principles and values upon which our country was based - principles and values that were commonly and universally shared by those who sought divine guidance and blessings in their quest for liberty. It is time to return to those principles and values. It is time for a renewal of the dream of America."

A smattering of applause rippled through the crowd and Jim

111

continued.

"Beginning tomorrow, we will start operating under a new system, a system under which you will have greater control of your lives and your future. And you will be able to start to rebuild your lives as individuals and families instead of just being cogs in a communal wheel. Beginning tomorrow, we will start operating under a system of credits; credits which will be earned by work and which may be exchanged for food, goods and services.

"Our food and supplies do not belong to you and your labor does not belong to us. A fair exchange makes an equitable economy in which a free market determines the value of labor and goods. Such a system is what made America what it was and enabled each person to build whatever life their talents, imagination and hard work allowed them to. It is to such a system that Stonemont will return."

The crowd was listening intently, some nodding their heads and some just listening.

Jim continued. "Beginning tomorrow, credit will be recorded for work done and traded for goods and services, including food. During the time many of us remember as America's golden age, it was possible for a man to support his family on the normal wages of his work. Certainly, some made more than others, some worked harder or longer than others and therefore were able to provide more for their families and build more wealth, but the basic salary of one adult was usually able to support a normal family.

"This is the standard by which we will establish our credit exchange. Each adult meal will be valued at two credits and each child's meal at one credit. That means that three meals a day for two adults and two children comes to eighteen credits. We will add two credits a day for rent of a tent, for a total of twenty credits. Using that as our baseline, twenty credits will be paid for each adult work day. In this way, a family can have its basic needs provided for by one working adult."

A woman in the crowd raised her hand. "What if both adults in a family work?"

Jim nodded. "Good question. Since an adult work day is credited at twenty credits, that family would receive forty credits for each day both adults work."

"What good are extra credits if the twenty credits take care of everything?" asked a man in the back of the crowd.

"Twenty credits would take care of three meals a day and tent rental," explained Jim. "But what if you don't want to just keep renting a tent and getting three basic meals a day? What if you want to buy your own tent, a bigger tent, so that your family is more comfortable and you're not as dependent on us in case you want to leave? What if you want to buy more food than just the daily rations or more clothes, better and warmer clothes when the weather starts to change? What if you want to buy a gun and ammunition to protect your family?"

"And where are we supposed to get these things?" asked another man, "and what good are credits?"

"Because we have those things." Jim said, turning and waving his arm at the barn and the trailers lined up next to it. "That is our business, salvage and trading. We prepared for an emergency before it happened and we continued to respond afterward with a lot of hard work and personal risk. We did this in order to ensure that these things would be available to us and to others who were willing to work for them. So, you will be able to buy them from us with the credits you earn working for us."

"So, you're holding food and supplies hostage!" yelled one man. "You're forcing us to do work for you in order to get food for our families! That's slavery!"

Jim thought for a moment. Was it possible that some people were really so stupid that they didn't understand such basic economic principles? Remembering the state of the country before the collapse, he had to admit that many were.

Jim looked at the man. "What's your name?"

"Tom Cramer," the man replied.

"Mr. Cramer, did you work before all this started?"

"Of course I did," Cramer said indignantly.

"So, you and your family weren't on welfare before the power went out?"

"Of course not!" the man responded.

"What did you do for a living?"

"I delivered newspapers."

"And why did you work?"

Cramer put his hands on his hips. "To make money!"

"Why?"

"What do you mean, why? To support my family, of course."

"You mean nobody just gave you food and clothes and a place to live?"

"Hell, no. I'm no sponge. I work for a living!"

Jim looked at the man. "Well, Mr. Cramer, I'm afraid I don't have any newspapers that need to be delivered."

Jim watched the crowd as some started to smile and others looked like they were just starting to understand.

Cramer at first looked confused, then angry again. "What do you mean by that?"

"What I mean, Mr. Cramer, is that I don't have any newspapers that need to be delivered. You said that was what you did, but I don't need that. Since you said you are not a sponge, and work to support your family, do you have any other skills we might need that you could trade us for food and supplies to support your family?"

"Like what?" Cramer was now equally angry and confused.

"We need medical professionals. Are you by chance a doctor, a nurse or a paramedic in addition to delivering newspapers?"

Cramer scowled and crossed his arms. "No."

Jim acted like he was thinking for a minute. "Well, we need engineers. Are you perhaps an engineer?"

"No."

Jim started walking through the crowd toward Cramer. "Dog breeder or trainer?"

"No."

"Heavy equipment operator?"

"No."

"Carpenter?"

"No."

"Builder?"

Cramer was silent for a moment, then said in a quieter voice, "No."

Jim stopped an arm's length from Cramer. "Well, Mr. Cramer, that's what we need right now. Since you aren't qualified in any of those areas, we also need people to unload trucks, cut trees, tend the fields and do whatever else we need on a daily basis. Now, Mr. Cramer, would you be interested in doing any of that work in order to provide for your family, or do you expect us to just give you food and a place to live without you doing anything?"

Cramer was looking less sure of himself and began to respond when Jim interrupted him.

"There is another option, Mr. Cramer. You can leave. No one is making you stay here. After all, you are not a slave."

114

Cramer looked stunned. He had thought others would feel the same way he did and back him up. Instead, those around him were pulling away from him. Even Patty was staying in the back of the crowd, though she had been complaining to him about her dissatisfaction with things for some time.

Jim turned around to the crowd. "Folks, we are happy to have anyone here who is willing to pitch in and help us start rebuilding some semblance of civil society. But that means everyone works for what they get. There will be no handouts to able people. In fact, we encourage everyone to not only take advantage of the work we have, but to build independence by working extra and building your own wealth, and also to market any skills you have that others might need. Our strength won't come from everyone working for one person, or even a few people, but from everyone building their own futures by their own imagination and hard work."

He turned back to Cramer. "Now, I'm getting hungry, and I imagine everyone else is too. What is your answer, Mr. Cramer? Would you like to continue to stay here at our home with us and do some work for the food and shelter we provide for your family, or will you be leaving us?"

Cramer was still angry, but was also embarrassed, which further enraged him. He had been sure he could back Wyatt down like he had so many others, and build a following of his own among the refugees at Stonemont. Instead, Wyatt had faced him down, shaming him in front of the crowd and his own family. He knew that he and his family would never survive outside Stonemont by themselves, so he realized he had to remain until he could build up enough support for another play against Wyatt. "Okay," he said through clenched teeth.

"What do you mean 'okay'?" Jim asked in a voice that could be heard by everyone.

Cramer glared at Jim. "I mean okay, I'll work."

Jim nodded and turned, speaking to the crowd. "Alright folks, let's throw the meat on and have a great evening. We're happy to have you at our home."

Then he turned to Cramer and spoke quietly in his ear. "Not you. You insulted me in my home. If I have any more trouble with you, you're gone."

12

Jim could tell by the angle of the sun that it was later than he usually awakened.

The barbecue had lasted late into the night, with everyone enjoying themselves and not wanting to leave the camaraderie that was growing within the group. He had had a chance to talk with all of the compound inhabitants and get to know a little about each of them. Just as importantly, and perhaps more so, they had had a chance to talk with him, Kelly and the others of the Stonemont core group.

All in all, he was pleased with the group. Most had understood and seemed to agree with the system he had explained to them, and those who hadn't understood seemed willing to see how it would work. Everyone appeared to get along well, with a couple of exceptions, but he would keep his eye on those exceptions.

After a quick shower and shave, he descended the stairs to the kitchen where he found Kelly and Ann putting away the breakfast dishes.

"Morning, sleepy head," said Kelly, smiling. "I kept a plate warm for you and Christian's waiting for you on the patio."

Jim smiled, walking toward the coffee pot. "Thanks, babe. Morning, Ann." He put his hand on Kelly's back and gave her a kiss. "I can't believe I slept so late. What did you put in my drink?"

Kelly laughed. "Everything must have finally caught up with you."

"I guess so." He poured coffee into a thick mug, grabbed the plate Kelly had put in the warmer for him and went out onto the patio.

"Well, I thought you might sleep the day away," smiled Christian. "But I know people your age need their sleep."

"It's why I'm better looking than you, young'un. You might want to consider getting a few more hours yourself. What's up?"

"We caught a thief last night."

Jim set his coffee mug and plate on the table and sat down. "Tell me about it."

"Tom Cramer. A couple of the new guys on security caught him in the barn. One of the security guys was going to flip and pitch in with him, but the other one faced him down. We have it all on video because the barn is the one place I put cameras inside as well as out."

"Who are the security guys?"

"The good one is named Andrew McClellan. He has a wife and two young kids. They're one of the families from Family Church. The one who was going to flip is named Jeff Waters. He came in with some others we came across on the road."

"Where are they now?"

"Cramer is cuffed in the barn. Mike is watching him. McClellan and Waters were relieved at six, so they're probably catching some shut-eye. They don't know we know Waters was going to flip."

"McClellan didn't say anything?"

Christian shook his head. "No, but he was staring at Waters real hard when they made their report."

"Okay, let me eat and then I want to see the video."

Christian pushed a small laptop toward Jim and turned it toward him. "I already downloaded it for you. The sound is even pretty good."

Jim watched the security video as he ate. It showed Tom Cramer enter the barn at approximately 0235 hours, start opening boxes and searching through them. McClellan and Waters entered the barn about ten minutes later and McClellan demanded to know what Cramer was doing in the barn. Cramer attempted to talk his way out of it, saying he was just looking around, then suggested that it was unfair Stonemount was hoarding all the supplies and keeping it from them. Pulling a bottle of bourbon out of his pocket, he told the two guards that he had found a case of it and offered to share it with them if they didn't turn him in. Waters agreed with Cramer and said he would accept it, telling McClellan they had a right to something extra for providing security. McClellan took a step back, charged his AR-15, raised the muzzle in Cramer's direction and instructed Waters to notify Christian. Waters started to object until McClellan told him again, then left the barn. Cramer continued to try to talk McClellan into letting him go until Christian entered the barn with Waters a few minutes later.

Christian leaned over and hit pause on the video. "There you have it. I stayed with him and sent McClellan and Waters back on patrol. Mike relieved me a little after six and I went to review the video."

"They still in the barn?"

Christian nodded.

"Tell me about McClellan."

"Mid-twenties. Nice but serious. Smart and a hard worker. Nice wife and two polite little kids."

"Is he any good?"

Christian nodded. "Damn good. I wish they were all like him."

"What did he do before LO?"

"El oh?"

"Lights out," Jim smirked. "I just made it up and am trying it out on you. Like it?"

Christian chuckled. He always got a kick out of how his uncle could throw something funny into an otherwise serious situation. "Love it. Does that mean we're in the year one LO?"

Jim smiled. "Sounds good. I feel younger already. So, what did he do?"

"He ran a rough-in crew for a builder. His wife just graduated from college and was going to be a teacher."

Jim nodded and thought for a moment. "Why don't you see if he's up yet. I'd like to talk to him."

Jim had just finished his breakfast and was pouring a second cup of coffee when Christian returned with McClellan.

"Jim, this is Andrew McClellan."

Jim looked at the young man but didn't ask him to sit. "Tell me what happened last night, Andrew."

Andrew stood straight, not quite at attention, and looked Jim in the eye. "Sir, Jeff Waters and I were on patrol when we saw the interior light in the barn was on. We went inside and found Tom Cramer going through some of the boxes stored there. I held Tom and sent Jeff to get Christian. Christian came and secured Tom, then sent Jeff and I back on patrol."

Jim nodded. "A very concise report. Is there anything else you think I should know?"

"Yes sir. Tom attempted to bribe us and Jeff wanted to go along with it."

Jim looked at McClellan for a moment. "Why didn't you include that in your initial report?"

"Because I didn't think it was the main issue, sir."

"Then why did you tell me at all?"

"Because you asked me if there was anything else you should know, and I felt you should know that."

"And why is that?"

118

"Sir, that is your property. Tom is a thief. Jeff was going to go along with it, which makes him a thief. I'm not a thief. You pay me to guard your property. I'm just doing my job, sir."

Jim looked over at Christian, who smiled and nodded in approval, then back at Andrew. "Have you had breakfast?"

Andrew shook his head. "No sir. I just woke up when Christian came to get me."

Jim turned to his nephew. "Christian, would you go ask Kelly if she could put together a plate of something for our new corporal of the guard, then go relieve Mike and ask him to come see me. Andrew will come relieve you after he eats."

Jim turned back to Andrew. "Grab a mug over there on the sideboard, Andrew. There's coffee or water. Then come sit down. We'll talk a bit while you eat."

13

Tom Cramer and Jeff Waters stood together at the front gate, Tom's right wrist bound to Jeff's left by crossed zip ties, surrounded by the inhabitants of Stonemont. The swiftness of their sentencing and its execution had left them both stunned, and Jim Wyatt now stood in front of them.

"Tom Cramer attempted to steal the property of others," stated Jim, in a voice meant to carry to the crowd around them. "Jeff Waters was on a security patrol, entrusted with watching over the safety and security of Stonemont while we slept. Instead of discharging those duties with honor and integrity, he agreed to participate in that attempted theft, thereby siding with an enemy of Stonemont. Because of the trust that was placed in him, his betrayal and crime is greater."

Jim reached out and grabbed Waters' unbound right hand, holding it in an iron grip against Waters' attempt to pull away. "Therefore, an additional punishment is appropriate." Quickly, he raised Waters' hand above his head and bent his fingers back to the breaking point.

The crowd heard only the first of several snaps before the others were covered by Waters' shrieks of pain.

Jim let go of his hand and Waters sank to one knee before he was able to stabilize himself and return to both feet. He tried to put his broken fingers under his opposite arm but the pressure was too painful and he just held his crippled hand across his stomach. He broke into a sweat and began to feel nauseous as he started to tremble, his breath coming quick and shallow.

Jim stood in front of the two, waiting for Waters to be able to focus again, then spoke again to the crowd. "Societies has dealt with thieves in different ways throughout history. Some cut off the right hand. Some executed them. Others declared the offender outlaw and banished them. This last method is the path we will take, since I don't believe in executing someone for a property crime and we can't allow them to stay after having attempted to steal from us. They are now outlawed and banished from Stonemont and any of Stonemont's holdings. Further, they are now outside the protection of Stonemont and its laws, and therefore there will be no punishment against anyone who takes any action against them, regardless of what that action may be."

He paused, looking around the crowd and spotting Patty Cramer. "One final thing. Is there anyone who wants to go with them?" He waited a full minute and no one moved.

Turning back to Cramer and Waters, he stepped closer to them so he could speak quietly. "Whenever someone attacks me or my family and I let them go, I make them a promise. If you ever try to come back at me or them, I will kill you. Now get out of here."

Jim stood aside and the two men started walking slowly away. Cramer turned around once, as if he were looking for someone.

Mike watched through a spotting scope from a hide he had just shown his newest trainee how to build, about a quarter mile from the gate. He watched as Cramer and Waters began to walk slowly toward them. "Here. Take a look," he said, backing away to the side.

Tracy Garner moved up to put her eye to the scope and watched for a minute. "Their wrists are zip tied together and something's wrong with Waters' right hand."

"Jim broke his fingers."

"Why?"

"I can't say for sure, but I think I can read the symbolism. Waters agreed to help Cramer, which would have made him Cramer's right hand man, so he's tied to Cramer's right hand. Then Jim broke the fingers on Waters' right hand for his additional punishment of betraying Stonemont, and to show him what happens to a right hand that serves an ill purpose."

Tracy turned toward him to see if he was putting her on, but he looked serious. "You got all that from how they're tied and some broken fingers? You're kidding, right?"

Mike shook his head. "Nope."

Tracy looked back through the scope and watched the two walk for a minute. "Good."

Mike chuckled. "Good?"

"Yeah. You know how in the movies the bad guys never got what was coming to them until the end, and then it was never as bad as they really deserved?"

"Yeah."

"Well, it seems like lately the bad guys are getting what they deserve. Jim doesn't put up with much, does he?"

"No, he doesn't. He can't afford to. He's responsible for his family and

121

now a lot of other people."

Tracy took her eye away from the scope and looked at Mike. "Yeah. He can seem mean sometimes, but I like him. So do my folks."

Mike nodded. "So do I. But he's not mean, he's just."

Tracy waited for him to finish what he was saying, but he didn't seem to be continuing. "Just what?" she finally asked.

"What?"

"You said he was just, and then you stopped."

Mike smiled. "I meant that he is just, as in justice. It may seem mean by a standard that thought it was mean to execute someone who had tortured and murdered an entire family, or that it was mean to expect able bodied people to support themselves, or that it was mean for one little league team to actually beat another one, or to tell a four-hundred-pound person that maybe they didn't need another doughnut. The thinking that truth and justice is mean is what made the world the mess it was before it all came crashing down, and it's also the reason so many people became unable to take care of themselves."

Tracy thought about that for a minute, then moved back so Mike could look through the scope.

"It's amazing," she said.

"What's amazing?"

"How far we let ourselves get away from reality. Do you know what the favorite TV shows were in college?"

"No."

"Shows about vampires and a bunch of women trying to get a guy to propose to them."

Mike looked at her skeptically. "You're kidding."

Tracy shook her head. "Huh uh. Nobody went out until those shows were over."

Mike shook his head in disbelief, then put his eye back to the scope. "They're almost to us. It's about time for you to go to the next location."

"Okay. Was Jim surprised when you told him you wanted to bring me?"

"I don't think so. He knows you're a capable person and I told him you were one of the best in your group."

"Really?" she asked with a smile, which quickly changed to a slight scowl. "Who's better?"

Mike gave a low chuckle. "That's not your business. You ready?"

"Yeah."

"Test your radio again."

Tracy whispered into the mic. "Who's better?"

Mike gave a thumbs-up and whispered back. "Not your business. Go."

Tracy returned the thumbs up and slowly backed out of the hide, then down the back of the embankment until she could get to her feet without being seen from the road. Giving Mike another thumbs-up, she turned and quietly walked north into the trees and brush.

Mike watched her walk away, approving of the stealth she had developed so quickly. He had been watching her out of the corner of his eye while she was on the scope. He thought her eyes were amazing, hazel with flecks of gold, and he usually avoided looking directly into them, as doing so often made him forget what he was saying. And the auburn highlights made her dark brown hair look like it was always shining. The weeks of hard work and training had tanned and strengthened her, and her light step only accentuated his realization that he had never seen camos filled out so well. She disappeared into the brush and he turned his attention back to the road.

The two men were almost even with him now. They were talking to each other, but too low for him to hear what they were saying. He watched as they continued up the road and soon heard Tracy's whisper in his earpiece, "All set."

Hearing that, he packed the scope away, backed down the embankment and went into the trees heading north. She should be about a quarter mile ahead and he would leapfrog her position by another quarter mile. They would do this a couple more times until they reached the first crossroad, at which they would stop together to see which way the two men went.

A berm had been built up along the east side of the road when it had been graded many years before, which allowed them to travel behind it and overlook the road wherever they wanted to crest it under the vegetation along the top. When he got close to where he thought she would be, he started looking closely into the shrub for her. After a couple of minutes, he saw her faint outline under some thick bushes. "Good job," he whispered into his mic as he passed, complementing her position.

"Thanks," came the response. Then after a second, "Does this camo make my butt look big?"

Mike flushed as if he'd been caught, and it was several seconds before

123

she heard his whispered "I didn't notice."

She smiled. Yeah, right. Mike tried to play it cool, but she had caught him looking at her several times. She just hoped he hadn't caught her looking at him. She watched the two walk past her and about ten minutes later heard Mike's whispered "I got 'em."

They leap-frogged two more times before Mike called her up to join him over-watching a small white house the two men had entered. Crawling into an area he had cleared behind some brush, she lifted her eyes above the crest of the berm and looked down on the house. It was situated about fifty feet off the road with a small out-building another fifty feet behind it. A silver car sat in a carport overgrown with weeds.

Mike leaned close to her and spoke quietly. "They just went in a minute ago. From the sound of it, they kicked in the back door. We checked this area about a month ago and this house was vacant. Should be still unless some refugees have moved in." He set up the spotting scope on the house.

"You haven't told me what we're supposed to do exactly," said Tracy,

"Jim wants us to follow them and make sure they leave the area. Also, to make sure they don't hurt anyone along the way."

"How long are we supposed the follow them?"

"Until we know."

"Good thing I brought my toothbrush."

They took turns on the scope throughout the afternoon, Mike taking occasional naps during his off times and Tracy trying to. By evening, the men had not come out of the house and Tracy was getting antsy. "What do you think they're doing in there?"

Mike lifted the boonie hat from his eyes and rolled from his back to his stomach to look over the crest of the berm. "The first thing they did was cut the flex cuffs off. Then Waters taped up his fingers. After that, they went through the house looking for guns, booze, food and whatever else they can use. They won't find any guns because we secured those. There's food and there's booze, so they've probably had something to eat and are now getting drunk and talking about how they'd like to go back and kill us all."

Tracy looked at him. "Wow."

Mike smirked. "Well, that's what I'd do if I were a thief and a dirt bag who had just been kicked out of my village."

Tracy nodded. "Makes sense."

Mike got into his rucksack and dug out some protein bars, giving two to Tracy and keeping two for himself. "Let's get a little fuel in us. When it gets dark I'm going down to take a look."

"What are you looking for?"

"I just want to make sure they're in there alone."

"And what do you want me to do?"

"If I'm not back in an hour, go back and get help."

"How do I know when an hour has gone by?"

"I'll show you when it gets dark."

They ate their protein bars and sipped water as they waited for it to get dark. When it did, Mike pointed up in the sky. "See that group of stars right there? See the biggest one?"

Tracy followed his finger. "Uh huh."

"When that big star passes the top of that big tree it will be about an hour after I leave."

Tracy raised her eyebrows in appreciation of the lesson. "Cool."

Mike reached into his ruck, pulled out a pair of NVGs and put them on.

"What the heck is that?" asked Tracy.

"Night vision."

"Double cool. Do I get one?"

"Yep." He dug another set out and helped her put them on.

She looked around her, amazed at the glowing green world around her. "Wow! How come 'wow' and 'cool' are all I seem to be able to say?"

She looked at him. "You look like some kind of alien anteater. How do I look?"

Mike tilted his head from side to side as if studying her, then smiled. "They make your butt look big."

He waited until an hour after the sun went down to leave the hide and check the house, entering through the broken back door and quietly making his way to the front. As he had expected, both Cramer and Waters were asleep and snoring in the living room, one on the couch and one in a recliner. Beer cans lay on the tables and floor around them and a mostly empty bottle of bourbon sat on the table next to the chair.

Making a quick check of the other rooms and finding nothing, he exited the house and went to the outbuilding where found the usual junk that accumulated on a farm over fifty years, including an old Massey-Ferguson tractor. Old tools and chains lay on work tables and hung from nails long ago pounded into the wooden support posts. Finding nothing of interest, he left and returned to the hide.

They split the watch, with Mike taking the first half and Tracy taking the second, or, as Tracy called it, "until the other big tree and after it."

At day-break they had some granola and another protein bar and started switching off on the scope more frequently. Finally, at what Mike guessed was about ten o'clock, Cramer and Waters came out from the back of the house. Each was carrying a bag.

"What do you think is in the bags?" whispered Tracy.

"Probably food. Maybe some other things they think they can trade."

They watched as the two men walked back to the road, headed north again then turned left at the cross road to go west.

Mike got to his feet. "Okay, here we go."

They stayed together this time, Mike using the opportunity to test Tracy on some of the stalking, tracking and tradecraft they had covered in her scout class and to introduce her to new skills and concepts. He had been impressed with both her abilities and her dedication in the class, and was even more impressed now that they were in the field. As the day wore on he let her take more of the lead, keeping her eyes on the pair while he ranged further away from the road, checking things in the quarter mile stretch south.

Late in the afternoon they saw a set of railroad tracks and a white two-story building just beyond. As they got closer they were able to see a sign that said "Boomer's" and smaller signs that promised live entertainment and "Girls! Girls! Girls!" Crossing through a small orchard and a stand of trees, they eased up the embankment of the railroad tracks and saw the parking lot filled with motorcycles. Cramer and Waters were just entering the building.

"Okay," said Mike. "That's good news and bad news."

"Yeah? More good or more bad?"

Mike gave a slight shrug. "You can never be sure until it's over. The good news is that they haven't run into any innocent people yet. Also, they're probably going to be in there for a while, which will hopefully give us time to get back to Stonemont."

"And the less than good news?"

"They probably have food, booze and women in there, but in amounts limited by their ability to loot. Now, there are two guys in there who are telling them where there's plenty more of each."

"Really?" she asked, feigning excitement. "We have plenty of booze?"

Mike couldn't help but laugh. "Well, I suppose that depends on the size of the party. Count the bikes."

"Forty-seven," said Tracy, after a minute.

"I agree. Let's go."

They headed cross country, keeping to a regimen of alternating jogging and walking, and by late afternoon were back at Stonemont.

14

Jim got up from the couch and walked to the windows looking out on the compound, watching those involved in their daily activities and getting ready for supper. Fathers were returning from their work and mothers were calling children to come and wash up before they ate. It was a satisfying sight, and he thought once again how fortunate they were here. Now, their first possible threat from the outside was imminent.

Behind him in the horseshoe of sofas sat the Stonemont core; Kelly, Christian, Mike, Bill, Ann and Tracy. Mike and Tracy had just finished their briefing, and Jim was surprised at how Mike had encouraged Tracy to take the lead, adding only occasional bits as needed. She had done a good job. There was more to this girl than he had first thought. He turned back to the group.

"I doubt they'll make a move at night, though they may send a scouting party. From my experience with this type, if they come it will probably be midday after they've recovered from the previous night."

He looked at Christian. "How many scouts and security people do you have?"

"We have twelve in all, but only about half of them are close to ready."

Jim nodded slowly, thinking. "Okay. Set your normal watch tonight, but add one over on the west fence at the creek. Waters was on security and he knows that's a weak spot. Have them take a dog. If they probe that spot the dog will raise hell and they'll probably discount that way. At morning watch change, switch out the guard so they can get some sleep but keep the dog there. In the morning, I want all the kids kept in the commons, ready to get into the house if trouble starts. All adults will keep their firearms on them and report to their assigned spots if the bell rings."

Christian nodded. "Got it."

Jim turned to Mike. "As soon as you clean up, get a change of clothes and have something to eat, head back out to overwatch the road at that abandoned house. They might try to scout the road or probe us tonight. Take Tracy and four others. You take an AR-10 and arm the others with three shotguns and two AR-15s. Double-ought in the shotguns. If you have to engage, I want them to think the world is coming to an end - because theirs will be. Keep us up to the minute on the walkie-talkies. We could hear you just fine, even in whisper mode." He paused for a moment, trying to suppress a smile. "By the way, Mike, if we ever form a diplomatic section, you'll certainly be considered."

It took a moment after Ann shot her a reprimanding glance for Tracy to understand the implications of Jim's last remark and to blush slightly. "Oops."

He turned back to Christian. "Go tell Ralph what's going on and invite them to stay here till this is over. They shouldn't be over there alone. Then block the road to their place just the other side of our drive and also the road going to the Eddington's. I don't want any of them being able to drive around to flank us.

"When the bell rings I want the four best of the remaining scouts behind me at the gate but behind the stone pillars. Split the remaining scouts to positions about fifty yards to the right and left of the gate. Fill in with another five men at each of those positions. Put any remaining with the scouts behind me at the gate. Have the scouts carry ARs and the rest shotguns. I want you with an AR-10 up the drive behind me where you can pick them off over the fence. If the ball starts rolling, I don't want anything getting out of there."

He paused for a minute, looking at each member of the group. "I know I don't have to say this to you, but I want to put it into words and give everyone a chance to say something if they want to. We discussed this when we first met, and you all", he nodded at Christian, Mike and the Garners, "dealt with it personally. If these people attack, they will be trying to kill us and our children. We don't have the capacity to keep prisoners. Any that get away will be able to attack us again or to bring others back on us. Therefore, any attackers who are not killed will be hung."

There was silence as each person nodded solemnly.

Jim nodded in return. "I'll announce this to the compound at dinner."

129

15

It was earlier than they had expected when they heard the first motorcycles.

Mike and his scouts had set up camp behind the crest of the berm overlooking the abandoned farm house and had taken turns watching the road with rotating two-man teams. They first saw the sparkle of sunlight reflecting off chrome as the bikes approached from the west, then heard the rumble of the engines as they turned south onto the road approaching Stonemont. Reaching the abandoned house below their position, the bikers slowed down and pulled into the drive, circling the bikes in the front yard and cutting the engines.

"I count twenty-three." said Tracy.

Mike looked through the spotting scope. "Me too. I wonder where the rest are. Call it in."

Tracy spoke into her headset. "Scout one to stone."

In a moment, they heard the reply. "Go ahead scout one."

"Twenty-three bikes just parked at the house."

"Any others in sight?"

"Negative."

"Okay, keep us advised."

They watched as the bikers dismounted and gathered in a group around one large, bearded man with massive arms and shoulders. Tattoos covered his arms and an American flag do-rag covered his head. A denim cutoff jacket bore a large patch on the back and smaller patches on the front. An AR-type rifle hung muzzle down over his back. The other bikers were similarly dressed, with various types of rifles and side-arms visible.

The bikers stood in a group for several minutes, then the large man and another biker unslung their rifles and handed them to a couple of others. They talked for a couple more minutes, then the two remounted their bikes and started them up with a roar.

"They don't seem to be trying to stay quiet," observed Mike. "One is a woman."

Tracy keyed her mic again. "Scout one to stone."

"Go ahead scout one."

"Two are headed your way. One male and one female. They left their rifles with the group, which so far is remaining at the house. Most are wearing patches that say 'Vikings'."

"Okay scout one. Keep us advised."

"Stone to scout two," Jim called the sentries at the west fence.

"Go ahead stone."

"You have any activity over there?"

"Negative, stone."

"Okay, stay sharp. We're missing a bunch of them."

Jim stepped up to the main gate and listened to the engines get louder with their approach. Soon, the bikes came into sight, growing larger until the riders finally pulled up in front of the gate, shut off their engines and stepped off their bikes.

The woman would have captured Jim's attention with her black leather vest and her long blonde hair held back with a black leather headband had the man not been one of the biggest men he had ever seen. The man looked at Jim and held up his hands to show they were empty.

"Howdy," said the man.

"Howdy," Jim answered, stepping through the gate and taking a few steps toward the couple. "What can we do for you?"

"We heard you had a doctor here," said the man. "We have someone who's hurt."

Jim watched the man's eyes, looking for hints of intentions.

"It's our son," said the woman anxiously. "He's been stabbed and he's running a fever."

Jim watched the two for another moment, deciding how much to say. "We don't have a doctor, but we have a paramedic. How bad is it?"

"We're not sure," said the man, shaking his head. "It took him in the lower left side. I don't know how deep it is."

The couple seemed sincere, but Jim knew what accomplished liars people could be. Leaving the rest of their party at the abandoned house could mean they weren't here to attack or it could be a tactical maneuver meant to assuage Stonemont's concerns. Jim continued to study the pair, noticing that they wore what appeared to be matching rings on their left ring fingers.

"Where is he?" Jim asked.

"He's back at a place called 'Boomers' about five or six miles from here." said the man. "It's an old strip joint some of our club has been staying at since everything went to hell."

131

"How did you know about us?" asked Jim.

"The guy who stabbed Austin, our son. He and another guy came past yesterday. They told us about you. Said you'd thrown them out. It didn't take me long to figure you had to be alright if you threw those two assholes out."

Jim thought for a minute. "Which one stabbed your son and why?"

"Said his name was Tom. He started drinking and messing with one of the girls. When Austin called him out he pulled a knife and stabbed him."

"What about Tom?"

"Dead. Austin killed him."

"How about the other one?"

The man shrugged. "Beats me. He took off running."

Jim nodded. One more question would help him decide. "Did you all come over here by yourselves?"

The man shook his head. "Nope. We had the others wait up the road at an old house. We don't travel anywhere except in a big group, but I didn't want you to think we were trying to move on you."

"Do you have a way to get your son here?"

The man nodded. "We have a camper. We can have him here in an hour if you'll let us."

Jim took a step toward the couple. "Go get him." He held out his hand. This would be the moment of truth and he was ready to drop to give Christian a shot. "I'm Jim Wyatt."

The man took his hand in a firm but non-challenging grip. "Mason Booker." He inclined his head to the woman beside him. "This is my wife, Bonnie."

Jim let go of Mason's hand and nodded to the woman. "We'll do everything we can for your son."

Jim keyed the mic on his radio. "Okay everybody, we may have a new plan, but stay on watch. Christian, relieve Mike. Mike, we're going to need you at the house."

It took them a little less than an hour to get Austin to Stonemont. As before, the bikes dropped off at the abandoned house while Mason and Bonnie brought Austin to Stonemont in an older pickup truck with a camper on it.

16

"I was a welder."

Mason and Bonnie sat on one of the couches in the den talking with Jim, Kelly, Bill and Ann. They had carried Austin into one of the rooms upstairs, where Mike had given him some painkillers and fever reducers, cleaned and sutured the wound and started him on antibiotics. Mike stayed with him while the others went back downstairs to talk.

"I had a shop in the back of my place and did a lot of custom work for people," Mason continued. "Gates, decorative ironwork and stuff like that. I built my own chopper, like those guys on TV, you know? When I started riding it I started running into all these other bike guys and started doing work for them too. It just kind of grew and my place came to be the place for a lot of the guys to hang out when they weren't riding." He gave a low chuckle. "Of course, I guess some of it might have been because we were just across from Boomers."

Bonnie gave him a playful jab with her elbow. "Ya think?"

"I notice you don't wear a one percent patch," said Jim.

Mason looked a bit surprised. "I'm a welder who rides a bike, not a biker who welds, if that makes any sense. How come you know about one percenters?"

"I rode when I was younger, but never with a club."

Mason nodded. "Most of our guys are like that. We've got carpenters, plumbers, electricians, pretty much everything." He chuckled again. "We even have an accountant and a history professor, if you can believe that.

"After we started doing runs together someone said we needed a name, so one of our guys who taught history at the college suggested 'Vikings' and it stuck. He said it had kind of a hidden meaning because the Vikings are known for being wild, but they were fairly domestic in their daily lives, like we are."

"That's true," said Bill. "They raided Europe, Britain and Ireland, but then introduced a more stable social structure of farming and trading to societies that had been more nomadic and cattle based."

Mason looked at Bill, then at Jim. "You have one too, huh?"

Jim laughed. "Bill was a judge, and is our resident expert on such things."

"Yes," smiled Bill. "It's amazing how much time you have to read if you don't play golf."

"I'm afraid we're going to see another major change," said Mason. "In fact, we're going to be part of it. What do you think is going to happen?"

"That conversation is going to take some time," said Kelly, getting up from the couch, "so I think I'll put together some sandwiches."

"I'll help you," said Ann, getting up,

"Me too," said Bonnie, following them.

The women walked down the hall, through the great room and into the kitchen.

"You have a beautiful home," said Bonnie.

"Thank you," said Kelly, opening the pantry and pulling out a canned ham. "Jim and I planned it for several years and built a lot of it ourselves. It really is our dream home."

Bonnie looked at the other women. They seemed so different from her on the outside, but the time she had spent with them since they had brought Austin here had shown her that they were down to earth and caring people. Just like their husbands, it seemed. She had spent so much time over the years dealing mainly with men, she had forgotten how good it felt to be with other women she could talk to about important things, and who didn't seem to judge her or her husband by their appearance. She looked at Kelly and Ann, and tears came to her eyes. "I want to thank you. All of you. Not just for helping Austin, but for bringing us in and making us feel welcome. We weren't sure what to expect. Most people shy away from us because of how we look."

Kelly and Ann both looked at Bonnie for a moment, then Ann took a step forward, placing her hands on Bonnie's shoulders and looking into her eyes. "Honey, when I look at you and Mason, I see a mom and a dad who love their son and are worried about him. That's what I see."

"Me too," said Kelly, looking at Bonnie over Ann's shoulder, then stepping around Ann to put her arm around Bonnie's shoulders.

At the women's touch, Bonnie broke down, her whole body shaking with her sobs. "Austin is ... he's ... he's everything to us."

Kelly guided her over to a chair. "Here, sit down."

The women held her for several minutes until her sobs subsided.

"Bonnie, Mike is doing everything he can and we're all going to pray for Austin. Don't worry, he's going to be okay."

Bonnie looked up, wiping her eyes and cheeks with her hands. "Thank you. I'm sorry, I'm usually not such a baby. But I spend most of my time around guys and I guess being with you two just brought it all out."

Ann patted Bonnie gently. "It's okay, honey, I'm sure the men are over there crying too."

Bonnie looked at Ann and saw a slight smile, then gave a small smile and stood up. "Okay. That did it. Baby's gone. What can I do to help?"

The women carried a tray of sandwiches and two pitchers of iced sweet tea into the den and set them down on the large coffee table in the middle of the couches.

"So, what did you decide?" asked Ann.

"We didn't," replied Jim. "We were waiting for you."

"Very wise. The fate of the world shouldn't be decided on an empty stomach."

They all grabbed sandwiches and poured glasses of tea. Mason took a long drink. "Man, I'd forgotten how good that is. How come you're set up so well when everyone else is scratching around like a bunch of chickens?"

"Jim saw this coming," said Bill.

Mason looked at Jim. "You did?"

"It was more like I was afraid something was going to happen. I didn't hunt, fish, play golf or watch sports, so I had plenty of time to watch what was going on in the world." He took a drink of his tea. "I don't know where you stand politically, Mason ..."

"About two clicks to the right of Ronald Reagan," said Mason.

Jim smiled and nodded. "Good. It sounds like you're in the same neighborhood as the rest of us.

"When I started seeing how our country was falling apart socially, economically and politically, I decided I didn't want my family to have to depend on anyone else for their safety or survival." He looked at Kelly. "I started reading some of the preparedness websites and TEOTWAWKI books. Then I started talking about it with Kelly and we started prepping. We started out slow, but got serious pretty quick.

"I didn't know what would happen, but when I learned about the catastrophic effects of an EMP and the probability of a CME I decided that's what we better prepare for, so we did"

Mason leaned forward, resting his massive forearms on his knees. "I used to watch some of those shows about preppers. Bonnie and I watched them together. I just thought those people were crazy."

Bill chuckled. "I did too. Ann tried to get me to understand how fragile our society and infrastructure were, but I never really believed it."

"At least one of you was thinking about it," said Bonnie. "I thought those people were crazy too. I never really paid much attention to what was going on in the bigger world."

"You were just normal," said Jim. "How did you all make it without preparing?"

Mason and Bonnie looked at each other, seemingly hesitant to answer. After a moment, Mason leaned back into the couch, placing his hands on his thighs.

"We really struggled for a couple of weeks. Ate everything in the pantry, killed some chickens and picked some vegetables before they were ready. Then one of the guys found a truck from a grocery store a few miles out. It was mostly empty, but there was some stuff left in it and that gave us the idea to go look for another one. We found another one a few miles farther out locked up tight, so we busted it open and spent a couple of days hauling everything back to our place and Boomers. We took a lot of it to folks around us but we still have a lot."

He paused for a moment and looked at those around him. "I guess that's stealing, but we were starving, and so were some of the people around us."

"That was good thinking," said Jim. "We've salvaged trucks ourselves and we're going to do more."

"Mason," said Bill. "the law defines stealing as the unlawful taking of the property of another with the intent to deprive them of the use or benefit thereof. The contents of that truck may not have belonged to you, but it is questionable whether it legally belonged to anyone. Companies no longer exist. Nor do banks, courts or governments to any practical extent. I think you can rest easy that you didn't steal. Salvage is much different, and that's what you did."

Mason and Bonnie looked at each other and seemed to relax. "I told you," said Bonnie.

Mason shrugged. "Well, that's the first time I've had a judge tell me I didn't do anything wrong."

"By the way," said Bill, "how come your bikes and pickup are running?"

Mason shook his head, remembering. "Man, that was a mess. Most of them wouldn't start after everything went off, except for the older ones with just kick-starts. One of the guys had seen something about this on a

136

TV show, so he suggested we strip all the electronics out of the newer bikes and take them back to basics. That worked, and we were rolling again." He smiled. "As to the pickup, I had kept that old thing because it was my dad's. Good thing, too. I guess he's still watching over me."

"No sandwiches for me?" Mike asked in a mock insulted voice as he entered the room and grabbed one. "Austin is still running hot, but he's asleep now. We'll just have to wait and see how he does through the night."

"You guys can have the room next to Austin's," Kelly said to Mason and Bonnie. "It's all ready and shares a bathroom with his. I'll bring you some toothbrushes and things in case you didn't bring yours."

Kelly got up early and went to check on Austin, finding both Bonnie and Mason sleeping in his room, Bonnie in the chair and Mason sitting on the floor leaning against the wall beside the bed. She moved quietly to the bedside, placing her hand on Austin's forehead.

"How is he?" whispered Bonnie, getting up from the chair quietly.

Kelly smiled. "His fever has broken and his breathing is back to normal."

She gently pulled the covers down and looked at the dressing. "It doesn't look like there's any new bleeding. Mike will check it later."

Bonnie clutched her hands together under her chin, her eyes welling with tears. She moved to the side of the bed, taking Austin's hand in one of hers and placing the other on his head, stroking his hair back softly with her fingertips. "I prayed all night until I fell asleep."

The women heard Mason getting up from the floor and moved over to allow him to stand by the bed.

Bonnie looked up at her husband. "His fever's gone, and Kelly says the bleeding seems to have stopped."

Mason stood by the bedside for a long minute looking down at his son, then slowly leaned over and kissed him on the forehead. Turning, he left the room.

Bonnie smiled at Kelly through her tears. "He didn't want us to see him cry. I heard him praying too."

Mason made his way downstairs, through the kitchen and out onto the patio where he found Jim pouring a cup of coffee. "Morning, Jim."

"Hey, Mason. Want a cup?"

Mason nodded. "Thanks. It smells good."

Jim poured a second cup of coffee and handed it to Mason. "Cream and sugar is on the table if you want it. How's Austin?"

"His fever's gone and Kelly says the bleeding has stopped." Mason said, sitting down. "She thinks he's going to be okay."

"Good."

The men sat for several minutes in silence, watching the sun rise and the compound awaken.

"Jim, I don't know how to thank you for all you've done for Austin. And for taking us into your home when you didn't even know us. If there's anything I can ever do for you, you just say it."

Jim shook his head. "No thanks are necessary, Mason. If it had been one of my kids I'm sure you would have done the same."

Mason nodded his head. "Yeah, I would have. But still, it's a different world now. We've run probes into the suburbs and the city, and people aren't what they used to be. Now, they're quicker to attack than to help.

"I know you were careful, but you welcomed us like in the old days." He paused, taking a sip of his coffee. "It's hard to believe that the old days were only a couple of months ago."

Jim nodded, remembering their experience in Topeka. "Yes, it is. Like we were starting to talk about last night, we're seeing a major change in the world. Probably the most drastic change the world has ever seen in so short a time. It took centuries to build what became the modern world and a split second to bring it all down. The question will be what kind of world will develop now. Which reminds me, when you think they're up, you can invite your riders up the road to come on in for breakfast. It can't be too comfortable out there at that house."

Mason wasn't able to hide either his surprise or his embarrassment. "You knew, huh?"

"Like you said, it's a different world now, and I'm careful. We can't afford to take chances. We knew those two could be more trouble when we threw them out, so we had a couple of scouts follow them. They followed them to Boomers and they've been watching your guys since you arrived yesterday."

Mason shook his head and grinned. "Well, I sure feel like a beginner. You don't mind them coming in?"

"Nope. I have a good feeling about you and Bonnie, and they're your guys. This is one of the first steps in creating the world we want to live in." Jim picked up his walkie-talkie from the table. "Stone to scout one."

"Go ahead, stone," came Mike's reply.

"Their leader is going to come out in a bit to bring them in for breakfast. His name is Mason. They are friendlies. Then you can come back in, but leave two scouts on lookout."

"Okay, stone. See you in a bit."

Breakfast was a major affair with the Vikings coming in. The deep throated rumble of twenty-one heavy bikes reverberated throughout Stonemont, announcing their arrival and drawing everyone to the commons to see what was going on.

The Vikings had been wary at first, hesitant to enter into the enclosure of Stonemont except for the trust they had in their leader and their concern for Austin. They had been welcomed by Jim, Kelly, Bonnie and the Garners, and were surprised when Jim told them they could either rack their weapons on the patio or keep them, whichever they preferred.

The long tables were set up and the Vikings joined the Stonemont residents in loading their plates with oatmeal, pancakes and ham. At first, the groups stayed separate, but they soon began to intermingle as curiosity grew among each group about the other, and, by the end of breakfast, the two groups were almost indistinguishable as they asked and answered questions about their lives and experiences over the last months. Jim and Mason had joined the group in order to help facilitate the mingling, then joined the Stonemont core on the patio for breakfast where the conversation soon returned to subject they had touched on the previous night.

"Mason and I were talking again about how things have changed and what we may have ahead of us," said Jim. "We all have a good idea of why things went to hell, and I think we pretty much agree on the reasons. Whether we agree on the solution is something I don't know, but I think it's important to discuss and find out."

Jim looked around and found that everyone was looking at him intently. He had known that this subject needed to be discussed, and had recently felt a pressing need to bring it up. Perhaps the others had too.

"Like so many my age, I was raised in a family that held strictly to one political party. I went along with it because I thought that my family must know best, of course not realizing that those with opposing views held them for much the same reason. When I started to pay attention and had more responsibilities, my politics became more conservative. Then when I really started paying attention I became much more libertarian."

Several around the table nodded their heads.

"We may be starting from a clean slate," Jim continued. "Or there may be a remnant of government, whether it be local, state or federal, that remains, and that may try to reestablish authority. We need to consider how we want to live and what each of us wishes to do in each of those situations, and to what extent those of us here either agree or disagree."

The table was silent until Bill cleared his throat. "I'll resist the temptation to stand, but I feel I must point out that, in the eventuality that no functional government exists, our discussion and subsequent actions carry with them the possible import of nothing less than the Mayflower Compact, which set the first foundation stone for what became the United States of America. If some vestige of government remains, our exercise may necessarily approach the character of the Declaration of Independence. That is a sobering thought, and I believe we should take each step with the measured tread its importance demands, as well as the petition to Providence, which our forefathers declared to be central to both their deliberations and their actions."

"I think that might have deserved you standing," said Christian, whose smile did not hide the sober appreciation in his eyes.

Bill gave a small smile. "Then I would like to suggest a few starting points for us to ponder in preparation for our discussions. The first is the legitimacy of government - any government. The second is the proper function of government. And the third is the proper structure to contain a government within that proper function."

The table again fell silent until Jim spoke. "Agreed. This is going to take a lot of thought, discussion and time. There are two other people I want to invite to join us, Pasquale Paoli and Sheriff Freelove. We'll contact them both, and set a tentative meeting date here at Stonemont in about two weeks."

17

The planned two weeks became a month in order to allow Sheriff Freelove to contact and invite another sheriff and an officer with the Kansas Highway Patrol with whom he remained in contact, but that month was a busy one.

Mason had taken the Vikings back to Booker's Crossing, as the Booker's place and Boomers had become collectively known, after he was sure Austin was stable and recovering, leaving Austin and Bonnie at Stonemont for another week. Bonnie became a constant helper and companion of Kelly and Ann, while Austin stayed as close as he could to Christian and Mike, picking up what he could as he watched them train the scouts and continue working on security measures. When Austin was healed enough to travel, Jim, Mike and four scouts took them back to Booker's Crossing, then went on to Osage County to invite Sheriff Freelove to the meeting. From there, they returned to see Pasquale.

Redemption was doing well, if its people were a bit leaner from the hard work and more natural diet. They had lost two members, one to an accident while cutting a tree and another to apparent natural causes, but several families from Family Church had joined them, as had more families from the surrounding neighborhoods, and all seemed to be fitting in well. The acres Ralph had tilled were starting to produce and it looked like they could expect a good harvest.

Pasquale was his usual self, cheerful and overflowing with energy, and agreed to attend the meeting as well as to conduct an archery class at Stonemont. When Jim asked him about the Hansons, Pasquale told him the Family Church members had kept them and their security detail on half rations and for twice as long as they had held the members, then led them out of town. None of them had been seen since. The one thing that concerned Pasquale was that the sprawling former Family Church now stood empty. Located on a hill only a quarter mile from Redemption, he felt it could be a threat if it were taken over by the wrong people.

At Stonemont, they had continued to run road salvage operations, securing more trucks filled with everything from food to household items to furniture, plus another tanker of diesel fuel. Jim had instructed that every load should be brought in, as there was no way to know what future needs might be and anything they couldn't use could possibly be traded as more groups of survivors were contacted.

Daily runs were made to several Home Depots, Lowes and smaller hardware stores, from which they brought back construction materials, tools, hardware, fencing, seeds, fertilizer and anything else they felt would be useful.

Construction was started on a main "long house" in the middle of the commons, a large root cellar and a chicken house. The long house would serve to house residents during the upcoming winter, until individual houses could be built for those who wanted them, at which time it would be converted to a central hall. The root cellar was constructed by digging into a hill, building the cellar with filled and reinforced concrete blocks and covering the post and beam roof with several feet of earth, and would allow the potatoes, turnips, beets, onions, carrots and other produce to be stored through the winter. The chicken house would hold up to two hundred laying hens.

The front gate entrance was redesigned to require two right angle turns to access the driveway from the road, and was built shoulder high with reinforced concrete and stone. Heavy iron gates were set into the concrete at both the outer and inner openings, and a steel reinforced bridge spanned the newly dug trench that ran outside the iron fence across the front of the property. The trench was twelve feet wide and six feet deep, and was designed as a vehicle obstruction as well as an anti-personnel barrier. Construction waste would be thrown into the bottom of the trench and soaked with oil, with wire fencing and welded angle-iron added later to create a combined flammable, tangle-foot and caltrop obstruction. The bridge itself was stationary, but would channel any attack from the front of the property to the reinforced zig-zag gate structure.

Two trailers had been taken to a spot just north of the abandoned house, one placed on each side of the road. Each was filled with dirt, then dirt was bulldozed under them in order to create a solid barrier. Steel gates were installed, spanning the road, and steel barrels were set into foot deep holes, secured with rebar driven through the bottoms and several feet into the ground and filled with concrete. They were placed along the road in positions to prohibit straight line vehicular entry, but to allow traffic, including the tractor trailers, to enter and exit in a serpentine course. The house was fitted out as an intake facility for anyone coming to Stonemont and as an office and squad room for those working at what was now being called the contact gate.

Christian and some of the sentry group had constructed tactical barriers around the entire property perimeter, creating approach channels that could more easily be defended than the entire fence line, and two ten-thousand-gallon water tanks they had found had been installed on a hill to the west of the house, providing good water pressure to the compound for daily needs and possible fire suppression.

Ann had supervised the building of a third ram pump to aid in filling and sustaining the large water tanks, and was building a hydroelectric generator that would be placed at a small waterfall in the creek to help keep the compound's batteries charged. She had also designed and overseen the building of pedal powered washing machines and clothes dryers that would be placed in an area of the long house designed as a laundry area. A refugee family had offered to operate the laundry for the community for one credit per load.

Mike had completed the initial phase of the first scout training class, with ten of the original thirteen trainees successfully completing it, and a secondary phase was about to start in the afternoons while a new class started training in the mornings. Tracy had completed the first phase at the top of the class, and would be helping Mike with the entry class in the mornings while going through the secondary phase in the afternoons.

Kelly had organized a school for the children and designed a curriculum that centered on the traditional classes of reading, writing, arithmetic and history. She had also put together a small library and asked Mike to bring in an assortment of educational books from the scouting and salvage trips. Additionally, she had opened a store operating out of the barn with items brought in from salvage runs. With so much work to be done around Stonemont, most of the residents were working more than the time needed to fulfill their food and housing needs so they were able to buy items to improve their comfort and quality of life, and many could now be seen wearing new clothes in the evenings.

Jim, often accompanied by Bill or Ralph, had spent much of the month contacting area farms and properties, and meeting those who lived in the area, introducing himself and explaining to them what was going on at Stonemont. Some were friendly and some were stand-offish, but he was surprised at how ill prepared many of them were. Though living on land, most had sustained themselves with jobs in the city and few had gardens or livestock operations sufficient to support themselves. Nor did they have sufficient stores for long term survival, having depended on grocery stores almost as much as those in the city. As a result, many were approaching the end of their ability to survive. This had shocked him, as he had assumed, and had always heard, that rural people were more self-sufficient than urban and suburban dwellers. Maybe they were when you got farther from the city, but here on the outskirts they didn't seem much different than those in the more congested areas.

Due to the pressing needs of people he met, he had been able to trade food and other supplies for several dozen cows, including some dairy cows, an Angus bull and some horses with tack. Though he hated benefitting from the troubles of others, he was honest with himself in recognizing that they could have invested their time and money into preparing just as he had, and honest with them in both trading and his advice to them for the future.

His offer was always the same; Stonemont would be there to help them to whatever extent they wished to become part of the growing Stonemont community.

18

The comparative roughness of the contact gate had not prepared the visitors for the thriving life at Stonemont. As each entered through the main gate complex and made their way to the main house, they looked with surprise and appreciation at the many elements of the compound that worked together to make a secure and vibrant community.

The longhouse was nearing completion, with family tents having been moved from their original central position to individual locations around the area, affording more privacy for each. Residents moved busily around the compound and the acres of crops spread expansively down to the large pond in the near distance.

By noon, everyone had arrived for what was planned to be a two-day conference, and had been settled in large tents set up around the main house. A fire had been built in the large pit, and the aroma of the pig being turned on the spit drifted over the entire compound.

Pasquale had been the first to arrive, bringing with him his wife and another couple from Redemption who had assumed leadership roles. Mason, Bonnie and a fully healed Austin Booker had arrived mid-morning, accompanied by two other Vikings, including the college professor Mason had mentioned. Interestingly, the Bookers came in their camper instead of on bikes, and all were wearing regular work shirts instead of their cutoffs.

The last to show up was Sheriff Freelove, who got there shortly after noon, bringing Glenn with him as well as Sheriff Rod McGregor of Coffey County and a Lieutenant Dehmer of the Kansas Highway Patrol. A surprise addition was a squad of Kansas National Guard headed up by a Captain Collins.

Jim and Kelly had met each group as they arrived, welcoming them to Stonemont, directing them to their tents and inviting them to the patio when they were settled in. By mid-afternoon, all the guests had joined the Stonemont core on the patio where Jim introduced everyone, then led them to the longhouse where a long table had been set up for the conference.

Once everyone was seated, Jim began.

"First off, I'd like to welcome everyone to Stonemont." He looked around the group. "It's nice to see those we've met before, and good to meet new friends."

He noticed that all seemed relaxed except Captain Collins, who appeared rigid and unsmiling.

"As I said to those I talked with, I thought it would be a good idea for us to get together to compare notes about our recent experiences, and share thoughts about how we intend to approach the future. We can get more into the details tomorrow, but it might be helpful to touch on some major points this afternoon so we'll have a general idea of the overall situation and what we need to spend more time on. Since I'm the one who invited you, I should probably start."

Everyone nodded their agreement.

"We're comparatively remote," he continued, "at least for being so close to the metropolitan area. As some of you know, we were fairly well prepared for something like this, so it didn't hit us as hard as it could have. Still, we have been out on scouting patrols in the immediate area, and we've found that most of the people we've contacted will not be able to sustain themselves on their own much longer.

"We have bartered supplies with them for things we can use, but they will soon be in a situation where they have nothing further to trade, and we will be unable to simply give them further supplies without re-starting the cycle of dependence to which our country had previously declined, thereby putting the future of our own community in jeopardy."

"What do you intend to do then?" asked Captain Collins.

Jim paused. The question, being asked so soon into his introduction, and in such a curt manner, surprised him. As one who believed strongly in courtesy and protocol, he was put off by Collins' attitude and watched the captain closely as he answered. "We'll offer to take them into our community if they are willing to follow our rules."

"And what are those rules, Mr. Wyatt?" asked the captain.

Jim continued to look at the captain. The two questions had carried a tone of inquisition rather than simple curiosity, a disrespect that would be remembered. "To treat other people properly, captain," he said evenly. "And to work if they are able."

The captain made no response, but kept looking at Jim.

Jim turned to Paoli. "Pasquale, how are things going at Redemption?"

"We're doing okay so far, though I think we've all lost a few pounds,"

Paoli answered with a smile. "The food and supplies trailer you sent us gives us some breathing room while we try to develop long term self-sufficiency. The crops from the seeds you gave us are looking good and we've already started harvesting some. We've collected as many canning jars as we can and one of our members is teaching others how to do it. Plus, I'm taking about a deer a week, so that helps.

"We've had quite a few people come by to get help," he continued. "Some move on after a few days but some wanted to stay, and we have taken in about thirty additional people since you were there last. A lot of the houses in the neighborhoods around us are empty now. I don't know where the people have gone, and we are now hearing of people dying almost every day from sickness, starvation or something else."

"Have you had any problems with thieves?" asked Jim.

Pasquale nodded. "Just in the last few weeks we've noticed some picking being done at night on the far side of the field. We are posting sentries, but I can't see hurting someone who is just trying to stay alive. The thing that concerns me most is that we are starting to see nightly fires to the north. I think we're going to start feeling pressure from the city as survivors start to migrate out. We're really not ready for that, either as relates to our ability to help them or protect ourselves from them."

Jim nodded. "What can we do to help?"

Pasquale gave a combination shrug and shake of his head. "You all have already done so much for us. I don't know what else we can ask."

"What's your perimeter security and weapons situation?" asked Jim.

Pasquale shrugged again. "We have a few rifles and a couple of shotguns," he replied. "We keep a guard at our front and back doors at night. That's about it."

"You're going to need more," said Jim, turning to Christian. "Can we provide Redemption with some weapons and security training?"

Christian nodded. "Sure. We can take some up there when Pasquale goes back and start doing some training this week if that's alright with him."

Pasquale nodded and started to respond, but Captain Collins interrupted.

"Excuse me, Mr. Wyatt. What you are proposing sounds dangerously close to the development of a private militia and vigilantism. One of the reasons I'm here is to establish communications with you and your people, and to advise you that the National Guard has been tasked by the governor to implement and enforce security measures within the state."

Collins looked around the table as if to establish his authority over each person there. "I have been put in command of this area, and I feel that the further training and development of private security elements could prove counterproductive to reestablishing competent legal authority. Therefore, I must request that any further such training or unit development be discontinued immediately."

The room fell silent. Jim saw that Freelove and McGregor were looking at Collins with a mixture of anger and shock. Dehmer was looking straight ahead with a blank look on his face and the others were looking back and forth between Jim and the captain.

"Well, that's good news, captain," said Jim, keeping his face impassive. He looked at Dehmer. "Is the Highway Patrol part of the enforcement mechanism, lieutenant?"

Dehmer looked straight at Jim. "The Patrol command structure has been informal for almost two months, sir. The state legislature adjourned the day after the grid collapse and the governor and executive staff left a couple of weeks later. To my knowledge, no one has received communication from any national command structure, or any command structure at all, until Captain Collins showed up at Forbes Field a couple of weeks ago with a couple of squads from Topeka. I was unaware of any such directive from the governor or any other authority until just now."

Jim nodded slowly, looking at the men. "Sheriff Freelove, were you aware of this new development?"

Freelove shook his head. "First I've heard of it."

"Sheriff McGregor?"

"Nope," said McGregor, studying Collins through narrowed eyes.

Jim looked back at Collins. "Captain, it seems we're all surprised. Have you been in touch with the governor?"

"No. My orders and authority come from disaster contingency directives signed by the governor and Kansas Guard Commanding General Paxton."

"And have you spoken with General Paxton?"

"No. Communications have not been reestablished throughout the guard. That is the reason for contingency directives, Mr. Wyatt. Direct communication is not necessary for directed measures to be implemented."

Jim leaned forward, steepling his fingers and looking intently at

Collins. "And what exactly are your directives, captain?"

Collins sat up a little taller, lifting his chin and looking around the table. "The National Guard is the representative of the United States government and is directed to establish order, enforce all laws, provide for the safety and welfare of the populace and secure all provisions necessary for the providence of such safety and welfare. In order to accomplish this, we will need an inventory of all provisions currently being held by private parties, including all food supplies, weapons, ammunition, livestock and active crop production."

The words sent a coldness through Jim, and he fought to keep a calm demeanor before answering. "I see. And why is such an inventory necessary, captain?"

"In order to facilitate the orderly distribution of resources as needed," replied Collins.

Jim knew exactly what that meant, but wanted Collins to put it into words for everyone to hear. "What does that mean, captain?"

Collins hesitated, then answered. "There are many people nearing starvation, Mr. Wyatt. Others have more than they need. My directives authorize me to receive surpluses from those with excess stores and distribute them to those who need them."

Jim let several seconds pass before continuing. "Receive, huh? You know, Captain Collins, I used to work for the government, and I was always amused at the beaurocrap language they used. You said you are 'directed to receive surpluses from those with excess stores and distribute them to those who need them'. Some might say that means 'take'. Others might say it means stealing from those who prepared in order to give it to those who didn't. How would you characterize it, captain?"

Collins started to reply when Mike came in the door. "Sorry to interrupt, Jim. Do you have a minute?"

Jim continued to look at Collins for several seconds, then excused himself and joined Mike on the porch. "What's up?"

"The captain brought some more people who didn't come in with him. We figure another squad outside the perimeter."

"Can you take them?"

Mike nodded. "Sure, we can take them."

Jim thought for a moment. "Think you can take them without hurting them?"

Mike shrugged. "That will be harder and take longer, but we can try."

"Okay, try. But not if it means any of our people getting hurt. Secure them somewhere and get what you can out of them, but try to keep it civil in case we can turn them."

Mike nodded and left.

Jim looked across at the patio where Tracy and some of the other young women were keeping the guardsmen's glasses filled with iced lemonade and sweet tea, made stronger than usual in order to mask the taste of the vodka they contained. It was hot, and the spicy salsa they were dipping their heavily salted chips into made sure they were drinking plenty. He smiled. They would know more about these guys pretty soon.

Jim turned and walked back into the room, hearing McGregor talking in a low voice.

"Let me explain something to you, soldier boy. In Kansas, hell, I think everywhere, but sure as hell in Kansas, the Sheriff is the highest-ranking law enforcement official in the county. That means my newest deputy can relieve you at his discretion, because I won't overrule him. But he won't have to, because nobody here is going to take you seriously."

McGregor looked up to see Jim returning. "Sorry, Jim. I don't mean to speak out of turn or be rude to another one of your guests, but captain kangaroo here is starting to chap my ass with his superior attitude."

"No problem, Rod," said Jim as he sat back down. He felt the same way, but he wanted to buy some time for Mike, and also for what Tracy and her friends were doing on the patio. He softened his voice and the look on his face.

"Captain, we've been a little out of touch out here in the sticks, so please forgive our caution. Sometimes we start to fight back when we should be listening. Of course we want to help out. Could you tell us a little more about the plan so we can better understand how we can help?"

Freelove and McGregor gave Jim a look like they couldn't believe what he was saying, then saw Bill hiding an amused smile by stroking his mustache. The others kept their faces non-committal.

They spent the next couple of hours listening to Collins explain the protocols of inventory and selection, and the mechanisms by which supplies would be secured and transported to feeding centers in the cities. By asking a myriad of questions, they soon had a basic understanding of the program and Collins' plans, and had succeeded in making Collins believe they were willing to cooperate.

When Jim felt that the time was right, he stood up. "We have a daily tradition here at Stonemont that we have found works better than a clock and a dinner bell." He motioned outside. "When the sun dips below the western tree line it's time for supper. And, in addition to that, the smell of that pig tells me he's done and needs our attention, so let's adjourn until tomorrow and go eat."

As they left the longhouse, Collins noticed that his men had melded in with the residents of Stonemont as they gathered around the pig roasting over the huge fire pit. They seemed a bit louder and more boisterous than usual, but he understood how the atmosphere might draw them out of the bored discipline they had been under lately, especially since each of them seemed to be talking to a pretty girl.

The tables were loaded with platters and bowls overflowing with corn on the cob, baked beans, mashed sweet potatoes, fresh baked cornbread and peaches. Jim led the conference group up to the pit where he grabbed a pit iron and banged it around the inside of the iron signaling ring that hung at one end of the pit. The crowd quieted their chatter and gave Jim their attention.

"Evening folks!" he started. "Everyone ready to eat?"

A cheer came from the crowd.

"Good. We'll get there in a minute, but before we start, I just want to let our guests know how happy we are to have them with us. I hope we're making you all feel welcome."

Another cheer rose up and Jim noticed that Collins looked irritated that much of the noise came from his guardsmen.

"I'm starting a new tradition here tonight, and I'm going to call it 'first cut'." He drew his large knife from its sheath. "As Stonemont host, I will carve the first piece and give it to someone we are especially happy to have with us tonight."

He took a large fork from the carving table to hold the piece and cut a thick slice from the pig's shoulder. Holding the slab up high, he spoke in a loud voice. "Austin Booker, bring your plate up here, son."

Everyone looked around for Austin as he started walking to the pit with an embarrassed smile on his face, and a round of applause broke out when he got to Jim.

Jim placed the slab on Austin's plate, put his hand on his shoulder and turned back to the crowd. "For anyone who doesn't know, Austin stayed with us a while back and we weren't sure if he was going to make it. He did the right thing when another man did the wrong thing, and he came out on top. He also brought his mom and dad with him, who are our kind of folks."

He turned to Austin. "It's good to have you here, son, so eat up."

Then, he turned back to the crowd. "Everybody let Austin through to the tables. That's a part of the new tradition I just made up too, the recipient of the first cut also gets first shot at the rest of the food!"

Another round of applause exploded as a sense of celebration ran through the crowd, and they lined up behind Austin to head to the food table before circling back to the pig and then sitting down.

Jim quietly moved to the patio table to join Kelly, the Garners, the Bookers, Freelove, McGregor and Dehmer, who were sitting down waiting for the line to shorten.

Kelly put her hand on his arm and smiled. "That was nice, honey."

Jim chuckled. "I thought I almost saw Mason smile there for a minute."

Mason chuckled back. "You'll see me smile around a piece of that pig in a minute. But seriously, that was nice Jim. Thanks."

"Did I miss Jim being nice?"

The table turned to see Christian stepping up onto the patio.

"I'm nice all the time, youngster, you just don't recognize nice when you see it. Showed up just in time to eat, I see."

"I learned from the best," Christian replied, winking.

"How did it go out there?"

"We got them all. Mike's holding them in the barn."

"Any trouble?"

Christian shook his head. "None to speak of. A couple of them got bumps on the head, but they'll be okay."

"How about our people?"

"Fine. Not a scratch."

"Did you get anything out of them?"

Christian nodded. "Yep, but that's an interesting thing. None of them habla'd the Englese too bueno, if you know what I mean."

Jim looked at him quizzically. "Really?"

"Yep. Mexicans. Or maybe Salvadorans or Hondurans, I don't know. But they all spoke Spanish. Fortunately, Emily Rodriguez was with us, so she could talk to them."

"Did she get anything?"

"Oh, yeah. It seems they were up here working; roofing, landscaping, you know. When it hit the fan, they were stuck here with no jobs and no quick way home. They finally started walking out of Topeka when they ran into Collins, who promised them citizenship if they served in the guard. Food and clean uniforms sealed the deal and now they think they're American citizens in the U.S. Army."

Jim looked at him for a moment. "You're kidding."

Christian shook his head. "Nope. They're pretty proud to be Americans too."

Jim looked around the table and saw everyone was as surprised as he was. He turned back to Christian. "Did they give you any trouble?"

"Not really. They were easy to sneak up on and most gave up when we told them to. Two of them tried to fight but that didn't last long. Collins had given them rifles, but no ammo. He probably didn't trust them. He told them we'd be scared just seeing the guns."

Jim looked out at the crowd and the food line, which was still long. He saw Collins walking through the crowd trying to disengage his men from their new female friends, and not having much luck.

"Aren't you all going to eat?" asked Tracy as she walked toward the patio.

Jim smiled. "Just waiting for you, Tracy. Can you give us a short briefing before we go load up?"

"Sure," she said, sitting down and pouring a glass of lemonade. She made a show of sniffing it. "Not spiked, is it?" she giggled and took a long drink.

"First off, that was a great idea. Those guys have been cooped up with each other for a long time drinking bottled water and eating those ready meals or whatever they call them. We can't shut them up."

She took another sip and continued. "Bottom line is that most of them are Kansas guys who Collins convinced they had to stay at the Topeka armory or they would be court-martialed for desertion. They've started questioning that lately, since no superior officers have come by since LO." She smiled at Jim. "I like that, 'LO'.

"Anyway, they say Collins has been getting weird lately, talking about how they are the only ones left in the area with national authority and how they needed to start implementing their emergency plan. Some of the guys were about to head back to their families when Collins heard that Lieutenant Dehmer was coming here and latched himself on for the trip."

"Are there any more troops back at the armory?" asked Jim.

She nodded. "Another squad or so, they said, but some of them doubt they're still there. They were ready to head home too."

"Well, isn't that interesting?" said Jim, looking out over the compound.

After a minute of silence, Bill asked, "What do you think, Jim?"

Jim smiled. "I think our Mexican friends could use some good Kansas barbecue."

"Mr. Wyatt welcomes you to Stonemont, his family's home," Emily Rodriguez said in Spanish to the stunned prisoners sitting on the ground in the barn. "He is sorry for the misunderstanding Captain Collins led you into, and regrets that he must ask you to remain here for just a little longer. But while you wait, he would like to share our supper with you."

Behind Emily stood Jim, Kelly, Bill, Ann, Tracy, Christian, Rebecca, Mason, Bonnie and Austin, each holding plates filled with barbecue pork, baked beans and corn on the cob. A small wagon stood beside them holding a large container filled with lemonade.

Emily motioned for the Hispanics to stand, which they did hesitantly. Once they were all standing, Jim walked over to one he felt was a leader.

"Bienvenuto, mi amigo," he said, holding out his plate to the man.

The man stared into Jim's eyes and slowly accepted the plate. "Gracias," he said with a brief nod of his head.

Each of the Stonemont group then stepped forward, handing a plate to one of the men. Once they all had a plate, Emily again spoke to the group in Spanish.

"If you would like some lemonade, Mr. Wyatt would like to pour you your first glass. After that, please feel free to refill your glasses as much as you would like."

The men moved as a group to where Jim stood by the wagon and filled a red plastic cup for each man while Kelly gave each one a napkin and plastic ware. When every man had been served, they returned to sit on the ground together.

Emily stepped forward again.

"What Captain Collins told you about getting citizenship for serving with him is not true, but Mr. Wyatt wants you to know that doesn't matter. Mr. Wyatt wants you to know that he will help you if you want to return home or if you want to stay here - either way. He is going to explain this to Captain Collins, and will invite you out to enjoy the barbecue in a little while. Until then, please enjoy your food and lemonade."

With that, the Stonemont group went back to the barbecue where they loaded their plates and returned to the patio.

As they began to sit down, Jim turned to Christian. "Bring Collins up here."

They were well into their pork when Christian returned with Captain Collins, seating him at a middle seat where the Stonemont group could see him from every angle.

Jim nodded at Collins. "We're just now sitting down, captain. Did you get some food?"

Collins nodded. "Yes, I did, Mr. Wyatt. Thank you."

"Good. We've been talking about the information you've given us and we've talked to your men." Jim gave a signal to Emily to let the men out of the barn.

"My men?" Collins asked, shocked. "You've been talking to my men?"

"Yep," Jim nodded. "They seem like a good bunch of boys, too, including the hispanic ones you had hiding out in the woods."

Collins' face started to flush, his superior demeanor starting to crack. "I have to protest you talking to my men." He looked around the compound, frantically wondering about his men's loyalty and what Wyatt might know. "Where are they? I demand to know where my men are. You are tampering with official army business!" Beads of sweat were forming on his forehead and upper lip. He started to rise from his seat but was held down by Christian's hand on his shoulder.

"Relax, captain," said Christian.

Jim took a slow sip of his lemonade and leaned forward, resting his forearms on the table and interlacing his fingers. He looked at Collins for a moment. "First off, captain, you didn't need to demand, which you are in no position to do anyway. You could have just asked. As you can see, your men are having a nice time mingling with our folks." He looked up, seeing Emily leading the group from the barn. "And here come the rest of them. They've already eaten, but I invited them to join us for the rest of the evening."

Collins looked around and saw the men following Emily from the barn.

"As to tampering with official army business, I'd like to see a copy of your directives, captain."

Collins hesitated. "I don't carry those with me, Mr. Wyatt," he said,

155

trying to regain some of his composure.

Jim nodded. "I'm sure you don't. When were you last in contact with your chain of command?"

"I don't see what difference that makes." Collins was beginning to regain some of his lost bravado. He always felt better when he was able to tell a civilian that something was none of their business. "Besides, that information is classified."

"Where are you from, captain?"

Collins paused before answering, momentarily thrown off balance by the sudden change in course of the conversation. "I'm from Connecticut. Why?"

"Well, as Sheriff McGregor said earlier, this is Kansas. Being from Connecticut, you may not know that you're sitting only a couple hundred miles from the original Boot Hill, which is filled with guys who tried to take stuff that didn't belong to them. Now, you say you have directives telling you to take our stuff so you can give it to other people. Tell me, captain, what gives you that right?"

"The law gives me that right. The government." said Collins, defensively.

"What government, captain?"

"The United States government, of course."

"Of course? What makes you think the United States government still exists, captain?"

Collins looked confused. "Of course it exists. How could it not exist?"

"Oh, I don't know, captain. Perhaps the same way the Roman Empire no longer exists. Or ancient Greece. Or the Mayan civilization. The U.S. government long ago turned away from serving the interests of the American people and declined into a despotic organism which took from those who were productive and gave to those who were not. In essence, captain, the government became a facilitator for parasites who eventually destroyed their host's ability and willingness to support them."

"I don't know what you mean," said Collins, obviously confused and irritated. "This is nonsense."

Jim leaned back in his chair. "I'm not surprised that you don't know what I mean, captain. You must have gone to public schools. But as far as being nonsensical, it is not. It was the government programs of the past fifty years that were nonsense, and which destroyed our country's ability and will to defend against the kind of thing that's happened to us. They were too busy making economic and political war on those who

156

believed in the founding principles of this country to focus on the real enemies. Or maybe they did it on purpose. Who knows? It doesn't matter now. What matters is that we may have been given an opportunity to start over. If so, we're sure as hell not going to start over again by taking some people's stuff away from them and giving it to other people. Around here, any giving, taking or exchanging of private property will be voluntary."

Jim stared at Collins, who stared back in silence.

"So, there won't be any receiving, securing, taking or redistribution of anything around here, captain, except as we, as free men and women, decide of our own free will. Is that clear?"

Collins glared at Jim, trembling with rage at the resistance he had encountered at Stonemont and the emasculation he felt as a result. Who were these people to question his authority? First, he had been sent from the civilization of Connecticut to this frontier of wheat fields and pickup trucks, and now he had to endure the humiliation of being lectured and dictated to by some John Wayne wannabe who had questioned his orders and usurped his command.

Jim stood up. "We will have you here as our guest, captain, until the day after tomorrow. Then we'll take you back to your armory."

Fury rose within Collins as he imagined his father, Colonel Jack Collins, witnessing the scene. Collins imagined his father's disappointment and disgust if he could see his son being treated so dismissively by this group of fly-over hicks. What would Jack Collins have done?

Suddenly, Collins was clear about what he must do. He rose to his feet, drawing his sidearm and pointing it at Jim. "Mr. Wyatt, you are under arrest, and are now a prisoner of the United States Army. You and your group will comply with the directives I issue, and will face just punishment for refusing to obey the orders of the emergency authority."

Jim looked at him coldly. Collins saw him start to say something, but he didn't hear what he said. Nor did he hear the report of the rifle that sent the 5.56 round that he didn't feel through his brain. He didn't see Kelly standing in the kitchen door holding the smoking AR, and he didn't feel his body hit the ground.

19

They buried Collins the next morning after breakfast in an area north of the contact gate they had voted to name Boot Hill. To everyone's surprise, it was Bill who had suggested the location and the name.

"Frontier justice acted as a much greater deterrent than anything we have tried since," he had said. "This may be the new frontier, and it was certainly justice."

It was also Bill who had suggested the inscription on the wood slab marker; "He tried to take what wasn't his."

Now, Jim was looking at Bill across the conference table and voiced a question they all had. "What if part of the country, the government, still exists?"

Bill let out a long breath and leaned back in his chair. "That's the big question, isn't it?"

He looked around the table. "The question has several parts. First, if some exists, how much and where is it? Lieutenant Dehmer indicates that there doesn't seem to be any functioning state government, and I think he would know. I would also think that if there were a functioning remnant of the federal government still operating we would have received or heard of some kind of contact, even if it were a leaflet drop, and even out here."

He paused for a moment, leaning forward and taking a drink of his tea. "That leaves the possibility that there may be an element of a national government intact, but of insufficient size, capability or inclination to contact us, in which case they are either incapable of projecting their influence here or have made a conscious decision not to.

"Now, that poses the question that, if they can't secure this area now, will they attempt to do so at some later date when they have grown stronger, what form will that take, and what kind of government will it be?

"On the other hand, there is the obvious possibility that nothing larger than local government or community influence exists. In that case, we're farther back than the wild west, we're in the pilgrim or first settlers days. And that means we have to decide exactly how we want to start over again."

He looked down the table at Fred Briggs, the college professor Viking who had come with Mason and Bonnie. "I'd be interested to hear what Fred has to say."

Everyone turned toward Fred, who leaned forward and nodded at Bill.

"Either you've been living in my head or I've been living in yours." He looked around the table. "I couldn't agree with Bill more. But I would like to throw in a couple of additional possibilities, probably certainties, which the original settlers didn't have to deal with.

"The first, of course, is a continental population of over four hundred million people, many of whom are unable to provide for themselves for any number of reasons, which has already started a die-off that will last for up to a year, maybe longer. Included in this are millions of psychopathic, sociopathic and just plain mean individuals who will probably survive the die-off at higher percentages than more normal people as a result of their personality traits.

"The second is that, between the military and the recent militarization of the police, there is an unbelievable number of weapons, including intermediate and heavy weapons, all over the country, from small towns to major military bases. Much of the higher tech stuff may no longer be functional, but millions of small arms will be available to those who wish to arm defensive groups or private armies. Without a functional civil authority, laws will essentially be whatever those with the most guns say they are. We might be dealing more with a Genghis Khan scenario than the pioneer days."

The table was silent as they digested the information. Jim turned to Mike. "Mike, what do you think will happen as far as the military is concerned?"

Mike shrugged. "That's hard to say, but I think the vast majority of NCOs and officers from lieutenant to colonel will try to get back to their families and form some kind of defensive and support structure that will provide security for their communities. Some, perhaps many, flag officers will feel they must remain at their posts and attempt to maintain command authority for their areas. This may be good or it may be bad. It could be good in that they will maintain order and security over large stockpiles of weapons. It could be bad if they see this as an opportunity to establish military governments in their area. Probably, it will be combination of the two. The danger in both cases is that I think most of the troops who stay with these commands will be low ranking enlisted who will follow whatever orders they are given, as long as they are fed,

159

clothed and allowed to enjoy the spoils of war without fear of civilian authority. Essentially, I think we might see the rise of warlords."

Jim looked around and saw the effect these opinions were having on the others. What had been a collection of people curious about the future had become a group focused on scenarios that many had not considered.

"What about law enforcement?" Jim asked, looking at Freelove, McGregor and Dehmer.

The three lawmen looked at each other, then Freelove spoke. "We talked about this quite a bit last night. We feel the cities are pretty much gone. Most city officers did not live in, or even close to, their districts. They went home within the first day or two and the cities have been burning ever since. We figure populations have probably decreased by half, but that's just a guess.

"Smaller towns and rural areas are different," he continued, "with officers living within or close to their patrol areas. Order has generally been maintained in these areas, since everyone knows each other and officers are an accepted and respected part of their communities. Besides that, social expectations are more uniform and people pretty much enforce those expectations themselves. The main problem is criminal gangs raiding into the rural areas from the cities and refugees fleeing from the cities into the rural areas."

"How bad is the problem now?" asked Jim.

"We had quite a few refugees a couple weeks after the power went out," Freelove answered. "Then there was a break and now we're seeing some more, but not as many."

"We figure the two waves were those who were totally unprepared and those who were somewhat prepared and lasted longer at home," said McGregor. "This second bunch is in pretty bad shape."

"What are you doing with them?" Bill asked.

"Some are being taken in by families and some by churches that have set up centers," said Freelove. "So far, we've been able to absorb them, but I think that's an indication of how low the city survival rate is."

The group sat silent for a minute, considering this information. Finally, Jim spoke. "How would you assess the current security situation?"

The lawmen looked at each other again. This time is was Dehmer who spoke.

"From interviews we've had with refugees, we think that most of the existing city survivors are criminal gangs who have survived this long by preying on the other residents. It's just a matter of time before they run out of food and start to push out of the city. That's what we're preparing for."

"Are you ready for that?" asked Christian.

Dehmer nodded. "I think we're in pretty good shape. They've already dealt with this out west of here. Remember how many illegals came across our southern border? Well, a lot of them ended up working in the packing houses in western Kansas and a lot of the gangs came with them. When they cleaned out Dodge City and several of the other towns they started migrating into the countryside. It was a bad move for them, as they were met by country folks who had been shooting since they were popping prairie dogs and jack rabbits as kids."

"What's the situation there now?"

"Dodge and the other towns are pretty much empty, the old Boot Hill should now be called Boot Mountain, and the country is nice and peaceful. Anyway, this is what we expect to happen soon with Topeka, Lawrence, Wichita and Kansas City, though on a larger scale. There is one area of concern, though, and I think this might go back to what Mike was talking about. Fort Riley."

Jim nodded. "Go ahead."

"Several troopers told me that Riley closed its gates after the event. They haven't come out or let anybody in since then."

"What's Fort Riley?" asked Bill.

"Home of the First Infantry Division," replied Dehmer, looking around the table. "The Big Red One. It goes back to before Custer. As a matter of fact, I think he was stationed there for a while. It's huge and has everything from armor to air power. If the Army has it, there's a good chance that Riley's got some of it. Anyway, they haven't come out and haven't let anyone in that we know of. We're not sure what to make of it, and the guards at the gates aren't answering questions."

"The Army's got a plan for taking a shit in a sandstorm," said McGregor, "so you can be sure this is part of a plan."

"True," said Freelove, nodding. "The question is what's next in their plan?"

Jim turned to Ann. "What would you guess is the status of their high-tech stuff?"

Ann shook her head. "I'd say they probably have millions of tons of stuff that might start but won't go."

"Why is that?"

161

"We did some work for a defense contractor a couple of years ago. One of the projects was a bid for HEMP protective measures."

"What's hemp?" asked McGregor.

"It stands for high altitude electromagnetic pulse," Ann answered. "In other words, an EMP caused by a nuke detonated at high altitude. There's no nuclear danger, but it's line-of-sight lights out. Anyway, the DOD put out an invitation to bid on vehicular and aircraft electronic protective measures that could only be construed as HEMP-specific. It wasn't hard to figure from the parameters of the bid specifics that they had pretty much nothing to begin with. We know that top tier stuff like the presidential and nuclear capable aircraft are protected, and probably some stuff we know nothing about. But the millions of circuit-rich electronic-dependent systems from night vision goggles to missile systems to tanks to helicopters and fighter jets are probably just big paperweights now."

Jim thought for a moment. "Well, there's no way to know whether that's good news or bad news. We'll just have to wait and see."

They spent the rest of the day discussing specific needs and concerns, letting each other know what areas they felt they needed help in or could offer help to others. By late afternoon, they were ready to wrap up, but Jim had a remaining question he wanted to ask the group.

"Pasquale has asked me something and I'd like to get everybody's input on it." He turned to Paoli. "Pasquale, would you explain it to them?"

Paoli leaned forward, resting his forearms on the table and folding his hands. "We have a large building across the road from us that used to be another church. It is now empty, and I am concerned that it could prove to be a danger to us and the entire area if a bad bunch took it over because it is very large, it is made of concrete and it sits on over fifty acres on one of the highest hills in the county. It overlooks us and the major intersection of the area. I asked Jim if he would consider taking it over and running a trading post out of it. Stonemont has the resources to run it, and would ensure the location serves the area instead of threatens it."

Jim then spoke. "I think it makes sense, and if Stonemont did take it over I would consider putting a medical facility in it as well as installing a security team there. But I don't want anyone to think that Stonemont is making a move to expand at other people's expense, or that expansion is our goal. It isn't. Our goal is the establishment and expansion of safety and security for free people. That's why I would like everyone's thoughts and hear any objections or reservations."

Everyone at the table looked at each other, some shrugging and some nodding approval. Uncharacteristically, it was Mike who verbalized a response.

"Someone will eventually occupy that location, and it is important that they not be a threat to others in the area. As a result of the Wyatts' planning and subsequent management of the crisis response, Stonemont is the one entity that can establish and operate a facility that can provide both security and service elements for everyone's benefit. I think this is a no-brainer."

"I agree," nodded Mason.

"Me too," said Freelove, with McGregor nodding beside him.

"Are there any who have a question or concern about it?" Jim asked, looking around the table. "I assure you there won't be any offense taken or hard feelings."

All around the table shook their heads.

"Let's give Jim an active vote of confidence," said McGregor. "Everyone who approves of Stonemont taking possession of and operating the site in question raise their hand."

Everyone raised their hand.

Jim nodded at Pasquale. "Okay, we'll get started right away."

Then, to the entire group, "Winter is coming pretty soon and this will be a major test. It will show who has prepared well and who is truly able to provide for themselves. I would expect an increase of refugees and perhaps the final large die off before spring. Let's all stay in touch and help each other get through it. If there's anything Stonemont can do for you, let us know."

20

Everyone rose early, those who had traveled to get an early start back and those who lived close by to get started on the many projects that had been laid out the day before. Jim had accompanied Freelove, McGregor, Dehmer and their men to the gate, wishing them well, and now walked to the barn with Christian, Bill and Mason.

Entering the barn, they looked around at the stacks of food and supplies that filled the massive building. The loft was full and very little floor space was left.

Jim stood with his hands on his hips. "We're out of room here. The rest of the trailers will have to stay where they are, but we need to get an inventory of them so we know what we have. From now on, all trailers will go directly to the new Church Crossing location. We need to kick up our road salvage operations as many notches as we can. I want there to be plenty of work for people to do and plenty of things for them to buy to make their lives better. I'll cover that with Mike later."

He turned and led the men out of the barn and back toward the common area. "Bill, how long till the long house is done?"

"About a week," Bill answered. "We just need to put in the interior partition walls and hook up the drains in the bathrooms. Everyone currently living in tents will be able to stay in it through the winter, though it may be a little cramped and short on privacy."

"Okay. That takes care of the immediate need. As soon as the longhouse is done, let's get started on cabins ringing the compound. Go ahead and start platting out the locations now. Depending on the weather, we may be able to start putting people in them before it gets cold and have everybody in one by spring. That will help people get back to feeling like families again instead of refugees."

He continued walking as he turned to Mason. "Are you all squared away for winter, Mason?"

Mason gave his head a half shake. "I don't know, Jim. I thought we were, but now I'm not so sure. I hadn't really thought that far ahead and now I'm starting to worry."

"What do you think is your biggest need?"

Mason took several steps before answering. "I'd say housing. I think we're okay on food with the trucks we've snagged, but a lot of the guys have been staying at Boomers and the rest are spread out over a couple counties with their families. We really don't have a central place we can defend and live as a group."

Jim nodded. "We're going to need some permanent staff and security at Church Crossing. Do you think any of your people would be interested, and would that help you out?"

Mason shrugged. "Yeah, I think so. Some of our single guys might be interested, and maybe even some with families. You want me to ask them?"

"Yeah, ask them and let me know. We'll put them through our security training and put them on Stonemont credits for their work. I'd also suggest you get as many of your people in close together and start working on building a defensible central location."

"I will. After what I've seen here I'm going to give us a kick in the ass."

"Good. Let me know if we can help."

They had crossed the commons area, exchanging waves and greetings with those going about their daily work, and were now heading into the woods on the east side of the pasture. Following a narrow path through a mixed stand of oak and dogwood, they soon entered a clearing in which the national guardsmen who had accompanied Captain Collins sat on the ground. Mike, Tracy and Emily Rodriguez were standing in front of the group and Mike was speaking.

"So, the bottom line is that we will equip you if you want to try to get back home, or we will find work for you and you can stay here if you want to."

Emily spoke for a minute in Spanish, translating what Mike had said for those who didn't speak English.

Mike noticed Jim and the others, and motioned them forward. "Mr. Wyatt and some of our other leaders are here," he told the group, as Emily translated quickly. The group looked around, watching Jim and the others walk to the front.

Mike turned to Jim. "I had just finished telling them what we had discussed and was about to open it up for questions."

Jim nodded and stood beside Mike.

A young guy with blonde hair in the front row raised his hand. "My dad is overseas and I want to get back to my mom and little sister out in western Kansas."

"Good for you, son," said Jim. "We'll give you some more ammo for your AR and get you fixed up with food and gear for your trip. We'll pray that your family's okay and that you get to them safely."

"Thank you, sir," the young man nodded. "But I'm just wondering, sir, what happens if I get out there and can't take care of them. What do I do then?"

Jim looked at the young man and realized they hadn't considered this. What if these men made it back to their families only to find that their families were gone or dead. Or what if they found them alive but unable to sustain themselves much longer. He knew that this would be the case in many instances. He looked at the young man for a long moment, thinking before he answered, then raised his hands to indicate he was talking to all of them.

"For those of you who are going to try to get back to your families, we will give you enough food to get home and to also try to get your family back here if necessary." He looked at Bill, who nodded. "It won't be possible for you guys to carry enough water, so Mike will teach a short class for you all in survival, water purification and scouting."

Mike nodded.

Jim continued. "For anybody going to Mexico or farther south, you won't be able to carry enough food for the whole trip, but we'll give you what you can carry."

Emily translated, and some of the Hispanics nodded. The one to whom Jim had handed his plate two nights before spoke to Emily, who listened and then turned to Jim.

"Manuel says that although they would like to get back to their families, trying to make such a long trip right now might be impossible, especially when they get closer to the border and areas controlled by the cartels. He wants to know if they could stay here and work until spring before they try to go home."

"Of course," Jim nodded, looking at Manuel and the others. "The same applies to everyone. You are welcome to be a part of us for as long as you like and to leave when you like." He looked around at the entire group. "Our rules are simple. First, everybody works. Second, observe the Golden Rule; treat others as you would like to be treated. Third, our laws are the Ten Commandments. If you don't know them, a plaque is being attached to the front of the longhouse."

He looked at Emily, who translated.

"To those of you who will be leaving, we wish you the best of luck and a safe journey. We hope you find your families alive and safe, and you are welcome here any time. To those of you who will be staying, welcome to Stonemont."

The Kansas guys nodded appreciation as Emily translated to the others. When she had finished, Manuel rose to his feet. "Gracias, senor Wyatt. We are with you." The other Hispanics rose to their feet as if on cue. "Gracias," they said in unison with a collective nod of their heads.

Jim nodded back to all of them. "You're welcome."

As they walked back to the commons, they could hear the sounds of kids playing and the hammering coming from the longhouse where the interior partitions were being installed. Each family would have a room measuring twelve feet by twelve feet; not large, but large enough for them to sleep comfortably and have some private space. Since the walls were not meant to be permanent, the construction was going quickly and the rooms would be ready in just a few days.

Jim and Ann had designed the building to be heated with a combination of passive and active solar, with four wind turbines installed on the roof to help charge the building's battery bank during the winter when sunshine decreased and the winds got stronger. Large windows on the long south side allowed sunlight to heat the stone floors of the south facing rooms, as well as large black water-filled barrels at the exterior corners of each room. Heat would be stored in the thermal mass and radiate into the room as the temperature dropped. Additionally, heat would rise from the open ceiling of each room to collect in the apex of the vaulted ceiling of the longhouse, where low voltage fans powered by the batteries would blow it back down to the living level throughout the building. As the sun set, insulated panels would be set into each window frame, preventing the heat from escaping back through the windows. In each room, a two-foot square sheet of aluminum set in a vertical frame stood in a corner about six inches off the floor. A heat lamp, running off the batteries, would shine on it from the back, causing the heated aluminum to radiate heat into the room. When the cabins were finished and the partition walls were removed, the aluminum radiators would stay to help heat the hall.

Jim explained all of this to the others as they entered the longhouse. At the east end, workers were busy laying stone for a massive fireplace and chimney that would dominate the wall.

"It's called a walk-in," he said, demonstrating the term by walking into the fire box and extending his arms out from his sides. "Seven feet high and twelve feet wide. They were common in castles and some of the old mansions back east. It will take massive logs that will burn for days and will heat this end of the hall by itself, plus you can roast a whole hog or half a cow in it."

"Damn, are they getting ready to cook you, Jim?"

The group turned to see Mike walking in with a smile on his face. "No offense, but you look a little tough to me. I think I'll wait for the pig."

Jim stepped out of the fireplace shaking his head. "You sound like you've been hanging around Christian too long. You used to be such a nice kid."

Mike laughed. "I thought I'd go ahead and get started on training this group if it's okay with you. I can get them geared up in about an hour and head up to secure Church Crossing in preparation for tomorrow. That will give them a day and a half of training instead of just one day, and I can cover additional environments with them."

Jim nodded. They were going up to the new location the next day to start getting it ready for re-purposing. Ralph was coming over with his truck, and, with one of the scout team leaders driving Stonemont's rig, they were going to push their road salvage operations out farther into the country. "Sounds good. Who are you taking?"

"I'll take the Kansas guard guys and the Mexicans, Tracy, Emily and a couple of our scouts."

"Mind if me and my guys go along?" asked Mason as they left the building and headed back toward the house.

"Not at all," Jim answered. "That's a good idea."

"Here comes Aedan," said Bill. "He looks like he's trying to outrun something."

The group turned in the direction Bill was looking and saw Aedan running toward them over the recently harvested field, his pellet rifle in one hand and a rabbit hanging by the ears in the other, with Max and Pink loping along beside him. They stopped, waiting for Aedan to reach them.

"Dad, dad!" Aedan yelled breathlessly as he got closer. "There's two ladies in the woods! I saw them! I think they're hurt!" He rushed up to the group, stopping and trying to catch his breath, his face flushed with exertion and hair wild from running.

Jim put his hand on Aedan's shoulder, looking down at his son. "Where are they, buddy?"

"In the little gully just over the no-go hill." Jim had told him he was not to go past that hill without an adult with him, and they called it the no-go hill.

"Why do you think they're hurt?"

Aedan took a deep breath. "Because one of them is laying down and the other one is sitting next to her crying."

"Did they see you?"

Aedan shook his head. "I don't think so. I just peaked over the hill to see what Max was barking at and saw them down at the bottom of the hill."

Jim patted Aedan on the shoulder. "Good job, buddy. We'll go take a look. You'd better get that rabbit up to mom so she can get it in the stew." Then he looked at the others. "Let's get our rifles. Mike, go get Tracy."

Thirty minutes later, Aedan was leading the group through the woods to the place he had seen the women. As they approached the hill he had peeked over, he looked at his dad and whispered, "Right over this hill."

The group stopped and switched on their headsets. "Everybody on?" Jim whispered. Everyone whispered back in the affirmative.

He moved slowly up the hill till his eyes cleared the crest. Seeing the two women as Aedan had described, he backed away and rejoined the group.

"Okay, they're there. Mike, take the right and Tracy take the left. Let us know what you find."

Mike and Tracy both nodded and slipped off quietly.

Jim returned to the crest of the hill and took his small binoculars out of a side pocket. With them, he could make out more details of the women. Both appeared to be in their twenties or thirties and dressed in shorts and halter-tops, not adequate for the cooling weather. Both were wearing flip-flops, though the one laying down was missing one. An orange backpack lay on the ground beside the one sitting down, her head on her crossed arms resting on her drawn up knees. Both women remained motionless as he watched.

After about ten minutes, Mike's whisper came over the headsets. "Nothing on my side."

A minute later, Tracy's voice came through. "Nothing on mine, either."

"Okay," Jim whispered into his mic. "We have two females, one sitting next to another one laying down. Neither is moving. No weapons visible. Mike, come take an over-watch on them. Tracy, come in from your side and approach them. Sling your rifle and go in with your hands empty. If either of them move on you, we'll take them out."

"Okay," both whispered back.

It was several minutes before Mike whispered, "Ready."

Tracy acknowledged, and a minute later came around a small stand of scrub pine to approach the women.

Jim and Mike watched as Tracy slowly approached the women, hands a bit out from her sides with the palms facing toward them.

When she was about twenty feet from them, she stopped and spoke. "Are you okay?"

The sitting woman slowly raised her head, looking for the voice. Her head moved languidly, as if she were very tired or drunk. She tried twice before she was able to move her blonde hair away from her eyes to continue looking for the voice.

Tracy started walking very slowly toward the women. "I said are you okay?"

The blonde woman saw Tracy and started to shake her head slowly, gesturing toward the woman lying on the ground.

Tracy moved more quickly to the woman, checking for signs of a weapon before getting close enough to touch her. The woman was covered with cuts and scratches and was quietly crying.

"Where did you come from?" Tracy asked.

The woman just kept shaking her head. "I…I don't know." Her voice caught. "A school."

Tracy put her arms around the woman and held her while Jim, Mike and the others came down the small hills. Jim continued covering the woman Tracy was holding while Mike checked the woman lying on the ground.

Mike shook his head. "Dead. Not long."

Jim looked around. "See if you can follow their back trail and find out where they came from. We'll get them up to the house."

Mike nodded and left.

Jim knelt down and opened the backpack. Candy wrappers. A bottle of water, half gone. A pair of men's underwear, a blue work shirt and a pair of socks. A flashlight that didn't work. A pair of wire cutters. He zipped up the bag and stood up, looking at the others. "We can take turns carrying her," he said, indicating the dead woman, then turned to Tracy. "Tracy, can you get her on her feet and help her walk?"

Tracy nodded.

Jim knelt beside the dead woman. Her face bore bruises both old and new. Dried blood trailed from her mouth and nose, and one discolored eye was swollen shut. He pulled her torso up by her wrists and put a hand on her back in order to steady her, feeling wetness.

"Oh, my god," breathed Bill, staring at the woman.

Jim laid the woman back down and turned her over. Dark brown stains covered the back of the shirt and shorts, and the backs of the woman's thighs and calves were sliced and torn with dozens of what appeared to be whip marks. He lifted the back of the woman's shirt. If anything, the damage on her back was worse, and he knew it would be the same under the shorts.

The brutality of it hit him like a punch, with the sickening sadness that comes with witnessing the brutalization of another human being. It reminded him of a case he had worked many years before in Kansas City where a pimp had beaten one of his girls to death with a fan belt.

He turned her back over and lifted her to his shoulder in a fireman's carry. It wasn't the most dignified or respectful method, but he didn't want to take the time to construct a stretcher and use two men to carry her since they didn't know if anyone might have been following the women. Rigor had not yet set in, so the body draped limply over his shoulder with that singular heaviness a body acquires when the spirit has left it. He settled the body on his shoulder and looked at Tracy, who had the other woman on her feet. Tracy nodded and he turned toward the compound. "Okay, let's go."

Between the weight of the dead woman and the unsteadiness of the woman Tracy was helping, it took them almost an hour to get back to the compound. The men took the body to the barn in preparation for burial and Tracy took the woman to the house where Kelly and Ann helped get her into bed.

Kelly brought a bowl of soup, to which she had added a shot of bourbon, but the woman was already asleep so they covered her with a light blanket. Kelly and Tracy went back downstairs while Ann stayed with the woman.

"Where did you find her?" asked Kelly as they walked into the kitchen.

"About a mile southeast of here in the woods. Actually, Aedan found them and came back to get Jim."

"Them?"

"Uh huh. Another woman. She's dead. The guys took her to the barn."

Tracy took a spoonful of the soup Kelly had set back on the counter. "Wow, so that's what my soup has been missing all these years. Bourbon."

"Did she say anything?" asked Kelly. "Do we know where they came from?"

Tracy shook her head. "Not yet. She hasn't said anything, but Mike is looking for their back trail." She paused, then continued in a quieter voice. "The other one was beaten up really bad. It looked like she was whipped with something for a long time."

Kelly looked at Tracy for a minute, then turned to look out the window. She and Jim had talked about how bad things would get, but this was the first time such brutality had come so close to them. She knew they had been lucky. They had worked, planned and prepared in order to insulate their family as much as they could from the animals they both knew waited at the bottom of this disaster, but they had both known they would have to deal with it eventually. Eventually had apparently come.

21

It was after midnight when Mike returned. Seeing light coming from Jim's den, he entered the house and knocked on the den door.

Jim's voice came quietly from inside. "Come in."

Mike opened the door to find Jim sitting on the right-hand sofa with his feet on the coffee table and a drink in his hand.

Jim waved him in. "Want a drink?"

Mike shook his head. "No thanks," he answered, sitting down on the couch across from Jim.

Jim took a sip of the bourbon. "Tell me about it."

Mike rolled his neck to work out the kinks. "We may have a problem. They came from what used to be an elementary school a few miles to the southeast. It looks like a Mad Max movie. Lots of motorcycles, old trucks and slapped-together what-evers. Even a few horses. Chain link fence has been installed around the entire perimeter and it looks like a second row is being added. They have sentries on the perimeter and the roof, and guards at all the doors."

Jim remained silent and Mike continued.

"The action really started after dark and it sounded like they were raising seven kinds of hell in there." He paused and smirked. "Listen to that. I'm starting to sound like you."

Jim gave a small smile.

"Anyway," Mike continued, "this place is filled with some very bad boys. If they don't know we're here yet, they will eventually, and we'll have to deal with them."

Jim drained his glass and stood up. "Come with me."

They walked to the barn, the three-quarter moon lighting their way. Jim could feel the slight nighttime cooling that indicated fall was coming. When they reached the barn, he rolled the heavy door to the side and switched on the low voltage interior lights, then walked to a table with a sheet laid on it. He gently drew the sheet back, revealing the pale body beneath it.

They had cut off the woman's clothing to inspect the wounds, and the paleness of the skin combined with the LED light gave the gruesome sight a surreal quality.

Both men stared at the body in silence for a minute.

Finally, Mike spoke. "I saw stuff like this in Iraq."

Jim pulled the sheet back over the body. "I've seen it right here in the city." He paused for a moment, then looked at Mike. "We've gone longer than I expected without facing an attack or having to go out after potential threats. But this needs to be dealt with and we're the only ones I know to do it."

Mike nodded. "Do you want me to go back and run some more recon?"

"No," said Jim as he turned the lights off and walked to the barn door. "You take your group up to Church Crossing tomorrow as planned. Hopefully, the woman in the house will be able to tell us some things tomorrow. That should give us something to start with. Then we'll work up a plan. Tell the Kansas Guard guys they're welcome to join us if they want to, but no hard feelings if they don't."

Mike nodded. "Okay."

"We have eleven people going with you tomorrow," Jim continued, "in addition to the people you're training. They're going to start getting the place set up after you sweep it. They'll all be armed, but I'd like you to select two scouts to take with you and leave there with them as additional security."

"Do you still want me to come back tomorrow night?" Mike asked.

Jim thought for a minute. "No. Stay there overnight in case they can use your help and come back day after tomorrow. That will give you a little more training time, and we should be able to talk to the survivor by then."

Mike left with the Churches Crossing contingent early in the morning and Jim spent the next few hours checking the compound with Christian. The rooms in the longhouse were almost finished and pipes were being laid from the septic tank to the drain field at the far end of the pasture below the pond. The chicken house had been completed and several dozen eggs had been moved to incubation trays in order to increase the number of producing hens by spring. The root cellar was full and they were hurriedly adding makeshift additions to hold the overflow.

The cows were doing well, but they needed to add more dairy cows to satisfy the needs of the growing population. They had found several female German Shepherds and Max was taking to them well, though Jim thought he detected a bit of jealousy in Pink since her July litter had

174

weaned. The one thing that concerned him was horses.

As they approached the corral, he let Christian know what he was thinking.

"You know we're all going to be riding these pretty soon."

"I've been thinking about that myself," replied Christian. "How much longer do you think the gas will last?"

"Hard to say. Supply's not a problem, but it's all going to start degrading soon, and there's a limit to how much stabilizer we can add. I figure two years at the most, probably less. After that, it's going to be foot, peddle or horsepower – the old-fashioned horsepower."

"That's going to be weird."

Jim leaned on the top rail of the corral and looked at the horses inside. "Yep, it's going to be. You know what Kelly said to me last night?"

Christian grinned. "Do I want to know?"

Jim smirked. "Well I don't know if you do or not, wise ass, but you're going to hear it. She said all this was hard, but it was exciting, too."

Christian nodded. "Kelly's tough. She seems to fit right into all this."

"Yeah, she is and she does. You should find one like her."

Christian looked at the horses for a minute. "Well, I've been meaning to talk to you about that."

Jim looked at him out of the corner of his eye, "Well, I'm flattered, Christian, but you're not really my type. Besides, we're related. Let's just stay friends."

Christian laughed, shaking his head. "You're going to make a joke with your dying breath, aren't you?"

Jim chuckled. "I hope so. Anyway, back to your love life."

"Becky and I want to get married, and we'd like you to marry us."

Jim nodded slowly, as if thinking. "Well, again, I'm flattered, but I'm already married. And even though things are different now, I don't think it's a good idea for three people to marry. Four, actually, since we'd have to bring Kelly into the deal."

Christian hung his head between his arms, groaning and shaking his head with exasperation. Straightening up, he looked at Jim. "Let me try to put it in a way you can't twist around. We would like you to be the minister, the officiant, at our wedding. The wedding at which she and I will be marrying each other, and only each other. I figure if the captain of a ship can do it, the head of Stonemont ought to be able to. Besides, weren't you ordained as a minister on the internet a few years ago?"

Jim laughed. "That's right. I forgot. I always meant to send in another twenty-five bucks to be a bishop." He shrugged. "I guess it's too late now."

He turned to Christian and slapped him on the shoulder. "You bet, buddy. I'll be happy and proud to do it. When do you want to hitch up?"

"We were thinking New Year's Day."

"Perfect. We've been wondering when you two were going to come out of the shadows. Where are you going to live?"

Christian shrugged. "I figure she and Bobby can stay here with me until I get a place built for us. That is, if it's okay with you."

Jim nodded. "Sure, you all can stay here for as long as you want, but we were hoping you would take the Eddington place."

"The Eddington place?"

"Sure. It makes sense. It's a nice place and it looks like they're not coming back. We can't leave it empty or someone else might move in, and that would put someone we're not sure about on our fence line. It will increase our immediate area of control, gives us another water source and it has over a hundred acres of tillable land. It's fenced and cross fenced, and has corrals and a good barn. Which brings me to the second part. Rebecca trained horses and Becky took after her before she went to college. Had quite a knack, from what I remember. The point is, we need to start a serious horse breeding and training program, not only for our own use but as a future business. The Eddington place would be perfect for it and I think Becky might be the right one to run it."

Christian looked at his uncle with a squint. "Seems like you've really been thinking about this."

"Yep. So, what do you say?"

Christian smiled and nodded. "It sounds good to me, and I think Becky will be excited. Plus, it will be great for Bobby."

"Yeah, he's a good kid."

Jim looked at his nephew for a minute. Something seemed to be missing. "Buddy, I don't mean to pry, and it's really none of my business, but are you sure about this?"

Christian kept looking at the horses for a moment before answering. "What do you mean?"

"I mean are you sure about this? Marriage is an important commitment. I'm not saying anything against Becky, she's a fine girl, but do you love her?"

Christian looked at Jim and shrugged. "I like her. We've known each other for years and I really like and respect her. Plus, Bobby needs a dad.

176

It just makes sense."

Jim looked his nephew in the eye for a few seconds. "Liking and respecting are great for a friend, but a wife is different. If it's going to be right, you've got to feel like this is the one person in the world you don't want to live another day without. Is that how you feel about Becky?"

Christian slowly shook his head. "No, I can't honestly say that I do." He looked at his uncle. "Is that how you feel about Kelly?"

Jim smiled. "Yep. Have since the first time I took her out, but don't you ever tell her that. I still claim that I was slow to come around."

Christian laughed. "Well, now I've got something on you. But seriously, things are different now. There's kind of a shortage of mate material. Don't you think people like Becky and I should get together so we can start building families?"

Jim thought for a moment. "Tell me this. How does Becky feel about you?"

Christian shrugged again. "About the same way I feel about her. We've talked about it."

Jim nodded. "Good, you're good enough friends to be honest about it with each other."

He paused for a moment, looking at the horses, then back at Christian. "You and Becky are both great people. She's a great mother and you'll be a great dad someday. But getting married without the right kind of love would be a mistake. What if you meet the one who really trips your trigger in a couple of years? What if she does? Don't get me wrong, I respect what you're thinking, but you two getting married could make one passable marriage instead of two great marriages when you each find the right person."

Christian looked out at the horses, nodding his head slowly, then looked back at Jim. "That makes sense. But what about Bobby?"

Jim smiled. "I can tell you love that kid, but you can be a great uncle and get him started in the right direction until Becky finds him the right dad who loves his mother more than anything else in the world, and that will make all the difference"

Christian kept nodding slowly and smiled. "You're pretty smart about these things for being such a hard ass."

Jim nodded. "Yep, and maybe by the time you and Becky find the right ones I'll make myself a bishop and we can really do you up right." He turned away from the corral. "Now let's go see if that girl's awake yet."

177

They walked back to the house to find Kelly and Tracy sitting at the table drinking coffee with the girl they had brought back. She had obviously showered and washed her hair, which she now wore in a ponytail, and was dressed in a clean orange t-shirt, jeans and running shoes. Jim noticed that although she was scratched up, she held herself well, looking at them with a steady, strong gaze when they entered the kitchen, and didn't have the beaten down look he had expected.

"Hey guys," said Kelly as they entered the kitchen, "we were just having coffee. This is Brinlyn, but she goes by Brin. Brin, the big mean looking one is my husband, Jim. The big pleasant looking one is our nephew, Christian."

The girl rose from her chair and came around the table, extending her hand to Jim. "Brin Anderson, Mr. Wyatt. I'm very happy to meet you. I'm afraid I fell apart yesterday and didn't thank you properly."

Jim took her hand, surprised and impressed by her poise. Her firm handshake matched the steadiness of her voice and the look in her green eyes, and the muscle tone in her arms and shoulders indicated she had not lived a sedentary life of shopping and sitting around. "No thanks are necessary, Brin. I'm sorry we didn't find you in time to save your friend."

Brin shook her head. "Actually, I didn't really know her. I was just trying to bring her with me when I escaped from that bunch of psychos at the school."

She turned to Christian and extended her hand. "And thank you, Christian. It's nice to meet you. I'll never be able to repay you."

Christian shook her hand and was also impressed. "We didn't do it to get paid, Brin. I'm glad we came along. Actually, it was Aedan who found you."

Brin smiled and nodded. "That's what Kelly told me. I met him earlier, along with Brody and Morgan. He's quite a kid."

Christian laughed. "You don't know the half of it. Wait till you get to know him."

"I think you guys need to hear what Brin has to tell you," said Kelly. "It fits with what Mike said, but it sounds worse than we figured."

Jim looked at Brin. "Do you feel like going into it now?"

Brin nodded. "Sure, Mr. Wyatt," she said, sitting back down.

Jim and Christian got cups of coffee and sat down at the table.

Christian raised his cup to Brin. "However you want to tell it."

Brin took a deep breath, then let it out as if trying to calm or focus herself. "My friends and I had been trying to get home since this whole thing started. We had gone down to Padre after graduation to celebrate one last time together before we had to go our separate ways and become responsible adults." She smiled as if at herself and her recent comparative innocence. "We made it to just this side of Fort Scott when we were raided one night. I guess we must have been careless looking for food and a bunch must have followed us to our camp.

"I just happened to be away from the others doing some personal business when they attacked. They turned on these really bright flashlights and were pointing guns at them and yelling for them to get on their stomachs. When they realized one person was missing they asked where I was, and when my friends said they didn't know, they started beating them. They tied their hands behind their backs and put ropes around their necks. Then some of them tried to find me, but I kept backing further into the woods and finally they took my friends and left."

She paused to take a sip of coffee. "I waited until it got light, then went back into camp and stuffed all the food and water bottles I could find into my pack and tried to find where they had gone. I stayed around there for four days but I never saw them again."

"That took presence of mind," said Jim, "and guts."

Brin shrugged. "I just did what I knew I should do. My dad always told my brother and me that if there was a problem, to keep our heads and have a plan. So, that's what I did."

"Your dad sounds like a smart guy," said Christian.

Brin nodded. "Yeah, he is. Anyway, I started heading north again, traveling at night and resting during the daytime. I guess I must have gotten sloppy again, or maybe they just got lucky, because a few days ago I woke up and three guys were standing over me pointing guns in my face. I figured they were going to try to rape and kill me, or maybe take me with them, but they handcuffed me and took me to this school building."

Jim and Christian were watching her closely as she told her story, and both noticed abrasions and bruising on her wrists, obviously from cuffs being applied too tightly and not being double-locked.

Brin took another deep breath, let it out and continued. "They took me to a basement room that looked like it had been a cafeteria and put me in a chain link dog kennel. I know that's what it was because we have some back home where we put the females when they're in heat and we don't want to breed them."

179

"Your family breeds dogs?" asked Christian.

Brin nodded. "My dad does, but we all help."

"What kind of dogs?"

"German Shepherds, mainly, though we also work with some Belgians for some of the police departments."

Jim and Christian looked at each other. "Did you all train guard dogs?" asked Jim.

She nodded again. "Guard dogs, patrol dogs, service dogs, search dogs, you name it. My dad knew an army dog handler and got interested in it. We don't train hunting dogs, though. That's a whole different thing."

"Where's home?" asked Jim.

"Coon Rapids, Minnesota. It's south of Minneapolis."

Jim smiled. "That's nice country. We went through there on our way to Kelly's cousin's wedding. But go ahead."

Brin took another sip of coffee. "They left me in there, in the dark, for a long time. All day, I think. Then they came down and gave me a candy bar and a cup of water that smelled awful, but I drank it anyway. They took my clothes and gave me a halter top, a pair of shorts and a pair of flip flops and took me upstairs to what I guess had been the gym. It was dark. But they had a lot of lanterns going, the old kind that uses oil and also some newer battery-operated ones. Plus, they had a couple of big metal barrels with fires going in them.

"The place was packed, mostly with men but some women, and it stunk so bad I thought I was going to throw up. A lot of people were sitting at tables and others were just hanging around. Everyone was drinking and things were starting to get a little wild. Some girls dressed in halter tops and shorts were working the tables, serving drinks and getting mauled, and other girls were dancing, some in the crowd and others on the stage.

"They took me to a table on a raised area up by the stage and made me stand in front of a man they called Elvin. I heard his name was Elvin Barnes. They told me to turn around slowly, and when I didn't they hit me across the back with a strap, almost knocking me down. I must have screamed, because Elvin said he was sure I could scream louder than that. He told me to get up on the stage and dance, and when I refused they hit me with the strap again, then handcuffed me behind my back and fastened the handcuffs to a metal ring that was nailed onto the edge of the stage. There were other rings nailed to the stage, but I was the only one fastened to one, so I got all the attention as they messed with me all night." She looked at the coffee cup clutched between her hands, staring hard, "At one point, they pulled the halter over my head so I couldn't see and started slapping me all over." Tears welled in her eyes and one trickled down her cheek. "They did that for a long time."

Jim watched her closely, then looked at Kelly, who nodded, answering the question she knew he was asking; were there marks on Brin consistent with her story? "You must have been very scared," he said.

Brin didn't answer immediately. Taking deep breaths and continuing to hold the cup tightly. "At first, I was scared," she said quietly. "Then I became more worried than scared, as I started to think more clearly. Then I felt sad that my life might end in a place like that." She looked up at Jim, her eyes still full of tears but with a focused strength. "Then I just got mad. Mad that they were doing this to me, mad that they were doing it to the other girls and mad that I was so helpless. I swore to myself that I would survive and make them pay for what they had done, and were going to do to me."

Jim held her gaze, watching for any telltale sign of untruthfulness or hidden motive, but her eyes were clear and unwavering and her anger seemed deep and real. "How did you get away?" he asked.

"When it got late and things were starting to slow down, they took me back down to the basement with some of the other girls and put us back in the kennels. They brought another girl down, Stacie, the one who was with me when you found us, made her take off her clothes and tied her to another kennel standing up. She was crying and screaming, because I guess she knew what they were going to do to her,"

She was staring hard at her coffee cup again, as if looking at the scene she was describing, but the tears had been replaced by a cold stare. "Then Elvin came down and told us we were going to see what happens to girls who don't do what he tells them to. He picked up a light chain from a table and started whipping her with it. He whipped her for a long time, all over her back and down the backs of her legs. At first, she screamed, but after a while all she could do was moan and whimper and finally she passed out. Then all we heard then was the sound of the chain hitting her and Elvin breathing hard."

The table was silent as Brin stared at her cup, but then she continued. "They left her hanging on the kennel by her wrists and left us in the dark. I could hear some of the other girls whispering, but I couldn't make out

181

what they were saying. Sometime later a guy came in the outside door and unlocked my cage. I knew what he wanted and I knew I'd only have one chance, so I acted like I was willing because I was scared and he let his guard down a bit. When he shoved my top up, I asked him to protect me from the others and put my hands on his face like I wanted to kiss him. When his hands went to pull down my shorts, I took his left eye out. He jumped back, gasping and wailing, his hands to his eye, and I kicked him in the balls as hard as I could. Then I took his knife and killed him."

Jim, Christian, Kelly and Tracy stared at her, the women with wide eyes and the men with hidden smiles.

"You took his eye out?" asked Jim.

Brin nodded. "My dad told me a person needs to be able to do three things in order to be able to hurt you - see, breathe and move - and if you take out someone's eye, they'll usually panic. So, I took his eye first, to make him panic and make it harder for him to see, I kicked him in the balls to make it harder for him to move, and I shoved his knife in his throat to make it harder for him to breathe and to kill him."

Kelly looked at Jim. "I think we've found your long-lost twin brother."

"How did you do that, take out his eye?" a wide-eyed Tracy asked.

Brin looked at her for a moment. "It's best to go in from the nose side," she said, crooking her index finger next to her nose. "Then shove it in as hard as you can and pull it out."

"Where did you learn that?" asked Christian.

"My dad. He had me do it once on a pig head." She paused, thinking. "I don't think I got this guy's eye all the way out, because he jerked away when I touched his eye. I got it enough, though."

Tracy looked both fascinated and as if she were going to throw up, Kelly nodded approvingly, and Jim and Christian both smiled. "Go ahead, Brin," said Jim.

She nodded. "I took his gun and went to a dark corner and waited. I thought somebody was sure to have heard the noise, but nobody came down. Some of the girls in the other cages were whispering to me to let them out. I went back to the guy and got the key he had unlocked my cage with and tried it on the others, but it didn't work. I searched his pockets, but all I found was a pocket knife, a candy bar and a can of chewing tobacco. I told the other girls I would try to find help and started to leave, but I heard the girl Elvin had whipped trying to say something so I went over to her and she was starting to come around. I knew I

182

couldn't get the other girls out, but I thought I ought to try to help her so I used the knife I took off the guard to cut her loose. She collapsed onto the floor, but I was able to get her clothes back on her."

She took a sip of coffee and continued. "I looked outside the basement door and didn't see anybody. I think the guy I killed might have been the guard for that door. I saw a pack on the ground and grabbed it in case it had anything in it we could use, then waited some more, but I didn't see or hear anybody, so I got Stacie to her feet and out the door. There was nobody at the gate and we just walked out."

They looked at her for a minute, Jim and Christian mentally reviewing the things she had said and checking them against each other, looking for contradictions or inconsistencies. "That was an exceptional report," said Jim.

Brin gave a small smile. "My dad taught me to give a complete report, including details that would explain the major actions and allow de-briefers to formulate pertinent follow-up questions to fill it in to the degree they wanted."

Jim and Christian looked at each other. They hadn't heard anyone talk like that in a long time. "Was your dad police or military?" asked Jim.

Brin shook her head. "He worked with and trained both, and did some stuff years ago in something he called an OGA. He runs a dojo, does survival training and trains dogs."

Jim and Christian looked at each other again. "A dojo?" asked Jim. "What does he teach?"

"He teaches his own system. He started off in judo and karate, but saw that they didn't work in real life, so he developed his own system."

Kelly raised her eyebrows at Jim. "Like I said."

"When did you escape?" asked Jim.

Brin scrunched her eyes in concentration. "The day before yesterday, I think."

"We didn't find a gun with you," said Christian. "What happened to it?"

"The first day, Stacie slipped going down a hill and I tried to catch her. I was carrying the gun in my hand and dropped it. It slid down the hill and I couldn't find it."

"When did Stacie die?"

Brin looked back down at her cup. "A couple of hours before you found us, I think." She took several deep breaths. "We had slept during the night and she couldn't get up again in the morning." Her eyes began to well with tears again. "Maybe if I had left her there she would still be alive. I thought I could help her, but maybe by trying to help her I killed her."

Jim shook his head. "When we checked her wounds, we found older ones. She had been whipped before. This latest one was either meant to kill her or maim her for good as a lesson to the other women. They didn't mean for her to live much longer, and any more time she had spent there would have been hell for her. You gave her the only chance she would have had."

He got up from the table and walked over to her, placing his hand on her shoulder. "We're going to bury her this evening if you'd like to be there." Then he leaned down and gently kissed the top of her head.

22

They had buried Stacie that evening in an area designated for Stonemont internments. Although no one but Brin had known her, they considered her a guest of Stonemont, and she rested now on top of a hill to the west of the compound overlooking the fields and rolling hills of eastern Kansas.

Mike had returned shortly after the funeral, having left a contingent at Churches Crossing and bringing back the guard members and Hispanics, and Jim had sent him right back out with a team of scouts to recon the school Brin had escaped from.

Now, two days later, the Stonemont leaders sat on the couches in Jim's den, leaning forward to look at the drawing Mike had made of the school and listening to him and Brin describe what they knew about the place.

Mike trailed a pencil around the school perimeter. "They're finishing up a second perimeter fence about ten feet outside the first one, but it's no problem because it's just basic chain link. It might make them feel secure, but it won't be a problem.

"I watched them for two nights and their pattern was the same both nights. It starts getting busy around dark and starts to thin out a little after midnight. Apparently, they have a closing time. Once all the customers are gone, it takes about an hour for the place to settle down and another couple of hours before all the guards are asleep. Good for us, sucks for them.

"There are two guards on all four doors now," he indicated the main door, the basement door and two rear doors, "maybe a reaction to Brin's escape. Customers come in the front door and are patted down before they're allowed in. There are the same sentries on the roof and perimeter as the first time."

He looked at Brin. "Tell us what's inside this door," he said, tapping the pencil on the basement door through which she had escaped.

Brin took the pencil from Mike and drew a square inside the door. "This is the room with the cages in it."

"How many cages?" asked Christian.

Brin thought for a moment, trying to form a picture in her mind.

"Four, I think, including the one I was in. No, make that five, including the one Stacie was tied to."

"How many girls in each one?"

"Four or five. I'm not sure. It was dark, and I think some girls are kept upstairs."

"Okay," said Mike. "Show us the steps and the gym."

Stacie drew steps coming off of the basement room and a larger rectangle at their end. "The steps make two turns," she said, indicating with the pencil. "The gym is at the top of the stairs. There are hallways going off in these directions," she drew lines leading away from the gym, "but they never took me down them and it was too dark to see."

"About how many men would you say are in Elvin's group?" Jim asked.

Brin thought for a moment. "I'd say about a dozen inside. I figure they're with him because they were carrying guns."

"So call it about thirty guns total," said Christian, looking at Jim.

Jim nodded. "Sounds like a good night's work. Mike, get the scouts ready, as well as the Latino squad. Tell them to get a little rest and to be ready to leave a couple of hours before dark. We'll hang back until after dark and then take our positions and rotate surveillance and sleep. We'll hit them at about four o'clock. I want Tracy and Emily with us to deal with the women."

He looked at Brin. "Do you feel like coming with us?"

Brin nodded. "Damn right. Thanks,"

Jim nodded back. "You bet."

The school had been built to serve the expanding suburbs which had stopped expanding after the housing crash, and was left about a half a mile beyond the nearest neighborhood at an intersection of two major roads which had never become streets. Its rear was toward the intersection, which put it facing the low hill from which Mike had watched it, and behind which Jim now spoke to the Stonemont attack force while Mike watched the school from a bush hide on the hill's crest.

"We're going to hold here until about three o'clock," said Jim. "At that time, scouts will move to their positions and begin watching their individual targets. Sometime around four o'clock, I'll give the order to take out the sentries. Now, so we don't sound like a bag of popcorn in a microwave, I will answer the age-old question, 'do we go on 'three', or 'one, two, three, go'?"

A few chuckles came from the group, probably from those who had been in previous snafus from such a misunderstanding.

"We will fire on 'fire'," Jim continued. "We will count down, ending with 'three, two, one, fire.' You will fire on 'fire'. We want this to sound as closely as possible to one shot. You will be given sufficient opportunity to watch and acquire your target, and to let us know if there are any problems. In situations where two of you are positioned together to take out target pairs, the one on the right will take the right target and the one on the left will take the left target. Make sure you verify this with each other. Are there any questions so far?"

Silence and shaking heads answered there were no questions.

"Good. After the initial shots, scouts will apply follow-up shots on a second order of 'three, two, one, fire'. If any sentries are observed to still be active after the second shot, scouts will advise us of the situation before firing again. The only exception to this is if a sentry is firing, in which case fire at will until they are inactive. Everybody still on the page?"

Everyone nodded.

"After all sentries have been taken out, an order will be given to advance to your pre-designated positions. Those who were assigned to secondary doors are to secure those doors, including the guards and their weapons. Those assigned to the perimeter sentries are to secure those sentries and their weapons, then join the main entry team."

A scout raised his hand. "When you say to secure the guards, what do you want us to do if we find a live sentry?"

"Good question. First, secure all sentries, whether dead or alive, with wrists zip tied behind their backs. Second, we will not finish off sentries we find to still be alive. They may be executed later, depending on what we find, but we will not kill them if they are already neutralized. This is a fine moral line, but an important one.

"Also, keep your rifle trained on all downed enemies as you approach them. A couple of us have had the pleasure of having someone we thought was out of the fight pop up to take another crack at us. If they move as you approach, give them another round. And if you come upon one whose hands are underneath him and can't be seen, don't roll them over. You don't know what they might have under them. Just give them a round in the head and move on. Everybody still with us?"

The crowd of nods affirmed that they were.

"The team assigned to the basement door to the cage room is a four-man team and will secure that room from both inside and outside. Securing and freeing anyone held against their will is a priority. No one gets in there but us. As far as the main level, we're going to have to play that by ear. We don't know the lay-out, how many people are in there or where they are. That's a recipe for a big mess, but all of you have night vision and they don't. Assume anyone with a gun and no night vision is a bad guy and take them out. We're going in to liberate hostages, not take prisoners, with one exception. We will take Elvin alive, if possible. Listen to your leaders, be as quick and quiet as possible, and we'll get it done. Any questions?"

No one spoke.

"One last thing. I will be leading the entry team. Mike will be my second. We will attempt to locate Elvin and extricate him without waking the others. You will understand the reason if we are successful, but if any others wake up silence them as quickly and quietly as possible, however you have to do it. Last chance. Any questions?"

No one moved.

"Good. Get some rest."

Jim watched the school as it got dark and customers began arriving. Mike had been right when he said it was Mad Max stuff. Fire barrels were burning at the entrance and sentries patrolled or stood post with weapons ranging from ARs to single shot shotguns. Customers arrived on foot, bikes, horseback, tractors and old trucks. At the door, customers offered a variety of things that would buy them entry, from food to liquor to ammunition, and those that didn't have enough to get in were roughly shown the gate. Occasionally, when a weapon was found during the entry frisk, the weapon was seized and a beating administered before the offender was thrown out into the road.

Jim watched and wondered who the customers were and where they came from. He assumed they had to come from close by, but wondered why they would come here and trade away things they needed when they probably had families to provide for. He had known of plenty of men before LO who had spent their time and money on themselves instead of their families, and, in his opinion, that had been one of the things that had destroyed society. But things were different now, and he couldn't understand how men could do this when their family's very survival was at stake.

As he watched and thought about this, an idea formed in his mind and he walked over to Christian, who was watching the school from another position. "What do you think?"

Christian shook his head. "Well, as they say, if you wanted to give this area an enema..."

Jim nodded. "Pick a few guys to get a little less sleep. I want a few customers interviewed after they leave, and I want to know the reason, the real reason, they go there."

Christian raised an eyebrow. "You mean other than the obvious?"

"Yeah."

At 0300 hours, Mike and Christian rousted the raiding party and formed them up for last minute instructions. Patches of clouds obscured the moon, and without night vision the sentries would have a hard time seeing anyone approach, even if they were awake. To the Stonemont troops, though, the world was bright green and they could see everything. As they watched and waited, Jim stepped up in front of them.

"Morning guys. I hope you all got your beauty sleep, 'cause a few of you could sure use it."

"That means you, Riley," said a voice in the back, which brought a few quiet chuckles and an expletive from Riley.

"While you were dreaming of sugarplums, Christian and a couple of your compadres went out and had a chat with some of the customers on their way home. I'll let him tell you about it."

Christian stepped to the front. "We grabbed three different guys after they left the school and asked them why they went there. We were as persuasive as we needed to be to get truthful answers fast. The first one went to drink and look at the girls. The second one is in love with one of the girls there, who he dated before LO. The third is the father of one of the girls there, who was snatched when she was walking to visit a friend. Evidently, the women there are a combination of locals and travelers who have been grabbed by Elvin to staff his little den of desires. The local girls' fathers, brothers and boyfriends bring Elvin stuff every night in order to be able to see them and ensure their so-called safety. So, this puts a little different spin on things.

"Remember, we want to be careful not to hurt or endanger the girls if at all possible. We also want to take as many of the assholes alive as possible, without endangering ourselves or the mission. For this reason, Jim and I will each be leading an entry team, one going in each direction and meeting in the middle since the school seems to be designed in a

189

square. As we clear each room, we will secure each bad guy by knocking them out if possible, zip tying their wrists and taping their mouths. As you watch us do it, you'll notice we strike the side or back of the head. That's the quickest way. If we don't get a clean shot or if they start to fight, we'll punch their ticket right there. We will secure any girls we find and move them to the gym until we're done and can sort out who's who. Tracy and Emily will be in the gym to help with them. Questions?"

Nobody spoke, so Jim stepped back to the front. "Alright everybody, time to go. Radio check, in order."

Each scout whispered his alpha designation in order.

"Any problems with night vision?" asked Jim.

No one spoke.

"Alright, guys, move out and let's do it right."

The scouts slipped quietly away toward their assigned positions, and within a couple of minutes started reporting they were on their spots. Within ten minutes, all had reported.

The next half hour moved slowly as each scout acquired and watched their assigned target. Jim, Christian and Mike watched from the hill and saw that most of the sentries seemed to be asleep. Such was the danger of many quiet nights and the feeling that one was the big dog on the block.

At the five-minute point, Christian began giving the scouts one-minute marks. As the designated time approached, he talked them down to the mark, finally announcing "Three, two, one, fire."

The shots, though nowhere close to sounding like one, were sufficiently compressed to please Jim, and Christian was about to count the follow-up shot when a single, flat report sounded, obvious in its singularity. Christian continued. "Follow-up, three, two, one, fire."

This time, the shots were more compressed and there was no lone report after the main group.

"Advise of any problems," said Christian into his mic. Getting no response, he said "Advance to your positions."

Jim, Christian and Mike walked slowly down the hill accompanied by Tracy and Emily. As they approached the bottom, Jim stopped them. "Wait a minute." Then he keyed his mic. "Slight change of plans, everybody. Main entry group position at basement door. Everybody else continue as planned."

Christian and Mike looked their question, which Jim answered. "I should have thought of this before. Where's the nicest place in a grade school?"

Both Christian and Mike shrugged.

"The office," said Tracy,

"And where is the office?"

"Right inside the main door."

Jim nodded. "Yep, and that's where Elvin will probably be. So, those doors will be locked and opening them could get loud. We'll go in through the basement and see if we can come up and take Elvin first."

He led them around the side of the building and down the terraced flower beds to the basement door, where the basement and main entry teams awaited them.

"Got the key," one of the scouts said, holding up a key on a ring.

"Good," Jim whispered into his mic. "New plan. Everybody hear me?"

All thumbs up told him they could.

"You," he pointed at the scout with the key, "open the door. Christian and I will take the entry team in and upstairs. Mike, stay at this door to interface inside and outside. Tracy and Emily, follow us in to keep the girls settled down if they wake up, but leave them in the cages till we get things secure. I don't want any of them to go crazy and start running around before it's safe. Door team, your job stays the same. Everybody got it?"

More thumbs up told him they did.

"Okay folks," he said, nodding to the scout with the key, "let's go."

The scout unlocked the door and pulled it open far enough for Jim and Christian to slip quickly and quietly through it and into the room, Jim going to the right and Christian to the left. Both squatted with their backs to the wall and surveyed the room. There were five cages, three to the right and two to the left. Each contained several girls, though they didn't take time to count how many. All of the girls appeared to be asleep.

Jim nodded to Christian and moved quickly to the base of the stairs. He had wondered about the resilience of the newer soft tactical boots he was wearing, but they sure were quieter, and a hell of a lot more comfortable that the old hard leather boots he had trained in forty years earlier. Moving into the stairwell so he could watch the stairs to the upper level, he saw Christian move to the door of the stairwell where he could cover both Jim and the scouts who were about to enter.

"Scout team move," whispered Christian, who watched the team quietly enter the room and form up behind him. Tracy, Emily and Brin followed, but knelt silently next to the cages, watching the girls inside. Christian gave Jim a thumbs-up and Jim advanced up the stairs to the main level.

The door to the gymnasium was at the top of the stairs to the left and two hallways ran away from the lobby at right angles, just as Brin had said. Both hallways had boxes stacked along the walls, making the passages narrow. The office was across the lobby to the right, and the metal framed glass doors and windows allowed him to see that no one was in the main area and no light was coming from the offices behind it. Feeling Christian's touch on his shoulder, he crossed the lobby and crouched by one of the doors to the office. Christian came up behind him and crouched beside him while the other scouts fanned out across the lobby, some training their rifles on the office and some covering the hallways and gym door. Jim motioned to two of the scouts covering the office, indicating that they should follow him and Christian. Both nodded.

Jim pulled on the door gently. It opened freely, making no sound, and Jim went through it followed by Christian and the two scouts, the second one controlling the closing of the door.

There were three doors down the short hallway behind the main counter, one on each side of the hall, which were open, and one at the end which was closed. Jim slowly approached the one on the right and found it to be a bathroom. Crossing to the opposite door, he looked in and saw two men sleeping, one on a couch and one on the floor. Motioning the two scouts to watch the men, he approached the door at the end of the hall.

Putting his hand on the door handle, he was surprised to find it give way to the slight pressure he put on it. Turning the lever till it stopped, he slowly pushed the door open, pausing at a squeak, then continuing until the door was wide enough for him to step through with Christian following him.

A man and a woman lay on a mattress on the floor, the woman laying on her side facing away from the man who lay on his back snoring loudly. Both were naked.

Christian moved to the side to cover them while Jim moved forward, picking up an AR-15 from the floor beside the man and handing it to Christian, who slung it over his shoulder.

Jim slung his own rifle and drew his .45. Kneeling down next to the mattress, he looked at the tattoo on the man's arm that said 'Elvin' on the

192

blade of a bloody knife, then tapped the man three times on the forehead with the barrel of the heavy pistol. "Hey Elvin, wake up. There are people here to see you."

The man snorted and jerked. As he tried to raise himself off the mattress, Jim struck him full force under the chin with a palm heel strike, making his head snap back and knocking him out cold.

Christian stepped closer and looked down at the man. "Damn, Jim, you might have killed him."

Jim took off his assault pack and opened a side pocket. "I haven't hit anybody in a long time. Guess I was saving up." Pulling a coil of wire out of the pocket, he turned back toward the man.

Christian watched as Jim turned the man onto his stomach and zip tied his wrists behind his back.

Next, he turned the man over on his back. "Glad I have gloves on for this part," he said under his breath.

Unrolling the spool of wire, he wrapped one end tightly around Elvin's genitals, then rolled the man back onto his stomach. Pulling the wire between his legs, he pulled the length up Elvin's back and around his neck, winding it around itself to secure it. He then took a length of rope and tied one end around the wire at Elvin's waist level. A tug would make the wire bite into both of its points of attachment. Then he picked up the man's shirt and tore off a piece, wadded it up and stuffed it in Elvin's mouth, securing it with a piece of wire wrapped tightly around his head.

"I always meant to ask you where you picked up all this stuff," said Christian, lowering the muzzle of his rifle and walking over to look at the girl.

Jim stood up, holding the coil of wire in his hand. "A combination of Uncle Sam and a fertile mind, buddy."

He looked at Christian and thought for a moment. Christian would need to understand what he was doing, both for now and when he took over as leader of Stonemont. "We could just execute him for what he's done here, and that would solve the immediate problem. But there are more like him out there, and more who are thinking about being like him. They are a danger to us and every decent person out there. What we do here needs to send a message. It needs to be a story that will be told over and over, and will spread and grow with time."

He looked down at the man, then back at his nephew. "He's going to suffer, but it won't be anything like the suffering those girls and their families have gone through, or what others will go through if we don't deal harshly enough with this now."

Christian looked at his uncle and nodded. "I agree." He looked at the girl. "You want me to wake her up?"

Jim shook his head. "Let her sleep. She probably needs it. Wake up those two in the next room, tie them and gag them. Leave one scout here to guard them, then take the rest with you to clear the rest of the building. Tie and gag them and bring them back here as you go. Wait a minute."

Elvin was starting to stir and his eyes were opening. Jim knelt down, putting his face a couple of feet to the side of Elvin's and shining a flashlight under his chin, which he knew would look disorienting to his slowly wakening prisoner.

"Morning, sunshine," Jim said to the suddenly awake and frightened man. "You hear me? Good."

Barnes' eyes were bulging with a mixture of anger and terror, and he started to try to get up until the zip ties and wire bit into him.

"Oh, I wouldn't do that." said Jim, "It could leave a mark. Just buck a little bit and you'll be able to feel what the wire's attached to."

He stood up, making Elvin strain to look up at him.

"It's going to be a big day for you, Elvin, so I knew you'd want to get an early start." He looked at Christian. "Get those other two up and we'll take them into the gym." He looked at the woman. "Wake her up and secure her, too. We'll figure out who she is as we go along."

Christian woke the woman and secured her while she was still groggy. She didn't resist, making him think she might be used to this treatment. He led her into the next room and Jim leaned over and grabbed a handful of Elvin's hair. "Come on, princess, up you go. We're going to your throne room. You know, where everybody has so much fun. It will be the perfect place for you to receive your subjects."

Barnes struggled to get to his feet while trying to keep the wire from cutting into him. Seeing that Christian and the scouts had the two guards tied, gagged and ready to go, Jim gave a light tug on the wire. "Okay princess, let's walk real nice like you're a little debutant. If you try to resist, I'll give this wire a good pull and you really might become a princess. Let's go."

Christian and the scouts led off and Jim followed with Barnes. As they opened the gym door and entered, the stench from hours of housing minimally washed bodies hit them. They looked at each other, thinking the same thing, then Jim pushed Barnes toward the stage.

"I heard about these cool rings you have nailed to the stage, Elvin. What a great idea. It lets a person know right where they're supposed to be, doesn't it? Saves all that confusion of 'should I be here, or should I be there?'" He walked a shaking Barnes to the ring at the middle of the stage. "Well, tonight, I'm the decider, as one of our former presidents once said, and I decide you will be right here."

He pulled Barnes backward against the stage and started to tie his wrists to the ring when he saw a pair of handcuffs on the stage. Picking them up, he saw the insides of the cuffs had been sawed a number of times to create sharp edges that would cut into a prisoner's wrists if they moved around, causing increasingly agonizing pain. "Gator cuffs, Elvin? You really are one sadistic bastard, aren't you? Well, let's see how they fit."

Barnes tried to pull away when he saw the cuffs, but a tug on the rope held him trembling but motionless and Jim soon had the cuffs on him and fastened to the iron ring.

Jim moved in front of Barnes, looking him in the eyes and patting him on the cheek. "How ya doin', Elvin? Not so good? You want to dance for us? No? Well, maybe later." He turned to Christian. "Okay, go get the rest of them."

Christian motioned for the scouts to follow him and led them back to the lobby from which the two hallways ran. Signaling for two scouts to remain and watch the hallway on the left, he led the rest of the squad down the hallway on the right.

Advancing slowly down the hall, they passed the boxes stacked head high bearing labels and logos for everything from food to toilet paper to sporting equipment. Obviously, Elvin and his crew had done some salvaging too, though much had probably been brought in by customers.

They found the first two rooms stacked with more boxes and bags of supplies. In the third room, two men were asleep on a gym mat with a woman between them. Christian motioned for three scouts to enter the room with him while the rest remained on guard in the hallway. Stun strikes were administered to each man's head, their hands were zip tied behind their backs and tape was placed over their mouths. When both had regained enough consciousness to follow the order to put their knees and foreheads on the ground, Christian shook the woman awake. She woke up slow and groggy, and it took her a minute before she understood that Christian was asking her if she wanted to get out of there. She nodded, found her shorts and halter-top on the floor and put them on, then went with the scouts taking the men back to the gym.

Jim was waiting when the scouts brought the first prisoners and the woman in, instructing them to place the men on their knees in front of Elvin and having the woman sit at a table off to the side. He had one scout stay to help him guard the prisoners and sent the other back to rejoin Christian and the squad. Every ten to fifteen minutes, scouts would bring another man or two in, sometimes accompanied by a woman.

A couple of hours passed, and over twenty men had been brought into the gymnasium, along with a slightly smaller number of women. The men were all positioned on their knees in front of Barnes and the women were clustered around tables at the back of the room. As Jim was expecting the next group to come in, he heard a shot, followed by several shots in close succession. The scout went to the door and quickly ducked through it, returning a couple of minutes later with Christian and the rest of the scouts leading two bound men and dragging a third. They put the bound men on their knees with others and dragged the third one in front of the group while Christian walked over to Jim.

"All clear, boss. We might want to bring Max in after the sun comes up but I think we got them all."

"Good." Jim nodded toward the man they had dragged in. "Anybody but him hurt?"

"He's dead," replied Christian. "As to whether anybody is hurt, let me check." He lifted his shirt to reveal a dark wet stain on the side of his tan t-shirt just above the belt.

Jim lifted the t-shirt to check the wound. "Did I forget to tell you not to get shot?"

"Yeah, so it's your fault. Wait till aunt Kelly finds out you got me shot."

Jim examined the wound and found clean entry and exit wounds just a few inches apart. "It barely grazed you. Does this hurt?" Jim asked, poking the entry wound.

"Shit!" yelled Christian.

"Guess so. Have Mike take a look at it."

Christian pulled his shirt back down. "Man, you old timers are mean."

Jim gave Christian a pat on the back and a shake on his neck. "That wasn't mean, that was funny. It'll give you a funny story to tell your kids." He looked around the room. "Have Brin bring the girls upstairs and let them help guard these punks. That will do wonders for them. Have Emily get the girls' sizes, then send her back with a few scouts to

196

get clothes and shoes for them. Then have Mike patch up your scratch, and have Tracy find some food in all those boxes and get the girls and the scouts something to eat. Don't worry about them," he nodded toward the prisoners. "They won't be hungry for very long."

By sundown, all the women had been clothed and fed, and Mike had treated several injuries among them. Brin had maintained a guard on the prisoners using the women who had been held there, and the clothes, food and dominion over the guards had brought about some of the mental and emotional resurrection Jim had hoped for. The women had dealt out a bit of retaliatory punishment to the prisoners, which he had not stopped.

As the night's customers arrived, they were escorted to the gymnasium where relatives and friends of the women were reunited with them and men who were not friends or relatives were escorted to a classroom and held under guard. After a couple of hours, Jim felt that most of the night's customers had arrived, and had the men being held in the classroom brought to the gymnasium where they were ordered to kneel behind Barnes' men. He then mounted the stage.

Looking out over the crowd of people, he thought about the torment and misery some of them had inflicted on the others. The victims and their families would carry the mental and emotional scars for the rest of their lives, some of them never fully recovering. Justice for this would be impossible, but punishment was not.

He waited until everyone saw him standing on the stage and quieted down, then spoke. "Men from outside the area came into your community, took women and girls from their families, raped, enslaved, beat, tortured and starved them, and set up this house of horrors where these girls had once gone to school. They did so because they were evil and had the power to do it. Justice for this is impossible, since no amount of punishment would have the same lasting effect on these animals as their brutal and sadistic actions have had, and will continue to have, on their immediate victims and the secondary victims of their families. However, punishment is within our ability to deliver."

He stepped over to Barnes and gave him a light kick in the head, bringing a low grunt from the now crumbling gang leader. His purpose was not to inflict pain or punishment, though he didn't care if he did, but to mentally reinforce the new order of things to everyone in the room.

He spoke a bit more somberly. "Before we continue, I want to ask if anyone here was looking for a friend or relative named Stacie." No one spoke up, but he waited a minute before continuing.

"Several nights ago, this piece of shit," he kicked Barnes in the head again, this time harder, "had Stacie tied to a dog kennel and whipped her with a chain until she passed out. She soon died of those injuries. Your wives, daughters, sisters and friends were kept in dog kennels in the basement when they weren't being used up here. All local men who came here to visit, whether as friends, relatives or customers, get on your feet. You're going to take a tour. Ladies, please stay here until we get back."

All the local men got slowly to their feet, obviously nervous or afraid of what they were going to see.

"While you are down there, I want you to imagine what these women went through. Imagine their fear, their despondency, being kept in the dark, in cages like animals, waiting and terrified of when they would be taken out to be used again and wondering why nobody was coming to help them." He pointed to the door with his rifle. "Get going."

The men slowly shuffled out the door, led and herded by the scouts. As they passed through the lobby, one of the men who was not a friend or relative made a break for the main door but was caught by a scout, zip-tied and returned to the group with a lump on his head. When the group reached the bottom of the stairs the scouts switched on their flashlights and directed the men to enter the basement room and stand among the cages. As the men looked around the room, some showed looks of horror while others tried not to see.

Jim came up from behind the group. "Listen to me carefully. Do exactly as I say, when I say it, or you will be shot. I won't repeat myself. All those who did not come here as a friend or relative of one of the women upstairs, step into a cage."

One man started to say something, but Jim drew his pistol and the man entered a cage, followed by the others. After all the men were in the kennels, the scouts secured the cage doors with padlocks and stepped back.

"Those girls upstairs were kept in these cages because you paid to have them kept here for your entertainment. You bear blame for their treatment."

"It wasn't our fault," said one of the men in the cages. "They were keeping them anyway. We just came to drink and have a good time. It wasn't our fault they kept those girls here."

Jim looked at the man. How often had he heard similar excuses over the years? "I'm sure you won't understand this, any of you, but that excuse would not have been acceptable forty years ago. It would have been correctly judged as a quibling excuse from someone too cowardly to accept responsibility for his own actions. The fact that it became common place, and acceptable to so many, is an indication of how far our society fell from what it used to be and should be. Well, it's time to start over."

Jim turned from the men in the cages and shined his flashlight on the friends and family members of the girls. "You are the fathers, brothers, husbands and friends of the women upstairs. Is that right?"

The men nodded and a few mumbled in the affirmative.

"Then why are you still alive?"

The men looked confused. Then, one in front asked, "What do you mean?"

Jim moved his flashlight from face to face as he spoke. "What I mean is that people you claim to love were being held here against their will and abused daily. Why didn't you get them out or die trying, instead of bringing their captors little presents every day?"

Some of the men mumbled while others just stood there hanging their heads. Finally, one of the men spoke up. "What were we supposed to do? They had guns. We couldn't do anything."

Jim looked at the man. "You all don't have guns? I'll bet some of you have guns. And if you don't, why the hell don't you? Are you some of those who expected strangers to always protect you and had that ridiculous attitude that guns were bad and you wanted nothing to do with them?"

"We were afraid they would hurt the girls if we tried something," said another man.

"We couldn't come up with a plan," said a third.

Jim switched his flashlight into the faces of the men who had just spoken. Revulsion rose within him, mixing with the anger and the sadness he already felt. He started to speak, but his disgust choked him silent as he looked around at the men. This is what had happened to society. People had become so isolated from their own responsibilities, so used to the government protecting them and providing basic services to them, they had forgotten that the real obligation to provide for and protect their families rested in their own hands. A nation of tough men and women who had built a country had devolved into millions of people who preferred watching others play sports, dance with a star or play act

199

that they were surviving on an island. Finally, a calm came over him, and with it a certainty of what he must do.

He shined his flashlight into the faces of the men as he spoke. "Those women had a right to expect you to protect them, to fight to keep them safe or get them back. Instead, you hid behind excuses and the cover of consensus. You did this just as you excused politicians you liked, athletes and sports teams you rooted for like idiots, and friends without standards. You have no core values and no moral strength. You're all flash and no substance. You blow in the wind and think you're right because every other imbecile you know is blowing in the same direction. You blew down flat when a bunch of morons with guns threatened you and you're lucky I don't cut you down to stubble, as worthless as you are."

He paused for a moment to make sure all of them were listening. "The only reason you won't share the fate of these others is that you may be of some small use to those you let down. Now get back upstairs and try to do your job as men. Maybe you can earn back some of the respect you've lost."

23

Barnes and his men were hung in the school yard three days later after spending those days and nights in the cages guarded by the friends and family members of the women they had held there. They were buried in a common grave formed by shoveling dirt over their bodies in a ditch a short distance from the school, the labor being done by the former customers who had spent the previous three days moving boxes and doing other manual labor while being guarded by the scouts and supervised by the women. The role reversal had a marked effect on the attitude and demeanor of both the women and the laborers in the newly formed work details, and a new sense of comparative worth was beginning to develop.

An inventory of the boxes stacked throughout the building yielded a wide variety of merchandise from clothing to housewares to canned food, in addition to the various items brought in for admission, and everything was being stored and recorded in an organized way in various rooms so it could be easily found and accessed when it was needed. When they weren't needed to move the boxes, the former customers were tasked with cleaning and disinfecting the entire building, including the gymnasium, while guarded by the women. Over a period of days, they were broken into smaller and smaller work groups until each man was working alone while being guarded by one of the women and a scout. At night, they were returned to the cages in the basement where strict discipline against talking was enforced.

After a week, scout teams of four, accompanied by the women and their family members, took the customers back to their homes where their families were told about their visits to the school and their recent punishment. In cases where there were children, and the man's admission donations had created a hardship for the family, double restitution was made to the family from the merchandise found at the school and the man was returned to the school for additional incarceration and forced labor for jeopardizing his family's welfare. The leader of each scout team explained that the area was now under the protection of Stonemont, and the men would be returned to their homes in another month, after which, weekly checks would be made on the family by Stonemont scouts to ensure their welfare and the man's adherence to his familial responsibilities.

The reintegration of the women back to their families was mixed, with some returning smoothly and without any apparent recriminations while some carried various degrees of anger, disappointment and resentment that their male family members had not done more to rescue them.

A woman from a third category now stood in the doorway to the office where Christian sat behind the desk looking over the recent inventories.

Christian looked up at the sound of her knock. The woman was striking. The sand colored t-shirt and faded jeans she was wearing showed a strong, though not overly large musculature, either from years of hard work or working out, and from her hands and several faint scars on her arms he figured it was from hard work. Her dark hair was pulled back into a long pony tail, which, in addition to her deep tan, gave her a native look.

"Do you have a minute?" she asked in a strong but quiet voice, her dark eyes steady as she looked at him.

Christian nodded. "Come in."

She walked to his desk and looked at a chair in front of it. "May I?"

Christian nodded again. "Of course. How can I help you?"

The woman took a seat and looked at Christian. "Gymnastics, ballet and rodeo."

Christian looked at her quizzically. "Excuse me?"

"You were watching the way I walked. I took gymnastics and ballet, and I raced barrels."

Christian raised an eyebrow. It was true he had been watching how she moved. He had never been accused of turning a blind eye to good looking women, and the grace and controlled strength of her movements was hard to miss.

"You also didn't look where and how most men look, and since I sat down you haven't looked below my face. I think you are a man who looks at the important things about a person."

Christian continued looking into the woman's eyes, trying to discern her purpose. "You seem to pick up a lot quickly, miss ...?"

The woman smiled and nodded slightly, her eyes softening a bit.

"Naomi Moore."

"And what can I do for you, Miss Moore?"

"I won't say the usual 'please call me Naomi', but it's fine if you want to. As to what you can do for me, nothing really. But you can do a lot for the people around here."

"And what's that?"

"Take over."

Christian leaned back in his chair. "Take over?"

"Yes." She paused for a moment, looking out the window behind him. "Most of the people around here are good people. They work hard and do the best they can. They thought they had made it through the tough times and were beginning to rebuild. Then Barnes showed up and they weren't ready, physically or mentally." She looked back at him. "They need someone to take control. They are angry and humiliated right now, and more fractured than before, doubting themselves. But they can be reformed with the right leadership and this area could be stabilized with a strong community able to defend itself."

Christian leaned back in his chair, impressed with the woman's poise and her thought processes. "You seem to have given this a lot of thought."

Naomi nodded. "I'll give you the short version to answer most of the questions I'm sure you have. I was up here staying with my aunt and uncle while doing some graduate work at Haskell when everything went to hell."

"Haskell? You're Native American?"

She gave a small derisive laugh. "Yeah, according to all the lib activists and guilt-ridden politically correct folks. But, in reality, so are you and everyone else who was born here. We say Indian, and I'm only enough to squeak in on a special program with some fancy talk anyway."

Christian smiled. He was starting to like this girl. "My great, great, grandmother was Cherokee. A lot of us have a bit in us."

"You just missed being a squeaker by a generation. At least your part is from one of the so-called civilized tribes. My great grandmother was Comanche, the tribe even the other Indians hated. My dad says that's where I get the abrasive part of my personality."

Christian chuckled, but said nothing.

"Anyway," Naomi continued, "I was staying up here with my aunt and uncle, getting ready to try to make it home, when a couple of the assholes you just hung and buried came to our place. My uncle tried to talk with them. He taught communications and political science at the community college and thought everything could be talked out. They knocked him around a little for fun, and he just kept holding up his hands and saying it didn't have to be like this, that we would give them what they wanted if they just left us alone. When they started grabbing my niece, he tried to pull her away and they started beating him. Carol, that's my aunt, jumped on them, trying to pull them off. I ran into the house to get my gun and when I came out they were done with Jerry and starting on Carol so I killed them."

"You killed them?"

"Uh huh."

Such matter of fact reports were normal to Christian, but not from a woman. He watched her eyes closely. "How were you able to do that?"

Naomi's eyes never wavered as she answered. "They were busy with Carol. They never saw me till I started shooting."

"Where did you shoot them?"

"The first one in the ass and then the head. The second one in the right side, then the head."

"You're lucky you didn't hit your aunt."

Naomi shook her head. "I hit what I aim at. Those were the targets I could acquire without hitting Carol."

Christian thought for a moment. "What kind of gun did you use?"

"1911 from Wilson Combat."

Christian raised his eyebrows and let out a low whistle. "That's a professional's gun. You don't find those just floating around. No offense, but how is it that you have one?"

"My dad gave it to me. He's a Ranger in Texas. Lawman, not ballplayer. He taught me to shoot when I was little."

Christian nodded his head slowly, watching the girl and thinking. She certainly had confidence, and if everything she said was true, she was an exceptional woman, an exceptional person. Finally, he reached a decision. "Do you have plans for dinner?"

Naomi raised her eyebrows. "Why? Are you asking me out?"

Christian chuckled again. "Not exactly. I think you should meet my uncle."

Jim took a long drink from his glass of sweet tea. It had taken Christian and his team a couple of hours to wrap things up for the day at the school, another hour to get back to Stonemont, then an additional hour to get ready for the dinner they were now sharing with their new guest. Jim had been paying close attention to her and was impressed with the easy, confident manner that made Naomi fit in almost seamlessly with the Stonemont core. Her statements and questions were direct and guileless, a pleasant change from the overly offensive or defensive manner of most new contacts, and she seemed to be completely comfortable eating and talking with the group she had known for only a few hours. Still, the statement she had just made out of the blue was why he had extended his intended sip to a long drink. Finally, he set his glass down and looked at her with feigned confusion. "Excuse me?"

"I know who you are," she repeated, taking another bite of Kelly's apple pie.

"You do?" He wasn't sure whether this was headed in a good direction or not. He looked straight at her. "Who am I?"

"You used to teach defensive tactics and combatives. My dad read all your stuff and passed copies out to his guys. He's a big fan of yours."

It had been a long time since Jim had crossed paths with someone who knew about that part of his life. He didn't consciously hide it, but didn't feel the need to share it with anyone who hadn't known him then. That was in the past, and he preferred to live in the present while planning for the future. He gave a small smile. "That's nice to hear. Who were his guys?"

"My dad was the commanding major of Ranger Company C in Lubbock. Still is, actually. He said you were one who knew and taught real stuff, not the watered-down politically-correct magic-dojo crap that became so prevalent." She raised an eyebrow in an amused smirk. "He said you sounded like an old hard-ass, just like him."

Jim chuckled. "Well, if he's a Ranger, I'm a big fan of his too. I've only met a few, but every one of them was a straight up man I'd be happy to side or have siding me. How do you think things are going down there?"

Naomi stopped her fork full of pie halfway to her mouth and thought for a moment. "I think things are probably okay. My dad wasn't as prepared as you, but I never saw a situation that scared or confused him. He'll have organized his Rangers and the other LEOs around Lubbock to make sure everything is stable. West Texans are pretty self-sufficient people."

"Are you going to try to get back home?" asked Kelly.

Naomi nodded. "I was about to head back several months ago when our place was raided. Since then, I've been living out in the woods with Jerry and Carol and the kids, helping them get set up at an old abandoned barn we found. We knew we couldn't stay at the house after what happened, so we've been trying to figure out what to do."

"How have you been able to survive?" asked Ann.

"After Jerry came to that day, we hid the bodies, gathered up everything we could carry in the way of food and camping gear and took off. We had heard about what was going on at the school and we knew we couldn't hang around. We found the barn the next day. It was well hidden, but not very far from the house, so each night Jerry and I snuck back and got more stuff. During the day, we worked on the barn and now it's set up pretty well." She looked at Jim. "Plus, I've been teaching them how to fight."

"Are you still going to try to get home?" asked Christian.

"I'm going to try again in the spring. I don't want to make that trip in the winter, and Jerry, Carol and the kids could still use my help for a while. I think it will be okay to move back to the house now, and they should be in pretty good shape by then if the food holds out." She took another bite of pie and looked at Jim again. "Mr. Wyatt, did Christian tell you what I suggested?"

"Well, Naomi, first off, I already feel old on occasion, so if you could find a way to call me Jim that would be great. As far as your suggestion, Christian said something about taking control of the area?"

Naomi nodded. "Once you get a few miles farther south into the small towns and farmland things are okay. The people came together and set up defenses for their areas. In fact, in many ways it's better than before because outsiders aren't coming out or travelling through on the highways. They've salvaged trucks on the highways, as well as some trains, but most of the people were self-sufficient anyway, with plenty of livestock and land to provide for their current and sustained needs. The city burned and exploded, spilling thousands of people out into the suburbs where they killed and were killed by the suburban folks. Pockets in the suburbs have survived where strong leadership emerged, but most are dead from starvation, disease and violence."

Seeing that everyone was paying close attention, she continued. "The city gangs that survived coming through the suburbs are mingling with, and in some cases fighting against, assorted country outcasts, bike gangs and other bands of misfits as they try to take over the soft areas between the suburbs and the small towns. These are the areas where large lot developments and isolated planned neighborhoods jumped a few miles past the suburbs so the up and coming new professionals could get first crack at the land before prices shot up. They had a high quality of life with their own schools and a sense of safety and detached identity, but this made them soft targets for the gangs. Most of them had never touched a gun, much less owned or fired one, and they found out that their Range Rovers, Rolexes and alarm systems weren't much good in stopping the kind of violence that showed up."

She paused, placing her fork on her plate and leaning forward, her hands clasped together on the table in front of her. "Those people will eventually fall prey to future attacks if they aren't brought together and trained to protect themselves and their communities. But if they are properly trained and led, they can not only protect themselves but serve as a first line of defense against any future threats from the city. You, Stonemont, can provide that training and that leadership."

The table was quiet, everyone looking at Naomi and Jim as they each leaned back in their chairs, looking at each other. After a moment, Jim pushed his chair back and stood up, walked to the large window that looked out on the compound and stood there with his arms folded. He thought about what Naomi had said as he watched the residents of Stonemont walk around the common areas, each on their own business. It occurred to him that in the old days, before LO, he would have had a hard time seeing them because of the glare from the inside lights. Now, even though they had electricity from solar, wind and hydro, they had developed a habit of keeping the lights low. He liked it better this way. It was more relaxing and made the separation of inside and outside less distinct.

Naomi was right, he knew. It was necessary to form the residents into a cohesive group capable of protecting and providing for themselves, as well as being able to assist other area groups. He had hoped someone from the community would step up, but no one had.

His gaze transitioned from outside to the reflection in the window of the group behind him. They remained silent, watching him, knowing that the decision was his to make. He thought for another minute, knowing that his decision would forever change the future of Stonemont and his family. He did not want the added responsibility and all he knew it would entail, but he knew that the security of his family might depend on it. Finally, he turned around, looking first at Naomi, then at the rest of the table. "Naomi is right. If this area is to remain secure, someone has to step up and assume responsibility and authority. Since no one else has, it falls to us."

He walked back to his chair, but remained standing. "Responsibility is a burden, and the authority that comes with it can be a doubled-edged sword that can harm those who possess it as much as those to whom it is applied. I have never trusted anyone who wanted power or authority over others. Nevertheless, authority is sometimes necessary in order to fulfill responsibility."

He looked around the table at each person before continuing. "If Stonemont accepts this responsibility and the attendant authority it requires, we must always hold responsibility above authority and strive to use influence before overt power." He looked around the table again. "Questions? Comments? Concerns?"

Everyone remained silent.

24

"It's not so much the structure of government that's important," said Bill as they walked toward the barn and corrals where Christian and Naomi were readying a scout squad to return to the school. "Certain monarchies and dictatorships served their people fairly well while some democracies and representative republics devolved into little more than mob rule and cronyism. Look at what our own country had become. The important thing is the moral strength and compass of the ruler or representatives."

They took several steps before Jim answered. "I'm starting to favor no institutional government at all."

Bill looked at him curiously. "Anarchy?"

Jim shrugged. "I'm not really sure. I've never trusted anyone who wants power or control over other people, and they seem to always rise to the top in whatever type of government structure is used."

"But there must be some formal leadership, some authority, if any social group is to survive."

"Maybe, but the extent of that leadership and authority is what I wonder about." He smiled and nodded to a group of young people heading back to the commons from the corrals, then looked at Bill. "Let me ask you something. What keeps you from attacking anyone else around here, or stealing from them? Is it fear of punishment or a personal value system that tells you it's wrong?"

"I understand the argument you're making. Of course it's a personal value system. But that doesn't work in a larger society."

"Why not?"

"Because not everybody has the same values."

"Why not?"

"Well, because not everyone is raised the same way. They come from different family structures and cultures with different values."

Jim nodded. "Uh huh. When you and I were kids, most everyone, regardless of political persuasion, religion, race or economic level, felt pretty much the same way about major issues. That's changed dramatically, but one thing remains the same. That is that people do the right thing for one of two reasons: either they do what's right because that's simply what they believe in, or they do what's right because they're afraid not to. They're scared of the potential punishment, whether that's a fine, jail or ostracism by their community."

He stopped walking and turned to look at Bill, who had stopped beside him. "I had had it up to the gills with the fragmented society we were living in before everything collapsed. You had too. A lot of people had. We were disgusted by the way society had devolved into a no-values, no-responsibility socialist society that rewarded those who slept in the entitlement hammock and punished those who paid for it. That's not how our country was founded and it's not how it was ever intended to be." He looked around at the people bustling throughout the commons and corral complex. "Well, to the extent that I'm able, I'm not going to let that happen again, at least not in my world."

Bill stood with his hands in his pockets and looked at Jim. "I agree with you, and I think most of the people around here do too. So, what kind of government would protect against such a societal devolution occurring again?"

Jim looked up at the barn and surrounding corrals, lost for a moment in thoughts he didn't share with Bill. Then, almost as if he were talking to himself, "I've thought about that. I've thought about that a lot." He turned back to Bill and gestured to the commons. "Do you realize how little trouble we've had here? Why do you think that is?"

Bill thought for a moment, turning around to look at the commons. "Well, I guess it's probably because they're all living close together and working together. They all know each other and appreciate the fact that they're safe here at Stonemont."

Jim nodded. "That's a lot of it, but there's more. They see examples of common values here, they know our expectations, and they know that violating the rules will be dealt with. Plus, they know their contributions are important and appreciated, and they feel good about being a part of a positive, working community."

Jim turned and walked toward one of the corrals where a teenage boy and girl were working with a couple of fillies. "Look at those beautiful animals," he said, as Bill walked by his side. "On their own, they think of nothing but their own basic needs. But with proper training they are able to do amazing things."

Reaching the corral, he hung his arms on the top rail and rested a boot on the bottom one. "People are no different. Left on their own, they're not much good to anyone including themselves. That's what happened in the inner cities, and to a lesser extent in the rest of society. Parents were missing or too busy, lazy or stupid to provide the proper training to children who needed it and deserved it. Now we're dealing with it."

He turned to look at Bill, then back at the teenagers working with the horses. "It breaks my heart to think that every one of those thugs and gangbangers heading out of the city started out as a perfect and precious little child of God. They could have been anything, done anything, but they were damaged by bad parents and a corrupt and enabling society. We have to deal with them now, but more importantly, we have to make sure it doesn't happen again."

"Patrimonialism," said Bill.

Jim looked at him. "What?"

"Patrimonialism," repeated Bill. "I did a paper on it in a comparative justice class. It's the tribal ancestor of monarchies. Power originates in and emanates from a central leader, or father, who rules his domain as a natural and indistinguishable extension of his personal life. Think Alexander the Great, or Abraham in the Bible." He looked at Jim with a wry smile and a slight twinkle in his eye. "Or in more recent history, Joe Bonanno."

"Who?"

"Joe Bonanno. The old mafia boss they based The Godfather on, or so some claimed."

Jim squinted at Bill. "You know, you have a real interesting knowledge base." He pushed himself away from the fence and started walking toward the barn.

Bill laughed. "Well, look at what's developed so far," he said, falling in step beside Jim. "We're all living on your place, most of us having had our asses saved by you or yours. Our food comes from you, our shelter comes from you, our work comes from you and our protection comes from you. You had prepared so that your family would be protected and provided for, and, as a result of your leadership, you and your family have become the hub of a large and ever-expanding wheel. What would you call that?"

They had reached the barn, and before Jim could answer, Christian came out leading a large black gelding followed by Naomi leading a grey Arabian mare and six scouts leading horses of their own. Each had an AR slung over their shoulder and a holster carrying their preferred pistol on their belt, in addition to a rucksack and bed rolls.

"You all set?" Jim asked.

Christian nodded. "We're going to scout a circle around here and the school and should get there before dark."

He looked at Naomi, then back at Christian. "You letting her take the Arab?"

Christian nodded. "She took right to her. Says she can handle her."

Jim looked at Naomi. "Did my nephew tell you this girl isn't finished yet?"

Naomi nodded. "He did. But she's beautiful. I can finish her if that's okay with you."

Jim looked at Christian, who shrugged, then back at Naomi, who smiled. He nodded slowly. "Okay, but don't break anything."

"I'll try not to," she laughed.

Jim turned back to Christian. "Take your time and be careful. We want to get a better idea of what's around us, but we don't want to lose anybody if we can help it, okay?"

"Will do," said Christian, placing a foot in the stirrup and swinging up into the saddle. "I'll see you when I see you."

Naomi mounted the Arab, which gave a snort and a testing half-rear before dancing around in a circle. Naomi kept her seat and smoothly guided the grey back to position, stroking its neck and talking softly to it. The rest of the squad mounted up behind her.

Jim raised his hand in part wave and part salute to the group. "Y'all be careful."

All of the scouts nodded and a few returned the half salute as they trotted past Jim to fall in behind Christian and Naomi.

"By the way," Jim yelled after them, "don't get shot!"

25

Christian could feel the big gelding's excitement and held it to a dancing walk as they passed through the commons and across the south meadow. He felt a bit silly when he realized he was softly whistling *Gary Owen*, but allowed himself the fun of it, thinking how crazy this would have seemed less than a year ago, and how ironic it was that someone would be whistling the tune made famous by George Armstrong Custer, who had commanded the seventh cavalry at Fort Riley, Kansas, then been court martialed at Fort Leavenworth just north of where he now rode whistling the tune. He turned in his saddle as they approached the tree line, and, checking the squad formed behind him, signaled for the lead scout to take point as they entered the trees.

The coolness of the shade was welcome as they wound their way through the attack channels that had been designed and constructed months earlier, and the comparative quiet of the woods made the sounds of the horses' hooves and creaking saddle leather seem almost soothing. It made Christian remember a saying he had heard years ago, though he couldn't remember who had said it, about the best thing for the inside of a man being the outside of a horse.

When they reached the rolling hills beyond the trees, the squad halted until the lead scout had taken the point about a quarter mile ahead of them and the flankers had reached their positions to the right and left. When the squad entered the open area, the rear guard remained behind until they were about a hundred yards ahead of him, then moved out, maintaining his position at the drag of the diamond.

It had been a long Indian summer and the day was warm for so late in the fall. As they rode the waves of hills and prairie grass they saw occasional small groups of deer feeding leisurely and hawks drifting on thermals watching for a chance at dinner on the ground. By noon they had seen no one, though they had checked a couple of farm houses that appeared to have been abandoned for some time, and stopped at a small creek to take a break in the shade of a tall cottonwood to let the horses drink.

The afternoon brought them in a broad circle to the south, where they contacted several inhabited farms and a mounted Sheriff's posse ranging up from Linn County. The farm families seemed in pretty good shape, a couple of them having taken in stranded travelers, and reported no trouble other than an occasional straggler trying to steal some fruit off of a tree or a chicken, which they gave them anyway before sending them on. The deputies told them that things were fairly stable as far south as Fort Scott, but that gangs from Wichita and Tulsa had been raiding west of Pittsburgh. They exchanged contact information with the posse and gave them an open invitation to Stonemont before moving on.

An hour before sunset they made camp at the base of a short cliff face slightly below the crest of a hill that commanded a three hundred sixty-degree view for miles around. Christian sent two scouts to the crest to dig in observation posts about fifty yards apart while the remaining scouts prepared what would be a dry and dark camp for the night. They tied the horses along a picket line that spanned their avenue of ascent and the two dogs that had accompanied them trotted in and out of the woods, interested in exploring the new territory but constantly checking that the scouting party was where they had left them. No one would be able to approach them during the night without their knowing it.

As the main party broke out their cold rations and situated themselves in their bed rolls along the cliff base, Christian climbed to the crest of the hill to get a look at the surrounding area before darkness fell and to join the first rotation of scouts on watch. Looking out across the miles of rolling hills of mixed forest and grassland, he thought again about how much he liked this part of Kansas. A hundred miles to the west started the vast prairie of wheat, golden in the summer and blowing in waves that made you feel like you were floating in a terrestrial ocean, finally rising gradually through cattle country until it met the foothills of the Rockies. But here, it was like a continuation of Missouri, with forested hills and rock outcroppings that overlooked the shallow draws and stretches of fields between them. The terrain had provided cover for the bloody guerrilla border fighting before and during the Civil War, and again he felt a sense of history, imagining Quantrill's Raiders, Bloody Bill Anderson and Jesse James riding the same hills and woods his group had travelled earlier in the day. He checked each of the scout's positions, finding them to be well situated and prepared, then settled down in a spot half way between them.

As the sun disappeared behind the hills to the west, he let himself mentally meld into the increasing darkness, slowing his breathing and concentrating on the sounds around him. It had been years since he had spent time in the woods away from the city and he had forgotten how dark it could get without much of a moon. The small sliver of a new moon gave very little light, but, as the darkness increased, the stars were amazing.

He stayed on the crest until halfway through the second watch and, having seen no sign of activity, returned to camp. As he descended the last few yards, he saw a figure standing on the edge of the small clearing looking over the fields and forests to the north.

"Can't sleep?" he asked quietly.

At first, he thought she hadn't heard him. Then, without turning, she answered, "I'd forgotten how dark the night can be." Then looking up, "Can you imagine?"

He looked up at the stars but remained silent.

"Can you imagine," she asked, "what the native people must have thought of the stars, not knowing what they were?"

He continued looking, trying to put himself in the mindset of an Indian, or ancient European, hundreds of years ago. Yes, what must they have thought?

"It puts things in perspective," she continued. "The universe, the world, is complete without our knowledge or understanding of it, or our so-called improvements to it."

He waited for her to continue, but she didn't. "You think things were better before industrialization and modern technology?" he asked, immediately realizing that his question seemed stilted and clumsy.

She still hadn't turned around. "Don't you?"

He thought about it. It had been a while, and seemed like forever, since his days were filled with email, phone messages, checking craigslist several times a day, keeping up with rent, utility bills and insurance payments, traffic, rude people, constant news of war, political corruption, a collapsing society and endless asinine commercials for things no content person wanted or needed. A smile crossed his lips and he nodded. "Yep."

He stood there, looking at her back, until he felt as if he were intruding on her privacy, but before he could turn away she turned around to face him.

"Your son will be to Aedan as you are to Jim Wyatt," she said. Then her head tilted as if she were confused about something, but she straightened and looked at him in silence.

The sudden statement took him by surprise. Though his affection for

215

Becky was friendship rather than romantic, he had come to think of Bobby as almost his own son. He shrugged. "Bobby's a great kid."

She took a step forward out of the shadow and he could now see her face. She looked out into the night as if trying to understand something, then back at him, her gaze probing. "No," she said slowly, again turning her head to look into the night as if trying to find the answer in the darkness.

After a moment she turned back and, with steps he couldn't hear, walked past him, her fingertips touching his arm gently as she passed. "Good night."

He turned and watched her walk silently back to her bed roll. "Goodnight," he said, too quietly for her to hear.

Christian awakened from a dream about traffic and emails to the sound of a horse walking softly. Opening his eyes as he tightened his grip on the pistol in his hand, he saw Naomi sitting on the Arab, silhouetted against the rising sun.

"Sorry if I woke you," she said, sliding smoothly from the saddle and onto the ground.

He looked up at her and saw that she looked as fresh as yesterday, which made him conscious of how he must look, which irritated him. "How long have you been up?" he asked, throwing his blanket off and getting to his feet.

"Most of the night. I thought I'd scout around a bit. Didn't see anything"

He put on his hat, glad that it covered his messed-up hair. "I'd rather you didn't do that."

"What?"

"Go off by yourself. It's dangerous, and the sentries might have shot you."

She smiled. "I told them I was going out. They said you'd kill them if they let me go but I told them they didn't have a choice short of shooting me and that I'd try to talk you out of killing them." She turned to get something out of her saddlebags. "But if you don't want me to go out by myself again, I won't."

He looked at her digging through her saddlebag, a bit surprised. He had expected an argument. "Okay. Good."

He dug his toothbrush out of his rucksack, slung his AR over one shoulder and his camelback over the other, then walked toward the trees to take care of morning business, kicking the feet of each scout as he passed them. "Rise and shine, beauties. Things to do and people to see, or maybe the other way around."

The morning took them farther east, close to the Missouri state line before they swung north again. Just as the day before, they stopped at a number of abandoned farm houses, some of them ransacked, and a few occupied ones. Those they spoke to said they had suffered some livestock theft, and in one case a raid by a small party they had been able to fight off. Some of the families had consolidated into central locations for greater security, explaining some of the empty farm houses, but others had just disappeared.

A public safety unit had been formed in Louisburg, headed by the Miami County Sheriff and made up of deputies, town police and volunteer firefighters, but they weren't able to do much patrolling beyond the town and concentrated on keeping it secure. The sheriff told them he had heard from Missouri deputies that gangs out of Grandview and south Kansas City had raided southward, but had mostly been wiped out by the folks in Belton and Raymore, and the deputies had taken care of the rest. "Those assholes trying to shoot their guns sideways didn't do too well against good old boys with ARs and deer rifles who know how to use them," he said.

A couple of his deputies smiled and one of them spat tobacco juice next to the toe of his boot. "Heard they picked up quite a few pistols off those dead gangers. Too bad they didn't let a few get through for us."

By mid-afternoon, they were a mile out from the school and were contacted by one of Mike's scouts who led them in. The place already looked squared away and the level of activity explained why. As they dismounted at the front door, Mike came out smiling.

"Couldn't stay away, huh?"

Christian smiled back. "Well, I figured you could make it a day or two without me, but beyond that might be pushing it."

Mike laughed. "That's probably true. I haven't shot anybody yet, but a couple of these idiots are testing my patience. Are you staying?"

Christian shook his head. "No. We'll break for a few minutes and then we have to go get Naomi's family." He looked around the school grounds and the bustling activity. "Jim wants me to talk to all the people here about something. How long would it take to get everybody together?"

Mike thought for a minute. "It will take a while to get everybody in from the outlying places. I'd say day after tomorrow."

Christian nodded. "Good. Let's go inside and I'll tell you all about it."

After briefing Mike, Christian and the squad followed Naomi, first to her family's home, which they found empty and vandalized, then on to the abandoned barn. When Naomi indicated that they were close, Christian ordered the scouts to remain behind the tree line and assume compass points on the small open area to set up surveillance on the building. After an hour, an auburn-haired woman wearing jeans and a dark blue work shirt emerged from the pedestrian door and stood with her face to the sun as if basking in its warmth.

Naomi touched Christian's sleeve. "That's Carol. Everything's alright."

Christian looked at her quizzically. "How do you know?"

"She knows we're here. She's facing the sun to tell us it's all clear. If there was a problem, she would be looking down or facing the woods."

Christian continued looking at her.

"It's a Comanche thing," she said, seeing the doubt on his face. "Trust me."

"Uh huh. So, it's your dad who's part Comanche?"

"Uh uh, my mom. But Carol is her spirit sister. It's like she's of the blood. Sometimes she's better than me. I'll go out to her, then motion you in."

Christian put his hand on her arm, stopping her while continuing to watch the woman, who now seemed to be looking directly at him. "Then why doesn't she just wave us in?"

"In case other people are watching. Also, because that's what someone would be ordered to do to suck us into a trap."

Christian nodded. "Makes sense. You all are pretty tricky, aren't you?"

He watched the woman for another minute. "Okay, but ride in in case you need to get away fast or need something to hide behind. And have everybody come outside before you wave us in."

She looked at him.

"It's a careful thing. Trust me."

Christian continued to watch the woman and the barn as he heard Naomi mount up, then watched as she walked the Arabian out of the trees and across the meadow. As she got closer, the woman smiled warmly and stretched out her arms. Naomi stopped by the woman and dismounted, moving into the woman's arms where they held each other in a brief embrace. After a moment, the woman turned toward the barn and a man emerged, accompanied by a teenage girl and a young boy. Naomi walked into the barn, then re-emerged to wave him in.

"Everybody stay put," he said into his mic, mounting the black and riding slowly across the field with his AR hanging at his right side and his right hand resting on his thigh inches from his pistol.

He reached the group and stopped, but didn't dismount.

Naomi looked up at him. "Christian, this is Carol, Jerry, Elizabeth and Logan. Guys, this is Christian Bell."

Christian nodded to everyone and touched the brim of his hat to Carol with his left hand. "Ma'am."

Jerry nodded, Elizabeth smiled shyly, Logan looked up in awe and Carol squinted at him. "You from Texas, Christian?" she asked with a slow smile.

"No ma'am. Kansas."

Carol smiled wider. "You've got Texas manners, touching your hat to a lady, but not with your gun hand."

Now, Christian smiled. "Well, around here, ma'am, we just call it being polite and being careful."

Carol chuckled. "Well, as soon as you decide that nobody here needs shooting, step on down and come on in. It ain't much, but we call it a barn."

On entering, Christian could see the amount of work that Naomi and Jerry had done carrying food and supplies to the barn. Stacks of canned goods and dehydrated meal packages filled an entire stall, and a rear area had been sectioned off with blankets to form a common sleeping area. An old iron wood stove had been cleaned and moved into the sleeping area, where it was used to cook on and provide warmth at night. They had not vented it, so that the smoke could not readily be seen from outside the barn, but the ceiling was high enough and the sidewall boards loose enough that the smoke dissipated and didn't collect inside. Pots and pans hung neatly on nails in the wall, and plates, cups and silverware were stacked on a side table.

Another stall was filled with makeshift shelves that held stacks of clothing, and a stall opposite the sleeping area had been transformed into a shower with a raised brick floor and fed by a barrel on stilts through a garden hose and spray nozzle.

Carol invited them to stay for dinner and the night, so Christian called in half of the scouts to take care of their horses and prepare a place for the squad in the barn. As they worked to set up the area, he took a second look around the barn and watched the family.

A lot of work had been done to make the place both livable and defensible, at least within the limitations of an old wooden barn, and the family seemed to get along well. It was apparent that Carol was the leader, though she did it in a loving, if firm, way. Jerry seemed affable and willing to work, and more than willing to follow Carol's lead. Elizabeth seemed like a good kid, ready to help as needed, and Logan was a ball of energy constantly bouncing from one person to another as he tried to keep up with what everyone else was doing. Naomi seemed to be an entity unto herself, close enough to the others to be included in the circle of familial love, but apart enough to be treated with a degree of extra-familial courtesy. Carol treated her as an equal, Jerry with deference, and Elizabeth and Logan with loving awe.

"You look like a man trying to figure something out."

Christian looked over to see Carol smiling at him. "I'm admiring what you've done to make this place livable," he replied. "You all have done a lot of work."

Carol tilted her head and raised an eyebrow at him. "You're being polite. There's not much here to admire, but we get along. Would you like some coffee? Real Folgers instant."

Christian grinned. "That would be a slice of heaven."

"Good. That will give me an excuse to have a cup too." She nodded at a long table. "Have a seat and I'll whip it up."

Christian took a seat on a wooden box with a feed bag folded on top for a cushion. Logan was hanging around the scouts, wide eyed and asking about their equipment and what it took to be a scout. Elizabeth was helping Naomi get supper ready. Jerry wasn't around.

"Here you go," said Carol, setting a cup of steaming coffee in front of him and sitting down. "Sugar?"

Christian smile his thanks. "I'd love it but I'm trying to kick the sugar habit. Jim says it will make my life simpler and I'll actually be able to taste the coffee."

Carol laughed. "I agree with him." She took a sip, then, as if reading his mind, "Jerry is a good man, a strong man. This situation has made him doubt himself because the skills and strengths needed in this new world are different than the ones he had, which were important in the old one."

Christian nodded. "I can understand that. People like Jim and I, and probably your family, were 'throwbacks' in the modern world. We didn't quite fit in. Now, the world isn't modern anymore and we're more in our element while those who were mainstream before are now out of theirs." He looked around. "Where is he?"

Carol looked out the barn door. "He's outside." She thought for a moment. "I think he wants to kill somebody. He's been angry and ashamed that he didn't protect his family when those raiders came. He hasn't said that, but I can tell. Now, he spends most of his time out in the woods keeping watch in case of another raid. I think he actually hopes for it so he can do what he feels he should have done the first time. It will kind of cleanse his soul, if you know what I mean."

Christian nodded. "I've seen it before. It's understandable."

He thought for a moment before continuing. "Our society had changed to a point where traditionally masculine traits had become looked down on. Instead of loving, leading, providing and protecting, men were told that these roles were chauvinistic and that they needed to develop kinder, gentler ways of participating in society. Some actually believed it, probably because it was the easier way to go, and others forced themselves to fit in so they could advance in their careers. Life became more about feeling than thinking, and more about talk than action. Men had to get along with women, often while in subordinate roles, more than with each other." He took a sip of coffee. "No offense, but I hated those days. It was the decline of manhood and our whole country suffered for it."

Carol shook her head. "No offense taken, and I couldn't agree more. I feel like I'm back home talking to my family. Jerry always disagreed, but I think his mind is changing pretty fast."

She looked over at Logan. "A lot of mothers would think I'm crazy for saying this, but I'm almost glad this happened. It will be more dangerous for my kids, but at least they'll live in a world where real values and principles apply, instead of insane political correctness and conniving back-stabbers in an office."

Christian nodded. "We've said pretty much the same thing." He took a sip of coffee. "You and Jerry seem pretty different in your world views."

Carol chuckled. "You're wondering how we got together." She looked out the door as if she were looking back in time. "Yes, we're different in some ways. We're each products of our environments, me from a wild west Texas clan of brothers and he from a family of college professors moved to Kansas from back east. But we're alike in the important ways. He's honest, hardworking, solid in his beliefs and totally committed to his family. He's just evolving now as harsh realities set in. Like you said, I was a bit out of my element before and now it's his turn."

"How did you get together?" Christian asked.

Carol burst into a full laugh, remembering. "We met at a rodeo at K-State. I was there with some friends and he was there covering it for the school newspaper. I think his original angle was cruelty to animals or something. Anyway, a drunk bull rider was trying to paw me out by the corrals and I was just about to take care of him with a knee to the church bells when Jerry came along and told him to leave me alone." She looked down at her coffee and shook her head, smiling at the memory.

"What happened?"

Carol sighed, but kept smiling. "Oh, that cowboy stomped Jerry good. But he left, and when Jerry finally got up he insisted on walking me to my car. He was a mess. His shirt was torn, his face was bleeding and his left eye was already starting to swell shut, but I could see he wasn't scared. He walked us to our car, and when the bull rider saw us in the parking lot and started yelling at us Jerry didn't flinch. He just stayed by our car till we left."

She looked up at Christian. "A couple of weeks later I saw Jerry's article in the paper. It wasn't the animal rights hit piece I had expected. Instead, he explained the history and importance of rodeo in western American culture, and talked about the respect the riders and spectators had for the animals. He even spoke of the toughness and the cowboy code he saw in the riders. I was really surprised, and impressed."

"Did he say anything about the bull rider who whipped him?"

Carol shook her head. "Not a word."

"It sounds like he doesn't hold a grudge."

"He doesn't. We're different that way. I can hold a grudge until hell freezes twice, but to Jerry every day is a new day with no baggage from the past. In some ways that's good, but in other ways it can be dangerous."

Christian nodded. "Yeah, it can."

"Anyway, I called the paper's office to thank him for that night and compliment his story. He wasn't in, but I left a message and he called me back. I don't know what made me do it but I invited him out for coffee and he accepted. We became friends, and after about a year we were inseparable."

222

Christian grinned. "I bet you two were an odd couple."

Carol waved her hand. "Oh lordy, we were. We'd go places, me in jeans, boots and a halter top and him in a polo shirt, plaid shorts and flip flops. People would look at us, trying to figure us out. His family seemed stilted and overly controlled to me, while my family seemed like a John Wayne movie to him. But in time we got used to each other and we could see the values in each way."

Christian started to say something when Naomi came over to the table. "Supper will be ready in about half an hour. You want me to go find Jerry?"

Christian stood up. "I'll go find him. What should I do with my cup?"

"Leave it," said Carol. "Around here, those who fight get waited on."

Christian smiled and nodded. "Just like home."

The sun was low when Christian exited the barn and the shadows were getting longer by the minute. He took a moment to orient himself, then entered the trees. He knew the scouts were at their positions, but he didn't expect to see them since that was their job, to be there but not be seen. After several minutes of walking carefully through the woods he found a high spot to sit down with his back to a tree and watch.

It only took a few minutes before he saw Jerry moving from one spot to another. Getting to his feet, he quietly walked toward the man, stepping behind a tree before he called to him in case Jerry spun around and shot before thinking. "Hey Jerry," he said quietly.

Jerry started to turn around and bring his shotgun up, then quickly realized that the voice had said his name and sounded friendly.

Christian stepped out from behind the tree and walked to Jerry's position. "See anything?"

Jerry shook his head. "No, nothing but some squirrels."

"Well, if you saw squirrels that means you're doing pretty well. They're skittish in the woods and any noise will spook them."

Jerry looked at him skeptically. "How did you find me, then?"

"I sat down and waited to see movement."

Jerry nodded. "Yeah, Naomi warned me about that. First to move first to die, right?"

Christian smiled. "Sometimes." He nodded at Jerry's shotgun. "What have you got?"

Jerry held up the shotgun as if he was still trying to figure that out himself. "Shotgun. Twelve-gauge. I know how to load it, how to point it and how to pull the trigger. Beyond that, you've got me."

Christian chuckled softly. "Well, that will do the job. Do you have a rifle?"

Jerry shook his head. "None to speak of. We have a .22, but even I know that's not enough for this situation."

They stood there for a few minutes in silence, watching the woods get darker. Finally, Jerry spoke.

"Naomi has been teaching us some stuff, but I know I have a long way to go. I'm just not naturally a combative person. In fact, Carol's more of a natural fighter that I am. I was always taught that fighting meant you had already lost the argument. Now things have changed. A lot."

Christian looked at him. "You're familiar with Neville Chamberlain, I assume."

Jerry nodded. "Oh yeah, 'peace in our time'."

"How many millions of people do you think died because he thought he could talk to Hitler?"

Jerry was quiet for a minute, not wanting to admit the answer. "Millions," he said quietly.

"How many innocent people?"

Another short pause, then, "Millions."

Christian nodded. "There are evil people in the world, Jerry, and other people who act good during good times but will revert to a more animalistic nature when the veneer of civilization cracks or wears off. It isn't an argument you win or lose, it's life and death, and those who don't recognize that don't last long." He looked out into the woods. "If more people had recognized the evil of Hitler sooner, and been willing and able to fight him sooner, millions of lives might have been saved." He looked back at Jerry. "Do you think you're mentally ready to fight now when it's necessary?"

Jerry nodded. "Yes."

"Good. Then the rest is just training and experience." He looked back toward the barn. "Naomi says supper's about ready. Let's go eat."

The scouts had rotated while he was gone, and the team that had taken the first watch was now in the barn getting ready to eat. Naomi and Elizabeth were putting bowls of ham and beans on the table, along with a platter of cornbread. Logan was pestering the new group of scouts with the same questions he had asked the old group, and Carol was trying to shoo him away. The scouts were grinning and one patted Logan on the shoulder, promising to answer all his questions after supper. After a few minutes, they were all seated around the table.

Carol folded her hands and closed her eyes, followed by the others. "Lord, we thank you for this food and for your continued blessings and protection. Watch over these men who have come here to help us, and sustain us all in these difficult times. Guide us in all that we do, and if fighting needs to be done, make our hearts strong, our eyes sharp and our aim true. In Jesus' name, Amen."

"Amen," said the rest in unison.

26

Morning brought a slow, steady rain that tapped a rhythm on the barn roof, making it hard to wake up. Still, the smell of fresh coffee and hot biscuits broke through Christian's haze and a drip of rain hitting him on the forehead made him open his eyes to see Naomi looking down at him.

"Good morning." she said. "Late sleeper, huh?"

Christian made a noise between a growl and a groan as he threw off the top of the sleeping bag and rolled to his feet. Waking up to her looking down at him was getting irritating. "I'm nocturnal."

Naomi smiled. "From the way you were snoring, you seemed more endothermal."

Christian paused while putting on his tactical vest. It was bad enough to wake up from a good sleep to see someone standing over you, let alone using words you didn't know the meaning of. "What the hel.., uh heck, does that mean?"

"An endotherm is an animal that hibernates. I was starting to think I was going to have to hold this cup of coffee till spring."

He looked at the cup in her hand. "For me?"

Her smile seemed to balance on the edge of a laugh as she held the cup out to him. "Unless bears don't like coffee when they wake up."

He tried to retain his morning scowl, but her smile, her friendly teasing and the cup of coffee cracked through his irritation and forced a smile to his face. He took the cup from her. "Thanks."

She nodded. "Anything to stop that snoring." She turned away and took a couple of steps, then stopped and turned to look back at him. "Just kidding."

The scouts who had been inside were waking, rolling their beds and sitting down at the table, filling their plates with oatmeal, biscuits and sliced ham while Elizabeth filled steaming cups of coffee for each of them. Carol was making sure everyone had enough food, Logan was asking all of the scouts questions and Naomi was putting on her gun belt, slinging her rifle over her shoulder and putting on a poncho. As Christian sat down at the table, he saw her walk out the door into the rain.

"What are we doing today, Christian?" one of the scouts asked.

Christian took a sip of coffee. There wasn't really a lot to do until the meeting at the school the next day, and a rainy day would be good for some more scouting. "You guys scout north and east a bit. The rain will be keeping most people inside and will give you some concealment. See if you can get to the outermost edges of the neighborhoods and see what you find. I'm going to stay here and see what I can do to help."

The scout nodded and smiled. "Staying close to the biscuits. I don't blame you."

Christian smiled. "You're reading my mind."

They took half an hour for breakfast, enjoying the good food, coffee and pleasant conversation of Carol and the kids. When all the bowls and platters were empty, the scouts got to their feet, donned their equipment and ponchos and headed out the door with a wave. As they left, Naomi came back in, shedding her wet poncho at the door and walking to the table.

"It looks like this is going to last all day. I was going to work with Jerry on some stuff today. Want to help?"

Christian nodded. "Sure. What kind of stuff?"

"Basic outdoor stuff. He's just getting started."

"You ready now?"

"When you are."

Christian enjoyed watching how Naomi moved through the forest and explained things to Jerry, and, pulling drag, he waited until they stopped for a short break before he spoke. "Jerry, you're doing pretty well. One thing; don't step over logs. If there's a snake curled up on the other side it could nail you. Step on top of the log and then a couple feet past it when you step off, unless it looks like it might give way under your weight. Same thing with rocks."

Jerry nodded. "She told me that. I was afraid I would slip on that big one I stepped over because it was wet."

Christian looked at him, not saying anything.

"Got it," nodded Jerry, realizing his mistake. "Step on logs and rocks, not over."

"If you slip and twist an ankle or bust your butt, we can fix you up and you can hobble along," continued Christian. "If a copperhead or rattler gets you, you're in a world of hurt. You may or may not die, but we'll have to help you make it out and that takes all three of us off first string."

227

Jerry nodded again. "Got it."

"Any particular direction you want to head?" Naomi asked.

Christian looked around. "Anything close by that you know of?"

Naomi pointed to the northeast. "There's some development about a mile that way."

Christian nodded. "Good enough. Lead on."

It took another hour for them to reach the edge of the woods on the crest of a hill overlooking a sprawling residential neighborhood. The houses were big, with three and four car garages, situated on large lots that at one time had probably been expensively landscaped. Now, grass and weeds were high. Some houses looked in good shape, as if their owners might step out of them at any moment. Others had burned to the ground. Most were in some sort of disarray, curtains blowing through broken windows, front and garage doors open, clothing, toys and personal items strewn across yards and tangled in bushes and trees. Cars sat at odd angles in driveways and streets. Nowhere did they see movement.

"My god," said Jerry.

Christian took a small pair of binoculars out of his pack and began a slow visual sweep of the neighborhood.

"See anything?" Naomi whispered.

"Nothing but a big mess."

"Should we go take a look?"

Christian shook his head. "Let's have a little patience training first. Sometimes, when you rush into something, you can't rush right back out again if you need to. We'll watch for a bit."

Naomi bit her lip. "You discovered my one imperfection."

Christian smiled but kept his eyes to the binoculars. "Only one, huh?"

"And I'm missing half of my little toe on my right foot."

Christian took the binoculars away from his eyes and looked at her with a raised eyebrow.

"One summer when I was little we had a bad rat problem in the barn. Not enough dogs and cats I guess. Anyway, my dad put out a bunch of rat traps. One day I was out at the barn and was curious how sensitive the traps were, so I touched the bait with my little toe." She paused for a moment. "They're very sensitive."

Christian stared at her, trying to figure out if she was kidding. "What happened next?"

"I ran to the house screaming. Momma patched me up and then went and reset the trap. She couldn't find the rest of my toe."

Christian continued to stare at her. "Rat ate it, huh?"

Naomi's face went blank, then a look of nauseated understanding took over as her hands flew to her mouth. "Oh, my gosh!"

"You alright?"

"I ... I never thought of that. Oh, my gosh!"

Christian put the binoculars back to his eyes and tried to suppress a smile.

"Oh, my gosh..."

"You're not going to puke, are you?"

After a minute of silence, he turned to see her staring intently off to their right. "What is it?"

She squinted, as if trying to see better. "I thought I saw something moving over there." She seemed to have forgotten about her toe and was pointing to the outskirts of the development.

Christian shifted the binoculars to the direction Naomi was pointing and watched. After a couple of minutes, a figure moved quickly from one house to another, followed closely by two others. Several minutes later three more figures moved from the first house to the second. After a few more minutes, three of the figures moved from the second house to a third, again followed by the other three a couple of minutes later.

"They're our guys," he said, still watching.

"Your scouts?"

"Uh huh."

"Should we go down with them?" asked Jerry.

Christian hesitated before answering. Jerry's question, even his readiness to ask a question that suggested a course of action, combined with his earlier excuse concerning the log, irritated him. Jerry needed to be watching, listening and learning, not excusing his mistakes and making suggestions. Still, Christian felt he was trying. "No. They know what they're doing. We'll provide over-watch, even though they don't know we're here. Going down there would only complicate things for them and remove whatever tactical advantage we can provide them from a backup position. We'll move down a bit, though."

"I just thought it would be better if we joined up with them," said Jerry. "You know, strength in numbers and all."

Christian counted to about four and turned to Jerry, but it was Naomi who spoke. "This is a new world, Jerry. It's not like the one you knew.

229

These guys know what they're doing. Watch, listen and learn."

"I just thought ..."

"Jerry!" she hissed, her eyes drilling into him.

Christian studied the slope below them. There was very little cover and not much more concealment, but he saw where they might be able to get about a hundred yards closer, which would put them about two hundred yards from the scouts and still a bit elevated above them. He turned to Naomi. "Follow me. We're going to take up a position behind those two small evergreens." He looked at Jerry. "You stay here."

Christian started moving down the slope, not seeing the sharp warning look Naomi gave Jerry. Within a minute, he was behind two small pine trees, looking through the sparse lower branches at the houses the scouts were in. Naomi joined him ten seconds later.

Christian handed her the binoculars. "Keep an eye on our guys and the right side." He then brought his rifle up and started scanning the left side with the ACOG on his rifle.

Several minutes went by before Naomi whispered, "Our guys just went to the next house."

"Okay." He thought he had seen something in a window a block over from the scouts. He kept watching, thinking about the neighborhood. Six months ago, it was one of the prime places to live. Mothers would have been standing in driveways chatting and holding babies while watching their older children kicking soccer balls and driving battery operated cars around the cul-de-sacs. Fathers would come home from their offices at dinnertime and the rest of the evening would be idyllic suburban life until it all started over again the next morning. Now, it looked like a modern ghost town without the tumbleweeds. "Scout one to scout patrol," he whispered into his headset.

There was no response. The radios they had were pretty good for open area communications, but they were civilian consumer grade and didn't do well if line-of-sight was compromised. He tried again. "Scout one to scout patrol." Still, there was no response.

He looked at Naomi. "I think I saw movement in a window on the next block. I have to get closer to the team so I can let them know." He looked at the two hundred yards of open field between their position and the first houses. "You stay here in case I get my ass in a crack."

"I'll go with you."

He looked at her. She looked like she was worried and trying not to look like it. "No."

"Why not?"

"Because I need you to cover me."

"What if you get shot?"

"It'll hurt like hell." He pointed to the house where he thought he had seen movement. "See that big beige house on the next block with the open window on the second floor?"

She gave him a half-glare for his flippant remark, then looked through the binoculars. "They're all big and they're all beige."

"The big beige one with lighter beige trim with an open window under the peak. You can see it between the big beige houses in front of it."

"Oh, yeah, that one."

"Watch that window. If someone shoots at me from there, or anywhere, shoot at them and give me cover. But don't expose yourself. If I'm down, let the scouts come get me when they can."

She looked back at him and nodded. "Okay. You know I'm going to be ticked at you if you get yourself shot again."

Christian chuckled. "Okay, if it will make you feel better, but I'll try not to let that happen." With that, he rose to his feet and took off.

It took him almost a minute to make the hundred and fifty yards to a depression he found and jumped into to call the team again. The uneven terrain had made his run jerky enough to keep anyone from getting a good shot at him and he started to call Naomi to see if she had seen any movement at the window, then remembered she didn't have a radio. "Scout one to scout patrol," he whispered into his mic.

"Go ahead scout one," came the whispered reply.

"I'm out back of the house you're about to get to. Have you seen any movement in the area?"

"Negative, one. There are some dead bodies, but the only thing moving is us."

"I think we have someone at a second-floor window on the next block. When you get to the next house, let me in the back door."

"Okay, one. See you in a few."

Fifteen minutes later, the back door of the house opened and a scout wearing a bandana over his face motioned him in. He ran the final fifty yards and entered the back door to be met by an overpowering odor he hadn't smelled in years. He looked at the scout. "That mask helping much?"

The scout shook his head. "Not much."

"Find some menthol chest rub and wipe it on your upper lip and on your mask. That's what we did in the old days. It helps." He looked around. "What are you finding?"

"It's a mess. Everything has been ransacked. All food is gone. Some houses are empty, but we're finding bodies in others. From the look of things, they died real thin, but I don't know if they starved to death or were killed. Some of the bodies have been torn up pretty bad by animals."

Christian looked around him. The kitchen was the typical upscale of the area with stainless steel appliances, cherry cabinets and granite countertops. It was obvious that attempts had been made to keep the place clean, but without running water and an increasing concern with just staying alive it was cluttered with dishes and old empty food containers. Dust was heavy on the furniture, showing that no one had used it for some time. "Have you checked upstairs?"

The scout shook his head. "We figured we'd let you in first."

"Okay. Secure the basement and let's take a look."

Leaving two scouts to cover the basement door and first floor, the rest of the team mounted the stairs to the second floor.

The first three rooms turned up nothing. One was a boy's bedroom, another a girl's and the third an office. The lead scout opened the door at the end of the hallway and entered, followed closely by another. "They're in here," he called.

The other scouts remained at the doorways of the rooms they had cleared while Christian walked past them and entered the master.

The family was in bed. A man, a woman and two children. The man and woman bracketed the children, who lay in the middle, turned toward them as if to comfort and protect them. In one of the children's arms was a stuffed bear, in the other's, a doll. A Bible lay among them, as if it had slipped from the man's right hand. Christian looked at them, then stopped himself. Just as he had years ago when coming onto a death scene, he had started to look closely at the deceased to try to imagine their last moments and hours, but this was too heart-breaking. He knew he could do nothing for them, and also knew they were together in a far better place where hunger, fear and sadness didn't exist.

He turned to the younger scouts. "Don't let this get too deep into your heads. It won't help them but can really affect you. Do your job and concentrate on the living."

Turning back to the family in bed, he drew the sheet up over their

232

heads, then went to the window. From here, he could see the house he had been watching. He raised his rifle to his shoulder and looked through the ACOG. Acquiring the window from which he thought he had seen movement earlier, he saw a scoped rifle pointing back at him.

"Gun!" he yelled, moving quickly to the side and dropping to the floor. He waited several seconds, expecting incoming fire, but none came.

He moved farther away from the window. Why hadn't the man fired? He obviously had Christian and the team in his sights before Christian saw him. He probably knew, or should know, that the wall behind which Christian hid wouldn't stop a bullet. Was he short on ammo, or out? Was the rifle even manned? Prudence made him assume that it was. "There's a rifle pointing at us from a house on the next block. Let's get back downstairs. Stay low."

They returned to the first level and had two scouts check the basement, but they found nothing of interest. Looking out one of the front windows, Christian saw that the house with the rifle was obscured by the houses across the street. The street corner was three houses away, and he judged that their target was two or three houses up on the other street.

He turned to the team. "We can't see him from here, which means he can't see us either. We're going to clear the houses down to the corner where we'll be able to get a better look. Be thorough, but don't go toward the back of the houses where he might be able to see you through a window. Any questions?"

There were none.

"Okay, two by two, let's go."

The first two scouts exited and ran across the street, followed by the next pair ten seconds later and a third pair ten seconds after that. Christian followed them a few seconds later. As the second pair reached the open front door of the house, the first pair entered, followed by the second pair when the third pair arrived. Within thirty seconds, all were inside the house.

It took them five minutes to clear the house, then the movement was repeated on the next two houses until the team found themselves in the corner house. Two scouts cleared the basement, two the upstairs and two the main floor while Christian carefully made his way in the shadows to where he could look out a kitchen window and see the target house.

"I'll be damned," he said in a low voice. "Look at that."

Four flags flapped in the breeze, each on its own perfectly spaced flagpole in the front yard. On the left was the American flag, followed in descending order to the right by the Kansas flag, the Marine Corps flag and the Gadsden. The front yard, including the driveway, was encircled by sections of chain link fence of varying heights topped with barbed wire. In the driveway sat a white Ford pickup with decals of the Marine Corps and the National Rifle Association on the back window. The personal license plate said SEMPER.

Christian smiled. "Looks like a quality individual."

"What do you want to do?" asked the team leader.

Christian thought for a minute as he continued watching the house. "Guess I'll go talk to him."

The scout eyed him skeptically. "What do you want us to do?"

"If all goes well, sit tight. If he shoots me, drag me out of the street. If I go inside and don't come out in half an hour, come get me."

The scout looked at the fortified house, then back at Christian. "How do we do that?"

Christian shrugged and patted the scout on the shoulder. "Beats me. You'll think of something."

Christian left the house through the front door and walked to the middle of the street, then turned toward the corner. Raising his hands above his shoulders and holding them wide, he walked to the intersection and turned toward the fortified house, staying in the middle of the street. When he reached the house, he stopped and faced it, slowly lowering his arms to his sides. He looked up at the second-floor window, trying to decide what to say, then thought of something from a John Wayne movie.

"Hello, the house!" he yelled, feeling a bit silly hearing it come out of his mouth.

"Hello, yourself!" called a man's voice from inside the house.

"How ya doin'?" Christian yelled back, smiling at the inanity of the exchange.

"Not bad," said the voice. "How 'bout you?"

"Not bad."

"What can I do for you?"

Christian almost chuckled as he thought of a reply. "I was just in the neighborhood. Thought I'd stop by and see if you needed anything."

A laugh came from the house. "Can't think of anything right off, unless you've got some electricity to spare. Or a cheeseburger."

Christian smiled. "Afraid not. Sorry. I'm from Stonemont."

"Oh, yeah? What's stonemont?"

"Well, it started out as my uncle's farm with a stone house west of here. It's kind of developed into a community of people who came together to help each other out."

"What are you doing here?"

"We're scouting the area to see what's around us, and to make contact with anyone who's left." He looked around. "Doesn't look like many are."

There was a short pause before the man answered. "No, not many. I think we're about it."

Christian looked over at the pickup. "You a Marine?"

"Yep. You?"

"No. Cop."

The man laughed. "The only time I got my ass kicked was by a cop."

Christian smiled and shrugged. "Sorry. I don't think it was me."

The man laughed again. "I deserved it. Eighteen and drunk on Hotel Street. HPD cop didn't like me taking a swing at him and let me know it. What do you want?"

"First, information. We want to know the state of things around us. Second, to help you if you need it and if we can. Third, to let you know about Stonemont and offer whatever kind of relationship you'd like, including relocation closer to us if you want. By the way, I'm Christian Bell."

"I'm Tom Murphy. Hang on a minute."

Less than thirty seconds passed before the front door opened and a man stepped out onto the porch. His blond flat top was getting a little long, but his bearing, his t-shirt and the way he held his M-4 all said 'Marine'. He looked around the neighborhood. "Where are your guys?"

Christian cocked his head back behind him. "Back in a house watching us." Then he looked up at the flags. "I like your flags."

Murphy nodded. "I went round and round with our HOA over those. They said they were going to put a lien on my house if I didn't remove them, then this happened." He chuckled. "Looks like I won. You know what the yellow one is?"

Christian nodded. "Gadsden. Created by Christopher Gadsden of South Carolina and given to the head of the Continental Navy, whose name I forget, and also to the South Carolina legislature. It was also used by the Continental Marines. To us it means liberty. I had a sticker on the back window of my truck, across from the NRA."

235

Murphy raised his chin and an eyebrow. "I doubt that more than a couple out of every thousand people who flew the flag or wore the t-shirt knew that." He lowered the muzzle of his rifle to a down position and pointed to a section of fence next to the driveway. "You can open that small section with the 'Keep Out' sign on it if you'd care to come in and meet the Murphys."

Christian entered the house ahead of Murphy, glad that Murphy hadn't asked him to give up his weapons, uncomfortable that Murphy was behind him, and surprised at the darkness inside the house.

"We'll stop here for a minute and let our eyes adjust," said Murphy. "Patty, toss a light stick, will you?" Then louder, "Kids, come on down. We have company."

Christian heard a snap and a shake, and a green chemlight arched through the air from the back of the house to land in what it revealed to be a large family room with a massive fireplace. With the glow of the light stick, Christian saw that he was standing in a large foyer which opened into the two-story family room. A dining room, dominated by a long table with eight chairs, was to his right. An office was to his left. Sheets of plywood covered all the windows, explaining the darkness inside the house.

"We don't get many visitors anymore," said a woman's voice from the far back corner, "so excuse the mess."

Christian watched as a woman emerged from the dark corner into the green light. The woman was blonde and had the same pre-competition body builder look of her husband. She was wearing jeans and a black t-shirt, and carried a bullpup rifle. The sound of footsteps drew his attention to a staircase on his right, where two teenagers, a boy and a girl, descended from the second floor. Both were well set up kids resembling their parents, and both carried rifles.

"Guys, this is Christian Bell from a place called Stonemont," said Murphy. "He says it's a community of people working together on his uncle's place and has invited us to join them if we want to. Or just be friends in whatever way we'd like. Christian, this is my wife Patty and our kids, Tommy and Saoirse."

Saoirse said "hi" quietly, and Tommy nodded. Both looked serious.

Christian nodded back. "Good to meet you all." He looked at the girl. "To be named for freedom is a special thing. Especially now."

The girl cocked her head at him. "How did you know that? I've never met anybody except my family who knew what my name meant."

"My uncle was involved in the Irish republican community. He talked a bit about it."

"IRA?" Murphy asked.

Christian shook his head. "He knew them and agreed with their efforts to fight British oppression, but he didn't like their socialist leanings."

"This is the uncle at your Stonemont?"

"Yeah." Christian waited to see what effect this information would have on Murphy.

Murphy looked at him for a moment, then nodded slowly. "My great, great, great grandfather came to America on one of the coffin ships. His stories of British oppression were passed down through the family. I did a stint doing urban training with the SAS in Belfast and Derry and saw it was still going on." He paused for a moment before continuing. "Your uncle sounds like a good man. What's his plan?"

"His main plan was to take care of his family and friends. He would have preferred to leave it at that, but he recognizes the situation calls for more. To put it simply, Stonemont is welcoming any who want to become a part of our community and agree to adhere to our rules. Secondly, we're establishing or assisting satellite communities to support those in surrounding areas for mutual benefit. Thirdly, we're establishing relationships with other communities in an effort to rebuild a society worth living in."

Murphy had been listening intently and nodded slowly. "That's what's needed. What are your rules?"

"We expect all able adults to work and be responsible for themselves and their families. Those who are unable to take full care of themselves will be assisted, but will be expected to participate and contribute to the extent they are able. We go by the Ten Commandments, The Golden Rule and what my uncle calls the laws of common decency."

Murphy looked at his wife, then back at Christian. "We've talked about that ourselves, how good it would be to return society to that model."

Christian nodded. He was getting a good sense of these people, and thought he would put something out to see their reaction. "My aunt said she thought this all might turn out to be a good thing, because regardless of all the suffering, it might have been the only way to get society back on the right track."

237

Murphy nodded and looked at his wife again, this time longer, then at his kids. "I think we might be interested, Christian. But we have a problem maybe you can help us with."

"What's that?"

"Follow me."

Murphy led off down the stairs to the basement, followed by Christian, then Patty. Tommy remained on the first floor and Saoirse returned to the second as if they had been trained to do so. At the bottom of the stairs, Murphy opened a door and turned on an LED lantern, then entered an unfinished section crowded with paint cans, tarps and miscellaneous tools. As the others followed, he went to a large sheet of wallboard leaning against the wall and moved it aside, revealing a door behind it. Opening the door, he stepped through.

Christian went through the door after Murphy, followed by Patty, and stared around the large concrete room. Shelves lined the walls to the ceiling, and more ran down the center. All of the shelves were empty except for one which held a few packages of toilet paper, three gallon-size jugs of hand soap and several cases of green beans.

"We planned to stock two years of food," said Murphy, "but we were only at about four months when it happened." He nodded at the few items on the shelf. "This is all that's left."

He turned to Christian, holding the lantern up so each could see the other's face. "Patty and I have been on reduced rations for a while so the kids could have enough, but we finally told them about a week ago." He nodded again at the few cans of beans. "We were getting ready to head out in a couple of days to try to make it in the woods."

Christian studied the man. The inner strength and rock-hard resolve were obvious, as was his love for his family. He nodded. "We can help, Tom. Come with us to Stonemont. We need people like you and your family, and I think you'll fit in just fine."

Murphy looked at his wife, who smiled and nodded, then seemed to relax with the making of a decision. "Okay. But we'll need help carrying some stuff."

He handed the lantern to Patty and turned to pull out a section of shelving, revealing another door. Unlocking and opening it, he took the lantern from Patty and stepped through the door, followed by Christian and Patty.

"Holy cow...," breathed Christian, looking around the room.

Racks of rifles and shotguns stood along the walls, interspersed with shelves of ammo corresponding to the various weapons. Above each group were signs; .22, .223/5.56, .308, 30.06, .50, 12 g, 20 g. A smaller area held boxes of handguns with their associated ammo; 9mm, .40, .45.

"I guess I went a bit long on the guns before I switched to groceries," Murphy said.

Christian was still looking around the room in awe. "No RPGs?"

Murphy gave a dry chuckle. "When I got out of the Corps, I had a pretty good chunk of change in addition to my retirement. The stock market didn't look that good and neither did real estate, but I figured that guns and ammo were always going to go up, so you're looking at our investments."

Patty spoke up with surprising humor. "As you can see, we have a diversified portfolio."

Murphy put his arm around his wife and looked at Christian. "We were going to have to leave most of this anyway, so could we trade this to Stonemont in exchange for a place in the community?"

Christian tore his attention away from the weapons and turned to the Murphy's, shaking his head. "That's not necessary. You're already welcome. We've established an economy we think is right and fair, that everyone has ownership of themselves, their possessions and their labor, and trade with others on an entirely voluntary and mutually agreeable basis. These are yours, to sell or trade with others however you see fit."

Murphy nodded slowly and looked around the room. "How would that work with this?"

"Well, we're going to need a truck to move all this." He saw the surprised look on Murphy's face. "Yes, we have trucks. Plus, people to help load it all and guard it on the way to Stonemont. Jim, my uncle, will figure out a fair trade for the use of the truck and the personnel, which Stonemont will provide. All the rest will remain yours to sell or trade as you see fit. Food, clothing, housing, medical care, whatever. Believe me, your investment is going to pay off for you."

Murphy nodded again. "Okay. How do we work this?"

"First, let's get you some food. We all carry scout rations, so I'll call in the squad and we'll start getting some protein into you all. How are you fixed for water?"

"We're okay. Probably two weeks' worth."

"Good. I have to go meet with a community tomorrow to explain what we're going to do in the area. I'll be back at Stonemont the next day, then it will probably be another day before we get back to you."

Murphy nodded. "We'll be here."

27

Christian woke the next morning to what seemed to be a recurring theme. "Late sleeper, huh?" Naomi asked.

It had taken less than an hour to get the scouts' rations to the Murphy's and back to Naomi's position, then another hour to get back to the barn after picking up Jerry. Both had seemed quieter than usual, with Jerry staying a bit farther away from Christian and Naomi a bit closer. Now, she stood over him again with a cup of coffee in her hands.

"That for me?" he asked.

"I was beginning to think I'd have to hold it till spring."

Christian smiled and got to his elbows. "Thanks."

She handed the cup down to him. "Today's the big day."

Christian took a sip of the coffee, wondering what she was talking about, then remembered the meeting at the school.

"How do you think it will go?" she asked.

Christian took another sip and shrugged. "We'll know soon enough. I'll just tell them what Jim told me to. I think it's a good idea." Then, remembering that it had been her idea in the first place, he looked up at her. "How about you talking to them, too?"

She gave him a quizzical look. "Me? Why me?"

"Because it was your idea to begin with. You'll put a softer feel to it. You have a good way about you."

She was surprised at what he said, but tried not to show it. "Okay, if you want me to."

"I do." He got to his feet and drained the cup. "May as well get started."

By noon, they were standing on the front steps of the school, looking out over the crowd that had gathered to hear them. Christian looked at individual faces, wondering what they were thinking and what their lives were like now. He wondered how they would take what he had to say and how things would work out in the long run, but realized that was beyond his control. His job was to represent Stonemont and explain to the local residents Stonemont's position and plans for the area. He looked at Mike, who was watching the crowd, then walked to the center of the top step, standing there until the crowd had seen him and quieted down.

"Can you all hear me?" he asked in a voice he hoped would carry to the ones in back. Murmurs and nods indicated that everyone could.

"My name is Christian Bell. I'm from Stonemont. For those of you who may not know, Stonemont is a fortified community a little west of here which developed and grew on the land of Jim Wyatt with people who were drawn to it because of the help he gave those who came to him. We are the ones who liberated this community from those who turned this school into the chamber of horrors it was a short time ago."

He paused before continuing. "When I was here shortly after the liberation of this school, a woman of your community came to me with a suggestion and request. I'm going to let her explain it to you." He looked at Naomi and stepped back.

Naomi looked at him, stunned. She had expected him to lay out Stonemont's plan and just let her put a little icing on it. Instead, he had thrown the whole thing into her lap.

Why had he done that? She was certain it wasn't because he was hesitant to do it himself. It had to be a test, to see whether she would stand up for her own idea. Mustering a confident look, she stepped to the spot vacated by Christian and took a deep breath. She had always been confident, even cocky, with individuals or in small groups, but this crowd had to be several hundred people. She collected her thoughts and looked straight at the crowd.

"My name is Naomi Moore. I'm not really one of your community, but I've been staying with my aunt and uncle for a while. We were raided by some of Barnes' men. I killed them and we lived in the woods until Stonemont came."

She took another deep breath and squared her shoulders, preparing for what she was about to say. "When Barnes and his men came, they were able to take over and victimize this community because you all weren't able to stop them. Why that was, only you can answer. But the fact is that you didn't. When Stonemont came, I told Christian, and later Jim Wyatt, that Stonemont needed to take over if you all were going to survive."

She looked around at some of the grumbling crowd before continuing.

"I'm sorry if that offends some of you, but that's the truth. You were not able to defend yourselves or your families. If another predator group comes through, you'll be victimized again unless you have the help of others who are willing and able to protect you, and teach you how to protect yourselves. And having an easily victimized community here will draw predators to this area, thereby putting others in the area in danger."

More grumbling came from a couple of pockets in the crowd, some confused and some angry. Christian put his hand on Naomi's shoulder, gently pulling her back as he took her place. "So much for a 'softer feel'", he said quietly.

"What she said is true," he said in a voice loud enough to carry over the noise of the crowd. "Those of you who are grumbling come up here and tell me how she is wrong."

No one moved, and contempt began to rise in him again. Some in this group were like so many he had dealt with in his previous life, unable or unwilling to take necessary actions themselves, but always ready to complain about those who did. His original intent to be as diplomatic as possible dissipated under the grumbling. Naomi had told it straight, and now he would too.

"What she said is true," he repeated. "When Barnes came through, he enslaved your women and reduced your men to subservient pissants who kow-towed and rewarded him for his brutal treatment of your community."

He noticed a large man in a red shirt grumbling and talking angrily to those around him. "You!" he called, pointing to the man. "Tough guy in the red shirt. Come up here and tell me how wrong I am!"

The man looked up and yelled. "You can't talk to us like that! Who the hell do you think you are coming in here and telling us what to do?"

Several others around the man yelled in agreement, and Christian could see others in the crowd nodding. He had seen this kind of thing before, in the city, where one loud mouth could get a whole crowd stirred up until it exploded into a collective violence that never would have happened individually. He glanced at Mike, who nodded, then walked down the steps and into the crowd.

The people separated as he made his way toward the man, and moved back a bit to create an open circle around them. Christian stood facing the man, close enough to touch him. "You asked who we were to tell you all what to do. We are the ones who saved your sorry asses from Barnes. Now personally, I don't give a rat's ass what you do, but right now you have two seconds to apologize for yelling at me."

"What the hell are you talking about?" snarled the man.

243

"Time's up," said Christian as his arm shot up and he struck the man under the chin with a palm heel.

The man collapsed as if the string that had been holding him up had been cut and he lay motionless on the ground.

Christian looked around at the crowd, which was trying to back away from him. "Anyone else?"

There was silence for a moment until a man in shorts and a purple polo shirt spoke up. "You can't just come in here and hit people," he said in a superior tone. "That's not the way to do things."

Christian turned and walked toward the man. "What's your name?"

The man backed up hesitantly. "Dennis. John Dennis."

"Okay, John Dennis, when Barnes came in, what did you do?"

The man looked around, looking for support from a crowd that was gradually pulling away from him. "There was nothing we could do," he answered. "They had guns. They never gave us a chance."

"You mean you didn't try to discuss things with him? Reason with him? Maybe have a big group meeting with him like you apparently want to do now?"

Dennis' eyes shifted from side to side, looking for a way out. He wasn't used to being challenged when he stated what he felt to be a reasonable opinion. "They weren't really the kind of people you could reason with."

"So, what's your plan for the next group like them that stops by?"

Dennis' eyes had turned from arrogant indignation to confusion. "I ... I don't know. I just know that going around hitting people isn't the way to handle things."

Christian looked at the man intently. "What did you do for a living before life dealt you this hand you are so obviously unprepared to deal with, John Dennis?"

The man was shocked by the accusation of incompetence, but found some confidence in being able to talk about a previous career he was proud of. He drew himself up and lifted his chin, his eyes meeting Christian's with renewed assurance. "I was a healthcare administrator."

"I see. So, you spent your days typing emails and sitting in meetings where everyone stroked each other with politically correct horse-shit about how smart and thoughtful you all were while trying to cut budgets to the bone so you could get nice bonuses."

Dennis bristled. "I'll have you know that I was in charge of admissions for the largest hospital in the city."

"Very impressive, Mr. Dennis. Perhaps you'd be kind enough to tell us about the biggest emergency you handled as the head of admissions for the largest hospital in the city."

Dennis' eyes betrayed his returning uncertainty. "It wasn't about emergencies. Good management techniques mitigate emergencies."

"Well then why weren't you able to mitigate Barnes, Mr. Dennis?"

Before the man could respond, Christian raised his voice again to the crowd. "We're not here to take over. We're here to establish a commerce center, a trading post of sorts, at the school, and a safe zone around it where everyone can come without fear of being attacked or otherwise threatened. Beyond that, Stonemont will place the area under its protection. We have given everyone back an equal amount of what Barnes took from them. The surplus items that were left over, plus more that will be brought in, will be available for sale or trade."

He walked back through the crowd, hearing the approving murmurs around him, and remounted the stairs. He motioned Carol and Jerry to join him, then turned again to the crowd. "This is Jerry and Carol Miller. They will be managing the center for Stonemont. The center will be open to all who act in a civil manner. Uncivil behavior will not be tolerated. We welcome everyone who wants to trade, but will not require anything from anyone who does not want to."

He saw that the majority of people were nodding in agreement and others were listening intently.

"The center is an extension of Stonemont," he continued, "and the same rules will apply. We go by the Ten Commandments, the Golden Rule, and normal standards of human decency. Those who agree with these principles will find a safe, supportive environment. Those who do not will not do business with us.

"Many of you have skills that can be important assets to the community. Others have trades that will help their neighbors and the community as a whole. Rather than trying to explain it, let me demonstrate how this will work. I accidentally looked in a mirror yesterday and noticed that I look a bit scruffy." A chuckle ran through the crowd. "Are there any barbers or haircutters here?"

A woman toward the back raised her hand. "I had a shop before all this happened."

"Good," said Christian. "How much would you charge to cut my hair?"

"Well, I charged fourteen dollars for a man's haircut."

Christian shook his head. "Dollars are worthless now. Would you cut my hair for a can of peaches?"

The woman looked confused, but realized it had been a long time since she had tasted peaches. "Sure, I guess so."

"Good." He turned to the scouts behind him. "Would somebody get a pair of scissors, a comb and a can of peaches, and bring out a chair for me to sit on?"

Five minutes later, Christian was seated in front of the crowd with the woman starting to cut his hair. Ten minutes after that, he stood for the crowd to see his new haircut.

"What do you think?" he asked. "Do I look pretty?"

The laughter in the crowd got louder and more light-hearted.

He turned back to the woman. "I noticed that the other scouts look even worse than I did. If we establish that a can of peaches is worth one Stonemont credit, and that other goods and services will be priced accordingly, would you be willing to cut their hair for one credit each, which you could redeem at the center for whatever goods you like?"

The woman looked at the can of peaches, felt the weight in her hand and imagined how good they were going to taste to her and her family. Thirteen more scouts meant thirteen more cans of peaches or whatever else she wanted for a couple of hour's work. "You bet," she said, nodding and looking up at Christian with determined eyes.

"Good. And looking around, I think quite a few more people here will want your services as things start to get back on track. What would you say to setting up a shop in one of the rooms here at the center? You set your own prices and pay Stonemont ten percent of what you take in."

The woman smiled. An hour ago, she had wondered how her family was going to survive the winter or the next attack. Now, she had a can of peaches in her hand, thirteen more coming and a new business in a secure location. "I'd say you've got yourself a hair cutter, Mr. Bell."

"Good deal." Christian held out his hand to the woman, who took it. "What's your name?"

"Laura Baker."

Christian turned to the crowd. "Folks, let me introduce the owner of the new barber shop and hair salon, 'Laura's', which should be opening soon. And by the looks of you, you ought to be lined up at the door."

The crowd laughed again and a man yelled, "How are we supposed to pay for it?"

"What skills do you have?" asked Christian.

"I'm a carpenter."

"Come by Stonemont. We're building, and skilled carpentry pays two credits an hour."

"I'm a master gardener," said another.

Christian waved his hand around the area. "One of the first things we need to do is to make this land productive with fields of vegetables and fruit orchards. I know we can't plant most things until spring, but there are some things we can do and it looks like there's a lot to do to prepare. You could get started right away. Are you interested?"

The man smiled and nodded. "You've got yourself a gardener."

Christian raised his hands. "That's how it works, folks. Everyone who will work will be able to make a living and be a functioning, contributing part of this community. Anyone who wants to be a sponge, to soak up benefits from the work of others, will find no place for themselves here."

He noticed that the big man in the red shirt was slowly getting to his feet. "Somebody tell sleeping beauty what I said, and tell him he has a choice to make."

A young boy in front yelled, "I know what we can name it. 'School Center'!"

Christian laughed. "So be it. Give this young man a can of peaches!"

28

Jim walked Christian down the stone steps of the house and out to the box truck that was getting ready to pick up the Murphys.

"It sounds like everything went well. We'll talk in more detail when you get back." He glanced around, making sure no one was within earshot. "Pasquale sent a messenger two days ago. They've been getting sniped at and had a few probes against Redemption from the houses to the north of them. They've lost a couple of people and had several more wounded."

"Do they have the harvest in?"

"Most of it. But winter is coming and attacks will get more frequent and forceful as the raiders get hungrier and colder. We have to clear that area."

"That's going to be a lot of work, going house to house up there. Then we'll have to post security around the whole area to make sure they don't get back into the neighborhoods. That's going to stretch us pretty thin."

Jim shook his head. "We'll burn it."

It took a moment for Christian to realize what Jim was saying. "Burn the houses? Those are half a million to million-dollar homes."

Jim shook his head again. "No, they're not. They're empty shells, either abandoned or full of dead bodies. They're havens for rats, raccoons and raiders. We need to clear the area back so Church Crossing isn't over-watched by sniper positions or close staging areas for raiders. Besides, that's southern Johnson County. There are thousands of houses that big or bigger for miles around. The one thing we will do is spare any houses belonging to those now at Church Crossing if they think they might want to move back into them after the rest have been burned."

Christian thought about it. The idea of burning hundreds of beautiful homes had shocked him at first, but he realized that it made sense. He nodded. "When do you want to do it?"

"In about a week. We need a little time to prepare but we can't wait too long. What do you think about this Marine you're going to bring in?"

"My first impression is good. This might be a good operation for him to go with us on. We can get a good look at him."

Jim nodded. "Do you know his rank?"

"No, I didn't ask and he didn't offer."

Jim shrugged. "Doesn't matter. Go get them and get back here. We have a lot to talk about."

The convoy headed out after breakfast, led by six scouts on dirt bikes followed by the box truck, then Jim's Excursion driven by Christian and another diesel Excursion driven by Mike carrying six more scouts.

The temperature had dropped into the thirties the night before, but it was warming up under a bright autumn sun in a clear sky and they made good time. By mid-morning, the convoy was pulling up to the Murphy's house. As they came to a stop, the door opened and Murphy stepped onto the porch, his rifle slung down his right side.

"Hey, Murph," called Christian. "Glad to see you're still alive."

A shot sounded from up the hill toward the center of the neighborhood. "Yeah, me too," answered Murphy, squinting in the direction of shot. "Better get inside. This ass-hat has been taking potshots at us all morning. He can't shoot worth a damn, but even a moron can get lucky."

Mike looked at Christian. "You want us to go get him?"

Christian thought for a moment. One guy taking ineffective shots at a house from that distance didn't make sense unless he was crazy, which was a possibility, or a probe for a larger group. "Yeah, go get him. See if he's with a larger bunch."

Mike nodded, motioned his team to follow him and took off.

"They look like capable people," observed Murphy.

"Yep," Christian replied. "Let's get you loaded up and see if we can make it back to Stonemont in time for supper."

Murphy smiled. "Sounds good."

It took them over two hours to carry all the guns and ammo up from the safe room and out to the truck, and Murphy was in the process of lowering the flags when Mike returned with only two scouts, one with a field dressing on his left arm.

"What happened?" asked Christian.

"The guy said he was from a big outfit run by a guy called 'Grim', headquartered at an old shopping center somewhere north of here. I sent the other scouts with him to check it out. They'll meet us back at Stonemont when they get done. Alex here caught one in the arm, but it went straight through. He'll be okay."

Christian nodded. "Okay. Mike, this is Tom Murphy. Tom, this is Mike Carpenter, our head of scouts."

The two men shook hands.

"I noticed your flags before you struck them," said Mike. "First Recon."

"Fourth AT," answered Murphy. "How did you get that guy to cooperate so quickly?"

"We were maximally persuasive," Mike answered with a straight face. "He was happy to answer our questions. When the other scouts get back we'll see if he told us the truth."

They turned to see Patty, Tommy and Saoirse carrying large plastic garbage bags out of the house. "I told them to round up their best quality clothing," said Murphy. "Plus all boots with some miles left in them. Is there anything else you would suggest for moving to Stonemont?"

Christian shook his head. "You'll find we have pretty much everything you need. Just bring anything of personal importance like pictures, family documents and such."

"We have those," answered Murphy. "Too bad most of our pictures are on discs".

Christian smiled. "Bring them. We have working computers."

For a second time, Murphy looked surprised. "You're kidding me."

"Nope. My uncle is one who prepared for comfort and pleasure, not just survival. He used to tell us that if a catastrophe happened, he didn't just want to be ready, he didn't want to notice."

"He sounds like a man with a plan."

Christian chuckled. "That's the truth. You'll see when we get to Stonemont."

After Patty retrieved the family picture discs, they loaded up and headed out, the Murphys riding with Christian. Tom watched the countryside with the curiosity and critical eye of one who hadn't ventured far from home in a while. He noted the easy discipline of the scouts and how they communicated comfortably with Christian and Mike. It wasn't like the military, but it seemed to work.

As they drove, he looked at his wife and kids. For the past month, he had fought to keep the fear of them dying suppressed, shoved deep down inside. Now, watching their faces looking out the windows of a vehicle taking them to a new life, the fear was released to meet an almost ethereal joy. The erupting combination was almost too much for him and he breathed a prayer he had long hoped he could pray. Tonight, his wife, his son and his daughter would join him in a family prayer of thanks.

He gritted his teeth and turned to look out the side window to hide the emotions beginning to escape his iron self-control.

29

Patty Murphy took a bite of flame grilled peppered steak, savoring the flavor she had almost forgotten and thought she would never taste again.

The trip to Stonemont had been uneventful, a mixture of sadness and hope, but their arrival had been almost more than they could believe after months of isolation and watching their neighbors slowly die or disappear.

Their first contact at the intake gate had indicated an organized operation, and their arrival at the main gate brought the first feeling of real safety she had felt in months. As they drove up the long drive, they saw the large stone and log house that sat on the top of the hill, then, cresting the hill, the large commons dominated by the main hall.

The level of activity had been shocking. Hundreds of people were working, some on the main hall, some on cabins arranged around the perimeter of the field and others walking purposefully from one place to another. The noise seemed strange but welcome after months of near silence, and the sounds of laughter and friendly chatter was almost too much for her to retain her stoic facade.

They had been welcomed by the Wyatts with a warmth that contrasted with the cautious reticence of her own family, and settled in the lower level apartment of the house. Kelly, Ann and Tracy had helped her put fresh linens on the beds and towels in the bathroom while Jim, Christian, Mike and Bill had helped Tom and Tommy carry their personal belongings in from the trucks. The feel of crisp clean sheets, freshly vacuumed carpet under her bare feet and a long hot shower complete with scented body wash, shampoo and conditioner had been euphoric, not to mention the softness of the fleece top and cotton yoga pants Kelly had loaned her. Now she found herself running her fingertip around the edge of the sparkling dinnerware in front of her as if to assure herself of its reality.

She was so engrossed in her thoughts that she didn't realize someone had said something to her until she saw that everyone was looking in her direction.

"I'm sorry," she said, looking around confused.

"Don't be sorry, Patty," said Ann. "I think I was a zombie my first night here, and you've been out there for six months, not the two days I was. I just asked if you all are getting settled in alright."

Patty nodded. "Oh yes, I can't tell you how...," then her emotions overflowed, her voice broke and the tears she had been able to contain up to that moment escaped as she looked at the gaunt faces of her husband and children. "I can't thank you all enough. We can't thank you ... enough ..." Her shoulders heaved as her sobs racked her body and she hid her face in her hands.

Kelly got up and bent over her, followed quickly by Ann, and they wrapped their arms around her, holding her tightly until her sobs slowly subsided.

Tom watched his wife and the two women with his elbows on the table, clasped hands held firmly together in front of his mouth, his eyes welling with tears.

After a minute, Jim got to his feet with his glass in his hand. "I've always liked people who cry at the right things." He raised his glass. "To Patty, Tom and the Murphy family. Welcome to Stonemont."

As they drank the toast, Tom rose to his feet and looked around the table. It took him a moment to gather his thoughts and his will before he spoke.

"Four days ago, I was ready to take my family into the woods to try to survive and start some kind of new life. Though I never shared this with anyone, even Patty, I knew it would be a miracle if we all survived until spring. So, I prayed for a miracle. I prayed hard."

He paused, looking at each member of his family and remembering his heartsick dread that any of them would die. He caught the choke in his throat, then looked at those from Stonemont.

"Like he's done so many times in my life, God answered my prayers. He gave me a miracle, though not the one I was praying for. He gave me a better one. The miracle he sent us was Stonemont."

He raised his glass, noticing that his normally rock steady hand was shaking. He gripped his glass more tightly, both to stop the shaking and to focus his mind. Again, he looked around at the tear-stained faces of his family, taking a moment to look closely at each one and letting his love for them gain a full hold on his mind and in his heart. Taking a deep breath, he forced his body to a rigidity that he hoped would control his hand and his voice. When he finally thought that he could control them, he looked at each of their hosts and spoke with a voice that came out like a gravelly, choking whisper.

"To Stonemont."

253

Made in the USA
Middletown, DE
14 September 2020